SATAN'S WORK

The cats lay silent in their hidden places, waiting out the storm . . . and watching as strange, misshapen creatures rose from out of the ground, coming out of the dark swamps. The Beasts stood in the rain; they were not fearful of this rain, for they knew it had been sent by their Master. They stretched their arms and loosened their muscles. They had been asleep for a long, long time. And now they were free.

Huge, clawed hands waved through the wet air Powerful jaws that dripped stinking saliva snapped at nothing. The fangs of the Beasts were four to five inches long, and yellow. The creatures, well over six feet tall when erect, weighed between two hundred and fifty and three hundred pounds. Their eyes were small and evil, with Hell-sent hate shining bloodred. Their bodies were covered with thick, coarse hair.

The cats lay concealed and watched the Beasts as they stretched and growled. And the cats knew that the devil's work had just begun . . .

THE DEVIL'S CAT
BY WILLIAM W. JOHNSTONE

ZEBRA BOOKS

are published by

Kensington Publishing Corp.
475 Park Avenue South
New York, NY 10016

ZEBRA BOOKS
KENSINGTON PUBLISHING CORP.

ZEBRA BOOKS

are published by

Kensington Publishing Corp.
475 Park Avenue South
New York, NY 10016

First printing: June 1987

Printed in the United States of America

To James Butler. A friend, a fan, and a marvelous singer.

All hope abandon, ye who enter here!

—Dante Alighieri

BOOK ONE

BOOK ONE

1

They had drifted for a year, not stopping for very long at any one place. Nydia knew her husband was looking for something, and knew what it was. But they had yet to find it.

Xaviere Flaubert's coven.

Since leaving upstate New York, Sam, Nydia, and Little Sam had kept contact with others to the barest minimum.

They were hunters, but yet they knew they were also the hunted.

They were hunting Satan's followers, and Satan's followers were hunting them.

Once, Sam thought he had found them in a small town in Illinois. That proved to be false.

They drove south into Georgia, and once more Sam felt he had found the followers of the Evil One. But again he was wrong.

"Sam?" Nydia said. "Let's try Nebraska."

"Why there?" he asked.

"The beginning," she said simply.

Sam pointed the nose of the car west.

On the fringes of what had once been the town of

Whitfield, Nebraska, Sam stopped the car.

"They aren't here," he said to his beautiful, raven-haired young wife. "But . . . something is."

"Can we get closer?"

"We can try."

The young couple, with Little Sam asleep on the backseat, drove into the charred remains of what the massive fireball had left when it struck the earth, several years back. They found nothing. But both were experiencing a very odd sensation.

"Do you feel it?" Sam asked.

"Yes. But I don't know what it is."

They drove on, through the cracked county road that wound through the sand hills. Sam drove slowly, his eyes searching both sides of the little-used road.

For what, he still did not know.

Then he saw the dog, loping along the side of the road, pacing them. Sam slowed to a crawl; the dog slowed, keeping pace. Sam picked up speed; the dog picked up speed.

"What the hell? . . ." he muttered.

"Stop, Sam!" Nydia said.

Sam braked and looked at her. "What is it, Nydia?"

Nydia looked at the light-fawn-colored dog, sitting on the side of the road, looking at them. "He is a friend, and we're going to need him."

Sam never questioned his wife. Nydia was a witch. But the inherent good in her had overpowered the dark side and Nydia had accepted God Almighty as her only God.

That action had infuriated the Dark One. He had schemed and plotted and sworn to have her as his own. For years Satan had tried to kill Sam and possess Nydia as his own. He had flung his awesome powers toward

10

that end.

But whatever Satan did, it always ended in failure at bringing Sam and Nydia to their knees, to worship him.

Once he thought for sure he had them up in Canada. He failed, and the skies darkened and it stormed for days. Another time he was certain he had them in upstate New York. But Sam destroyed his coven and then blew up the town to spite him.

And through it all, Nydia had stood like a rock beside her husband and child.

And the Dark One cursed them.

"Call the dog, Sam," she said.

Sam hesitated.

"He won't hurt us. He is why we are here."

Sam opened the door and got out. It was warm for this early in the spring, and the hot winds fanned him.

He wondered if it was *just* the wind.

He thought not.

Sam squatted down beside the car and called for the dog to come to him. "Come on, boy. Come to me."

The dog did not hesitate. He rose from a sitting position and trotted to Sam, standing in front of the young man.

Sam stayed in a squat, looking at the dog. He couldn't tell what breed it was. It looked to be perhaps a hundred pounds, with a massive head and large jaws. The crushing power in those jaws would be tremendous. The dog appeared to have some German shepherd in him, as well as perhaps some boxer. His ears were pure hound dog. He was solid, with powerful legs. A thick neck.

But it was his eyes that fascinated Sam. One was light blue, the other one was a yellow-gold color. Sam wondered if the dog was blind in his pale eye, as is so often the case. He tested the animal. The pale eye seemed to be normal.

Sam turned around and looked back. Little Sam was awake, sitting up on the backseat, looking at his father and the dog.

"You like him, Sam?" his father asked.

The boy smiled and nodded his head.

"I wonder if he has fleas?" Sam muttered.

"I doubt it," Nydia said, a touch of the mysterious in her voice.

"Dog!" Little Sam said, his voice filled with excitement. "Dog!"

"I guess that's what we'll call him," his father said.

Sam looked more closely at the big dog. No collar.

"That you can see." Nydia spoke softly.

When they first met, it startled Sam to have her read his mind. Now he paid very little attention to it. And since sometimes he did not know the true meaning behind her words—as now—Sam elected to remain silent.

The sky began to swiftly darken, announcing the forming of a savage prairie storm. Thunder rumbled around them and lightning lashed the heavens, seeking introduction with the earth.

Not God's earth, Sam thought. For he knew only too well—firsthand—that while God ruled the Heavens, the galaxies, Satan roamed the earth, ruling it from time to time.

Dog looked up at the dark sky and growled deep in his throat, baring his wet fangs at the lightning.

Little Sam, now in his fourth year, laughed at the approaching storm.

It was still unclear to mother and father exactly what

12

power the boy possessed . . . Good, or Bad.

Both felt the boy was on the side of Good, for he had exhibited signs to that effect.

But neither could be certain. They would have to wait. Wait.

The winds began to howl, screaming over the sand hills and ripping the hot air, but not cooling it. The air became hotter, and with it came a foul, evil-smelling, putrid odor. The odor assailed the nostrils of all who smelled it.

Dog sneezed and growled.

Sam looked around him, sudden realization touching him with a numbing sensation.

They were parked in the middle of what used to be Whitfield.

He said as much to Nydia.

"Yes," she replied. "I know. I can feel Dad's presence."

"Yes. But he is far away."

Dog growled and turned his big head, looking at Sam.

"Sam?" Nydia said. "Let's go."

"Are you afraid?" her husband asked.

"No. But I know where they are."

Strength filled the young man. He rose to his feet just as the first hot, stinking drops of rain began pelting the barren earth. He opened the door and Dog jumped onto the backseat, lying down beside Little Sam.

Sam slid behind the wheel and turned around. "Where, Nydia?"

Her eyes were closed and her brow furrowed in deep thought. Sweat streaked her face. Sam remained silent, for he had seen her like this before.

The storm battered the car. The winds shrieked in a familiar language to those whose lives were dedicated to

13

fighting evil.

Sam looked back at Little Sam and Dog. The boy was patting the huge head of the animal. Dog opened his eyes and gazed into the dark eyes of the boy. Something invisible moved between them; some . . . understanding, Sam felt.

Sam took his foot off the brake and the car moved forward slowly.

"They're waiting, Sam," Nydia said. "They are firmly entrenched and waiting for us."

"What do you see, Nydia?"

He was suddenly aware of Dog sitting up on the backseat, his big head resting on the back of the front seat, his mismatched eyes studying Nydia.

"Cold unblinking eyes," she said, her voice husky.

"What is behind those eyes, Nydia?"

"I don't know. Yet."

"Which way, Nydia?"

"I see cypress trees and Spanish moss. Lazy streams. No. Bayous. It's very hot. The people are friendly and open."

"Bayous? Louisiana?"

"Yes."

"What else, Nydia?"

She opened her eyes and turned her head, looking at Sam. "Black magic."

2

The town of Becancour lay just to the north of the center of the state, and a bit to the east of the geographical center of Louisiana. Here is where the Cajun influence really took hold, in speech and music and philosophy.

And in Becancour was where the Dark One had chosen to face his old enemy: God.

Becancour lay off the beaten path; no roads ran east and west. A state road ran north and south, connecting some twenty miles later with Highway 28 to the north, and absolutely, positively nothing to the south.

Except swamps.

Dark, deep, foreboding swamps.

And the population number of Becancour was to some people . . . well, *odd*.

Odd, that it never seemed to change. It had not changed in the last six years. It remained a constant. When someone was born, someone either died, or moved away. When dying came first, someone either moved in, or was born.

Odd.

But since Becancour was so far off the beaten path, that little oddity never came to anyone's attention.

15

Until it was too late.

Such a pretty little town, it was said by those few who visited Becancour.

Sure was.

And the people were so friendly.

Sure were.

But there weren't many dogs, though.

Nope.

Sure were a lot of cats, though.

Yep.

A lot of cats.

"Sure is hot," Thelma Lovern remarked to her husband.

"Sure is," Frank agreed. "And it's so damned early in the season, too."

Frank and Thelma owned the local motel. It didn't have a name. Just **M O T E L.**

They also owned the café adjoining the motel. The café didn't have a name, either. Just **E A T S.**

"Reckon we'll get some tourists in this season, Mother," Frank said.

"I'm sure we will, Frank," Thelma agreed.

Neither one of them believed it. Any tourist who came to Becancour was either hopelessly lost or drunk. Or both.

Frank and Thelma had owned the motel and café for twenty years. They made a living, and that was about it.

"Sure is hot," Thelma said.

"Sure is," Frank agreed. If she says that one more time, Frank thought, I'm gonna kill the bitch!

Across the street, at the most popular bar in town, Lula's Love-Inn, Lula Magee was unlocking the front door to let in her clean-up man, Jules Nahan. Lula noticed that Jules looked even worse than he normally looked. She commented on that.

"I hate cats, Lula. I hate them worse than I do a cottonmouth. And this town is full of 'em. Where the hell did they all come from?"

"I don't know, Jules. But calm down. You need a drink."

"Damn shore do."

She gave him a beer and a broom. "I'll be in my office, Jules."

Jules sat down to rest before work.

Down the street, Chief of Police Sonny Passon sat in his office and stared at Deputy Don Lenoir. He opened his mouth to speak, closed it, then finally blurted, "Would you mind saying that again, Don?"

Don repeated it.

The chief shook his head. "Don, now I know you went off to college and got you a fancy degree in law enforcement, then you done a hitch in the Marines. I know you're a bright young man. You been all over the world and seen a lot. But, Don, don't come in here talkin' a bunch of shit to me! It's too damn hot for jokes."

"I'm not joking, Sonny," the deputy said.

Since Becancour was so far away from anything in the parish, a deputy was stationed there on a permanent basis.

And nobody wanted to be that deputy, 'cause nothing ever happened in Becancour.

Old Man Jobert sometimes dipped too deep into his muscadine wine, dressed up in his French Foreign Legion uniform, and marched through the streets of Becancour, singing "La Boudin" at the top of his lungs. But Jobert

17

never gave the arresting officer any problems. Just slept it off in an unlocked cell.

Sometimes the local good ol' boys got rowdy in Lula's Love-Inn, but Sonny Passon's patrolmen, and one patrolwoman, were very adept at handling rowdy good ol' boys. More than one good ol' boy around Becancour had bumps and scars on his noggin from tangling with the Becancour city police. Especially when one good ol' boy grabbed patrolwoman Rita Dantin by the tit and shouted, *"Grand teton! Teter, s'il vous plaît?"*

Rita bounced a hickory stick off his *tête de mort* and gave him a tremendous *mal de tête* of the headbone.

For a fact, Becancour used to be lots of fun. A fais do do many times during the summer. Church picnics, lots of good times.

But the townspeople had changed over the months. No one seemed to have much fun anymore. Oh, the regulars still came to Lula's Love-Inn and drank and played the jukebox and shot pool and got drunk. But it was . . . different somehow.

People were more wary now. And for no good reason that anyone could explain.

"Devil worship, Don?" Sonny almost whispered the question.

"Old Man Musto's missing sheep, Sonny?"

"Yeah. What about it?"

"I found it this morning. Mutilated. I took pictures." He tossed several Polaroids on Sonny's desk. The chief looked at them, paled, and placed them back on his desk.

"It was layin' in a circle. What the hell does that mean, Don?"

"I don't know. Now, about those dogs your people found, Sonny?"

"How do you know about them?" The question was sharply asked.

"Come on, Sonny! It's a big parish but a small town. People talk. Hell, Sonny! You can't keep nothing secret among Cajuns. Or damn little."

"Yeah, but it usually stays among us, Don."

"I haven't said a word to the sheriff."

"*Pour de bon*. OK, OK. It's kids, Don. Got to be kids. But why are they doing it?"

"How do you know it's kids?"

A sigh. "I don't. Don, I was with the Highway Patrol twenty years. Finally pulled the pin. Started out 'way to hell and gone up in Monroe. Ended up down in Lake Charles. I've seen everything anyone could throw at me. But I ain't *never* had a case of devil worship. Jesus Christ, I don't know anything about it."

"I think we'd better learn, Sonny. Both of us."

Sam, Nydia, Little Sam, and Dog pulled into Becancour at two o'clock that afternoon. It was early May, and already the temperature was in the nineties, with the humidity matching it.

"You take pets?" Sam asked Frank at the check-in counter.

"Mister," Frank said, "as long as it don't shit on the floor, you can have an ape in the room with you." He grinned at Sam. Just please don't say it's hot out! Frank thought. Please!

"Sure is hot out," Sam said.

Frank gritted his dentures. "Will you be staying long?" he managed to say.

"Until we find a house to rent for the summer."

19

Frank beamed. "I *got* a house!"

"Hey, that's great," Sam said with a smile.

"It's about five miles out of town." He pointed. "South. Right on the bayou. Two bedrooms, bath and a half, carpet throughout. It isn't nothing fancy, but it's clean. There's even a boat there ya'll can use."

"Okay if we wait until tomorrow to look at it?" Sam asked.

"Sure!" Frank handed Sam a key. "I'm givin' you and the missus the suite. Two rooms. It's Number 20. All the way down on this side. We'll drive out in the morning and look at the house."

"That'll be fine," Sam said, taking the key.

"Ya'll be sure and have supper with us in the café this evenin'," Frank told him. "We're servin' up red beans and rice."

"Sounds . . . delicious," Sam replied, not having the foggiest notion what the man was talking about.

Dog stood up and placed his front paws on the countertop, staring at Frank through those strange mismatched eyes set in the huge head. Frank took a step backward, momentarily startled.

"Does he bite?" Frank asked.

"He's never bitten me," Sam told him.

Located just inside the city limits, on the southern edge of Becancour, on Dumaine Street, was the largest house in town. The old Dorgenois home. Back in the early 1800's, when Becancour was just a tiny village, Romy Dorgenois moved his family from New Orleans up to Becancour. Rumor had it they moved out of New Orleans under protest. Seems the Dorgenoises had gotten involved with black magic, voodoo . . . and Satanism.

No one ever really knew; or if they did, over the years, they weren't talking. However . . . it was widely accepted throughout the community that the Dorgenois house was haunted. Most accepted it good-naturedly, as a joke, but there were those who took it much more seriously.

With good reason.

There had been some mysterious deaths over the years. And the people who died had been very vocal about the Dorgenois family. And although the priests involved would not talk about it, the incidents of exorcism, or attempted exorcisms, had increased ever since the Dorgenoises moved into Becancour.

How many exorcisms had been successful?

No one knew.

Or they weren't talking.

The last two generations of Dorgenoises had refused to live in the huge mansion set on twenty acres of land. And their explanations for not doing so were vague.

House was just too large, said Grandfather R.M. Dorgenois and his wife, Colter.

Maybe.

We prefer the more modern type of home, said the grandson, Romy Dorgenois, and his wife, Julie.

Sure.

So the Dorgenois family began renting out the lovely mansion.

A lot.

Back in the 1930s, when the house was first rented out, a young boy fell to his death, tumbling down the long, spiraling stairs. Damn shame, was the consensus of the townspeople. He was sure a cute little altar boy, too.

The sheriff said a cat had tripped the boy. The father

shot the cat. About a month later the father drowned in the sluggish bayou behind the house.

And some of the older townspeople still insist that goddamned cat reappeared.

Of course, no one believed that.

And then the house was rented to a New York City couple name of Franklin. They had two kids, a boy and a girl. The family was devout Catholics. And they didn't much care for cats. It seemed that the house came with a built-in population of rat catchers. Couple of dozen of them. All different colors.

One day the family went on a fishing trip back in the dark bayous. The family, along with the two local guides, never came back, and their bodies were never found.

The Dorgenois house stayed empty for several years after that. Then a young couple from up in Little Rock rented the place for a honeymoon. Three weeks into the month the couple had a bad quarrel and the young bride ran out into the warm night, crying. Sheriff said it looked like she tripped on some vines and hit her head on one of the fountain walls. Busted her head wide open. She died a couple of days later, in Old Doctor Livaudais's clinic right there in Becancour.

Then in the 1950s some local kids broke into the house one Halloween night. No one ever did figure that one out. That young Claverie girl went slap-dab crazy. Took a half dozen men to restrain her. Took her to the nut house. Still there. The young Savoie boy was found dead in the musty study of the old mansion. Not a mark on him. Just sitting on the floor, stone dead. The Rogers girl come out of it all right, the townspeople reckoned, and turned into a beautiful woman, but Jesus God, she turned . . . well, *strange*. Yeah, that was the word.

Bonnie Rogers was weird. Dave Porter was . . .

Oh . . . 'fore I forget, that Savoie boy? His parents wouldn't let the funeral parlor people do anything with him. Just stuck him in a box and shoveled the dirt over him. Turned cold that day the boy was planted. Mean, bone-chilling cold for that time of the year and for that part of the country. The wind was howling and whistling and the drizzle that fell from the sky was cold.

Dave Porter? Well, he seemed all right. Got out of high school and went off to college and then the Army and come back and married Margie Gremillion. Started him up an insurance agency and done all right for himself. Margie says her husband gets a little bit flaky at times . . . especially around Halloween. And sometimes when the moon is full, too. Likes to sit out in the yard and look up at the moon. Seems like maybe he could see something up there that nobody else could see.

And who knows? Maybe he can.

Anyway, there was, let's see, two or three more families tried to vacation in the Dorgenois house.

One family paid a whole summer's rent, then up and pulled out after just a week there. Didn't leave no forwarding address or nothin'. Just hauled ass in the middle of the night. Another family come down from way up north, Michigan, it was. They left one of their own down here in Louisiana, in the Becancour graveyard. No one ever figured out just how the young man died, but one of his friends who come down with him found him. Boy like to have gone stark ravin' nuts.

He claimed a bunch of cats was eatin' on his friend's dead body.

Now . . . no one really believed *that*. But . . . come to think of it, that boy had a closed-casket funeral. And Old

Mister Authement at the funeral parlor—his boy Art runs it now—never would talk about the boy.

Was there anyone else who come down to rent the Dorgenois house? Yeah . . . them people who have been livin' in it for the past, oh, maybe fifteen months.

Now, you talk *about* weird! Them folks take the cake for odd.

Whole passel of 'em. One guy who wanders around the grounds like a zombie. Jimmy something-or-another. One kid who couldn't be more than eighteen or nineteen at the most. Jon Le Moyne. A real cute girl called Janet. There's about ten or twelve people live in that ol' house.

Including one of the most beautiful women anybody around Becancour had ever laid eyes on.

Xaviere Flaubert.

3

"He has arrived, Princess," Xaviere was informed.

"Yes, I know," the woman said. She rose from her chair and walked across the room to a window, gazing out. She was tall, with rich brown hair that tumbled down her back. A magnificent figure, with full breasts and tiny waist. She was tall, her complexion flawless. Pale eyes and full lips.

She was also the daugher of Satan. She was the Princess of Darkness.

She was also Sam Balon's daughter.

Her mother, the witch Roma, had died giving birth to the monster. With that action, Roma had left her various earth-lifes to forever join her master, The Dark One. The birth had not been a natural one, the monster that would undergo a rapid metamorphosis had burst from the womb in a shower of blood and mangled flesh. The Mother Witch had only a quick glimpse of the monster before dying; but that one look was enough.

Already, just moments from the womb, the girl-baby had begun changing, growing quickly. In a year's time she would be a mature young woman.

For Satan is impatient.

Xaviere turned away from the darkly stained window—all the windows in the house were stained dark, for light hurt Xaviere's eyes—and looked at Janet. "They have an animal with them?"

"A big dog."

"He is much more than a dog, Janet. Believe that. He was placed here to protect my half-brother, Little Sam."

"Can he be killed?"

"I don't know," the Princess of Darkness replied truthfully.

"God . . ." Janet wrinkled up her face at the mention of His name. ". . . sent the dog?"

"Doubtful. Probably that meddling Michael. God's mercenary!"

Janet remained silent. Around her feet, a half dozen cats slinked and slithered, rubbing against her ankles.

"How is your child?" the Princess asked.

"Beautiful. Our Master slowed her growth. She is perfect."

"Sam Balon's daughter and Little Sam's half-sister. Is she ready?"

"Yes."

"We will not hurry. There is no need to rush matters. We have all the time in the world." Xaviere leaned down and picked up a cat. She stroked the fur of the animal and listened to it purr in satisfaction.

The purr contained a dark, evil sound.

Xaviere said, "It promises to be a good summer, Janet."

"Yes, Princess," the young woman replied, her lips pulling back in an ugly smile. "Very interesting, indeed."

26

The cats in the room began purring.

"Well, there she is, folks," Frank said, pointing to the home on the bayou. "What do you think of it?"

"It's lovely," Nydia said, slapping at a mosquito and missing.

"They'll be sprayin' around here in a few days," Frank assured her. "Then them things won't be so bad."

"Good," she muttered. She brushed back a lock of black hair and once more looked at the house. She was conscious of Frank gazing at her. Not in an ugly way, but in a man's very appreciative way of looking at a very beautiful woman.

"We'll take it," Sam said.

The men shook hands on the deal and it was set.

"That big mansion we passed on the way out here," Nydia said. "It's very old, isn't it?"

"Oh, yes'um. 'Bout a hundred and fifty years old. 'Course it's been done over a time or two. Rajeunir, you know?"

Nydia smiled. "*Oui, monsieur.* I understand perfectly."

"Ohh," Frank said with a grin. "You gonna get on all right down here, ma'am."

"We hope to," Nydia replied. "Well, let's see about getting settled in, Sam."

A car drove past and the driver tooted its horn.

Frank waved and said, "That's Dr. Tony Livaudais. His daddy was a doctor here, like his daddy 'fore him. Fine man."

"Anyone live in that old house?" Sam asked.

"Huh? Oh! The Dorgenois house. Oh, yeah. Some

27

folks been livin' there for, I guess . . . over a year, now."

"I was just curious," Sam said. "We like to tour old homes. Would it be possible?"

"Ahhh . . . I kinda doubt it. Them folks that live there are . . . well, odd. Hardly ever see none of them people. They just don't come out much."

Sam smiled. "Well, I guess that lets that out."

But Frank had a bit more to say about the Dorgenois house. "Place is haunted."

"The mansion?" Sam questioned.

"Yes, sir. Been haunted ever since it was built. I 'member my granddaddy talkin' about that place. He wouldn't go near it."

Nydia smiled at Frank. "Do you really believe it's haunted, Mr. Lovern?"

"Well . . ." Frank drawled the word with a grin.

Then he couldn't remember what they'd been talking about. He just drew up a blank.

"Something wrong, Mr. Lovern?" Sam asked.

"Huh? Oh! Why . . . no. I reckon not. Well, time for me to get back. Everything is turned on. I come out this morning and aired it out and then turned on the air-conditioning. Ought to be nice and cool in there for ya'll. I'll see you around."

He got in his car and left without looking back.

Sam and Nydia exchanged glances. Nydia said, "Could you feel the Dark One's presence, Sam?"

"Yes. But only slightly. I'm not sure I understand that."

"Nor do I." She looked toward the sluggish bayou. "I wonder if there are alligators in there?"

"Probably. And various types of snakes, including

28

Cottonmouth moccasins."

His wife smiled. "Are you concerned about Little Sam?"

He returned the smile. "Nothing can happen to Little Sam. But you and I can be bitten. So be careful, Nydia."

She took his big hard hand. "Come on. Mr. Lovern said the place had pots and pans and dishes."

"So?"

"We're going to wash them all, turn the mattresses, and vacuum the place."

Grumbling good-naturedly, Sam allowed himself to be tugged along, Little Sam and Dog following.

Only Dog spotted the cats slinking along the brush on the north and south borders of the property. His mismatched eyes narrowed and gleamed; but he neither barked nor growled. Just watched.

"Did you run them?" Deputy Lenoir asked Chief Passon.

"Yes," the chief replied. "The car is registered to Sam Balon. Checks out. Valid driver's license. No wants, no warrants."

Don poured a cup of coffee; strong Cajun coffee. He sat down across from the chief of police and said, "I wonder why they came here?"

Passon shrugged. "For a fact, they had to have had a reason. This place isn't even on a lot of maps."

"Why do I get the feeling you're holding back from me, Sonny?"

"I asked for his military records . . . if he has any, that is. I never got a reply on the teletype. But about ten minutes after I punched it in, the FBI called me—or the

29

guy said he was from the FBI. I don't think he was. He told me that Sam Balon served with honor in the Army Rangers." Sonny lifted his eyes to meet Don's. "Period. That's it. You been a cop long enough to know the feeling that you're being had, right, Don?"

"Sure. That's what you think?"

"That's what I think."

City Police Officer C.D. Capell walked into the office. "Who are those folks just rented the Lovern house out on the bayou, Chief?"

"We were just talking about them. They're from New York State."

Capell looked pained. "Yes, sir. I see that plate on their car. But what else?"

"Nothing," Don told him. "Sam Balon is clean."

"Balon?" Capell said. "How come that name is familiar to me?"

"Is it?" Passon asked. "I'm not familiar with it."

Capell was thoughtful for a moment. The patrolman was widely read, particularly enjoying and subscribing to every magazine on unexplained phenomena. He said, "It'll come to me. I know that name."

"You think of it, you tell me," Passon said.

"Oh, I will, Chief. And I'll think of it. Bet on it."

The morning passed very quickly for Sam and Nydia. The rented house was neat and well-kept, but Nydia insisted on washing all the silverware and every pot and pan and dish. Sam vacuumed the floor and turned the mattresses, then went into town to buy several sets of sheets and pillowcases. As he passed the Dorgenois house, he cut his eyes.

A young woman was sitting in the gazebo, playing with a small child. Sam knew the woman—Janet Sakall. Memories flooded him, memories of the night the young devil worshiper had drugged his drink and seduced him, in his own den.

He wondered if the young child was his?

He felt it probably was. And he wondered which side of the line separating Light and Dark the young child's loyalties might lie?

He thought he knew that, too.

He drove on into town and parked in front of a family department store. He got out of the car and stood for a moment, surveying the town.

Sam Balon was several inches over six feet tall. He was very muscular, with big shoulders and arms, thick wrists, a narrow waist. His hair was thick, dark brown. He was not of the pretty-boy handsomeness . . . he was rugged-looking, with a solid, square jaw.

And while he was quite human, and his flesh bled when cut, he had been blessed by God. Sam Balon was God's earthbound warrior. His destiny was clear to him. Admittedly, he had tried to sidestep that responsibility. And he found he could not. As his father, Sam Balon, Sr., had done, the son would spend his life seeking out and fighting Satan and the Dark One's followers.

Sam was under no illusions concerning his career. He knew no mortal could ever destroy Satan. Sam did not attempt that. And he knew, from experience, that one could not gaze upon the various shapes of the Prince of Darkness. For if one gazed too long, he or she would be destroyed.

Or enslaved.

Sam looked up and down the street. Something was wrong here, he thought. And not just the fact that a coven was here.

It was more than that.

Then it came to him. He had not heard a dog barking since he had arrived. Not one.

He felt eyes on him. Unfriendly eyes.

He looked up, at the top of the building housing the department store, and gazed into the cold eyes of a cat, staring at him. Man stared at beast.

Beast!

Sam wondered if the Beasts were here? He felt sure they were—but where? And when would they appear? Unanswered questions.

Sam recalled what he could about the Beasts.

His father had called them God's failures. But before God could allow them time to become extinct, Satan had taken control of them. The Bible doesn't make any references to God's mistakes—there was no one around to record them or confirm them. And the Beasts were cunning, for they survived the Flood and everything else God did to destroy the evil on the planet Earth. The Beasts belonged to Satan; they answer only to the Prince of Darkness.

Satan's Beasts can lie dormant for hundreds of years, and they have a native intelligence. They are part human, part animal—all evil. The Beasts will breed with anything—anything!—in order to keep their species alive.

But there was one thing that might reveal their position in or around Becancour: while the others slept, a chosen Sentry remained alert, on guard.

And they stink. God, do the Beasts stink. If Sam could find that hideous odor, he could track to the lair of the Beasts.

Sam cleared his head of the Beasts. One thing at a time, he cautioned himself. He once more glanced up.

The cat was gone.

But what connection did the cats have with those now residing in the Dorgenois house?

Another unanswered question.

A little? A lot? Or nothing?

Sam walked into the department store and did his shopping. First things first. Sam knew he could not make the first hostile move. Those who worshiped Satan would have to do that. And he knew from past experience that he would be laughed at if he tried to warn the townspeople of what faced them. And . . . he did not know who to trust in the town. How many had gone over to the Dark Side? He had no way of knowing.

But one thing he knew for certain . . . He would find out soon enough.

He paid for his purchases and walked back out into the early summer heat. He stopped on the sidewalk and stared at the hood of his car. The hood was dotted with numerous cat tracks.

But not a cat was in sight.

Sam felt eyes on him and turned to face whoever was doing the staring.

Sam smiled and spoke to the man.

"You're new in town," the priest said.

"Just got here yesterday," Sam said. He extended his hand. "Sam Balon."

"I'm Daniel Javotte. Staying long, Mr. Balon?"

"Oh, probably the summer. It seems like a nice place."

33

"Yes, it is. Perhaps you'll come to services this Sunday?" He noticed the wedding band on Sam's left hand. "And bring your family."

"We're not Catholic, Father."

"You don't have to be, Mr. Balon."

"Well . . . perhaps we'll come to see you at the rectory sometime."

"That's a start. Any children, Mr. Balon?"

"One. A boy. He's four."

"All the churches have gone together and formed a very nice preschool . . . well, almost all the churches, that is."

Sam chuckled. He did not have to ask what church would be absent. And he felt the priest knew it. "I was raised to be tolerant of another's faith, Padre. My mother taught me that."

"Oh. And your father?"

"He died before I was born. He was a preacher."

"What faith, Mr. Balon?"

"Christian Church, Padre. Do you object to my calling you Padre?"

"Not at all. A preacher, you say. Not a minister?"

"Mother told me that Dad said there was only one reverend person to ever walk the face of the earth. He was crucified."

"I see." The priest smiled. He was a few inches shorter than Sam, but with a rugged look about him. Stockily built, with dark, piercing eyes. His hair was peppered with gray, but he looked to be in excellent physical shape. "Then I'm sure your mother taught you that Catholics don't have horns and a tail?" Javotte smiled the question.

"Yeah. But you couldn't prove it by listening to some people."

"I think we're going to get along, Sam Balon. Welcome to Becancour. If you get a chance, do come to Sunday services. I think the sermon might interest you."

"Oh? What's it titled?"

Javotte's dark eyes locked with Sam's. Something was behind those eyes, but Sam couldn't quite make it out. The priest said, "'The Mark of the Beast.'"

4

"And you think we should enroll Sam in this preschool whatever?" Nydia asked.

"I think it would be good for him."

"Can I take Dog?" Little Sam asked.

"No," Sam and Nydia both answered.

The boy took it well. He did not pout. He never pouted, and rarely cried. He knew who he was and what he was. And when it was time, he would tell his parents. Or show them.

Whatever his Master wished of him.

"Is the program in session now?" Nydia asked.

"I don't know. I forgot to ask. I would think not. Probably start around the first of June."

Little Sam sat on the floor of the house and listened, his dark eyes giving away no inner thought.

"Feel like a walk along the bayou?" she asked.

The family walked along the bayou's edge, with Sam keeping a wary eye out for snakes. He had taken one phase of his Ranger training in the swamps of Georgia, and he had a healthy respect for Cottonmouth moccasins. He knew that a rattler, most of the time, would not strike unless provoked; Sam had walked within two feet of rattlers and they had not attempted to strike. A Copperhead was a mean snake, totally unpredictable. The Coral snake, also found in Louisiana, was a docile snake, seldom seen, but very deadly. But a Cottonmouth would stalk a person; a Cottonmouth would strike for no apparent reason. Of all the poisonous snakes indigenous to the United States, Sam hated Cottonmouths, and would kill every one he found.

"We'll have to buy some fishing gear and get licensed. We've got to behave as ordinary tourists. And we're going to have to meet people and socialize."

"Well," Nydia said. "That'll be fun."

Sam nodded. He pointed to Dog. "Do you know for certain what his role is to be?"

"No. Only that he is to be with us."

Dog stopped, swung his big head, and looked at Sam and Nydia.

Then he trotted on, catching up with Little Sam.

"I think he knows what we say," Sam remarked.

Nydia did not reply. She took her husband's hand and they walked slowly along. Sam's eyes swept the gloomy interior of the bayou. He had studied a map of the area and knew this swamp extended for miles, east, west, and south. Within the interior of the swamp there were dots and pockets of upthrusted earth, islands of dry land where . . .

. . . the Beasts might live.

"And a boat," Sam vocalized his thoughts. "How are the finances holding out?"

He smiled as he asked that, for his wife was a very wealthy young woman.

"Oh," Nydia replied, catching her husband's smile. "I think we can muddle by. Sam?"

37

"Uh-huh?"

"How do we handle the funds? Can I transfer monies to the local bank without bringing a lot of attention to us?"

"I've been thinking about that. Let's transfer enough to live on and use cards to buy whatever else we need." He shrugged his shoulders. "Either way it's going to cause talk, I'm thinking, since our cards—a few of them—have no limit."

"And if the police run checks on us? . . ."

"The way you had your people set things up, we're a very wealthy young married couple who don't have to work."

"Very well. That priest you talked to?"

"He knows something. But I couldn't read his eyes. After we feel around some, I think we should have him out for dinner."

"Let's get the law on our side, too," she suggested.

"Yes. I'll pay them a visit in the morning."

"You saw Janet." It was not put in question form.

"Yes. No doubt about that. I think it's going to be a waiting game this time."

"I was afraid you were going to say that."

Dr. Tony Livaudais looked at the young woman sitting on the bed in his clinic. She had been brought in by her parents just after he had returned from lunch. He had checked her, and found evidence that she had been raped. That supported what her parents had told him.

But the girl would not discuss it.

"Judy," Tony said. "Are you afraid that you'll be hurt if you tell me who did it?"

"Nothing happened," the girl said, a deadly flatness to her voice.

"Judy, I'm a doctor. I am also the medical examiner for this part of the parish. Don't try to kid me, girl."

Her eyes shifted to meet his. Tony fought to keep from taking a step backward. The girl's eyes were hate-filled . . . and something else lay lurking in their misty depths. Something that the young doctor could not read. And was not all that certain he wanted to read.

"Me and my boyfriend got it on, that's all," Judy told him.

"Judy," Tony said patiently, "I found evidence that you have been both vaginally and anally violated. There are enough minor tears and bruises to tell me that one person could not have done it. I have known your boyfriend since his arrival on this earth. Don Hemming may well be the biggest jerk in Becancour, but he is not Superman. I also happen to know that Don can barely manage to write his own name, much less be proficient enough to tattoo that cat on your buttocks. That is a fresh tattoo. Not more than twenty-four hours old. I saw a lot of them in the Navy. In places I don't care to reveal. I'm still trying to forget. Now you level with me, girl. Or I'll call Deputy Lenoir and Chief Passon in here and you can talk with them. It's all up to you; which is it going to be?"

"You want me to tell you something, Dr. Livaudais?"

"Yes, I do, Judy."

"OK. Dr. Livaudais?"

"Yes, girl?"

"Go screw yourself!"

*   *   *

39

Sonny Passon almost swallowed his cigar. "She told you to do what?"

Dr. Livaudais repeated what Judy had told him.

Deputy Don Lenoir shook his head. "Are we talking about the same girl, Tony? Judy Mahon is one of the sweetest kids in town."

"I always thought so," Tony agreed. "But she damn sure has a gutter-mouth now."

"And you're sure she was raped?" Passon asked.

"I was." There was open and ill-concealed disgust in the doctor's voice. "Now I'm not so sure."

"Meaning? . . ." Don asked.

"Well, I think she was a willing participant in what we used to call a gang-bang."

"Jesus Christ!" Passon said. "Where do you reckon her boyfriend was all this time?"

"I think he was a part of it," Tony said. "Don Hemming is one sorry jerk!"

"Great football player, though," Patrolman Black injected.

That got him a dirty look from everyone in the squad room.

"If that's all you have to contribute, Louis," Chief Passon said. "Shut your mouth."

"What'd I say?" the city cop said, astonishment in the question.

The doctor, the deputy, and the chief ignored him.

"So what do we do?" Dr. Livaudais asked.

"We can't do anything," Deputy Lenoir replied. "Not unless she brings charges. Or her parents. Judy is sixteen and Don is seventeen, so that opens up a new can of worms; he's legally an adult."

"How about Health and Human Resources?" Tony asked.

"I'll call Mac and see what he says about it," Passon said. "And he might get to it in a month or so."

"Why a cat?" Don asked. "Why would a bright, beautiful, well-brought-up girl have a cat tattooed on her butt?"

"God only knows," Tony said, striking much closer to home than he realized.

Sonny Passon felt eyes on him. But no one in the squad room was staring at him. Irritated, he glanced out the office window into the hall. No one there, either.

"What the hell?" he muttered.

Don glanced at Passon. *"Qu'est-ce que c'est?"*

He shook his head. "I don't know. I felt . . . *feel* eyes on me."

"Hell, it's just a cat," Louis Black said, pointing.

All the men looked. A calico cat sat perched on the air conditioner, outside the window.

"Shoo!" Passon said, waving his hands at the cat.

The cat yawned.

Passon picked up a magazine and beat it against the windowpane.

The cat sat and stared at the man through very cold, unemotional eyes.

"Well, damn!" Passon said, and solved the problem by lowering the blind. "I can't stand for anything to just stare at me."

"Anybody but me noticed the number of cats in town?" Tony questioned.

"There's a bunch of 'em," Louis Black agreed. "More than I ever remember seein'."

41

"Cats," Tony said softly. "And a cat tattooed on the buttocks of Judy Mahon. Is there . . . could there be some connection?"

"What would it be, Tony?" Passon asked. "Hell, they're just house cats."

"Yeah," the doctor said, standing up. "You're right."

After trudging along for more than five miles without seeing one single vehicle of any type, the hitchhiker began to realize that he'd been had. Those goddamned smart-mouthed kids back there in that hick town on 84 had told him a friggin' lie when they said this was a shortcut down to 71. This wasn't no friggin' shortcut; this was a highway to nowheres. Walt Davis kicked at a beer can and cussed.

Well, he thought. The goddamned road has to lead somewheres. Nobody, not even these funny-talkin' folks in Louisiana builds a road that goes nowheres.

He hoped.

Walt trudged on. He couldn't figure out how in the hell he'd let that guy convince him to ride down to Mississippi with him. Walt had never liked the south. Too goddamned hot for one thing. Too goddamned many cops for another. Goddamned cops always asking a bunch of damn-fool questions. Always wantin' to know if you was headin' somewheres for a job?

A job! The very thought of work made his stomach hurt. Screw a job. *Any* job. It was easier to steal. Sleep out in a field at night, watch to see how many folks was in the house. Then come morning, watch them all leave, then bust in and grab any money that's layin' around. Be surprised how many folks leave money around.

Sometimes he got lucky and found a chick they'd left in bed. Wrap her head up in a pillowcase so's she can't see you, knock off a quick piece of ass, and split. Stuff the chickie in a shed around the place, all trussed up, and a guy had all day and sometimes half the night to get clear.

Hitch to the next town wearin' nice clothes took from the house, grab a bus for the next town, then change directions, ridin' the bus right through the town you'd just left. Stupid fuckin' cops never checked the people who was already on the bus.

They'd ask the driver, "You pick up anyone on the road?"

"Naw."

Usually that was it. But even if a guy was checked by the cops, the trick was don't never take no rings and watches and guns and shit like that. Just money. It ain't against the law to be carryin' money.

But lately, Walt had been experiencing a run of bad luck. He figured money must be gettin' tight, 'cause there damn sure wasn't much of it left layin' around the houses no more.

But, he thought, walking along the deserted highway, at least I ain't been busted in a long, long time. He'd been arrested a couple of times as a kid, booked, mugged, fingerprinted. But that had been local shit. Way to hell and gone back up in Maryland. And all that shit in the movies about 'em checkin' prints in five minutes was pure garbage, man, and every con artist and crook and thief in the country that was worth a damn knew it. Sometimes it takes months. And if your prints ain't on record with the Feds, forget it, baby.

Another trick was to wear gloves. Just be careful bustin' in, then find a pair of gloves to wear. Every house

43

has four/five pairs of gloves layin' around. Straights are so stupid *they* oughtta be locked up.

Walt sat down to rest. The heat was bad, man. He looked up at the road sign. Becancour 2 Miles.

He shook his head. Damn folks down here had the dumbest names for their towns.

Out of the corner of his eyes, he caught movement to one side. He turned his head and took a better look.

A cat sat by the side of the road, staring at him. "Hey, pussy," Walt said. "What the hell you doin' way out here?"

The cat padded toward him on silent paws.

"Get your ass away from me," Walt told the animal. "You the wrong kind of pussy."

The cat made a funny kind of noise in its throat.

Walt crawled to his knees. "Get away from me, cat."

Something landed on his back with a soft thud. Walt screamed as claws dug through his sweat-soaked shirt and into the flesh of his back. He hurled himself to one side and landed on his back, crushing the thing that was clawing at him. Jumping to his feet, he frantically looked around him.

A dozen cats were gathered around him.

The cat that had leaped onto his back, clawing and hissing, lay kicking and dying on the shoulder of the highway.

Walt jerked up his suitcase and ran across the road.

The cats followed him, licking their chops, sniffing the air, smelling the hot blood from the deep clawmarks on his back.

Something growled from deep in the dark timber. Walt spun around and around, looking to see what had growled and trying to keep an eye on the cats, as well.

44

Then a terrible odor struck Walt's nostrils. The smell was so bad it damn near caused him to puke.

Walt looked at the ditch. It was full of water and about six or seven feet across. He tossed his suitcase across the expanse of dark, brackish water and jumped in, wading across. He grabbed his suitcase and ran up the other side of the bank, climbed the fence, and stepped into the woods, the earth squishy beneath the soles of his shoes.

And that smell! Jesus God . . . it smelled like . . . like . . .

Death!

Walt looked back at the cats. They were all lined up in a neat furry row, like silent soldiers, watching him.

"Fuck you!" Walt said.

He turned around and came face to face with the most godawful looking thing he'd ever seen in all his life.

The thing grabbed at him.

5

Sonny Passon was experiencing a feeling very much like that feeling he'd had just before his one and only shoot-out as a highway cop, back in 1963. One shoot-out in twenty years of carrying a badge up and down every highway in Louisiana wasn't bad.

He'd stopped a car for speeding and was walking up to the vehicle. The car had two guys in it, and they both got out. Mean-eyed-looking men.

Sonny had known—*known*—those turkeys were gonna pull guns. He couldn't tell you how he knew, but he knew.

Everything got all bright and clear to Sonny Passon. Things started moving kind of slow-like. He would swear to his dying day that he could hear every sound that was happening around him; every crawling insect, every flying bird, every hum, every chirp, every*thing*.

That was the way it was now.

He'd killed both those men, even though one of them got off the first shot. Sonny had gut-shot him twice, his second shot higher than the first, tearing out the guy's back, severing the spinal cord. Sonny had dropped to one knee just as the second snakehead was rounding the rear of the car. Sonny put two rounds into the guy's chest, one slug shattering the heart.

He'd got a big medal for that from the colonel and one from the governor. And no one in the troop ever knew that Sonny Passon, Trooper First Class, had pissed all over himself that day.

But that odd feeling just before the shooting . . . he'd never forgotten it.

And he couldn't quite figure out why he was feeling the same thing now.

With a sigh, Sonny turned out his desk lamp and went home. A beer would taste real good.

Dr. Tony Livaudais checked his waiting room. Empty. "Lock it up," he told his receptionist. "And have a good evening."

He returned to his office and shut the door. He couldn't understand the feeling of . . . well, he guessed it was depression that had wrapped itself around him.

For a fact, he needed some time off. But there was no way that would happen anytime soon.

But he didn't think that was it at all.

He just couldn't get over the Mahon girl. Things like that happened in the big cities; not in little towns like Becancour. Population three thousand six hundred and sixty-six.

Tony couldn't shake the feeling that something very bad was happening in and around Becancour.

He just didn't know what it might be.

Deputy Don Lenoir slowly drove through the peaceful-looking town. His radio crackled with calls, but they were all concerning other parts of the parish. Sometimes Don would go two or three weeks without a call from the sheriff's office, located almost thirty-five miles away, to the north and east.

Sometimes he got the feeling that no one really cared about Becancour. Of course, that wasn't true, but still he got that feeling at times.

Don's eyes swept both sides of the street. He had not seen a stray dog in weeks. People still had dogs, but they were the variety that were penned, or house dogs.

No stray dogs. Odd, he thought.

A carload of kids motored past him, heading in the opposite direction, the mufflers just legal, the radio—or tape player, probably—blaring rock and roll at an intolerable level of db's. Intolerable for an adult, that is.

Don caught a glimpse of the kids' faces. Not happy faces. Sullen.

Been a lot of that lately, too, he thought. The kids around town, most of them, that is, did not appear to be happy.

He drove on, his headlights picking up the darting shapes of cats.

Sure was a bunch of cats around Becancour.

He drove past the Dorgenois house and caught the flickering of candles. Those people who rented the place didn't use electricity . . . they used candles. Insurance rates, so Don was told, went sky-high when the company learned about that. Didn't bother the people at all, Dave Porter told Don. Rich, rich folks, he figured.

Don had seen the woman who was head honcho of the clan that lived there. A breathtaking beauty of a lady. But that day she had looked at Don from the rear seat of her limo, Don felt a chill run up and down his spine. The lady

48

was young, younger than Don's twenty-six years—but my God, those eyes. Cold and . . . something else, too. But Don had yet to figure out the other. It was just that she didn't appear to have any emotion in her eyes. They were flat, like when she was looking at him she wasn't really seeing him at all. Kind of like when a person looked at something without really seeing it.

Made a guy feel funny.

Father Daniel Javotte stepped out of his small apartment located next to the church and gazed out into the gathering dusk of early evening.

The priest could not .put into words what he was feeling. Could not, because he did not know exactly what it was.

It was a heavy, oppressive yet intangible sensation. It was like a stinking shroud recently taken from a rotting corpse.

But it was more than that.

What was happening in Becancour? This had always been such a friendly, open little town. Until . . . about a year ago. That's when Javotte first began experiencing the odd sensations. And those sensations had gradually built in intensity.

He had spoken to the other ministers in town . . . skirting the issue, just leaving it open-ended. Only one, the Methodist, Mike Laborne, had picked up on what Javotte was saying. Since then, Catholic and Methodist had become good friends, discussing their worries in private.

But neither could really put their finger on what was wrong.

Had there been a drop in church attendance?

No, none at all.

An increase in crime in the area?

No.

But there had been an increase in drinking around town. Booze sales were up about fifty percent from this time last year.

And the number of domestic crimes was on the increase, seldom reported to the police, but usually confided to the ministers.

A chill covered Javotte, a cold, clammy, numbing chill touched him. He knew then what it was he'd been experiencing for the past several months. It was . . .

. . . evil!

At Lula's Love-Inn, Lula looked at the packed bar and marveled at it. In all her years of running various bars around the parish, she'd never seen anything like it. Even a bunch of those psalm-singin' Baptists were openly knocking back the juice, coming in every evening to booze it up. Playin' around with the barmaids and with other's spouses.

Lula loved it!

"Sure is hot outside," Thelma said.

Frank Lovern reared back and knocked his wife clear out of her chair.

She was squalling at the top of her lungs as her butt hit the floor.

Grandfather Dorgenois knocked on his son's front door.

Romy's wife, Julie, opened the door and waved the man inside.

"I'll be brief," the older man said to his son. "Your brother Jack has escaped from the institution. They believe he is heading this way. We have to find him before the authorities do. You can handle him, Romy."

Romy brushed his face with a weary gesture. "I think it probably would be best if the police did find him, Dad."

"You can't mean that, Romy! He'd attack them and they'd kill him."

"Wouldn't that be best, Dad?" the son challenged.

The father's face hardened. "I will not dignify that with a reply, son. He's our flesh and blood; please keep that in mind."

Romy was not really the elder Dorgenois's son. R.M. and Colter were his grandparents. But they had raised him after his parents had been killed. Romy thought of his grandparents as parents, and that was the way it had been since he could remember.

"He's a monster, Dad. Face it, and admit it, please."

The older man stood his ground. "Are you going to help me, Romy?"

Slowly, hesitantly, Romy nodded his head. "Let me change clothes. You know I'll help."

Walt Davis squalled and cleared the fence with one leap, leaving his battered suitcase behind him. He ran right through the cats, knocking and kicking them spinning and yowling. Walt Davis, drifter, thief, rapist, and all around no-account, at that moment in his life could very well have qualified for the summer Olympics ten-thousand-meter run . . . and won, hands down.

51

After about a hundred yards the cats gave up the chase and disappeared into the woods on either side of the road. There would be other prey. There always had been before.

Except for a few meandering parish roads that unless one was familiar with would oftentimes prove more like a maze than roads, there was only the one road leading to Becancour. And it was on that road that R.M. and Romy Dorgenois drove, heading north. They were the first to spot the man running right down the center of the highway.

Romy pulled the car over to the side and called for Walt to stop, come over, and tell them what was the matter.

Walt collapsed on the hood, thinking surely he was about to have a heart attack. "Cats attacked me!" he managed to gasp.

Then he passed out.

"Cats!" Romy said.

But the older man's eyes were strangely hooded. He made no reply. He stood ramrod straight by the car, looking up the road, in the direction they'd been traveling.

"Dad?" Romy asked, kneeling down by the fallen, bloody man.

"No," R.M. said.

"What do you mean, *no?*" Romy asked. "Dammit, Dad, this man's back has been clawed to shreds."

"Not again," R.M. said. "It must not happen again."

"*Dad!*" Romy shouted.

The harsh voice cutting through the murky hot late spring air jarred the older man. He turned his head, looking down at Romy. "That poor man needs assistance.

52

Put him in the backseat of the car. We'll take him into the clinic."

Headlights cut the dusk. Romy and R.M. could make out the bar lights on top of the sheriff's department car. Don Lenoir jumped out and ran up to the men.

"What happened?" Don asked.

R.M. looked at Romy, warning in his eyes.

But Romy failed to see the warning. "Guy was running down the center of the road when we spotted him. He managed to say he was attacked by cats. Then he passed out."

"Attacked by *cats?*" Don questioned. "Like . . . well, cats?"

"That's what he said." Romy rolled Walt over, allowing Don to see the man's torn back.

"Deputy," R.M. Dorgenois said. "If this man's wild story gets out, people will be shooting at shadows . . . and a lot of them will be injured. If you get my point."

"Yes, sir," Don said. "I sure do."

"Would you take him to Dr. Livaudais's clinic, Deputy?" R.M. asked. "We'll be along presently to make our report."

Walt groaned and lifted his head. "Monster!" he gasped. "Some kind of wild man back there." He pointed. "You can probably see my suitcase on the east side of the highway. I never saw nothin' like that in my own life." He put his head on the road and began crying.

"Monsters?" Don questioned. "Attacking house cats and now monsters? What the hell is going on here?"

"I'm certain we shall get to the bottom of it all in due time, Deputy," R.M. said. "As a matter of fact, while you're taking the poor fellow to the clinic, Romy and I will cruise this road and see if we can find this man's

53

suitcase. Do you want us to leave it, or bring it in? If we find it, that is," he added.

Don knelt by Walt. "Mister, were you attacked by some guys?"

"No!" Walt sobbed. "It was cats. Plain ol' cats, man."

"Yeah," Don said, standing up. "If you find the suitcase, bring it in. But watch yourselves. I just got word that a nut escaped from that private institution over west of Alex. Some guy named Jack Dorg. You can't get much information out of those private places. Dorg probably isn't even the guy's real name. People pay big bucks to put family members in those places."

"Really?" R.M. said blandly. "I suppose that insures anonymity."

"Yeah, it sure does," the deputy said. "But makes it a lot harder on us if some nut escapes, though."

Don loaded Walt into his car and pulled out, heading back to Becancour.

"You think that monster is Jack, don't you, Dad?"

"It's a reasonable assumption. Poor Jack can twist his face into some awful masks. That disease he is suffering from is a hideous one, you know?"

Romy did not answer until they were back in the car. "Jack isn't suffering from any mortal disease, Dad," Romy said softly. "And you know it. And I've known it for some time."

R.M.'s face turned into a mask of conflicting emotions. He stared straight ahead through the windshield. "I don't know what you're talking about, Romy."

"It's truth time, Dad. It's way past truth time, don't you think?"

"Drive very slowly, son. Just creep along." He got a flashlight from out of the glove box and tested it.

"Dad, Jack has to be destroyed."

R.M. did not take his eyes from the darkness by the side of the road, that area the bright headlights could not penetrate. "He's your brother, Romy."

"He craves human flesh, Dad."

"He is suffering from a disease, Romy. It is medically documented. Lycanthrophy."

"You know better, Dad."

"I don't wish to discuss this, son. Let's just find Jack and have the people from the institution come get him. I have enough medication at home to sedate him until that time."

Romy stopped the car, put it in park, and twisted in the seat to face the older man. "Dad, I know that Jack killed our father and mother. I know that he then ate their flesh. I know that Jack dabbled in black magic ever since he was just a little boy. I know that he was born marked by Satan. You see, Dad, I know everything."

"How did you find out?" R.M.'s voice was no more than a whisper in the car.

"I finally got the truth out of old Doc Livaudais a few months before he died."

R.M. cleared his throat. "Rumors, son. Vicious unfounded rumors. There is no truth to any of them."

"When we get back home, Dad. I'll call Father Javotte. We'll go to the church. We'll kneel in front of the blessed Virgin and Jesus Christ, then you'll swear to that, right?"

"Preposterous!" R.M. said.

"Then you'll do it?"

R.M. turned his head to look at the man he had raised as his own son. He blinked away sudden tears. "You know I won't do that, Romy."

"Why in God's name didn't you or my real father and

mother stop him?"

"We tried, Son. But we found out too late what he'd become."

"And what was that, Dad?"

In the darkness by the road, from within the swampy timber, someone started laughing, evil-sounding laughter that came bell-clear through the open windows of the car.

6

Sam watched Dog's head come up and the big animal tense. His gaze was riveted on the front door.

Little Sam was in his room, watching TV on the portable Sam had bought that afternoon. Neither Sam nor Nydia cared much for commercial TV, preferring, when they did watch the tube, the PBS network.

Sam rose from his chair and walked to the book shelves. He slipped his hand behind a small row of books and took out a .22 caliber semiautomatic pistol. He jacked a round into the chamber and walked to the front door. He was conscious of Dog's eyes on him as he put a hand on the doorknob.

He could hear Nydia singing softly as she soaked in the bathtub.

He flipped on the porch light at the same time he jerked open the door.

He smiled as he saw an armadillo lumbering across the front yard, awkwardly making its way to the bayou's edge.

Sam turned off the porch light and stepped out onto the porch, and into the hot night. Peripheral vision caught fast movement to his left, near the yard's end, where it rapidly deteriorated into brush and timber.

Cats, several dozen of them. He watched as they streaked into the brush and heavy growth. Sam squatted down on the porch and waited, the .22 in his hand. Dog came out onto the porch and sat down, his eyes looking in the same direction as Sam's. Sam was sure the big animal could smell the cats, but he made no move to chase them.

A pack of them, Sam thought. One sees dog packs, but one seldom sees large cat packs.

Sam could never remember seeing one this large. A car came slowly down the road in front of the house. The headlights picked up dozens of eyes, gleaming in the night.

All staring in the direction of the house.

All looking . . .

. . . straight at Sam.

"No question about it," Dr. Livaudais said. "He's been badly clawed by some type of animal. Are you allergic to anything, Mr. . . . ah? . . ."

"Davis. No, Doc. Nothing that I'm aware of."

Tony cleaned the deep claw wounds and applied antiseptic. That brought Walt to attention.

"Where were you heading, Mr. Davis?" Don asked.

"I was headin' for Baton Rouge, lookin' for work. Some kids tole me I could take this shortcut. Turned out they lied."

"They sure did."

"Everything I got's in that suitcase, Deputy. 'Cept for the money in my wallet. I got money. I'm not a bum."

"No one said you were, Mr. Davis." Don had visually inspected the man moments before, noting that while

58

Walt's clothing was sweaty and wrinkled, it was not filthy clothing, and it was recently purchased. No road dirt was embedded in the man's hands or under his fingernails.

"I can't get your blood pressure down to an acceptable level, Mr. Davis," Tony said. "Have you a history of high blood pressure?"

"I . . . don't think so." Hell, he didn't know. Walt's BP hadn't been checked in so long he couldn't remember the last time. "I don't have any insurance, Doc."

"We'll worry about that later, Mr. Davis. No one has ever been turned away from this clinic because they lacked funds."

Walt was helped to a bed in a small clinic and was asleep a minute after his head hit the pillow.

It was still early, and Tony was keyed up. He asked Don to step into the small lounge. Over coffee, they talked.

"Now, about this monster he thinks he saw? . . ." Tony said.

"I don't know, Tony," Don replied. "I'm having a hard enough time accepting his story about cats attacking him."

"I think that much is true. I've treated dozens of kids and adults for cat clawing. But this was a very vicious attack. You noticed the spot where the flesh was torn out?"

"Yes. What about it?"

"That animal tore that out with its teeth. Now cats claw and bite, yes. But this appears to be an attack for food."

Don sat his coffee mug down on the table. "You're serious?"

"Very."

Don told Tony what R.M. had said about the people

59

panicking if the story got out.

"What were R.M. and Romy doing out that way?" Tony asked.

"I don't know. I was heading out that way because of that nut who busted out of that private bug house other side of Alex."

"What nut?"

Don shrugged. "All I got is his name, Jack Dorg. And the message that he's very dangerous. And maybe heading this way. Why would he be heading this way, Tony? I don't know of any family named Dorg in this area, do you?"

"Not . . . by that name, no."

Why did the doc hesitate? Don silently questioned. Why did his face suddenly change into a con mask? Or was that just my imagination?

"Tony? If you know something I should know, please level with me."

Tony sighed. He rose from the table and pushed back his chair. "Stick around for a few minutes, Don. Let me make a call. I . . . uh . . . I've been going over some of my father's old papers. Throwing away a lot of case histories that I have no use for. The families have all moved away, or died . . . whatever. I'll be back in a minute."

"OK."

What the hell was going on? Don mulled over many things during his short wait. Dorg? He didn't know a single person in the parish named Dorg. He'd never known of anybody named Dorg.

He sipped his coffee and waited. He looked up as Tony reentered the lounge.

"All right, Don. I called Chief Passon, asked him to

meet us over here. I'll wait until he gets here, then I'll tell you what I know about this man called Jack Dorg."

"It's Jack," R.M. said.

Romy reached under his seat and took out a .38 caliber pistol. As R.M. watched, his eyes horror-filled, Romy checked the loads and clicked the cylinder closed.

"My God, son!" R.M. said. "What are you going to do?"

"I'm going to do what you and the others did not do," Romy replied. He met the man's eyes. "I'm going to kill him!"

"Son, listen to me, listen for just a moment. Why do you think we had Jack confined in that institution? Why do you think we didn't let the sheriff's department handle the deaths of your real mother and father? Have you ever thought about that?"

"Many times, Dad."

Both men sat in the car, looking at each other, while the wild, insanely evil laughter rolled in waves from the dark-timbered swamp.

"You can't kill him, Romy." R.M.'s words were softly offered. "And I don't mean can not in any moral way. I mean you *cannot* kill him. You cannot, I cannot, the deputy cannot, the law cannot. Are you beginning to see?"

"I don't believe you! It's . . . you're just making that up."

R.M. shook his head. "No, son, I am not making anything up. You could empty that pistol into your brother's chest; you could tear his flesh and fire directly into his heart. But you *cannot* kill him. He will not die."

61

"Talk to him, old man!" Jack's voice ripped from the hot darkness. "Your time is near. It's time, old man. It's time, baby brother. My Master is near. Very, very near." He laughed and laughed.

Somewhere very close, a wild yowling began.

"Listen to my little friends!" Jack yelled. "Would you like to see some of them?"

"I've handled him before, Dad," Romy said. "He's broken out before and always returned here. And I've taken his hand and he's followed me as docilely as a lamb."

"He wasn't following you, Romy. He was listening to his Master; not you. As he just said, *now* is the time. The time was not right before."

Both men jerked in surprised fright as a cat leaped onto the hood of the parked car. The cat stared at the men through the windshield.

"Get off!" Romy yelled.

The cat sat and stared.

R.M. sighed and shook his head. "I could talk to no one," he said, speaking as much to the hot air as to Romy. "No one would have believed me. They would have put *me* in some institution. I've lived with this . . . horror all my life. Just as my father did, and his father before him, and his before him. As I am sure the others did, in France."

The cat on the hood of the car extended one paw, the claw out. The cat dragged its claws down the glass, producing a noise very similar to fingernails on a blackboard. The rasping noise invisibly cut the psyche of the men.

"Put up the windows, son," R.M. said. "Right now."

Romy pressed the power button; the windows closed.

"Now what?" Romy asked, his voice filled with a mixture of emotions: awe, disbelief, horror.

"Drive on until we find a place to turn around. Then return home and pray."

"Pray for *what?*" Romy screamed.

A half dozen more cats leaped onto the hood of the car. They sat and stared through the windshield.

"Forgiveness. Compassion. Understanding."

"Are you telling me we don't go to the police with this?"

"Would they believe you? Me? I can answer that. No, they would not."

"Is there no one to turn to?"

"Oh, yes, son."

Romy waited for some explanation. When none came, he blurted, "Well, dammit, Dad . . . *who?*"

"God," R.M. said softly.

"Jack Dorg is really Jackson Dorgenois. He . . ." Tony sighed, paused, then shook his head. "Men, I don't know how much of this is true. But you both knew my father. He was a very level-headed, pragmatic man. And he kept quite an extensive journal about this man now called Dorg.

"Jesus, this is macabre. Anyway," he said, clearing his throat. "Sonny, you're old enough to remember Romy's parents, right?"

"Sure. I went to school with Jackson. Romy was an accident. I think he's . . . oh, fifteen or so years younger than Jackson. I was one of the pallbearers at Jackson's funeral. What is this bullshit about Jackson being alive?"

"It isn't bullshit, Sonny. That casket was, is, empty. Jackson killed both his parents when he was about . . . oh, twenty years old, I believe it was. The chief of police here in Becancour back then was Borley. I remember him, but very vaguely."

"Jackson's parents drowned, Tony," Sonny said, protest and disbelief in his voice. "Their bodies were never found."

"What was left of them was found. It was a cover-up. You exhume those so-called empty caskets, and you'll find bones."

"What do you mean, Tony—what was left of the bodies?"

"Jackson ate his parents." Tony spoke the hideousness softly.

Sonny spilled his coffee on the table. He sat in stunned silence as the dark liquid rolled off the table and dripped to the floor.

"*Ate them?*" Don blurted, breaking the silence. "You mean like a cannibal?"

"Something like that."

"I do not . . . I absolutely refuse to accept, nor do I believe any of this!" Sonny said, considerable heat in his statement. "None of this can be true."

"It's all true," Tony defended his father's writing. "The chief of police back then, Borley, and the sheriff went along with it. Both of them are dead, and if you'll both remember, they died under, well, strange conditions."

"True," Sonny said.

"R.M. Dorgenois and my father, working with both those men, put a lid on the matter and had Jackson committed to a private institution. Jackson is supposedly suffering from what is called lycanthrophy. That is a form of insanity in which a human being imagines himself to be a wolf or other wild beast. In Jackson's case, he imagines himself a great cat. And from looking at the sudden changes in both your facial expressions, I think I know what just crossed your minds. Don't make any more of it than is there, please."

"Sure is a bunch of cats in town," Sonny said.

"Pure coincidence," the doctor said.

"And a drifter gets attacked by a pack of cats," Don added.

"A freak accident," Tony said.

Rita Dantin was one of those working the night shift that evening. She walked into the doctor's lounge. "Been looking for you, Tony," she said. "Need you in the emergency room." She cut her dark eyes to Sonny. "Frank Lovern just belted his wife. Busted her mouth. I say 'just.' Probably happened about an hour ago. Then she got up and conked him on the head with a lamp. Then they really started fighting. Tore up one room at the motel, then spilled over to the café. Busted tables and chairs all over the place. Both of them are bleeding all over the place."

Sonny looked down at Rita's uniform trousers. One leg was shredded near the cuff. "What happened to you?"

"Darndest thing, Chief," she said. "A cat attacked me. Just came right out of an alley, hissing and clawing. I popped it on the head with my stick and it ran off. I don't ever remember being attacked by a cat before."

Tony exchanged glances with Don and Sonny. "Coincidence," the doctor said. "Just stay calm, everybody."

65

"Why, Tony?" Sonny questioned. "You think things are gonna get worse."

"Yes," the doctor said. "I do."

And because of his earlier statements about coincidence, the words popping out of his mouth surprised even Tony.

7

Don went back to the sheriff's department's substation, arriving just a few seconds ahead of R.M. and Romy.

"We couldn't find the suitcase, Deputy," R.M. said. "How is that poor man?"

"He's all right. Clawed up and scared, but he'll make it."

"Well," R.M. said. "I suppose we'd best be getting on home."

"No, I think it best if we talk," Don said.

Both men understood that his words constituted an order, not a request.

"Oh?" R.M. said. "About what, sir?"

"Jackson Dorgenois." Don turned and unlocked the door to the trailer. He stepped back and motioned both men inside. "I think we have a lot to discuss, so let's get started."

Don noticed that neither man bothered to say that Jackson was dead, as the townspeople all believed.

"You're not going to believe what I have to say, sir," R.M. told him.

"I don't know what to believe, Mr. Dorgenois," Don replied. "But a lot of things—this is my opinion—seem to be slightly out of whack around this town. Now I don't claim to be a genius, gentlemen. I'm just a deputy sheriff in one of the biggest parishes in this state. Now, I can't speak for the rest of the parish, but I know, without being able to prove it, that something is very wrong in this part of the parish. And I'm going to find out what the hell it is."

Inside the coolness of the trailer, Don motioned the men to chairs in front of a long table. He hung up his summer straw hat and sat down opposite the men.

"You are, Mr. R.M. Dorgenois, among other things, an attorney. How do you want to handle this?"

The elder Dorgenois shrugged his shoulders. "Neither my son nor I have broken any laws, Deputy . . ."

"That's bullshit!" Don flared. "You covered up a double murder, you aided and abetted the murderer, you have given that murderer aid and comfort for years, you falsified official court records, you have perjured yourself countless times over the years. Now *do not* hand me any crap about your innocence."

"My son is innocent," R.M. said quietly.

"You talking about Romy, your grandson?"

"That is correct. I call him my son, he calls me father."

"I understand that, sir. Do you want an attorney present?"

"I have been charged with nothing, Deputy. And to be perfectly honest and frank with you, I doubt that you, or anyone else, could charge me with anything. And make it stick," he added. "After all these years . . ." Again he shrugged. "A grandfather protecting the family's good name. You will not, *cannot,* prove that Jackson killed his mother and father. And even if you could, what would it matter now? Besides, it will all be over in a very short

68

time anyway."

"*What* will be over, sir?" Don asked.

"A way of life. All hope," he added softly. "Tony found some of his father's old records, did he not?"

"Yes. What do you mean, sir, all hope?"

R.M. rose from his seat and began pacing the room. Back and forth, like a convict pacing his small cell. He stopped and looked at Don. "I remember you growing up, Don. You were a good boy. You and Frances have been married . . . how long now?"

"Two years."

"You have no children?"

"No, sir."

"Take your wife and get out, Don. Leave this town. If you wait much longer, leaving will be impossible."

Don sighed. The interview was not going as planned. And Don was beginning to think the old man was nuts. Maybe it ran in the family?

"Mr. Dorgenois, would you please sit down and tell me what in the hell you're talking about?"

R.M. ceased his restless pacing and sat down. "It's a very long story, Don. And one that I don't particularly care to discuss at this moment."

The deputy sat and stared in astonishment at the old man. "Well, I beg your pardon, Monsieur Dorgenois. *Je regrette d'avoir a dire que . . .*" Don lost his temper and banged his balled fist on the table. "I don't give a good goddamn whether you care to discuss it or not. I got a raving lunatic running around this side of the parish—he might well be in Becancour this minute—and you sit there cool as hell and tell me you're not going to discuss it! The hell you say!"

"Don, Don," Romy spoke. "Please. I can probably

69

answer a great many questions for you if R.M. chooses not to cooperate."

"Romy," R.M. warned. "I must ask you to hush. You don't know what you're getting into here."

Don hated to be disrespectful to the elder Dorgenois, but one way or the other, he was going to get to the bottom of this . . . mess. Just as he opened his mouth to speak, the front door opened and Patrolwoman Dantin walked in.

"Sorry, Don," she said, eyeballing the two men sitting before the deputy. "I got a call while driving by here and pulled in. I might need your help on this one."

The city police were all deputized and could work outside the city limits, but when available, they preferred Don to come with them.

"What's up, Rita?" Don asked.

She cut her eyes to the civilians and Don picked it up. Now he didn't know what to do.

"I beg you, Don," R.M. said. "Give us a few hours to . . . handle the matter. If we can't—God help us all."

Rita was looking first at Don, then at Mr. Dorgenois. She had no idea what was going on, and since R.M. Dorgenois not only owned damn near all of Becancour, but about fifteen thousand acres of land in the parish and adjoining parishes, she wasn't about to stick her mouth into it.

Besides, she'd heard stories about the Dorgenois family since a little girl. Besides being one of the most powerfully influential families in this part of the state—if not the whole damn state—some old folks said the Dorgenois's could walk on either side of the boundaries separating God and Satan.

Of course, Rita didn't believe any of that last bit.

Well . . . maybe a little of it.

"This going to take long, Rita?" Don asked.

"Hour at the most."

Don nodded. He looked first at Romy, then R.M. "I'll be at your house by eleven. I hope you have . . . ah, taken care of it by then."

"We'll do our best, Don," R.M. said, standing up and extending his hand across the table.

Don shook it. "I'll see you in an hour or so."

"Go with God," R.M. said gently.

When the door closed behind the two men, Don looked at Rita. "What'd you get?"

"A dead body. About five miles south of town. A few hundred yards north of Lovern's rent house on the bayou."

"We'll take my car. Let's go."

Heading out, Don asked, "Do you know who it is, Rita?"

"No. Old Man Fontenot found the body. 'Bout scared the crap out of him. He drove back to Lovern's place to use the phone, but they haven't had it hooked up yet. Tomorrow, they said. Mrs. Balon got Fontenot settled down and Sam Balon, the husband, drove into town and reported it." She smiled. "He sure is a handsome, rugged-lookin' guy."

Don grinned. Rita was a looker herself, and married to a mighty jealous man. Burt Dantin was, according to the stories, about to ruin a real good marriage with his jealousy.

"What are you grinnin' about, Don?"

"Just thinking, Rita."

"How you and Frances makin' it?"

"Still honeymooning."

71

"Stay at that as long as you can, boy." She sighed. "Me and Burt split the sheets this morning."

"I hadn't heard. I'm sorry, Rita."

"I'm not," she said flatly, and Don knew she meant it. "Burt's accused me of making out with everybody in Becancour that wears pants. It got so bad I couldn't even go out with the girls for a few hours. He tried to slap me around last week—again."

"Did he hit you, Rita?"

"He got one good pop in before I judoed his ass and damn near broke his arm. Hurt his pride more than anything else. Then he came back scratchin' at the door, beggin' for me to take him back. And like a fool, I did."

"You think it's done for good this time?"

"I saw my lawyer this morning," she said in summary.

"What's the condition of the body? Did this Balon see it, or did he say?"

"He saw it. He's a cool one, Don. I think I'd want him on my side if push come to shove. He told me it was hard to tell age or even sex. Said the body looked like it'd been attacked by lions."

"Lions?"

"That's what he said. He said it looked to him like the body had been clawed to death and then part of it eaten."

Don took that time to tell Rita about the drifter who claimed he'd been attacked by cats. He did not tell her anything about the sighted monster—yet.

"Cats, Don?"

"That's what the man said. And Tony stuck by the man's story."

"Might be some connection?"

"That's what I'm thinking. How long you on tonight?"

"All night. I'm workin' a double shift. Max has the flu,

or something."

"Ride with me tonight, Rita?"

"Sure, Don." She did not question why he would ask that. Rita and Frances were the best of friends. She knew Frances would think nothing of it. "You meet Balon's wife yet, Don?"

"No. But I was told she is some kind of sensational-looking woman."

"I saw her this morning. Believe me, she is all of that, and more."

"Those blinking lights up there belong to Balon, you think?"

"Yeah. He said he'd park by the body and not touch anything. You know, he said something else that was kinda odd."

"Oh?"

"Yeah. He asked me if it was common for cats to run in packs around here?"

"How'd you answer him?"

"I said I never had paid no attention. But come to think of it, they have been runnin' in packs. You noticed that?"

"Yeah. I sure have."

Both Don and Rita were experienced cops; they both had worked killer wrecks and shootings and stabbings and seen mangled and torn bodies.

But nothing to match this.

The body had indeed been clawed and partially eaten. Don took pictures of the scene and the body and then radioed in for Dr. Livaudais. A lot of cops would rather work something like this for a time before calling in the coroner, since they had a bad habit of screwing up evidence without meaning to do so.

"You know him, Rita?" Don asked.

"No. At least, I don't think so. Hell, Don, his face is torn off."

"Yeah." Don went through the man's pockets, finding nothing. He stood up. "Nothing. All right, Rita, get your flashlight and work that way, try to find out . . ."

"You won't find a thing," Sam said. "I looked. But about twenty or so minutes before Mr. Fontenot knocked on our door—by the way, he's sitting in the living room with my wife and son—I heard a car stop, then a door closing hard, then the car sped off, burning rubber. The tracks are right there." He pointed.

Don and Rita looked. "I'll get the camera," Rita said.

"You're very observant, Mr. Balon," Don said. "And very cool."

"My wife and I don't watch much TV, except for PBS programs. It is a quiet night, and we were talking. As for that," he said, pointing to the mangled body, "I've seen worse."

"Prior service, Mr. Balon?"

"Call me Sam, please. Yes. Army Ranger. Eyes and Ears Only clearance."

And not too many folks have that clearance, Don thought. "I was Marine Force Recon."

Sam nodded his head. "I was with some of them . . . south of here, so to speak."

Don grinned, his teeth flashing white in the night. "I heard that, Sam."

"This must be Doc Livaudais comin'," Rita called. "He's got it cocked back."

Tony pulled off the road and parked, leaving his caution lights flashing. Don pointed to the mangled body by the side of the road.

74

"Jesus Christ!" Tony said, squatting down beside the body.

"That's about the only person that could help him now," Don said.

"I.D.?" Tony asked.

"None. How's our buddy at the clinic?"

"He's resting. I just got through stitching up Frank and Thelma."

"Lovern?" Sam asked.

"Yeah," Don said. "They had what is commonly referred to as a domestic squabble."

"Sounds like they beat the hell out of each other," Sam said.

Everybody laughed at that and any tension that might have existed between cops and civilian vanished. Don was thinking that Rita had been right in thinking Sam Balon would be a good man to have on one's side.

"Yeah," Rita said, taking in Sam's rugged handsomeness in the flashing and whirling red, blue, and amber lights of the vehicles. "And those family squabbles are on the upswing around here, too."

Then Sam said something that puzzled them all. "That's usually the way it starts."

"The way what starts, Sam?" Rita said.

Sam shrugged his heavy shoulders. "Just talking to myself, ma'am. It's been a long day."

"Rita, not ma'am."

"OK . . . Rita."

Tony was looking at the young man, an odd glint in his dark eyes. There was . . . *something* about this Sam Balon that pulled one's attention to him and held it there. The young man seemed to be just too cool, too composed, too sure of himself . . . but, Tony decided, nothing in any

75

unlawful manner; he was sure of that.

Dog padded up to Sam, startling everyone with his silent, cockeyed approach.

"Jesus!" Tony said. From his position in the ditch, he was very nearly eyeball to eyeball with Dog.

"Relax," Sam said. "He's with me. His name is Dog."

Don picked up that Sam did not say, "He's my dog." Or, "He's the family pet." Or any other line denoting the dog belonged to anybody. Just, "He's with me."

Odd.

"What kind of a dog is that?" Rita asked. She knelt and Dog came to her, allowing himself to be petted.

"I don't know," Sam said. "He's only been with us about a week."

The cops let it stop at that point. It was obvious that Balon was not going to volunteer anything else.

"Want me to call Art for the ambulance?" Don asked Tony.

"Yes. And we'll tell him to keep his mouth shut about this."

"How long's he been dead, Tony?" Rita asked.

"Just guessing, I'd say between twenty-four and thirty-six hours. And all this," he indicated the mangled body, "certainly wasn't done here, by the side of the road."

Sam walked over to the side of the ditch. His eyes had caught a glint of metal. "Doctor, would you shine your flashlight on the man's closed fist. The other one. Thanks. What is that?"

Don and Rita gathered around, Rita having just called dispatch to notify Art Authement at the funeral home.

Tony forced the man's stiffened fingers open. A cross fell from the dead fingers. It shone brightly on the dewy grass of the ditch.

"Better call Father Javotte, too," Tony said.

Rita walked back to Don's car. Don looked at Sam and said, "You're very observant, Sam."

"I've learned to be," Sam replied.

He left it at that.

8

Sam asked if it was all right for him to return to his home. It was. Just to be at the substation in the morning and give his story.

Fine. See you then.

A still badly shaken Mr. Fontenot was sent home.

While the two cops and the doctor waited for Art to show up with his meat wagon, Don brought Rita up to date, and this time, he left nothing out.

Rita stood in the Technicolored darkness for a few seconds. The flashing, whirling, and blinking lights seemed to make the scene a surrealistic one. "Sonny needs to be in on this, Don," she finally said.

"As soon as we get back to town. No—you go on and have dispatch call him out. We'll all go see the Dorgenoises when we leave here. You, too, Tony."

"Fine."

While Rita made the call, Tony said, "What are you going to do, Don?"

"I don't know,' the deputy admitted. "I need to call the sheriff. But he's set to leave on vacation in two or three days. I screw that up for him, he's gonna be pissed."

"Well, if you're looking for an opinion, Don, here's mine. Sheriff Ganucheau and Chief Deputy Wines are both retiring. The new people take over July one. He's probably just going to tell you to handle it. I'd call him right now."

"I guess you're right." Don walked to his car just as Rita was wrapping up talking to Sonny Passon.

"Sheriff isn't gonna like this, Don," radio dispatch said, from the parish seat.

"Just get him on the horn," Don said.

Don could just see the sheriff, in his pajamas, bitching and cussing as he left his house heading for his unit. The sheriff came on the speaker.

"10-41, Sheriff," Don said.

The men changed frequencies and Don brought the man up to date.

Surprisingly, the sheriff was not upset with the young deputy. "You do have a problem, Don," Ganucheau said. "The news about Jackson doesn't come as any surprise. I've always suspected that. As for that drifter being attacked by . . . what he claims got him, I don't know. I'd be suspicious of that. Run him from ankles to elbows. Ice him for a couple of days. Not in jail. In the hospital. Tony can think of something. As for the . . . other matter, you're just going to handle it best way you see fit. Anything comes up, Wines will be at his house, in bed. He was workin' in his garden late yesterday and the heat got him. Doc put him to bed. He's really sick, Don. So don't bug him unless it's absolutely necessary. Myron will be in charge. Handle this real delicate, boy. Don't shake any trees that don't need shaking. You know what I mean."

"Yes, sir. Have a good time on your vacation, sir."

"Thank you, boy."

The sheriff broke it off.

Maybe in me, Don thought. He knew that unless it was requested, nothing on the alternate frequency was ever recorded by dispatch.

And sometimes—a lot of times—the goddamn tape recorder was broken and nothing was recorded. Due to the economic condition of the state, a lot of funds were being cut, and many SO's were in bad shape, in a lot of ways.

In the distance, Don could see the lights of Authement's meat wagon flashing through the night. Don hung up the mike and walked back to Tony and Rita.

"What'd he say?" Tony asked.

"Exactly what you said he would. Tony, I got a bad feeling in me. I can't explain it, but it's damn sure inside me. Some . . . *thing* is happening in this part of the parish. You know what I'm trying to say?"

Tony said, "Not entirely, Don. Personally, I think it's all this early heat that's getting to people."

"Something damn sure is," Don said, his voice low.

Mary Claverie sat up in bed at the institution located just outside a small Central Louisiana town. The moon was very full and shining very brightly through the high, barred window of her room. Many institutions now prefer to call them rooms, rather than cells. Rooms, barracks, quarters, apartments . . . it's still a maximum security hard lock-down.

Now! She heard the silently whispered word ring very clear in her head. *Now.*

She swung her feet off the bed and slipped them into

80

house shoes. Smiling, she thought about all those pills she had pretended to be taking over the past month . . . and had not.

First time in a long time she'd been able to think with a clear head.

For her, a clear head. Anybody else would be sitting in a corner blowing spit bubbles.

Mary reached into her nightstand, way into the back, under a box of tissues, and took out a small box of matches. She had found them in the exercise yard and had clutched them to her as a small child would do with a pretty doll.

Only problem was, she didn't know, then, what to do with them.

Those answers came later, in her sleep. She guessed they came in her sleep; she didn't really know. Maybe someone plugged some more of those wires to her temples and fed her Morse code.

She tapped her feet in what she imagined Morse code must be like and suppressed a giggle.

The voice had told her to stop taking her pills. So Mary had stopped.

The voice had told her to start paying attention to things around her, and Mary had done so.

Now, without the mind-dulling and spirit-ebbing drugs, she found that escape could be very easy.

But that voice had told her to wait. Wait. It would tell her when to leave.

Now it was time.

Mary reached under her mattress and pulled out a piece of glass. About seven inches long, wrapped at the base to keep the edges from cutting her own flesh, Mary moved toward the door.

It was so easy to find things once your head became clear. She had just walked over to where those nasty-talking men were building the new addition and found the glass.

Of course, she had to endure all the vulgar comments those men had to say.

"Look at that queen," one had said. "Goddamn, she's so ugly she could haunt graveyards."

Laughter.

On and on the men talked, spewing their filth. Mary just walked a bit, found what she was looking for, squatted down pretending to be looking at an early flower, and picked up the piece of glass. She wrapped the glass in a piece of paper, stuck it between the cheeks of her ass, and entered the building holding it like that. Made her walk kind of funny, but that was all right; everybody walked kind of funny around this place.

"Ooohhh," Mary moaned, her face pressed close to the base of the door. "Ooohhh!"

Since Mary had never been violent, she wasn't confined in the real hard lock-down wing of the institution. This was more like just a regular hospital.

"Ooohhh! Miss Somerlott, please help me. I'm sick."

"Is that you, Mary?" the night nurse called.

"Yes'um. Please help me. I'm bleeding."

"Bleeding!" A jangle of keys. "Where are you bleeding, Mary?"

"From my . . . privates, ma'am. I can't stop the bleeding."

Mary scooted away from the door, so Miss Somerlott wouldn't be able to see her through the glass and wire mesh opening in the door.

They had told Mary that she had been very hard to

handle when she first came to the hospital. She had been very strong and very violent. But she was a good girl now; had been for years and years. She guessed no one ever thought about how violent she had once been.

But Mary had never forgotten it. Mary had a lot of stored-up grudges. And tonight, tonight, she was going to get even.

At last.

Then she was going back to Becancour. And she was going to get even back there, too. She was going to get even with those filthy boys who had raped her in the big ol' spooky house. She was going to get them—all of them. And she was going to get those brothers of hers, too, 'cause they had signed the papers to put her in this rotten place. And she knew from reading the papers that that Margie Gremillion had married Dave Porter, so Margie was gonna get it, too.

Mary never did like Margie.

The door swung open. Mary lunged and drove the piece of glass into the right eye of Nurse Somerlott. She fell backward, not uttering a sound as the long piece of glass entered her brain. Mary jerked out the long piece of glass and tossed a blanket over the nurse's face so her uniform wouldn't get all bloody.

Mary had plans for that uniform. Trouble was, she thought, pausing, she couldn't remember where those plans came from.

Oh, well. No matter.

She stripped off the nurse's uniform and pulled her own shapeless sack of a dress off. The nurse's uniform was almost a perfect fit. Mary pulled Nurse Somerlott onto the bed and covered her up. She took the ring of keys and slipped out into the hall. Mary walked back to the nurse's station and punched the button that would unlock all the doors in this wing. Then she walked to the pipes running up the wall and turned off the water supply to the sprinkler system.

She was so *smart!* Mary congratulated herself. She wasn't crazy; she was just brilliant.

Then she ran from room to room with her box of matches, setting the blankets and curtains on fire. Then she locked all the doors and just . . .

slipped into Nurse Somerlott's coat and . . .

walked out the back door.

She could hardly keep from hopping and skipping and jumping as she walked to near the front gate, hiding in the bushes, waiting for the fire trucks. She knew that when the fire trucks came there would be lots and lots of confusion. She also knew from years of listening to the nurses talk among themselves, that the doctors almost never took their keys out of their cars. No need to. The doctors' parking area was well lighted and right in front of the guards' station. It had been almost thirty years since Mary had driven a car, but she thought she could still drive.

She looked at the building. Lovely fire was all over one wing. It was so pretty. She would have loved to stay around and listen to all those crazy bitches scream and holler as they burned to death.

But, she thought with a sigh, she had work to do, and one's work must come first.

Bonnie Rogers sat on her front porch with her cats, and gazed up at the moon. So pretty when it was full. And deadly.

84

She had waited for almost thirty years for this moment. Now it was almost time.

She touched the cross that hung around her neck on a long chain, nestling warm against her flesh, just above her full breasts.

The cross hung upside down.

She rose abruptly and walked back inside her house. Her house was pitch-black but the woman moved through it as if it were as light as noonday. Bonnie needed no light to see at night—night was her time. She shunned the light, hating it, fearing it.

She went into a large room at the rear of what had been her parents' house. Except for some brass cups and other ornately decorated brassware, the room was empty. The drapes were of heavy black velvet. Bonnie knelt in the center of a large circle, painted on the bare wooden floor, and began praying. But her prayers were not directed Heavenward.

"Oheh, Oheh," she chanted, beginning her invocation against God.

She chanted long, the sweat breaking out on her face, dripping down and dampening the inner circle.

> "The earth is damp, surroundings cold.
> Hear me now, speak these words of old.
> Soon thy corpse will stir the mud,
> To rise, and walk, and suck the blood."

Bonnie collapsed, in a trance, within the circle.

Margie turned in her sleep and put one arm out, expecting to find her husband there.

Her arm hit the cold bottom sheet and she came awake.

"Dave?" she whispered.

Her only reply was the hum of the air conditioner.

She slipped from the bed and put on a house coat, sliding her feet into house slippers. She walked through the ranch-style home, walking silently, not calling out for her husband, her eyes searching the darkness. Then she glanced out the sliding glass doors leading to the patio.

The moon was shining brightly in all its lush fullness. Then she spotted her husband.

Dave was standing naked in the backyard, his arms outstretched. His head was thrown back, face to the full moon.

"What the hell?" she muttered.

She was much closer to the truth than she could realize.

She slipped to the kitchen window, trying to get a better look at her husband's face, for he appeared to be saying something.

Yes. His lips were moving; she could see that in the moonlight.

But who was he talking to?

And what was he saying?

Softly, silently, she opened the window above the sink. Dave's words drifted to her on the soft spring air.

"Air, water, fire, and earth," he said. "Combine the elements and make me change."

Change into . . . what? Margie thought.

"Three times I shall say these words," Dave said. "On the night of the third day, I shall change forever, and I shall be one with all things. The air, the water, the fire, and the earth."

Then Dave hissed, the hissing loud enough for Margie to hear. Her fingers gripped the edges of the sink.

The yard seemed to flood with cats, of all sizes and colors. They slinked about, rubbing against her husband's bare ankles.

She watched in horrified fascination.

"Hear me, Satanachia, and carry my words to Rofocale!" Dave called out.

"Who?" Margie whispered.

Her husband whirled around, facing the rear of the house. The cats turned, their eyes glowing in the reflection from the moon.

Her husband and the cats began moving toward the kitchen window.

Margie fainted, hitting the tiled floor and not moving.

And Bob Savoie lay in his moulding casket and heard nor saw anything.

Yet.

87

9

Don and Rita drove past R.M.'s house first. Both cars were parked in the garage. The house was dark.

"Maybe R.M.'s at Romy's?" Rita suggested.

"Don't bet on it," Don replied.

They drove to Romy's house. All the cars were there, and the house was just as dark as R.M.'s had been.

"Now what?" Rita asked.

"Nothing," Don said sourly. "I take you back to your unit, and then I go home and try to get some sleep."

He picked up his mike and said, "Seven to B-1."

"Go ahead seven," Sonny's voice came from the speaker.

"Like you said, Sonny. Everything is dark at both places."

"Now what?"

"We pull their butts in after breakfast. You game for that?"

"Damn right!" Sonny spoke without hesitation. "I want to get to the bottom of this."

"See you in a few hours."

"Ten-four."

"But don't they realize what that nut might do?" Rita asked.

"I don't think they care, Rita. But I'll bet a month's pay on this: R.M. has covered his back trail. I been doing some thinking on it, Rita. You see, up until not too many years ago, it was easy to commit someone to a bug house. Practically nothing to it. Hasn't been that long since the legislature changed the procedure. You remember what Tony told us a few minutes ago? About Jackson being admitted?"

"Yeah. He said that according to his father's notes, the sheriff was the one who took care of it."

"That's right. The sheriff, and Chief Borley. According to what Dr. Livaudais had written, Jack Dorg was a drifter who went off his nut in this parish. Hell, I was just a little boy when that took place. The sheriff told the people at the institution that Dorg's family had been contacted and they had agreed to pay for keeping him down here. And you can bet your boots on something else, Rita: there is no way we, or anybody else, will ever be able to connect the Dorgenois family with that money sent to the institution for Jackson's care."

"I tend to agree with you."

"So tomorrow, Rita, I'm going to gather up some people I can trust, and start beating the bushes. And when we find Jackson Dorgenois, I'm going to try to take him alive. If I can't . . . what happens next is Jackson's tough luck."

"Hey, girl!" Dave said, bathing Margie's face with a cold cloth.

She opened her eyes and looked at him.

He was dressed in pajama bottom and T-shirt, his usual bedtime attire.

"What happened to you, Margie?"

The sight of him standing naked amid dozens of cats returned to her. "What happened to *me?*"

He grinned at her. "Yeah. Did you fall? Faint? What?"

"Dave," she said. "Where have you been?"

"Margie, I've been in bed. I woke up, flopped my arm over on your side, and you were gone. I came looking and found you down here, on the floor. Like to have scared me out of my wits."

"God, what a nightmare I must have had. Hold me, Dave?"

"Sure, baby." He pulled her close.

Must have been a hideous nightmare, she thought. It had to have been.

Oh, God! she silently prayed. Please let it be nothing more than that.

She didn't look at his bare feet. Had she done that she might not have wanted Dave to hold her.

His feet were filthy, and covered with grass stains.

"Come on, baby," Dave said. "Let's go to bed. You've had a rough night."

Sam fixed his breakfast, leaving Nydia sleeping. After eating, he carried a cup of coffee out to the screened-in back porch and sat down, enjoying both the view the bayou offered and the loveliness of new dawn.

Sam felt that matters would soon be reaching their boiling point in Becancour. He didn't know how he knew that, but he sensed the truth in it.

Nydia came out to join him.

"Did I wake you?" Sam asked.

"No. I woke up thinking the first day has passed us."

90

"You want to explain that?"

"What number do you usually associate with the Dark One, Sam?"

"Six."

"I asked Mr. Fontenot what was the population of Becancour. Three thousand six hundred and sixty-six."

"Six sixty-six."

"Yes. And he said it has not changed in more years than he could remember. He said people around here don't think much about it. Just one of those things, he said."

"And you think whatever is going to happen will happen in six days?"

"From yesterday. We have five more days."

"To stop it?"

"Yes."

"But that doesn't mean the entire town will suddenly transform on the sixth day."

"Oh, no. Not at all. But I read your thoughts a moment ago. You were thinking that the boiling point will soon be reached."

"Yes."

"I wonder if the Dark One is playing with us, Sam?"

"I thought about that, too. I don't think so, Nydia. He knows we are his sworn enemies. I think this is no longer a game with him. Not like it was in Canada, or up in New York State. I don't think the Prince of Darkness will tip his hand this time."

"I'm amazed that we haven't heard from Xaviere. I wonder why she's waiting?"

"I don't know," Sam said.

* * *

"We do nothing," Xaviere said to her followers. "We cannot stop what has already begun, but we do not have to be a party to it."

"Why has it begun so soon?" Janet asked. "We were to have all summer."

"I don't know," the Princess of Darkness said.

Mary had a perfectly awful time figuring out how to operate the car she'd stolen from the parking lot of the institution. She had never seen so many knobs and buttons and funny-looking things. And that damned voice that kept urging her to buckle her seat belt almost caused her to jump from the car in fright when it first came on.

But the voice finally shut up and Mary got the car started and was on her way.

She stopped at a filling station to pick up a road map and almost got arrested when she tried to walk out the door with it without paying for it.

"Fifty cents!" she said. "What happened to free?"

"There ain't nothin' free no more," the young man told her. "Gimme half a buck or gimme back the map."

Mary dug in Nurse Somerlott's purse and handed the smart-mouthed young man a dollar bill. "Paying for road maps!" Mary snorted. "I never heard of such a thing."

The young man gave her the change and said, "Will that be all, lady?"

"Don't be rude," Mary told him.

The young man rolled his eyes Heavenward. "Man, I am gettin' all the fruitcakes in tonight."

Mary drove the long piece of glass into the young man's throat and seesawed it, working a hole in his throat from front to back. She looked around the place. They were alone. Mary scooped up all the money in the open cash drawer and then her eyes saw the pistol just below the cash register, on a shelf, a box of bullets beside the gun.

She dropped the gun and the bullets into the purse and walked outside, leaving the young man gurgling and jerking on the floor. She drove for a few blocks and pulled over, studying the map. The roads had not changed very much. She pulled back out onto the highway and headed toward Becancour.

And revenge.

Margie remained in bed for a few moments after Dave left the house, heading for his office. She kicked off the covers and started to swing her feet off the bed. Her eyes caught a smudge of something near the foot of the bed, Dave's side. She scooted onto the center of the bed and looked.

Dirt. And something else. Some sort of green stain.

She couldn't possibly believe Dave had gone to bed with such dirty feet.

Then, with white-hot reality, she knew what had caused the stains. She had not suffered any nightmare. What she had seen was . . . *real.* Dave had been standing out in the backyard. With those cats.

She jumped from the bed and ran through the house. She was alone. She locked all the doors and fixed a cup of coffee with shaking hands. She drank her coffee and showered, feeling very vulnerable standing naked in the closed stall.

She toweled off and dressed very quickly. She

slipped her feet into the old tennis shoes she used when working in the yard and went out into the backyard. She walked to where she'd seen Dave during the night and knew, then, it for sure had not been any dream.

The soles of her shoes were slick with cat shit.

Sam was not surprised to find Father Javotte sitting with Don and Sonny Passon in the sheriff's substation.

"Sam," Don said. He waved a hand toward a coffeepot. "Help yourself."

Pouring a cup of coffee, Sam said, "I just heard on the car radio about that fire at the mental institution west of here."

"You think it's linked with what's happening here?" Sonny asked the young man he'd met just a few hours before.

"Why should I have any ideas about it?" Sam replied, looking up, a smile on his face. "I'm a newcomer here."

"I have a question, Mr. Balon," Sonny said.

"Sure."

"Why did you and your family come to Becancour?"

"Because we are enormously wealthy and don't have to work," Sam said. Except for God, Sam silently amended that. "We'd never been to Louisiana and thought it would be a nice place to summer."

"In a little town, at the very end of a dead-end road," Sonny said. "Don't misunderstand me, Mr. Balon. I'm not hostile toward you, and you're not wanted for anything. And you certainly don't have to answer any of my questions. It's just that we don't get many tourists here."

94

Sam was very conscious of Father Javotte's eyes on him.

Sam was caught up in a mental quandary. If Nydia was right, time was running out and these men should be warned. But would they believe him? No, he thought they would not. Not yet. But did he have the right to withhold the truth from them? No, he did not.

He smiled. "I'll level with you people. My wife and I have a rather, well, macabre hobby."

The two cops tensed; Father Javotte returned Sam's smile.

"We like to explore so-called haunted houses."

Don and Sonny each expelled a breath. Father Javotte was still wearing a smile.

"The Dorgenois house," Don said.

"That's right. It was quite a disappointment to us when we learned the Dorgenois place had been rented out."

Sonny Passon looked at Sam's eyes. The man was smiling, but his eyes were cold and unreadable. Not cold in any criminal way, the chief thought, but . . .

He's lying, it came to Sonny. But why?

Sam was saying. ". . . explored so-called haunted houses in several states."

"What was your most interesting house, Sam?" Father Javotte asked.

Satan-fighters, each with different methods, locked eyes. "Falcon House," Sam said.

The priest paled slightly. When he lit a cigarette, his hands were trembling ever so slightly.

Don noticed the priest's paling, his trembling hands. "Something wrong, Dan?"

The priest inhaled deeply, slowly blowing out the smoke. When he spoke, it was not directed to any one person. "The other evening, as I stepped outside for a breath of air, it came to me what I had been sensing for several months. Evil. Evil in its darkest form. When I first saw you on the street, in front of the department store, I sensed something quite different about you, Sam." He glanced up at Sam.

"Go on, Padre," Sam urged.

"Where were you born, Sam?" Father Javotte asked.

"Nebraska."

"You told me your father was a . . . preacher. I should have put it all together then."

"Put what together, Father?" Sonny asked.

"Be silent," the priest told the man. He had not taken his eyes from Sam's. "We're in danger, aren't we, Sam?"

"Yes." Then it came to Sam. Both he and Nydia were wrong. It was not six days; something was going to happen within that time frame, but it was the sixth month they had to fear. It was Little Sam's birthday. He had been born in the sixth month, on the sixth day. And this was 1986.

666.

The Mark of the Beast.

And Satan would try to take the child, one way or the other, between the first and the sixth day of June.

"Yes." Nydia's voice came to him, drifting over the few miles from house to town. "I realized it the same time you did. But how did we know? Who gave us the information?"

She knew she was not expecting a reply. The aura of her mind touching his faded.

Sam blinked to clear his head.

"I felt a . . . something in the room," Don said, his eyes wide. "I know I did. What the hell was that?"

"My wife communicating with me," Sam said. "We have the ability to read each other's minds."

"Say . . . *what?*" Sonny said.

"Before then," Javotte said, "you were experiencing something, Sam. Important to us?"

"Important to all of us, Padre." Sam, with a sigh, made up his mind. He warmed up his coffee with fresh and sat down with the men.

"All right, gentlemen," Sam said. "I don't know why the devil chose this particular town. I suppose he has his reasons . . ."

"The devil?" Sonny interrupted. "You mean, like Satan?"

"Yes."

"You got a weird sense of humor, Balon," Don said, none of the previous night's friendliness in his tone.

"When it comes to the Prince of Darkness, I have no sense of humor," Sam informed them all. "And when you see fully what he has planned for Becancour, none of you will have any sense of humor about it, either. I can assure you all of that."

Sam rose and walked to the front of the trailer. He looked out the window. When he spoke, his voice was husky with emotion. "My father died fighting Satan, back in Nebraska. He fought to the death with a Princess of Satan, Nydia. She finally killed him, but not before she impregnated herself with my father's sperm.

"Two children were born from that union. A boy, Black, and a girl, Nydia. I killed Black several years ago, in Canada. I married Nydia. Yes. She is my half-sister and the daughter of a witch. But our marriage was blessed by

God, and Nydia accepted Him as her one true God.

"Last year, in upstate New York, I again fought the Dark One, and his Princess . . ." Sam smiled; this was getting complicated. ". . . who happens to be my daughter. Her name is Xaviere. She and her entourage are now living in the Dorgenois house."

Not a word was said for one long minute. Even the two-way radio linking the sheriff's substation with the parish seat was silent.

Father Javotte finally signed himself and sighed. "Who was the priest out in Nebraska, Sam?"

"Dubois."

"The Tablet?"

"What tablet?" Don asked.

"Shut up!" the priest told him. "The Tablet, Sam?"

"I've never been able to find it. I don't want to find it. That means certain death. But bet on this: The Princess of Darkness is here in Becancour. That means a new coven is being planned. If that is the case, the Beasts are not far away, and neither is the Tablet."

Don stood up and looked at Sam. "You wanna know what I think, Balon? I think you belong in a fucking nut house!"

Father Javotte rose and, with his open hand, slapped the deputy.

10

Margie had driven to a friend's house. She was in a mild state of shock and panic kept touching her. She was alternately crying and shaking almost uncontrollably.

Her relief was almost overwhelming as she spotted Susan's car in the drive. Being the chief R.N. at Livaudais's clinic, Susan sometimes worked some odd shifts. Margie managed to pull in behind Susan's car and stop before she ran into the other vehicle. She jumped out of the car and ran and staggered up the drive to the side door.

Susan was sitting at the kitchen nook, drinking coffee. Margie pounded on the door, the wild hammering startling her friend.

"Margie!" Susan said, looking up. She took in her friend's wild eyes, her flushed face and tear-streaked cheeks. She quickly opened the door and pulled Margie in.

"Good God, Margie! What's happened?"

"Susan, you're not . . . going to believe this. But I swear to you it's the truth. I swear it."

"Look, you go wash your face and try to calm down. I'll pour us coffee. We'll talk in the den." She gave her

99

friend a gentle push toward the bathroom. "Go on, Margie. Then we'll talk."

"You young fool!" Father Javotte said to Don. "Not everything one encounters in this world can be easily explained away. Not all is black and white. Now sit down and be silent!"

Sonny Passon sat and stared in shock at the priest. He'd never seen Father Daniel Javotte behave in such a manner. He'd never seen *any* priest behave like this.

Don sat down, a look of astonishment on his face.

Javotte swung his eyes back to Sam. "Sam, I can believe what you said. I have no problem with it. But others? . . ." He let that drift off into silence.

"I know, Padre. I'm sure my dad had the same problems almost thirty years ago."

"The devil?" Sonny whispered. "Here? In Becancour?"

"You hit me, Father," Don said. "You hit me!"

"I got your attention, didn't I?" Javotte asked.

"Damn sure did," the deputy agreed.

"Now, listen to me, all of you," Sam said. The men looked at him. "I can tell you all almost exactly what has been happening in this town. I've seen it before. Drinking is up; incidents of depression are up; family violence is up; the young people have become sullen; sexual promiscuity is up . . . and people are behaving strangely. Right?"

Don looked at Sam, new interest in his eyes. The side of his face was still red where Father Javotte had popped him. "All right," the deputy said. "I'll give you that much. Yeah. You're right."

"Satan is insidious," Sam said. "The Dark One moves very slowly in his conquests. There is no need for him to rush matters. You see, the Prince of Darkness knows that he rules the earth."

"Let's assume that I accept all—or even a part—of what you've told me," Sonny said. "I mean . . . well, what's the next move?"

"Waiting," Sam said. He smiled grimly. "You see, Satan knows that Christians are virtually helpless, powerless to do anything—legally—concerning the situation. Drinking and partying and rejecting Christ and engaging in sexual activities . . . none of those things are against the law. And neither is forming a coven, providing no human or animal sacrifices take place."

"Animal mutilations," Don muttered, recalling the sheep and cattle he'd found in this part of the parish.

"That would be part of it," Sam said. "Was there any blood left in the animals?"

Don shook his head. "I didn't check, Sam. But there were strange carvings cut into the flesh of the animals."

"Stars, moons, stick-men?"

"Yeah. And that means . . . what to you?"

"That the coven is firmly established in Becancour."

"What the hell is a coven?" Sonny asked. "What do the people do at these . . . covens?"

"All depends," Sam said, looking not at Sonny but at Father Javotte. "Call out evil spirits. Worship Satan. And call for the Undead to rise and once more walk the earth."

"The *Undead?*" Sonny blurted. "You mean like in the movies and books and crap like that?"

"Yes."

"Rita told me that she's had to run kids out of the

101

graveyard several times," Don said, looking at Chief Passon.

"Yeah. There's been some vandalism in there, all right." Sonny rose, almost knocking over his chair doing so. "Look, people. I got to go for a drive. I got to clear my head. I got to think about all this . . . stuff ya'll been telling me." He paused. "Wait a minute. We're forgetting why we gathered here this morning. How about Jackson Dorgenois?"

"How about the Dorgenois family as a whole?" Sam asked.

"What about them?" Don asked.

"Their history. When they came here . . . and more importantly . . . why?"

Sonny shrugged. "I never was much of a student of history, Sam Balon. So I can't tell you the why of their coming here. But . . . there have been rumors about them over the years."

"What kind of rumors?"

"Rumors that the Dorgenoises are in league with the devil," Father Javotte said. "I don't believe it and never have. Not about R.M. and Romy. Talk was stronger about Jackson, though. But I don't know. I was not here when Jackson did . . . what Dr. Livaudais wrote he did."

"Who was the priest then?"

"Twenty years ago? Well . . . that would have been Father Landry. But he's dead. After him . . . Father Ramagos. Father Landry was ill when Father Ramagos came. I'm told the two men became good friends before Father Landry died."

"What did Landry die of?" Sam asked.

The priest shrugged. "Why . . . I don't know. Father Ramagos didn't say and I never thought to ask."

Nobody seemed to notice when Sonny Passon slipped quietly out the front door and was gone into the already hot morning.

The phone rang. Don jerked it up, glad to have something else on his mind besides all that hocus-pocus Sam Balon had been spewing. "Yeah? No. No, I haven't seen him this morning." He hung up and looked at Sam and Father Javotte. "The clinic. Looking for Tony."

"You've got to get hold of yourself, Margie," Tony told the woman.

Susan had called him after listening to less than one minute of Margie's story. Susan was afraid her friend was cracking up, emotionally.

Margie took several deep breaths. When she spoke, her voice was deadly flat. "I have told you both exactly what happened last night . . . early this morning, excuse me. I am not crazy." She cut her eyes to Susan. "I've told you for years that at times Dave's behavior is, well, suspect, at best. But he's never raised a hand to me—and still hasn't—don't get me wrong. But Dave needs help. And I mean, he needs it . . . *right now!*"

"Let me sound him out, Margie," Tony said. But he was thinking: Cats! They're popping up just too many times to be just mere coincidence.

"You wanna go wade through my backyard, Tony?" Margie asked him. "It's full of cat shit."

"I don't doubt you, Margie." And then Tony was mildly astonished to hear the words pushing out of his mouth. "I don't doubt any of your story."

Susan looked at the doctor, her boss, strangely. "I'm going to be at Margie's house when Dave comes home for

103

lunch. I'll do some checking of my own, Dr. Livaudais."

"Fine, Susan," Tony said, almost absently. He checked his wristwatch. "I got to go. I'm due at a meeting ten minutes ago."

He walked out the front door.

"Now, what's wrong with him?" Susan questioned.

"What's wrong with a lot of people, Susan?" Margie asked.

"What do you mean?"

"I was shopping yesterday down at Antini's. Mrs. Carmon passed me in one aisle. Margie, she smelled bad. She was . . . *grimy*. And she's always been one of the most fastidious people in town. Over in the next aisle, I saw that Bob . . . what's-his-name? . . . runs the garage? . . ."

"Gannon."

"Yes. Him. He was . . . well, fondling Alma Clayton. Brazenly. Henry would kill him, and maybe her, too, if he found that out. But they behaved as if they didn't care. Then . . . that got me to thinking about some things I've seen over the past couple of weeks. People are behaving . . . oddly, Susan. And I can't think of exactly how to describe it."

Susan sat down beside her friend on the couch. She was thoughtful for a moment. "You know, you're right, Margie. You're right. I just haven't paid any attention to it. But people are behaving . . . well, you said it, *oddly.*"

The thing that was getting to Sonny was that Don was the one who brought up all this devil worship crap in the first place. Now he acts like he's never heard of it before.

Sonny cut the wheel to avoid hitting a kid on a

motorcycle. Stopping, Sonny backed up to where the kid had pulled over. Fred Johnson.

"Fred." Sonny stuck his head out the window of his patrol car. "You better start watching where you're going, boy."

"Yeah, yeah, fine," the boy said.

Sonny looked at him. "Don't yeah-yeah-fine me, boy. I'll hang a ticket on your smart mouth before you can blink, you don't watch that lip."

Fred laughed at him. He toed his bike into gear and roared off.

Sonny sat with his head hanging out the window, a look of pure astonishment on his tanned face. "What the hell? . . ." he muttered.

A sharp banging noise startled Sonny. He jerked his head around to find old lady Wheeler banging a broom head on the hood of his car.

"Chief Passon!" she squalled. "I want you to stop these hoodlums from coming around my house at night, tormenting me. *Me comprenez-vous?*"

"*Oui, en effet,*" Sonny replied in the language the old woman had switched to in her anger. He winced as she pounded the hood of his car with the broom. He got out of the car. "Mrs. Wheeler, will you please stop doing that?"

She ceased her hammering with the broom.

"Thank you, Mrs. Wheeler." He cut his eyes, inspecting the hood for damage. No dents. "What's wrong? What's been happening?"

"What's been happening?" she squalled at him. "As if you didn't know, Sonny Passon. I took a stick to your behind when you were young, and I'll do it again you talk uppity to me."

"Mrs. Wheeler . . ." Sonny had to hide a grin. Mrs.

105

Wheeler had been one of his teachers in high school; and for sure, she'd laid the board of education to his butt more than once. "I don't know what you're talking about. *Pouvez-vous comprendre ce que je dis?*"

"Haw! You trying to tell me you don't read the reports people call into your office, Sonny Passon?"

Sonny's eyes narrowed. "You've called the police to report . . . what's been happening, Mrs. Wheeler?"

"Three times, Sonny. Three times I spoke with that white-trash Louis Black. Last time he said awful things to me."

"What things, Mrs. Wheeler?"

She told him, bluntly, as had always been her fashion.

Sonny balled his big hands into bigger fists and gritted his teeth. "You wait on the porch for me, Mrs. Wheeler. I'll be right back."

Louis Black's butt hit the carpet in his bedroom. He had been awakened rudely . . . by being jerked out of bed and dumped to the floor. He looked up at Chief Sonny Passon standing over him.

"Jesus Christ, Sonny!" Louis protested.

"You dumb son of a bitch!" Sonny cussed him. "I've put up with you because I thought you had the makings of a good cop. And because I felt sorry for you." He looked around him. The room, the house, was positively *nasty*. "Jesus God, you're living in filth! Now you tell me what's going on over at Mrs. Wheeler's house."

"Nothin'," Louis said sullenly.

"You haven't spoken with her?"

"Naw."

"*Menteur!*" Sonny shouted at him. "I talked to C.B.

106

not three minutes ago. He was on duty all three times she called requesting help. He said you handled the calls. But you never showed up. Then you tell old Mrs. Wheeler to get fucked. You wanna deny that, Louis?"

"Naw. It don't make a shit no more, Passon."

"*What* doesn't make a shit, Louis? What?"

Louis grinned, rolled over on one side, and pulled down his dirty drawers.

"He did what?" Don asked.

Sonny had called Don at the substation and asked him, and Sam, if Sam was still there, to come over to Mrs. Wheeler's house. And bring the priest, too. The four men now stood outside the old lady's house.

"Stuck his ass in my face. I kicked him right in his big butt. After I fired him."

Don shook his head. "Incredible. I always knew Louis was dumb; I never thought he was stupid."

"And you say his house was dirty?" Sam asked.

"No, Sam—it was filthy. Nasty. And his drawers looked like he'd been wearing them for a week. It was disgusting."

Mrs. Wheeler's screaming cut the hot morning air. The men ran for the house.

11

Mrs. Wheeler pointed with the handle of her broom. The men looked in that direction. Bloody internal organs from an animal were scattered on the old woman's back porch. Above the grisly scene, spray-painted on the outside wall, were the words: THE DEAD SHALL RISE AND WALK AT NIGHT.

"I'll get a camera from my car," Sonny said, fighting back the hot bile that threatened to erupt from his throat. "Bastards!" he muttered. "Tormenting an old lady."

But why were they—whoever "they" might be—doing it?

Sonny didn't know, but one thing he knew for damn sure: He was going to find out.

"When were you last out here in the backyard, Mrs. Wheeler?" Don asked.

"Late yesterday afternoon. I heard some noises out back last night, but I didn't come out to check on them. And I didn't call the police, either." She spoke the last with more than a trace of bitterness.

"Sonny just fired Louis Black," Don informed her. "And then kicked him in his rear end."

"Put the boot to his ass, did he?" the old woman said

with a smile. "Good. Sonny is a good boy. But that Louis Black is nothing but trash."

While Sonny took pictures, Don continued to question Mrs. Wheeler. "Do you know who has been tormenting you, ma'am? Have you seen any of their faces?"

"I've caught glimpses of them, Don Lenoir. But I don't know these kids anymore. They grow up so fast nowadays. I probably had their parents in school."

Mrs. Wheeler had probably had two-thirds of the population of Becancour in class. She had taught history and civics—among other subjects—for more than fifty years.

"Do you have a garbage bag, ma'am?" Sonny asked.

"Certainly. Are these . . . things from a human, Sonny?"

"No, ma'am. Animal, I think. I'll take them over to Dr. Livaudais."

"I beat his butt more than once, too," the old lady said with a grin. "Has he settled down any?"

"Yes, ma'am," Sonny said, returning the grin. "He married Miss Lena Breaux."

"I know that! I still read the papers, boy."

"Yes, ma'am." I'm pushing fifty years old and still act like a slew-footed kid around her, Sonny thought. Probably always will, too.

"Who are you, boy?" Mrs. Wheeler looked at Sam. "I thought I knew everyone in Becancour. But you're a new one on me."

"Sam Balon, ma'am."

"Balon? I don't know any Balons. Where'd you come from?"

"Originally from Nebraska, ma'am."

109

"Well, you're a big one. You look like you'd be hard to handle if somebody was stupid enough to pull your string. You visiting somebody I know?"

"No, ma'am. I'm down here with my family for the summer. We rented the Lovern place out on the creek."

"Bayou," she corrected. "You a lawman?"

"No, ma'am."

"You ought to be. Big as you are. Nice to meet you, Sam Balon. You and your family come see me anytime you like. Sorry we had to meet under these hideous conditions." She cut her eyes to Sonny. "Sonny, I got me a twenty gauge pump in the house. It's loaded. I got my late husband's old .38 in there, too. And lots of ammunition for the both of them. I'm serving you warning now—my backyard is fenced. The gate is locked with a chain and padlock. Anybody else trespasses on my property, tormenting me, gets shot. And I'm a good shot, Sonny."

Everyone present knew the old lady meant every word she said.

"Yes, ma'am," Sonny said meekly.

"Animal parts," Tony said, inspecting the organs. "Sheep, I'm sure. But why Mrs. Wheeler?"

"I don't know," Sonny said. Father Javotte remained at the home of Mrs. Wheeler; he'd walk back to town. Sam was riding with Don.

"Bring me up to date, Sonny."

Slowly, Sonny began talking, telling Dr. Livaudais everything he'd heard that morning from Sam Balon and Father Javotte.

Tony received the news with a stoic expression. He was

not especially a religious man, did not attend Mass very often. But there was something oddly unsettling about Chief Passon's words.

"And what do you, personally, think about it, Sonny?"

"I . . . think something is very wrong in this town, Doc. But I don't know what it is. I can tell you this much: there is something weird as hell about Sam Balon."

"Weird . . . how?"

"I can't explain it, Doc. I can't explain anything that's happening around town. And I don't know what Louis was talking about when he said 'it don't make a shit no more.' Doc, I've been in Louis's house dozens of times. It was always kind of messy. But clean. You know what I mean. Now his house is just plain nasty. And he's suddenly become nasty. Right now, we should all be out beating the bushes for Jackson Dorgenois. But he's become secondary. And you know what, Doc. I don't care. And I don't think Don cares either. That's weird, Doc. I don't want to leave this town, Doc. Me and the wife was going to drive over to Alex tonight for dinner. We always enjoyed doing that. But she told me this morning that she didn't wanna go. Jane has always enjoyed fixin' up and going out. Now she just doesn't want to go."

"Jackson Dorgenois must be found, Sonny. The man is dangerous. He could be killing right this minute."

"I know that."

Something in Sonny's eyes bothered Tony. Some little intangible . . . *thing* seemed to be drifting just under the surface. "Well, if that's the way you feel about it, Sonny. As Chief of Police, I don't know of a soul who can order you to go out looking for Jackson."

111

"But what I'm feeling is *wrong*, Doc, and what's worse is . . . I know it. But I can't seem to shake it."

Tony did not know what to say to the man. He was experiencing none of what Sonny claimed to be feeling. "What is it you want, Sonny? You think I have some kind of pill or shot that will alleviate the sensation?"

"Do you?"

"No."

Sonny leaned back in his chair. "It's gettin' worse, Doc. And I didn't feel this way an hour ago."

Tony thought of something, then almost immediately rejected it. None of what Sonny had told him about devil worship and covens and vampires and all that crap was true. None of it. Tony didn't believe in any of that nonsense.

Or did he?

Oh, what the hell! he thought. It's worth a try. "You want the best advice I can give you, Sonny?"

"I sure do."

"Go see Father Javotte and tell him what you told me. I don't have any medicine to cure you."

Mary Claverie had slept in the car, pulled off the road about two miles from Becancour. When she awakened, stiff and sore from the cramped space, she felt worse than stiff and sore . . . she felt awful. She got out and stretched until her joints popped. Boy! it felt so good to be free of that nut house.

Then she looked down at her nurse's uniform. All dirty and mussed and icky. Got to do something about that. Well, she had her piece of glass and her gun. So she'd just drive a bit until she came to a house, go up and knock on the door, and take whatever it was she wanted.

Sounded pretty good to her.

Then she saw the house. It sat to the south of where she had parked all night, just a little stand of timber separating Mary from the house. Getting her gun, she left the car and walked through the timber. At timber's edge, she paused. She could see window air conditioners, but none were on, and it was already hot. She hiked up her dress and squatted down, watching the house. Then she saw the telltale signs: several rolled-up newspapers were in the front yard. No one home.

Mary looked in all directions and then scampered across the yard, angling toward the back. She jumped up on the small back porch and tried the doorknob. Locked. She felt around the top of the door frame and smiled as her fingers touched the key.

In the house, she stood still for a moment, listening. She knew the house was empty; it had that feeling.

She stepped back outside and ran across the timber, to her stolen car. She crept up to the road's edge and looked both ways. Clear. She gunned the car, fishtailed for a second, then cut into the driveway of the empty house. Tucking the car behind the house, she got out.

"Your keys are in the ignition," the voice said.

"Screw you!" Mary said. "If I ever figure out where you're hiding, I'm gonna kill you!"

She was not aware of the eyes watching her from the shed out back of the house.

Sam was the first to spot the symbol that mutely declared war.

"Look on the water tower," he told Don.

Don looked. "What is that thing?"

"An upside-down cross. It means that whoever painted it there has rejected God and accepted Satan."

Don dropped the car into D and drove on. "I've got to find Sonny and apologize to him."

"Why?"

"I came to him the other day and told him I believed something like devil worship was going on in Becancour. Then this morning, well, it was like some . . . voice, but not really a voice, was telling me to reject what you were saying. I completely forgot about Jackson Dorgenois. Until just a few minutes ago. Sam, it's real, isn't it? I mean, the devil . . . he's here, isn't he?"

"No, not yet. But he's coming. The Princess is here though."

"Well, Sam, if you're so certain of that. Let's . . . well, do something about it."

"What would you suggest, Don?"

Don thought about that for a moment. Then he sighed and shook his head. "I don't know."

"I told you, Don. All we can do is wait."

"You know what, Sam?"

"What's that, Don?"

"I haven't seen a single cat all morning."

"Then look right over there," Sam said, pointing.

Don braked so hard he almost threw Sam against the dashboard. The two men sat and stared in open revulsion mixed with fascination.

The stone fence surrounding a house on the corner of the street was lined with cats. Cats of all sizes, all colors, all shapes. The cats sat silently, staring . . .

. . . at Sam and Don.

*　　　*　　　*

Nydia, Little Sam's hand in hers, stood by the bayou's edge and looked at the beginnings of the great swamp just a few hundred yards from where she stood. Dog sat a few yards away, gazing not at the swamp but back toward the house.

Silently guarding.

"He sees something we can't," Little Sam said.

"What does he see, baby?"

"Evil," the child replied.

Dog swung his big head and looked at Little Sam through his mismatched eyes.

R.M. sat in Romy's study and met the younger man's gaze. "Romy, if I knew what to do, don't you think I'd do it?"

"I don't know, Dad. But I don't believe you have ever leveled with me about our family. Why are you afraid to tell me the truth?"

"Romy . . . I'm not sure I know the truth. I . . . I do know that we—you and me and all Dorgenoises—are different. Our ancestors, Romy, made a decision two centuries ago; a decision that, according to what I have learned over the years, forced them to leave New Orleans."

"Why?"

"It isn't what you think, son. We're not vampires or werewolves or witches. It's very simple. Our ancestors accepted God as the only true God, turning their backs to the Evil One."

"How much of this is true, Dad?"

"Son, I can't prove any of it. I can only relate to you what my father told me, a week before he died."

"Why would accepting Christ force our ancestors out

115

of the city?"

"They were running, son. Running for their lives."

"From whom, Dad?"

"From Satan."

Walt Davis just did not know what was the matter with him. He was well fed, comfortable, and pampered by the nurses at the clinic. The cops in this town were nice; they didn't hassle like a lot of cops Walt had come in contact with over the years.

All in all, he thought, he had it made. He might be able to stretch this into a week's affair if he played his cards right.

He stretched on the clean, cool sheets. His back was healing nicely, so the doctors said. There was still just a bit of pain, but nothing that Walt couldn't live with.

It was just . . . No! that was stupid. People don't do things like that. He tried to force that thought from his mind.

It would not go; if anything, it became stronger.

"Damn!" Walt muttered.

Walt had this almost overwhelming urge to lick himself.

12

They met back at the substation, each with their own stories to tell about what they'd seen around town. The painted upside-down cross on the water tower. The cats lined up like soldiers on the stone fence. And the funny feelings some of them had been experiencing.

"How do you feel now, Sonny?" Sam asked.

"Fine, after talking with Father Javotte," the chief said. He looked at Don. "You?"

"I'm all right," the deputy said. "Let's make plans to find Jackson Dorgenois."

Sonny held up a hand. "Wait a minute. I just thought of something. My thinking has been so muddled for the past few hours it just came to me. Where is Mary Claverie institutionalized?"

"Who?" Don asked.

"It happened before you were born, Don," the chief said. "Over in the Dorgenois house. There were four kids—about my age. Little younger. Mary Claverie, Bonnie Rogers, Bob Savoie, and Dave Porter. Bob was killed and Mary went crazy. No one knows what happened in there 'cause none of the three left alive

117

would ever talk about it."

"Bonnie Rogers?" Don said. "She's that weird lady who never comes out of her house during the day, right?"

"That's her. Her parents were quite wealthy and Bonnie inherited a lot of money after they . . ." He paused. ". . . died."

"Why did you say it like that?" Sam asked. He looked up as Rita Dantin entered the trailer.

Rita was dressed in jeans and T-shirt, tennis shoes on her feet. Out of uniform, she looked much more vulnerable, much softer . . . and very pretty.

"I just saw the oddest thing," she said. "Mr. Slater just hauled it out and took a whiz right on the street corner; right over there." She pointed.

"Pissed in the *street?*" Sonny said. "The president of the bank Slater?"

"Yeah," Rita said, astonishment still clear in her tone. "Then he just zipped up and went on walking down the street. Went into his bank like nothing had happened."

Father Javotte looked at Sam. Sam shrugged his shoulders, silently saying, "Be prepared for anything to happen. It's going to get worse."

"What about this Mary Claverie?" Javotte asked.

"Was she in the institution that burned last night?"

"I'll find out," Don said, moving to the radio.

"Back to Bonnie Rogers," Sam said.

"Well," Sonny said, "I always felt that her parents' deaths were . . . odd. I was gone from here when it happened, but I talked with the trooper who worked the wreck a couple of years later. He said that accident bothered him 'cause there was no reason for it. Nothing was wrong with the car. The insurance people went over it from end to end. The car left the highway and sailed several hundred feet before impacting. It would have had to be traveling a hundred miles an hour to do that. And Mr. Rogers was a menace on the highways because he never, *never* got over forty miles an hour. And Mrs. Rogers couldn't drive. That trooper told me it looked to him like, well, these are his words, something just picked the car up and hurled it those hundreds of feet. That trooper worried on that wreck for two or three years. I never seen a man so obsessed with something. And I'll tell you what's really weird about it: that trooper was killed right outside of Becancour, in exactly the same way the Rogers died."

"My daddy told me about Bonnie," Rita said. "He said she didn't even attend her parents' funeral. My daddy said that girl really changed that night in the Dorgenois house. Took to doin' some really strange things."

"What strange things?" Father Javotte asked.

"She's never been out of that house during the daylight hours," the patrolwoman said. "And she's in the graveyard at least two nights a week, summer or winter, rain or starry nights—she's there."

Sam glanced at Father Javotte. "You know anything about this woman?"

"Only what I've heard. I've seen her, oh, half a dozen times during the years I've lived here. Always at night, walking. She never speaks."

Don stilled the ringing phone. "Sure, Max, he's right here. Hang on." He handed the phone to Sonny. "Encalarde." He had uncovered nothing about Mary.

"Max? What's up?" Sonny listened for a moment, his

119

face turning beet red. "Yeah? Well, the same to you! Look, Max . . . quit if you want to, but give me some notice, won't you?" The chief looked as though he might explode any moment. "Fine, Max. I really appreciate this, you . . ." He held the phone out. "Bastard hung up on me."

"Patrolman Encalarde quit?" Father Javotte asked.

"Sure did. Told me where to shove my job, desk, chair, badge, and all."

"Expect more," Sam said, recalling the siege at Logandale, New York, and the events leading up to it. "Everything might fall apart tomorrow, but I rather expect it to take several weeks."

"Will somebody please tell me what is going on?" Rita asked.

Don brought her up to date.

Rita sat down with a thump. "Last night was bad enough," she said. "Are you people *serious?*"

"Yes," Sam told her. "Deadly so. Sonny, how many people do you have working for you . . . before Max quit?"

"Including myself, six."

"And the single highway linking the town to the outside is number? . . ."

"Six," Rita said.

"And the town was first settled?"

"The French formed the first settlement here," Sonny said. "Back in 1766."

"And the population of the town is? . . ."

"Three thousand six hundred and sixty-six."

Father Javotte sighed audibly. "Here is wisdom," he said, speaking from Revelation. "'Let him that hath understanding count the number of the beast: for it is the number of man; and his number is six hundred threescore and six.'"

"Father Javotte," Sam said. "Why were you posted to this particular church?"

Did the priest's eyes become cloudy with that question? Sam thought so. He waited.

The priest said nothing.

"Why are you asking that, Sam?" Don questioned.

"I'm curious, that's all. I like to know as much as possible about the people I'll be siding with in any upcoming fight."

"I'm lucky to have a church," Father Javotte finally spoke. "I'm lucky to still be *in* the Church, for that matter."

"We're all flawed, Padre," Sam said. "And when the final battle lines are drawn, I can just about tell you the names of everyone on the side of God. And we'll all be flawed in some manner."

"You presume a lot, young man," Father Javotte said, with heat in his voice.

"I'm flawed," Sam said. "But still I was chosen to fight the fight here on earth. I'm flawed, yet I've spoken with Michael; heard his footsteps on earth. Did you know that Satan calls Michael God's mercenary?"

The priest appeared shaken. "*You* have spoken with Michael?"

"Yes, and he with me. You have not seen, any of you, what the forces of Satan can muster. But I have. I've seen the two-headed Amphisbaena, the reptilian Basilisks, the winged, clawed Griffins, the deformed and hideous Su, and the Gulon . . . straight out of the pits of hell. I have

121

personally witnessed human sacrifices, where still-beating hearts were cut out of living human beings . . . and I've seen the coven members eat it."

Rita burped and covered her mouth with a hand.

"Yes, I'm flawed, but still I was chosen. My wife is flawed—she was born a witch, daughter of a Princess of Satan—but now she fights on the side of God. You say I presume a lot, Padre. Then hear me: when the sides are picked, and that's happening now, believe me, here is who—of those I have met—will be standing with me. Sonny Passon, Don Lenoir, Rita Dantin, Daniel Javotte, Tony Livaudais. Satan will never break that old woman I met, that Mrs. Wheeler. She'll die before she renounces her faith. And she'll be hard to kill. She's tough. The Dorgenoises are not bad people. I think before our trials begin, we'll discover that the Becancour Dorgenoises renounced Satan and accepted God. That's why they came here. And that is why Satan is here. And Satan is why I am here." Sam sighed. "Oh, there'll be others to join our ranks. Seven or eight others, probably. Perhaps ten. No more than that."

"That is about . . . fifteen or so people, Sam," Rita said. "But who will we be fighting?"

"People who were once your friends, neighbors, relatives. Boyfriends, girlfriends, wives, husbands, lovers, brothers and sisters. My father killed his best friend back in Nebraska."

No one had heard Patrolman C.D. Campbell come in through the back door. He had stood in silence in the narrow hall, listening in horror. Finally, he spoke.

"Chief Passon?"

Sonny lifted worried eyes to the man. "I didn't hear

122

you come in, C.D. How long have you been standing there?"

"Long enough to know Sam Balon is who he says he is."

"How do you know that, C.D.?" Rita asked.

"I told ya'll I'd heard the name Balon before. I went back home and been lookin' through all those old books and magazines I got. Sam Balon, Sr., died up in Nebraska back in the late fifties. Big, big government cover-up about that. When the cops and the National Guard got there, they supposedly found a small group of survivors . . . driving stakes through the heart of any coven member who survived. Isn't that right, Sam Balon, Jr.?"

"That's the way it was told to me," Sam said quietly.

"Then," C.D. continued, "a great fireball struck the town of Whitfield. Who sent that fireball, Sam Balon?"

"God. He gave the town more than enough time to reject the Dark One. They didn't. My mother was tortured and raped and finally crucified. I saw it all, while I was lying on a hill overlooking Falcon House, in Canada."

"And now you're here," C.D. said, very softly.

"Now I'm here."

"Will Becancour be destroyed, Sam?" Don asked.

"It will, or we will," Sam told them all.

Sonny Passon shuddered violently. "We can all just leave and let them have the goddamned place!"

"God hasn't damned it yet," Sam said. "But you can leave. I don't think anyone will try to stop you. I'm thinking that this won't be like Logandale. I'm thinking this time around it will be far more insidious; a gradual building of horror. You can all leave. But I have to stay."

"Why?" several asked at once.

Sam stood up and removed his shirt. All present were impressed by his powerful build; but what caught and held their eyes was the deep burn in the center of his chest, burned and scarred amid the thick pelt of chest hair.

It was the outline of a cross.

13

They were all just into their teen years. Thirteen and fourteen years old. All but one. The girl. She was fifteen.

"Leave me alone," she said softly.

The bayou bank was green and hot. Above the knot of teenagers, the train trestle loomed skeleton-like.

"Take off your shirt, Andrea," the older of the boys said. "Let's have a look at your tits."

Andrea looked around her. No way she was going into that bayou full of cottonmouths and gators. And no way she could climb up that steep trestle bank without the boys catching her. She was trapped.

"You should have come to the meeting the other night, Andrea," the older of the boys told her. "You blew it. But maybe it's not too late for you."

"What do you mean, Chuck?" Andrea knew what he meant; she was just stalling for time.

Chuck licked his lips, a very strangely dark and evil look in his eyes. "You know," he said.

Andrea had heard of the meetings a lot of the kids were attending. And a little bit of what went on at those meetings. She wanted none of it. And just as soon as she got away from this . . . mess she was in, she was going straight to Earl Morris at the church and tell her preacher all she knew.

She felt eyes on her back. Turning her head, she looked at the trestle. The support beams under the tracks were lined with cats, maybe a hundred of them, all looking at her. Their tails were swishing back and forth in unison, like a silent metronome, all in meter, moving back and forth, back and forth.

"You take off your shirt, or we take it off for you," Billy said, his voice in the process of changing, breaking every now and then.

Thirteen-year-old Tommy was rubbing his crotch, his lips wet, his eyes shiny with anticipation.

The front of Peter's cut-off jeans were bulging with his erection.

What to do? Andrea thought, sweat beading her forehead. She didn't want to be hurt, but she didn't want to be raped, either. If there was just one of them, she could fight and probably win. But against four of them? . . .

Then she seemed to find inner strength as she made up her mind. They might rape her, but she'd make them pay dearly for it. Maybe they'd hurt her, maybe they'd even kill her, but she wasn't going to just lay down and give them sex.

She suddenly jumped toward Chuck and lashed out with one foot, catching the oldest boy in the crotch. He screamed in pain and dropped to the coolness of the bayou bank, his hands holding his crotch.

Andrea knew it had not been a good kick, for her foot caught him too high to pop him on the balls. Already, Chuck was getting to his feet, rubbing his crotch gingerly. "You get it all at once for that! I'm gonna make you holler."

Andrea turned and tried to scramble up the trestle bank. A strong hand grabbed her by the ankle and jerked. She fell backward, sliding down the bank. The boys pinned her to the ground and tore off her clothing.

"Lemme do it first!" Tommy said, dropping his cutoffs to his ankles and stepping out of them.

"Go ahead," Chuck panted. "I had me some last night anyways."

Andrea screamed as Tommy roughly poked at her. "I can't get it in!" he said.

"Get her wet," Chuck instructed, sitting on the bank and watching through hot, mean eyes. "Spit on it three or four times. Use your finger on her."

Andrea moaned as Tommy fumbled at her with his fingers. The others leaned close and spat several times.

Then Tommy was hunching on her.

"We got all day, boys," Chuck said. "Take your time; make it good for you."

And the cats sat and watched silently.

The angry young teacher leaned over the principal's desk, putting both hands on the desk. "Mr. Comeaux," she said. "You've got to do something. It's getting worse."

Comeaux looked at the very pretty young teacher. "Tess, it's the heat. It's just damn near unbearable. I've spoken with the superintendent about short days. He said no."

"Mr. Comeaux, it's not the heat. Ted Wilson just asked me if I wanted to fuck. Don't tell me the heat made him do that."

Comeaux's eyes widened at the young woman's blunt talk. He started to say she probably misunderstood the Wilson boy. But he knew that would be a lie. Never, *never,* in all his years of teaching and administration, had he seen discipline deteriorate so rapidly as was occurring in Becancour's school system.

No, he mentally, silently, corrected that. He'd seen it coming. And that fool of a superintendent should have seen it. If he'd ever take the time to visit Becancour more than twice a year. Even though Comeaux knew that wouldn't have done any good. Spineless turd had all the backbone of a leech.

He lifted his eyes, meeting the angry eyes of Tess Nardana. "Tell Ted Wilson to report to my office, Tess. That punk has coasted through four years of high school, and you and I both know why. Now I'm going to do something I have yearned to do for years."

"Don't blow your pension, Mr. Comeaux," Tess warned.

"My pension is secure, Tess. Get him!"

Ted Wilson swaggered into the office. "You wanna see me, Comeaux?"

The principal hit him. No warning given, just one good solid hard right fist to the jaw. Ted's feet left the floor and he bounced off a wall. On his sudden return to his approximate original position, Comeaux hit him twice, a left to the jaw and a right flush to the mouth.

Ted hit the floor and stayed down, blood leaking from his busted mouth.

Comeaux's hands hurt, but he felt better than he had in years. "Get on your feet, you smart-mouthed jerk!" Comeaux yelled at the young man.

Slowly, with glazed eyes, Becancour's hero of the gridiron managed to get to his knees. He remained there only by propping himself up by his chin on the edge of Comeaux's desk.

Comeaux pointed a finger at the young man. "New rules are now in effect, boy. Totally unconstitutional. But they will be enforced for as long as I remain the principal of this high school. You may take heart in the fact that after today my time is probably very short. And that suits me just fine. The new rules. You open your big mouth only when spoken to! And that bunch of punks you run with? . . . Boy, you better keep them in line. I better not have any discipline problems with any of them. If I do, it's your ass on the block. And anytime you feel like you can take me, sonny-boy . . . come on. How about it, boy?"

"No, sir, Mr. Comeaux," Ted said.

And for the moment, Comeaux felt, the boy meant it. "Get on back to class, boy. Then, when school is dismissed for the day, you can run home to mommy and daddy and moan and blubber while you tell them about how this mean ol' middle-aged man whipped your rough, tough butt all over his office. Now do you understand all that, you bucket-headed maggot!"

If Ted had known just the slightest about the Marine Corps, he would have realized that one ex-Marine Corps Force Recon had just hit the beach.

"Yes, sir, Mr. Comeaux!"

"Drag your ass, boy!"

When the door had closed behind Ted Wilson, Comeaux leaned back in his chair and rubbed his hands together.

Goddamn, but he felt *good!*

*   *   *

Father Javotte rose to touch the deep scar on Sam's chest. He signed himself and returned to his seat. "When did that happen, Sam?"

"Several years ago, in the Montreal airport. Nydia was with me. I also had . . . communication with my father that day."

"Touched from beyond the grave." Rita spoke very softly.

"I've been at war with the Dark One ever since," Sam finished it. "Nydia beside me." His eyes touched all present. "Don't delude yourselves into believing this will be the final battle. It won't be. That day will come when God decides to end it all. But prepare yourselves mentally, for this fight facing you—us—will be unlike anything any of you have ever experienced. You're going to see and hear things that up until now you've only seen and heard and read in make-believe movies and books. And it's very possible that some of you won't make it."

"It was a very small pocket Bible that saved me," Father Javotte said.

Now we get to it, Sam thought. He looked at the priest and waited.

"Saved you from what, Father?" Sonny asked.

"The embrace of the Dark One," the priest replied, his eyes downcast, his brow furrowed in what must have been painful recall. "I had a church in Lake Charles. A fine future. I was well thought of by my superiors. Then . . . a young couple approached me. They felt their child was possessed. After speaking with the young girl on several occasions, I agreed with her parents. I did everything exactly right, following Church procedure to the letter. In the few short years I'd been a priest, I have gained a . . . well, not to be modest about it, a reputation

130

as an exorcist. I believed my success factor to be very high.

"I knew from the very beginning this one was going to be very bad. The child fought me every step of the way. She was very powerful, and very much Satan's child.

"It took hours, and I accomplished so very, very little. I could feel her growing stronger, and myself growing weaker.

"Then . . ." Javotte paused. "He appeared." The priest looked at Sam. "You have seen the Dark One?"

"Briefly."

"That is all the time you can afford to gaze upon him. But I'm telling you nothing you don't already know. He laughed at me. The child laughed at me. I ran, fleeing like a thief in the night. I lost my faith, my hope. The child pursued me; simply broke her bonds as if they were cobwebs and chased me from the house. I knelt in the backyard and wept. I was ready to surrender to the Prince of Darkness." He shook his head. "The priest who had been assisting me was killed. I could hear his screaming. But I was powerless to do anything. I simply could not function. I think that was the worst moment in my life.

"The police found me wandering the streets, babbling like a fool. My clothing was filthy and I was unshaven. They put me in jail, believing me to be a vagrant drunk. What could I tell them? That I had been attempting to exorcise Satan from a child and failed? I would have been committed to the nearest asylum. And in my mental state, at that time, they would have been correct in doing so.

"The monsignor found me and had me released. The police apologized. I harbored no ill will toward them; they were only doing their job." He smiled ruefully.

"Then, in a manner of speaking, I *was* committed. I spent almost a year in a church-run hospital. Two years after the failed exorcism, I was given this small church. This is the end of the line for me. I can progress no further. Flawed?" he spoke to Sam. "Oh, yes, I'm flawed. I'm a coward."

"You were a coward once, Father Javotte," Rita said. "When you looked upon the face of Evil. What person wouldn't run. But how did a small Bible save you?"

Javotte sighed deeply. "I remembered that only after extensive treatment in the hospital. Kneeling in that yard, that night, I held up the Bible, in front of my eyes, as the Dark One approached. It stopped him. He recoiled as if hit by lightning. That's all I remember."

"And you feel that experience makes you unworthy, Padre?" Sam asked.

"It proved my cowardice."

"It proved you are a human being, nothing more. Don't you think I know fear?"

"But you stand firm against it," the priest countered. "You don't run away."

Sam smiled. "Padre, I run away if I feel that is the best course of action to take, at the time. Only a pure fool stands and dies when nothing is to be gained by it. What one does is circle around and come up from behind. Strike them from the blind side."

The priest grinned. "Why do I get the feeling that you don't fight fair, Sam?"

"Because there is no such thing as a fair fight, Padre. The words are contradictory when put together. If one knows they are in the right, not necessarily legally right, but morally right—such as protecting your life, your property, your loved ones—then one fights to win, with anything at hand. And when fighting Satan and his minions, you can toss fairness out the window."

C.D. pulled out a .357 magnum and held it out for all to see. "Will this stop them?"

"The mortal ones," Sam said. "The others? . . . No. You work with wood, C.D.?"

"Well, sometimes. I like to build things for the house. Shelves and that type of thing. Why do you ask?"

"Then you have a lathe?"

"Sure."

Father Javotte stiffened slightly. Sam and Rita picked up on it.

"I would like for you to start making some things, C.D. About a hundred of them will do, I think. Make them about three feet long and rounded. Sharpened on one end."

"Sure," the city cop agreed. "But what are you asking me to make?"

Sam looked at him, his eyes hard and flat. "Stakes."

133

14

Looks normal enough, Susan thought, as she observed Dave over a lunch of sandwiches and salad. Dave was chattering on about this and that and really saying little.

Then Margie dropped the bombshell square into his lap.

"I don't know if I'm going to be able to get those grass stains off the sheets, Dave."

The look Dave gave his wife was almost enough to cause Susan to back away from the table.

Dave quickly recovered his composure. His expression changed from one of hate to one of blandness. "What are you talking about, Margie? What grass stains?"

Margie had her anger up and battle flags flying. She wasn't about to back away. "The ones you had on your feet last night, or this morning. The ones you got while parading about in the backyard, naked, with all those goddamned cats around you."

Dave's left eye began to tic. Margie had told Susan it did that when Dave became very nervous. "Dear, have you been drinking this early in the day?"

"Stop lying, Dave! Now I showed the sheets to Susan. I

showed her the backyard, full of cat crap! Now it's your turn to stop the crap, Dave. What in the name of God were you doing out in the yard, naked, with all those damned cats? And what were you saying? What were you trying to change into? And those other names . . . Satanachia and Rofocale—something? What is going on?"

Dave leaned back in his chair. "I . . . uh . . . I'm being initiated into a club we're starting up here in Becancour. It's . . . kind of silly, isn't it, girls?"

"I wouldn't know, Dave," Susan said dryly. "I didn't see you parading about in the moonlight stark naked."

The look he gave her was ugly, hate-filled.

"What's the name of this club, Dave?" Margie asked.

"It . . . ah . . . doesn't have one yet."

"Aw, Dave!" His wife pushed away from the table. "Come on—you can do better than that."

"Yeah, Dave," Susan jumped in. "Who-all belongs to this . . . club?"

Dave smiled, once more regaining his composure. "Did either of you hear the news around town?"

"Your problem is not going to disappear by not talking about it, Dave," Margie said.

"I don't have a problem!" Dave shouted. "But what you've got, Margie, is an overactive imagination."

"A bed full of grass stains, a husband who prances around in the middle of the night naked, and a backyard full of cat shit was not my imagination."

"You want to hear my news, or not?"

Margie waved her hand in a weary gesture. "By all means, Dave. Tell us your news."

"Matt Comeaux beat up Ted Wilson. Used his fists on

135

him this morning."

"Good for Matt," Susan said.

"I second that motion," Margie said.

"You two are crazy! Ted's a fine boy and . . ."

". . . a great football player!" Margie and Susan joined voices with Dave.

"Yeah, we've heard it all before, Dave," his wife told him. "About a thousand times."

Dave slowly pushed back his chair and stood up. Both women thought his eyes looked just a bit crazy. "You sorry bitches!" Dave's voice was double-edged and sharp. He looked at his wife. "Have your ass out of this house by the time I get back from work."

"Whoa, boy," Margie told him. "You seem to forget something. It was my money that started the insurance and real estate business, and this house is in my name. You carry your ass, Dave. I've had it with you."

"Fine," Dave said tightly. "I'll pack up my stuff after work."

"No, you won't," Margie told him. "You'll do it now. And I'll help you."

"So will I," Susan said.

"You want me to call the office and tell Bette that you'll be late?" There was an equal amount of sharpness in that question.

Dave's smile was nasty. "I wondered when you'd get around to that."

"Oh, Dave, I've known about you and Bette for a long time. The whole town knows. At least you waited until Dave, Jr., and Sally were gone before you started screwing around. I thank you for that."

Dave leaned over the table, putting his face close to hers. It was then that she noticed his breath was very bad and he smelled as though he had not bathed in several days.

"Damn, you stink, Dave!"

He slapped her, the force of the blow knocking her out of her chair. Susan conked him on the head with the salad bowl and cut a small gash in his forehead.

And the fight was on.

Andrea heard the boys leave; listened to their ugly laughter and rough talk.

"Good juice, baby!" Tommy said.

"Yeah," Peter said. "Great gash, honey."

"We'll do it again sometime, baby," Billy said.

"Yeah, Andrea," Chuck said. "Only next time—and there will be a next time—move your ass a little bit more, will you?"

The boys scampered up the bank and were soon gone, laughing and talking.

Andrea sat up and looked at the trestle. The cats were gone.

For a fifteen-year-old, Andrea had uncommonly good sense and a fairly level head on her. Her one mistake had been in taking the shortcut across the trestle that morning. She would not make that mistake again.

With a painful sigh, she sat up and gathered her torn clothing around her. While doing so, she reviewed her options. Like most teenagers, she was TV smart when it came to the law. She knew if she reported the rape it would be her word against theirs. Four to one. And they would all alibi the others. But she wasn't going to let them get away with it. Regardless of the outcome, she was going to report it.

She looked at her torn panties, almost balled them up and threw them away, then thought better of it and stuffed them in her jeans pocket. She found a piece of old rope and used that for a belt to hold her jeans up; the zipper was ruined. With a deep breath, she began the climb up the bank to the tracks. First stop, she thought, Dr. Livaudais.

"Let's go!" Don said. "A neighbor just reported that Dave and Margie and Susan Brackett are having a fight in the Porter house."

When the cops arrived, they found Dave sitting on the floor in the den, bleeding from the head and face.

And City Patrolman Bid Grenier noticed something else while standing outside. Cats. Lots of cats all around the place. They were restless, and he did not like the look in their eyes. He didn't think he'd ever seen . . . quite that look before. He didn't know exactly what it meant, but he damn sure didn't like it a bit.

"Anybody want to press charges?" Sonny Passon asked the three combatants.

"I just want to get my stuff and get out of this house and those crazy women!" Dave said.

"I'd like to have that crazy jerk committed!" Margie said, pointing at Dave, who was glaring at her.

"Oh?" Sonny asked. "You care to elaborate on that a bit, Margie?"

"Yeah, I do," she said, taking a deep breath. Then she unloaded it all, Don and Sonny taking it in.

Odd, Susan thought, watching the faces of the cops. They don't seem surprised. Susan glanced out the big picture window to the street. And there sat Rita Dantin in civvies, with Father Javotte and that new guy in town, Sam something-or-the-other. Handsome fellow, whoever he is. But why would they all come over here?

Odd.

Margie finished, Sonny looked at Dave. "You want to say anything, Dave?"

"On or off the record, Sonny?"

"Dave, you're not filing charges, and she's not filing charges, so it'll have to be off the record."

"Fine. She's a lying goddamn bitch!"

"That all you got to say?"

"That's it."

"Margie?"

"I want it on record that he is to stay away from this house and from me, Sonny."

"Duly noted, Margie."

"And witnessed," Susan said.

"Just let me get my stuff together and I'm gone!" Dave said.

Bid Grenier stepped into the room just as Dave and the women were leaving the den, heading out to pack up Dave's clothing.

"Don," Bid said. "The clinic just called. Andrea Golden just staggered in. Says four boys just raped her." He looked at a small notepad. "Chuck Lee, Billy Downing, Tommy Patterson, and Peter Labarre."

"I'm on my way," Don said.

"That ain't all." Bid's voice stopped him. "Ted Wilson's parents have sworn out a warrant against Matt Comeaux. Said Comeaux beat up their little darlin' in his office this morning."

"You got any more good news, Bid?" Sonny asked.

"Yes, sir. Dispatch just called. Said the Alexandria

P.D. just teletyped a message. Mary Claverie busted out of the nut house during that big fire."

"All right, Bid. Call out our reserve officers. I think we're going to need them."

"I can't, sir. Dispatch said they all called in 'bout five minutes ago. They quit."

15

Leaving the cops to deal with cop business, Sam and Father Javotte got in Sam's car and slowly drove the streets of the small town.

"Are you certain of the timetable, Sam?" Javotte asked.

"You can't be certain of anything when dealing with Satan, Padre, as you well know. Everything could blow up tonight, or six months from now. I voiced a theory, that's all."

Becancour lay still and hot under the fierce early summer sun. Most people were still at lunch; perhaps taking a nap under air-conditioning, refreshing their bodies for the afternoon's work that lay ahead of them.

"I thought I would spend the rest of my life pastoring in a quiet little town," Javotte mused aloud. "One never knows."

"Ever think what is shaping up here, facing us, was all planned, Padre?"

"The thought has crossed my mind during the last few hours. I'm being very selfish taking up this much of your time, Sam. You must be terribly worried about your wife."

Sam grinned boyishly. "Nydia is a witch, Padre. Any mortal who tries to mess with her will be in for a very unpleasant surprise. I don't know where Dog came from, but he's no ordinary animal, and my son has powers that will boggle your mind. They're all right."

"You would know, mentally, if they were not?"

"Yes."

"Growing up, Sam . . . you were not aware of, well, your fate?"

Sam shook his head. "Perfectly normal childhood. Cars, girls, rock and roll music."

"Mine was cars, girls, and Tommy and Jimmy Dorsey." Javotte smiled at Sam.

"Always wanted to be a priest?"

"Oh, no. That came while in college. I set out to be an actor. But I soon realized I had zero talent for that. Slow down." Javotte's voice hardened. "Look over there." He pointed.

A man was staggering along the sidewalk, a bottle of whiskey in his left hand. He stopped and took a swig, then staggered on his stumbling way.

"You know him?" Sam asked.

"That is, *was,* one of the finest young doctors I know. Dr. David Whitson. Let's pull over and see if we can help."

"Be careful," Sam warned. He pulled over to the curb.

"Peter!" the priest called. "Could we give you a lift home?"

The young man lurched to a stop and turned, his misty eyes focusing on Javotte. "Well, now. Look who's here. I think I'll pass, priest."

Javotte did not change expression. "How long have

you been drinking, David?"

"Well, let me see." He leaned against a trash can. "Since last night. I came in and found my wife humpin' our neighbor. Isn't that cause to get drunk, buddy?"

The trash can tipped over, spilling the young doctor to the gutter.

Sam and Javotte got out and helped David into the backseat of the car. The doctor started giggling.

"Where to?" Sam asked.

"Let's try his house."

"Let's put him in that room," Tony said, pointing. "Jesus, what is happening in this town?"

"I think you know, Tony," Javotte said. "You just won't admit it."

"If you're implying that the devil is taking over Becancour, Father, I'm sorry, but I sure as hell won't accept that answer."

"You will in time," Sam said.

Tony gave him a dark look.

"How is Andrea?" Javotte asked.

"Resting. Her parents have yet to show up, and I find that odd."

"She was raped?" Javotte asked.

"Repeatedly. Brutally. But unlike Judy Mahon, Andrea is cooperating fully." He looked at Sam. "Sonny told me all that you discussed this morning. You may have convinced all of them, but you've got a ways to go with me."

"I'm not even going to try to convince you," Sam told him. "If you want to walk around with blinders, that's

143

your business."

Tony opened his mouth to speak, then closed it as Andrea's parents walked in.

The first thing all three men noticed was the filthy clothing on the parents. As they approached, their body odor struck the nostrils of the trio.

Sam glanced at the doctor. "Maybe they just don't like to bathe every day," Tony muttered.

"There ain't gonna be no charges against them boys," Mr. Golden said. "Andrea just showed off one time too often and finally got what she deserved, that's all."

His wife giggled. "Yeah. Just think of it. Four guys at once."

The husband giggled. "I'll have to round up some of the boys and we'll try that, baby. Is that a good idea?"

"Great!"

"Send the kid home when you get done with her, Doc. Me and the old lady got to lay in a stock of booze. We're havin' a party tonight. Come on out if you've a mind to."

Husband and wife turned around and walked out of the clinic.

Tony stood with his mouth open. He seemed unable to speak.

"Their parental concern was quite touching," Javotte said. "Don't you agree, Tony?"

A nurse walked swiftly up to Tony. "Doctor? You've got to see this. I saw it, but I'm not believing it."

They all followed the nurse to Walt Davis's room. The four of them stood in open-mouthed shock at the sight before them.

Walt Davis was naked, on the floor, on his hands and knees, lapping at a bowl of water. He looked up at the quartet.

He purred in contentment.

Mary Claverie looked up as she heard the back door opening. She lifted the .38 pistol.

"I know you got a gun," a guttural-sounding male voice came to her. "But don't shoot. If you're who I think you are, we can deal."

Mary cocked the big .38. The clicking was very audible in the small and silent house. Mary had not turned on the air-conditioning, and it was very hot.

"Little Mary," the voice said. "Has to be Little Mary Claviere. It's Jackson Dorgenois, Mary."

Mary lowered the .38 and smiled. "The voice told me you'd be here."

Jackson stepped around the corner. He grinned at Mary. She knew that grin. She loved that grin for what it was. Evil.

"You're still a handsome man, Jackson."

"Didn't do me much good in that nut house, Mary. Damn, why don't you turn on the air? It's hot in here."

"The owner might come back."

"We can deal with him." Jackson leaned close to Mary and whispered in her ear, his big hands roaming her body, squeezing her breasts, pinching the nipples. She moaned and moved against him.

"That's a good idea, Jackson. I've been waiting for you for so long."

She wriggled around and hiked up her nurse's uniform and the two mated in the chair, in the den of the hot house.

*   *   *

145

Xaviere Flaubert said, "It's slowed some, Janet. But events are still moving much too fast to suit me."

"They got restless," the girl said.

"The people?" the Princess of Darkness asked.

"Yes, Princess."

"I don't think that's it entirely. I think Evil sensed that Good was near and is challenging Sam Balon to make a move."

"Then let us hope he does that soon."

"He won't. Not Sam Balon. He's going to play right by the rules. Sanctimonious son of a bitch!" she cursed her father.

Janet remained silent. The Princess was growing very angry, and when the Princess of Satan grew angry, matters tended to become very nasty, very quickly. Janet knew that the Princess was still a virgin, saving herself to breed with Sam Balon, to produce a pure evil child, a boy-child to rule on earth. It would be wonderful if that were possible . . . but Janet doubted it would ever happen.

She pushed those thoughts from her mind before the Princess could read them.

A knock sounded on the heavy oak door leading to the darkened chambers of the Princess.

"Come!" Xaviere said.

A man shuffled into the darkened room, moving with zombielike steps. Jimmy Perkins was one of the survivors from Whitfield, back in '58. He had been serving the Master ever since. First as the servant of Roma, and then Roma's daughter, Xaviere.

Jimmy was not looking forward to once more meeting Sam Balon.

"What is it, Jimmy?"

"Blood." Jimmy spoke in his heavy voice.

146

"You may leave the grounds tonight, Jimmy," Xaviere told him. She shook her head in anger. It was very nearly time. For Jimmy only craved hot human blood when the Master was approaching. He had not requested blood for well over a year.

"We're moving too quickly, Jimmy," Xaviere said.

"I cannot help it, Mistress. I know only that a strange new force has entered our perimeter, speeding up our inner clocks."

"Sam Balon?"

"No, Mistress. Someone much stronger and much more powerful than he."

"Good or Evil, Jimmy?"

"I cannot tell, Mistress. But the Beasts are awake and stirring."

Xaviere suppressed a groan. She had heard that the Dorgenois male who practiced black magic had escaped from his prison. But she doubted that was what Jimmy and the Beasts were feeling. But . . . she couldn't be sure. Bonnie Rogers was very strong and very faithful to the Master. But there again, she doubted it was Bonnie.

Xaviere brushed back silken hair from her pale face, her dark eyes glowing with evil and bottled-up hatred. Dave Porter was only a minor figure in the scheme of things, so she was sure it was not Dave.

Of course, it might *possibly* be someone from the side of Light. But she doubted that.

Unless there had been a rules change between the Dark One and that, that . . . *puke* who ruled the Heavens. But she very seriously doubted that.

She cut her eyes to Janet. "Janet? Didn't you say Balon brought a dog with him?"

"Yes, Princess."

147

"I wonder," Xaviere muttered. "I just wonder about that dog."

A few miles out of town, on the porch of the rented house, Dog raised his head and looked toward the town of Becancour.

And if an animal could smile, Dog did.

16

"He's got to be institutionalized," Tony said. "There is no question but that he's lost his mind."

"Perhaps," Father Javotte said softly.

"Don't start, Father," Tony warned. "You're my priest, and I respect and follow your teachings, but don't start with the devil worship bit."

Sam was one of God's warriors on earth, but he was still a mortal. And he had to fight back a quick surge of anger directed at the doctor. "Let's go," he said to Father Javotte.

Tony watched the men leaving the building. He even followed them as far as the door, his eyes watching them get into Sam's car and drive out. Was he being a fool? he questioned silently. Was the devil . . . making a play for the souls of Becancour? Was that *possible?*

"Hell, I don't know," he said wearily. He reached into his pocket for a cigarette, then remembered he'd quit several years ago.

"You say something, Doctor?"

Tony turned, meeting the eyes of R.N. Noreen Daly. "Talking to myself, Noreen. What's our . . . patient doing now?"

149

"Curled up into a ball in a corner of the room, sleeping—and purring."

"He's crazy. He is not possessed. He is just plain nuts!"

"Possessed?"

Tony did not reply to that. "How's David doing?"

"Well, he's either passed out or sleeping. I did a blood alcohol on him."

"And? . . ."

"Doctor, it's a wonder he isn't dead. Tony . . . can I ask you something?"

"Of course, Noreen. You got a cigarette?"

"In my purse, in the lounge. But you quit years ago!"

"I just started again. Come on, let's get some coffee."

The first inhaled puff almost knocking him out of his chair, Tony managed to gasp, "What's on your mind, Noreen?"

She shook her head at his antics and said, "This town."

Tony's second puff was not so harsh. He sipped coffee and met the R.N.'s gaze. "What about the town, Noreen?"

"Let's not play games with each other, Tony. We've known each other all our lives. Tony, add it up and tell me what's the total in your mind?

"Tony, in twenty-four hours, look what's happened. A drifter is attacked by cats, and now he's flipped out . . . he thinks he's a *cat*. Old Lady Wheeler has Satanic words spray-painted on her back porch. Matt Comeaux uses his fists on a high school senior after said senior asks Tess Nardana if she'd like to fuck. And by the way, Tess is coming by after school; she phoned, told me what happened. Said she needs some nerve pills."

Tony nodded. Personally, he thought, I'd like to have

150

a drink.

"Now . . . Andrea is raped by four kids, who, just last month, were some of the nicest kids in town. A lot of kids are skipping school; about twenty-five percent of them, to be exact. Rita Dantin told me that Mr. Slater, this morning, hauled his kazoo out on Main Street and took a whiz in broad daylight. David's wife is shacked up with a seventeen-year-old. Dave Porter, according to his wife, was parading about in their backyard last night, naked, wading through cat shit, mumbling to the stars and moon. Frank and Thelma Lovern practically wrecked their place having at each other. Dave and Susan and Margie went at each other not two hours ago. The entire reserve police force just quit. Chief Passon fired Louis Black, and then Max Encalarde up and quit. The parents of the raped girl don't care if she was raped or not. Judy Mahon, or so it looks, willingly took part in a mass gang-bang. We have what's left of a body in the cooler. Attacked and eaten by . . . something. Word is that Jackson Dorgenois is still alive and heading this way. And so is Mary Claviere. And in case you don't remember, Mary and Dave were in that house together when Bob Savoie was killed. And the people in this town have stopped bathing. Tony, look at your waiting room. It's empty. Have you *ever* seen it empty? Ever? And who is Sam Balon?"

Tony sighed and bummed another smoke from Noreen. "It's a wild story, Noreen."

"I got nothing but time."

"You're fired!" Matt Comeaux was informed by telephone.

151

"Good!" Matt yelled into the phone. He hung up and began packing his gear.

The phone rang again.

"Yeah?"

Same man. "And your temporary replacement is Carl Nichols. You're a disgrace, Comeaux!"

"Carl Nichols," Matt said. "That figures. The dumbest person on the staff." He hung up.

Matt quickly packed up all that he wanted to take with him. He'd get the rest later . . . maybe. He looked up as the door opened. Carl Nichols.

"Uh . . ." Carl said.

"That is just about what I expected from you, Nichols. Did you bring your Silly Putty to play with? God knows, you're too stupid to do anything else."

"I'll come back later."

"Man, no!" Comeaux waved the assistant coach to his chair. "Please stay and take over, Nichols. You're welcome to it."

Comeaux walked out the door. Had he turned around, he would have seen the hate shining out of Nichols's eyes.

"It's gonna be a pleasure killin' you, Comeaux," Nichols muttered.

Tess stopped Matt in the hall. "Where are you going, Matt?"

"I have just been fired, Tess. It's been good working with you. You're a fine teacher."

"Who is in your chair now?"

"Carl Nichols."

"Carl Nichols is an idiot! He once told me that for years he thought Dante was a rock group."

Comeaux leaned against a locker and laughed. The laughter felt good. Almost as good as had whipping Ted Wilson's ass. Comeaux wiped his eyes and looked at Tess.

"I'm not staying here if you're leaving, Matt."

"For a fact, Tess, I'm leaving. But don't do anything you'll regret later."

"School will be out in a few weeks anyway. Hell with it."

"Anything you want to get?"

"I must have been thinking about doing this for some time, Matt. I took all my personal stuff home several weeks ago."

"Fine. Come on over to the house and have coffee with Martha and me. She needs someone to talk with, I think. She's been . . . well, behaving rather oddly the last several weeks."

Tess watched Matt's nose wrinkle as he opened the front door and stepped into the house. The smell was terrible. Tess thought she might be sick. She fought back the nausea and stepped inside.

Matt kicked a cat aside and took a swipe at another cat with his briefcase. He missed the fleet-footed feline.

"Dammit," he cursed softly.

"I didn't know you had pets, Matt."

"We didn't until about three weeks ago. Then Martha started dragging in every cat she could find. At last count we had ten. Martha!" he called. "Martha!"

Only hot silence greeted his words.

"Tess, I'm sorry about this odor. Martha ran off our maid and she just refuses to do much cleaning. The

153

woman needs help, mentally, but I can't get her in to see the doctor."

Tess's eyes took in the mess in the den. The place was positively filthy. Matt had gone off walking through the house, looking for his wife. Tess stepped over the cats who were winding around her ankles. The sensation was annoying.

She stepped into what she knew was Martha's bathroom, clicked on the lights, and recoiled in revulsion.

The bathroom was just plain nasty. Worse than filthy. She stepped to the mirror and looked at her reflection. But it was not her reflection. The thing staring back at her was hideous-appearing, with matted hair and rotting and mottled flesh. Male or female; Tess couldn't tell.

Tess started screaming.

Noreen leaned back in her chair in the lounge. "Tony, that's the wildest tale I've ever heard."

"I warned you."

"And you think . . . what?"

"Noreen, I don't know what to think. But somebody's going to have to come up with some hard evidence before I accept this devil worship stuff."

"Well, whatever is happening might work out best for us at the clinic."

"What do you mean?"

"None of the nurses' aides showed up. Only one orderly, and the kitchen is closed."

"I thought the place was rather quiet."

Noreen glanced at her watch. "Tess should be coming along shortly. Want me to send her right to your office?"

"You? Where is the receptionist?"

"She didn't show up."

A foul, sickening odor was drifting out of the mirror; the image in the mirror had opened its mouth, exposing needle-pointed teeth, the tongue blood-red.

"Jesus Christ!" Matt said, jerking Tess out of the bathroom. He slammed the door.

"Wha . . . what? . . ." Tess managed to stammer. Her heart was hammering.

"I don't know, Tess. I don't know. And I don't know where Martha is. She's never been one for practical jokes."

"That was no joke, Matt. Matt? Drive me to the hospital, will you? I've got an appointment to see Dr. Livaudais."

"Sure. Come on. I can't take the smell in this house any longer."

They drove straight to the hospital, meeting Sonny Passon in the lobby. One look at the chief's face and they knew the man was very angry.

"You heard about Andrea Golden?" Sonny asked.

"No," Tess and Matt replied.

"I just got fired and Tess just quit," Matt told Sonny.

Sonny digested that for a few seconds. "Goddamn town has gone nuts," he said. "Where was I? Andrea was raped this morning. Her parents are refusing to press charges. I can't get in touch with Juvenile. People are fighting and shacking up and getting drunk and . . . and . . ." He waved his hand in disgust. "Shit!" he said, then walked out the front door.

"He's got a point," Matt said so only Tess could hear.

"What, Matt?"

"Whole town going nuts."

Tony Livaudais walked up to the couple. "Please tell me you don't have some supernatural experience you want to relate, Tess?" But he said it with a smile.

The smile soon vanished as Tess began talking. She didn't wait for Tony to show her to his office, just began talking, standing there in the lobby of the small clinic. She spoke in a gush of released emotions. As Tess talked, the third doctor at the clinic, Oscar Martin, and the other nurses gathered, standing quietly, listening, most with disbelief clearly visible in their eyes.

Matt saw the disbelief in their eyes. He said, "Don't smile too much, people. I saw that thing in the mirror, too. And it was real."

One of the younger nurses shuddered at his words.

When Tess finished speaking, no one among the hospital staff said a word. Before anyone could manage to speak, a loud crash came from down the hall. A gurgling scream ended in a wet bubbling sound. Doctors, nurses, and former schoolteachers ran toward the sound.

Tony threw out his hand, halting those behind him. The one orderly who had shown up for work that day lay in a spreading pool of blood. His eyes had been ripped from his head and his throat had a great gaping hole in it. Blood was squirting from the wound with each beat of the young man's heart. The orderly began jerking as death drew nearer with each labored beat of his heart.

Looking around, Tony could not find the man's missing eyes.

"Walt Davis is gone," Noreen said, looking into the room where Walt had been housed.

"Where did those come from?" Matt asked, pointing

156

to the tracks in the blood; tracks that led toward a door at the end of the hall.

They were not human footprints.

"What made them?" a nurse asked, as the orderly's heart stopped beating and death took him winging.

"Cats," Dr. Martin said. "But how the hell did cats get into the clinic?"

"And how did a cat open that door?" Noreen asked.

No one ventured an opinion.

The corridor was suddenly filled with a strange sound. The men and women listened for a moment. Finally, Tony said, "What the hell is that sound?"

"Purring," Noreen said. "Purring."

BOOK TWO

But first on earth, as vampires sent,
Thy corpse shall from the tomb be rent,
Then ghastly haunt thy native place,
And suck the blood of all thy race.

—Byron

THE FIRST NIGHT OF THREE

1

A violent thunderstorm shook the land, nature's way of relieving the fierce heat that had been baking Becancour and the immediate area around the small town.

And as suddenly as the storm appeared, the people of Becancour took to their homes and stayed there.

Well . . . *almost* everybody.

Walt Davis crouched naked under a house near the old Dorgenois mansion. He was quite comfortable despite his nakedness.

He was surrounded by cats. The silent felines kept him quite warm and dry.

Jackson Dorgenois and Mary Claviere left the house when full night touched the land, coming a bit earlier because of the darkened storm clouds. They left the stolen car and walked toward Becancour after Mary changed out of her nurse's uniform and into some jeans and shirt she'd found in the house. Both were barefooted. The stones and twigs and sticks under their feet did not seem to bother them as they walked through the woods and fields toward Becancour.

Bonnie Rogers stepped out of her house to sit on the porch. She enjoyed the storm; it was like an immensely satisfying sexual experience. As the lightning seared closer to earth and the thunder pounded, Bonnie shook with one climax after the other, for she knew who was sending the storm, and she loved the Master for it.

"The first night," she whispered, her voice not audible above the raging thunder and lightning storm. "Now they will begin to stir and move and seek escape from their rotting homes."

Bonnie threw back her head and howled with laughter as the storm raged.

Dave Porter lay on the bed in the motel room and thought savage thoughts of his wife and her friend, Susan. He had plans for both of them . . . plans that would soon become reality . . . just as soon as the Master signaled.

Jimmy Perkins silently prowled the stormy night, oblivious to the storm around him. The rain did not bother him, for it was not sent by God. But by his God. Jimmy laughed silently, the lightning flashes glistening off a blood-red tongue and teeth that were as pointed as daggers. He lightly ran his tongue over his teeth. For the first time in a long time he was hungry for the taste of warm living human blood.

"The first night," Jimmy muttered. "The first night."

He laughed as he hunted.

And young Bob Savoie, who would never grow older, heard the silent call of his Master.

"*Vous arrivez juste a temps.*" Bob spoke for the first time in decades. His voice was raspy and deep. The words echoed about his dank and satin-lined home.

And the Master spoke to him. Bob listened intently.

"*Oui,*" Bob said. "Now?"

Soon, the silent message reached him through the grave.

Bob opened his dead eyes. He flexed stiff fingers. He grew impatient.

Soon, the message came to him, calming him. Bob relaxed.

Soon. Very soon.

Bob closed his eyes and waited.

There were no patients in the clinic. For the first time in his memory, Tony Livaudais's clinic was empty. He sent those who had shown up for work back home.

"Don't make me go home, Dr. Livaudais," Andrea begged him. "Please don't."

"I won't, Andrea," he assured her. He called Don at the substation.

"I'm going to take Andrea home with me," he told the deputy. "Lena won't have it any other way. I just can't send her back to her parents. And I don't give a good goddamn what Juvenile thinks about it."

"They'll never know about it, Tony. I damn sure won't tell them."

Tony shut down the clinic, and with Andrea's hand in his, they stepped out into the thunder, lightning, and rain-lashed night. They stopped under the canopy protecting the ambulance. The storm was so intense it made normal conversation impossible. Tony could feel the girl's fright as she stood close to him.

And Tony wasn't all that inwardly calm himself. He kept an outwardly calm facade for the girl's sake, but he was jumpy.

163

The orderly's body had been taken to the funeral home after Sonny and Don had made their reports and taken the stories of those present. Neither man had shown any signs of surprise at the cat tracks or the stories of hearing that . . . that *purring* sound.

To Tony's mind, that meant the cops had accepted the idea that the devil was at work in Becancour.

Nonsense!

Lightning unfurled its sulfuric illumination, momentarily lighting the night, the raindrops appearing like translucent pearls pocking the darkness.

What the hell was that? Tony thought, catching a flash of . . . something moving beside the far corner of the clinic.

It had looked like a man . . . sort of. Then it came to him. Whatever it was, and Tony was certain it had been a man, the man appeared to be hunting something. No, that wasn't quite right. *Stalking,* was the word.

Come on, Tony! he berated himself. Get a grip on yourself. It's just your imagination running wild, nothing more.

But he couldn't quite convince himself of that.

Andrea tugged at his arm. He looked down at the girl. "Where is your car parked, Dr. Livaudais?" She practically had to shout the words.

"'Way over there!" he returned the near-shout, pointing. "Let's wait it out, Andrea. This rain can't keep this torrent for much longer."

She nodded her head, her eyes wide with fright. Tony felt sorry for the girl. After having endured a savage rape, she had stepped out of her room and seen the dead orderly, sprawled in a pool of blood on the floor. An awful lot for a young mind to accept.

Lightning flashed again, and again Tony's eyes caught movement to his right. Whatever it was, it was a lot closer than the last time he'd seen it.

He looked around for a weapon of some sort. Nothing. Then, as the lightning silently crackled, his eyes found a broken broom handle, about three feet long, sticking out of the trash bin. With Andrea not leaving his side, Tony walked to the container and pulled out the sturdy industrial broom handle, hefting it. Damn nice shillelagh, he thought.

Andrea tensed, then let out a squall that brought the short hairs on Tony's neck to attention. He spun around, let out a sigh of relief, and relaxed his knuckle-whitening hold on the club.

"Will," Tony said, recognizing the man as the mayor of Becancour, Will Jolevare. "What in the world are you doing out in this weather?"

Will Jolevare said nothing, just stood in the pouring rain, just outside the canopy, and stared at the man and young girl.

"Are you sick, Will?" Tony asked.

The man said nothing. He stepped under the canopy, facing Andrea and Tony.

"Mr. Jolevare," Andrea said. "What's the matter with you?"

Andrea suddenly screamed as something very wet and slick rubbed against her bare ankles, slithering like a furry snake around her feet. She looked down. Several cats squatted on the concrete, looking up at her.

And they brought back memories she would have preferred to forget. The framework of the trestle, lined with cats, silently watched the boys rape her.

She stepped away from the cats, closer to Tony. She

was wondering what in the world was the matter with Mayor Jolevare.

"Will," Tony said, exasperation clear in his tone. "What do you want?"

"You," the man said, and lunged toward them.

Jimmy released his hold on the man, allowing the near-lifeless body to thump to the grease-splattered concrete of the garage.

"You won't die," Jimmy whispered. "You shall never die." He smiled as the man's blood trickled down his chin to plop on his wet shoes. Jimmy licked his lips, not wanting to lose a drop of the still-warm blood. He squatted down and kissed the lips of the man. "Join us now," Jimmy said. "To serve the Master forever. You will remember nothing until you are called. Rest now." Jimmy straightened up, a bit of dark humor touching him. He glanced down at the minister. "Thank you for having me over for dinner, sir. It was quite tasty."

Jimmy Perkins stepped out into the drumming rain and disappeared into the night.

At Lula's Love-Inn Bar and Grill, Lula Magee shook her head in disgust, her eyes taking in the near-empty lounge. Jules Mahan was the only customer this night, and you sure as hell couldn't call Jules a customer.

Business was booming for several months, rain or shine. And now . . . nothing. Where in the hell was everybody?

"Hey, baby!" Jules called.

Lula looked around her. Had she missed somebody?

No. Was that old fool talking to her?

"You!" Jules called. "I'm talkin' to you, babe!"

"Don't baby me, you damned old coot," Lula said. "What do you want?"

Jules told her. Bluntly. He punctuated his remarks by rubbing his crotch.

"Jules," Lula said wearily. "You better watch your mouth. If I was to strap some on you you'd have a heart attack. Besides, you ain't had a hard-on in twenty years."

Jules grinned. "You wanna bet, babe?"

Lula shook her head and glanced down at the highly polished bartop. Her mouth dropped open in shock as her eyes took in the reflection shining back at her. She blinked; looked again. The image remained the same.

Jules and Lula, screwing on the pool table.

She cocked her head and looked again. Very interesting. A strangeness touched her. An odd feeling that she had never before experienced.

"You want me to lock the door, babe?" Jules asked.

"Yeah," Lula heard herself saying. But the voice did not sound like her own. "Yeah. You do that, Jules."

Bonnie Rogers sat on her front porch. She was exhausted from her sexual experiences. She had torn off her clothing as one shattering climax after another had ripped her. Panting, exhausted, she rose from the chair and picked up her torn clothing. Slowly she walked back into the house. There was still much she had to do this first night.

Sam and Nydia waited out the Satan-sent storm snug in

167

their rented home. They both knew the forces of evil were working all around them. And they both knew there was little they could do this early in the game. And it was, they also knew, a game. The Dark One's favorite game.

Little Sam looked away from the toys on the floor and glanced up at his parents. Dog lay a few feet from the boy.

"Don't be afraid of the storm, Son," Sam told him.

"I'm not afraid of anything, Father," the boy replied. Then he resumed his playing.

"Ballsy little kid, isn't he?" Sam looked at Nydia.

"Takes after his father," Nydia replied with a smile.

Sam returned the smile. "What I was thinking a moment ago? . . . You don't agree with me, do you?"

"No. It's too obvious. The Prince of Filth tried blocking all the roads up in New York State. It didn't work. He tried isolating us up in Canada; didn't work there. According to what you've told me, Satan tried about the same in Nebraska, back when your father fought him. It didn't work then, either. This is going to be a very interesting fight, Sam."

Sam stroked his chin with big fingers. "But a slow-building one."

"Yes."

Sam smiled again.

"I don't know whether I like that or not, Sam," his wife told him, correctly reading his thoughts.

"Give me your objections."

"No one has made a hostile move toward any of us. You know the rules."

"Nydia, we have been told by mortal men that those are the rules. The smoking hand of God has not written them in stone for us to see. I . . ."

Little Sam stood up, stilling his father with that action.

"Satan is a murderer, and was a murderer from the beginning. And he abode not in the truth, because there is no truth in him. When he speaketh a lie, he speaketh of his own; for he is a liar, and the father of it."

"How do you know that, Son?" Nydia asked.

"Because Jesus said it."

"How do you know that, Sam?" his father asked.

"I know," the child said. "I know that Satan will blind the minds of those that do not truly believe. I know that Satan tempts men to disobedience; that he seeks man's destruction and opposes God's servants. I know that he incites men to evil and can appear as the angel of light. And I know that he is to be resisted."

"Have you been saying your prayers every night, Sam?" Nydia asked.

"Yes, Mother."

"Has God been answering you?"

"Not . . . really."

Sam began to smile.

Nydia glared at him, unable to read his thoughts. "What do you find so amusing, Sam?"

"I think I know who is answering our son's prayers. Has this man ever come to you in your dreams, Son?"

"A few times."

"Can you describe him for us?"

"He's big, and carries a big sword. He talks kind of . . . hard, but his eyes twinkle. And he sometimes tells me funny stories about how he slips out of Heaven."

"And that makes God mad, doesn't it, Son?"

"Yes. But God doesn't stay mad at him."

"Michael," Nydia said.

Sam nodded. "Michael. Has he come to you lately, Son?"

169

"Last night."

"Did he talk to you?"

"Yes. But I can't tell you what he said 'cause I'll get a spanking."

Dog abruptly rose and walked between the boy and his father. He laid down and looked at Sam through those mismatched eyes. Sam didn't think he wanted to try to punish Little Sam with Dog anywhere near.

Dog's eyes never left Sam's face. They followed each movement of his hands.

"No one is going to spank you for repeating anything said to you by an angel, Son."

"I never thought angels would look like this man does."

"Well, Michael is an . . . a very unusual angel. Some even say he's God's bodyguard. Not that God needs a bodyguard. Michael is a warrior, Son."

"Like you, Father?" the boy asked.

"I'm not in his class, Son."

"Mister Michael said you were too modest."

"And you thought I'd spank you for repeating that?"

"No, it was the other thing he said."

Sam and Nydia waited.

"He said that when the hard rains come, they will not be sent by God. He said that on the third day, the dead will walk. And . . . he also said something else . . ." The boy paused.

"Go on, Son," Sam urged.

"He, uh, also said it was time for you to start kicking ass and taking names."

2

Tony sidestepped Will's lunge. The doctor did not know what in the world was wrong with Will Jolevare, but he knew he was damn sick and tired of all the strange happenings. And his patience had reached the breaking point.

Spinning, Tony gripped the broom handle as he would a baseball bat and swung with all his strength—which was considerable. Broom handle came in contact with ass and Jolevare squalled in pain, the blow knocking him off the concrete and back into the rain.

"You wimp!" Jolevare yelled.

Having been an athlete all during high school and into college, Tony had never considered himself to be a wimp. He didn't have any idea what Will was talking about. But he knew if Will got up and charged him again, he was going to beat him to a pulp.

Will got up and charged. The man was screaming the vilest of obscenities.

Will was windmilling his arms, his hands balled into fists. Tony backed up and jabbed him hard in the stomach with the broom handle, the jabs bringing yelps of pain from Will. Tony shortened his grip on the handle and whacked Jolevare on top of his head. The scalp parted and the blood flew.

Screaming in pain, Will staggered from under the canopy and ran out into the rain-swept night.

"We'll be back, Livaudais!" Will called. "We'll get you. You just wait and see."

Tony looked around for Andrea. The teenager was backed up against the outside wall of the clinic.

"You all right, Andrea?"

She nodded her head, not trusting her voice.

"Let's get out of here." He held out his hand and the girl took it. "Come on, we'll run for the car."

A few minutes later, both of them drenched during the short run to the car, they pulled into the garage of Tony's house. "Safe," Tony said with a grin. "You know my wife, Lena, don't you, Andrea?"

"Yes, sir."

The garage light came on and the door opened. Lena Livaudais stood framed in the light from the kitchen. Tony thought she was smiling rather strangely.

Tony got out to face his wife, standing two steps above him. "Unusual outfit, hon," he said.

Lena was dressed in black pants, some sort of pointed and curved-toed slippers, and a black shirt with strange characters sewn into the material. Tony took a closer look at the characters. He had never seen anything quite like it.

"Don't you like it, Tony?" she asked.

"Uh . . . yeah! Sure. Is it new?"

"Actually, it's quite old." She opened the screen door wider and smiled. Was it Tony's imagination, or was there something hidden in that smile? He brushed that

172

aside and motioned for Andrea to step into the house.

"You have anything that will fit Andrea, Lena?"

That damned odd smile again. "Oh, yes, Tony. I assure you, Andrea will be well cared for here." She put her arm around the girl's waist and led her through the kitchen. She called over her shoulder, "Oh, Tony, I fixed you a drink. It's there on the counter. I made it kind of strong."

"Good. I need it. Thanks."

But he was speaking to an empty hall.

He pulled off his wet shirt and hung it over the back of a chair. Picking up the drink, he lifted it to his mouth. The whiskey smell was there, but something else cut through the bourbon odor to reach his nostrils. He took a very small sip. It tasted all right, but that very light and strange odor didn't seem right to him. He spat out the sip and dumped the drink into the sink. He rinsed out the glass and built a fresh whiskey and water. Not really knowing why he felt he should, Tony turned on the hot water and melted the ice cubes in the sink. Carrying his drink, he walked down the hall to his bedroom. He could hear the shower running in the hall bathroom. Glancing into the bedroom Andrea would use, he could see clothing laid out on the bed.

Tony was home. Here, he was safe. Here, he could relax, unwind. So why was he feeling the unsettling sensation that he was not safe?

He stepped into his bedroom. Lena was standing by the bed, smiling at him. "How's your drink?"

"Fine. Just right."

"I didn't know what time you were coming home; so much has been happening around town. I'll start dinner now. It'll be rather late when we eat."

"Fine with me. I'll shower now."

"I'll get right on dinner."

Tony nodded his head, his eyes once more taking in the strange shirt his wife wore. Where in the world did she get it? And more importantly, why did she buy it? It was not attractive at all. It was . . . it was . . .

. . . hideous-looking.

Lena strolled out of the bedroom, leaving the hall door open. Tony sat his drink down on a coaster and peeled out of his still-wet clothing. He started for the shower, paused, and picked up his drink, taking it into the bathroom with him. For some reason he didn't want to leave it out where . . .

. . . Lena could get to it.

"Now why would I think something like that?" he muttered.

He walked naked back into the bedroom and closed the door. Suddenly, for no real reason that he could think of, Tony was suspicious, and wary. Suspicious? Of whom? he pondered. He didn't know. Lena? Maybe—but why?

Glancing at the closed door, checking to see if it was still closed, he walked to his wife's dresser. He quickly searched the drawers, finding nothing that would cause him to be suspicious of Lena. Then, in the very bottom of the last drawer, he found an envelope. He picked it up and opened it. Full of pictures.

Tony's stomach churned in revulsion.

The pictures were a mixed bag of hideousness. Naked people being whipped. Of dark, candle-lit, black-draped rooms. He felt he should know those rooms, but the people in the pictures drew most of his attention.

There was Lena, naked, with an also naked Will

174

Jolevare, their faces contorted in sexual frenzy. There was Will's wife, Betty, with Louis Black. He knew every man, every woman, every teenager in the telltale pictures. There was Dave Porter . . . entertaining—if it could be called that—Lena. Very interesting sexual position, Tony thought. Looked damned uncomfortable to him.

But what was that thing that each person wore around his neck? Some sort of medal or medallion. Tony couldn't make it out. Didn't think he'd ever seen his wife wear it before.

He looked at another picture. There was Max Encalarde with Lena and Judy Mahon. Disgusting. Perverted. And as he looked through the pictures, each became more perverted than the last.

He almost vomited looking at the next picture.

It was a naked man, tied spreadeagled to a black-draped altar of some sort. He was covered with cats . . . and they were eating his living flesh.

In the next picture, Tony could make out the faces of many of those gathered around the now-bloody altar. There was Ted Wilson standing beside Mrs. Carmon. Bob Gannon was there, with Alma Clayton. Fred Johnson standing beside Dave Porter's secretary, Bette. There was that pompous ass from the bank, Nate Slater, one arm around the naked shoulders of Judy Mahon, his hand cupping a young breast. The teenager was grinning foolishly.

Oh, yeah, Tony knew them all. All the good folks of Becancour. And he knew who the man was lying dead on the altar. It was that poor man they'd found out by the Balon rent place.

175

Tony put the pictures in the pocket of a pair of slacks and closed the drawer. He quickly showered and dressed. Stepping out into the hall, he bumped into Andrea.

"Mrs. Livaudais stepped out for a few minutes," the girl told him. "Said she had to see somebody. Said if she wasn't back in time for dinner, not to worry. The casserole is in the oven, and for us to help ourselves."

"She took her car?"

"Yes, sir."

Tony walked into the kitchen and turned off the oven. Damned if he'd eat anything fixed by Lena. Not until he figured out what the hell was going on around here.

He looked at Andrea looking at him. "You hungry, Andrea?"

"No, sir. Not a bit."

"Me, either." He found a bottle of unopened Crown Royal and broke the seal, fixing a fresh drink. "You want a coke, Andrea?"

"I'll fix it, Dr. Livaudais."

"Make sure the cap hasn't been opened."

She glanced at him. "What's going on, Dr. Livaudais?"

"That's what I want you to tell me, Andrea. But before you do, I'm going to make a couple of calls."

"Yes, sir."

Tony called the rectory and asked if Father Javotte could come over. He would leave immediately. And pick up Sam Balon, please? Fine. Tony called Sonny Passon and Don Lenoir and asked them to come over.

"Aw, shit!" Tony said, startling Andrea.

"What's the matter?"

"I completely forgot about Dr. Whitson. Christ, he's

176

"No, sir. He left a long time before we did. I saw him leave."

"What? How . . . I mean, well, how?"

"He walked out. Well, he kind of staggered out. I don't know where he went."

Tony jerked up the phone, cursing under his breath at his carelessness. There was no doubt in his mind that David was still drunk, and unpredictable. "Jean? Is David there?"

"He staggered in here about an hour ago and packed some clothes. I don't know where he's gone, and I don't care. Hey, Tony—you wanna come over and join our party?"

"I think I'll pass, Jean." He had seen Jean's face among the sweaty and naked participants in the photos.

"Your loss, baby," Jean said. She broke the connection.

"It's all these secret meetings that's been going on around town, isn't it, Dr. Livaudais?" Andrea said.

"I don't know anything about them, Andrea. But if you do, then that's what we'll talk about. I know that the young people of today, just as we did when I was a kid, have their own grapevine, and miss damn little."

"I don't know much about them, 'cause I never went to one."

Tony held up one hand. "Wait until the others get here and you can tell it just the one time."

"Fine with me, Doctor."

Tony took a deep breath and looked at Andrea. Such a pretty girl; the kind who would grow up into a beautiful woman. Tony began to experience a light-headed sensation. Not at all unpleasant; a euphoric, sort of erotic sensation. He rather enjoyed it. He looked at Andrea.

Wonder if she liked it? Tony thought. Wonder how many times she got her cookies off?

Andrea turned her head and smiled at Tony.

Wild, erotic, perverted images flew through Tony's mind . . . all concerning Tony and Andrea. She was naked, they were in bed, with Andrea straddling him, riding up and down on him, her young breasts bouncing, the nipples erect . . .

"No!" Tony shouted.

Andrea jumped to her feet. "Dr. Livaudais?"

"Stay away from me, Andrea," Tony said, trying his best to keep his voice level and the erotic images from taking control. "Find a Bible. Right over there!" He pointed.

Andrea ran to the shelf and grabbed up the Bible. "What do you want me to do with it, Doctor?"

Tony was struggling to speak; his head was filled with eroticism . . . all concerning the young Andrea. "Ope . . . open . . . it!" he gasped. "Re . . . read to . . . me."

Frightened, with trembling hands, she opened the Bible and began to read. "'. . . Thy navel is like a round goblet, which wanteth not liquor; thy belly is like an heap of wheat set about with lilies. Thy two breasts . . .'"

"*Andrea!*"

She looked up.

"Read . . . something . . . else."

"I know!" she said, and quickly flipped the pages. She began to read the Lord's Prayer, slowly and calmly.

Tony's head began to clear of the eroticism. His breathing evened out, and he could speak.

178

"I'm all right now, Andrea. Thank you very much, girl."

"What happened to you, Doctor?"

"I don't know, Andrea. But I'm beginning to believe Flip Wilson was right."

She grinned at him. "What do you mean?"

"The devil made me do it."

3

Lula lay on the pool table, naked, her legs spread wide. She was truly amazed; she didn't think the old goat would have had it in him.

She giggled.

Well, actually, he didn't have it in him; she had it in her.

"Hey, babe!" Jules called.

She turned her head. Old bastard had a blue boner. Sticking out like a small flagpole.

"Want to go again, babe?" Jules asked.

"Does a cat have a tail?"

With those words still echoing about the barroom, a strange sound drifted to Lula. She wasn't sure what it was, with all the rain out, but it wasn't bad-sounding. Kind of soothing. Kind of familiar-sounding, too.

But she couldn't place it.

"Get your ass up here, Jules," she said. "And get to pumpin'."

Jules hopped up on the pool table and started working, both he and Lula hollering like kids. The green felt soon became soaked with sweat.

And then Jules cried out once and laid his head on Lula's damp shoulder. Dead. On top of her. In her.

Lula started squalling when she found she did not have the strength to lift him off her.

That strange sound became louder. And Lula knew then what it was.

Purring.

"There's where we're going," Jackson said, stopping Mary with his hand.

"Who lives there?"

"My darling brother, Romy."

"I don't remember much about him."

"Well, baby, you're about to see a lot of him. Scattered all over that house."

Mary squealed in delight and anticipation. "Do I get to help?"

"That's why you're here."

"Do we do it now?"

"No . . . first we have some fun. Come on."

Matt's wife had ordered him from the house. She screamed and yelled and began hissing like a cat when he showed up with Tess in the car.

"Will you please tell me what is the matter with you?" Matt asked her. "I do not understand this change that's come over you."

"Oh, you will," she said, smiling at him. "Sooner than you and your friend might like; but you'll understand."

"What was that . . . that *thing* in the bathroom mirror, Martha?"

"Oh, good!" she cried, clapping her hands. "You saw it!"

"What is it?"

"My friend. My confidant. My Mas—" She stopped.

"Why did you stop, Martha? What were you about to say?"

"You'll find out," she said sullenly.

"Why not tell me now?"

She hissed at him and slammed the door in his face.

Walking back to the car in the driving rain, Matt thought about her hesitation. "Mas?" he said. "Mas? What does that mean?"

"Not a very friendly welcome home," Tess said as Matt got in the car.

"It appears I don't have a home, Tess."

"Oh, yes, you do, Matt—mine."

With the cats leading the way through the rain-drenched streets, Walt Davis walked naked among them. He did not know where they were going, nor did he particularly care. He knew only that he must obey them.

The violent storm had knocked out the streetlights in the downtown section of Becancour, and there was no traffic, vehicle or foot.

No traffic that pure mortals could see, that is.

The cats stopped Walt in front of Lula's Love-Inn.

"Here?" Walt spoke, his one-word question more like a purr in the stormy night.

Walt tried the doorknob. Locked. He followed the cats around to the rear of the bar, to the back door. The doorknob turned in his hand. Walt could hear the sounds of someone crying and moaning and whimpering. Sounded like a woman. He followed the cats into the main room.

Lula's eyes widened in fright when she spotted the naked Walt. She whimpered as the cats jumped up onto the pool table and began licking at her nakedness, brushing up against her, rubbing their wet fur against her body. She had screamed herself hoarse; she had practically no voice left her.

Walt walked to the dead Jules and lifted his head by the hair. Bending over, Walt kissed the man's lips, breathing into Jules's mouth. Walt spoke words he neither understood nor knew where they came from.

Lula watched him through eyes that held just a touch of madness. Her horror-filled eyes watched as Jules moaned and stirred. She could feel him once more growing within her.

She once more began whimpering and squalling hoarsely.

Walt pulled Jules away from the woman. Lula closed her eyes and began crying, not believing any of this horror was actually taking place. It was all a dream; had to be.

But deep down inside her, she knew it was no dream.

She opened her eyes. Jules was looking at her. But what in God's name was the matter with the old fart's eyes. They looked . . . dead! Most of the color was gone from them.

Then he touched her belly. Lula sucked in her breath. Jules's hands were like ice. Jules cut his eyes to Walt. Walt smiled and moved to the head of the pool table, holding Lula's hands firm.

The cats lined the pool table, sitting on the leather-covered raised edge. They watched through unblinking eyes.

Lula began screaming as Jules took her sexually.

"Cold!" she gasped. "Cold!"

Walt leaned over and kissed the woman's lips. Fire and ice leaped into her brain. A strange odor filled her nostrils. The smell of smoke nearly overwhelmed her. She fought Walt's strong grip; she could not break free. She tried to twist her head away from the man's slobbering, stinking mouth; she could not. Jules's erection seemed to be made of long slick ice.

Lula Magee passed out.

"People have been having meetings," Andrea said to the roomful of people. "I was told they started on Christmas day, last year. I have not attended any of the meetings."

"What do they do at these meetings, Andrea?" Sonny asked.

The girl shook her head. "I don't know. But I've heard talk they have sex parties. I've also heard they're practicing black magic. But I don't know anything for sure."

Tony reached into his pants pocket and pulled out the envelope of pictures. He handed the envelope to Father Javotte. "Brace yourself," he warned the priest.

The priest looked at the photos, a look of disgust and revulsion on his face. "Hideous," he said, and handed the pictures to Don.

The men all looked at the pictures, all but Sam recognizing the participants. Sonny walked to a lamp and took a better look, his face paling and his eyes narrowing.

"That's Jane," he said. "My own wife is getting pronged by that punk Don Hemming." He stood for a moment, trembling with anger. All could see the tears in

184

Sonny tossed the pictures on an end table and walked out of the room.

Don picked up the photos. "Well, there's Rita's husband, Burt. He's busy entertaining that little Pat Bennett. Gosh, just look at these people. It's nearly everybody in town."

Tony said, "Carl Nichols, Nate Slater . . ." He let it drift off and tossed the photos back on the end table.

Sam picked up the pictures. "Anyone would be hard pressed to prove this . . . human being tied to the altar was alive when this was taken. I've seen, and so have all of you, more realistic-looking bodies in horror films. So what law has been broken?"

"Crimes against nature," Don said. "Sodomy is against the law in Louisiana. And that's what is happening between . . ." He broke it off as Sonny reentered the room.

"Go ahead and say it, man," the chief said. "That's what Don is doing to my wife. Yeah, it's against the law. But all Jane would say is that she was willing. There is another way we could go, legally—contributing. A lot of those kids are juveniles."

"And once charges are brought, the Dark One would just pull back for a few months," Sam said. "But I'd be willing to bet these pictures, and that's all the proof there is, would disappear."

Father Javotte nodded his head in agreement. "I concur. I think we're back to square one."

The cops looked at the priest. Finally, Don said, "Are you *serious?*"

"Quite," Javotte said. "We are now, unwillingly, I'll

185

admit, playing Satan's favorite game." He glanced at Sam.

"Waiting," Sam finished it.

Sonny plopped his hat on his head. "Not me," he announced. Before anyone could stop him, he was gone out the door, into the storm-slashed Louisiana night.

Don tried to stop the man. The door had closed before the deputy could reach him.

"Let him go," Sam said. "He's angry and he's hurt. If any of us tried to stop him now there would be trouble."

Javotte said to Andrea, "How many of your friends are involved in this . . . madness, child?"

The girl sighed. "I don't know. I do know that I don't have many friends anymore. Ever since I refused to attend those meetings, the other kids kind of shy away from me."

"I guess we have to conclude that most people in the town are involved in this thing," Tony said.

"If they're not," Sam said. "They soon will be."

"On what side?" Tony asked.

"That depends entirely on how strong their faith is."

Someone rang the front doorbell. Tony hesitated, then walked to the door and cracked it open. Rita Dantin stood on the small porch, Dr. David Whitson beside her. The man was dirty, unshaven, but steady on his feet. Tony could smell no alcohol on the man.

"Does this belong to you?" Rita asked, nodding her head toward David.

"Come in, Rita, David." The door closed, shutting out the wind and rain. Tony said, "Why do you ask that, Rita?"

"'Cause his wife damn sure doesn't want him. She

186

too busy entertaining half a dozen men over at her house."

"Alcohol solves nothing," David said. His speech was clear. "Hell, I knew that to begin with. I have some things out in the car, Tony. Could I spend the night here?"

"Of course you can, David."

"I'll get his things," Don said. He walked out into the night, closing the door behind him.

David's eyes focused clearly on Tony. "What's going on around this town, Tony? What in the world has happened?"

"Let's get some food and coffee in you, David," Tony said. "You, too, Rita. Use the phone in the den to call in and tell the station where you'll be. Rita, you know some of what is going on. I . . . OK, I'll accept Sonny and Father Javotte's theory about the . . . devil. I'm still not totally convinced, but I'm getting there."

"The devil?" David said. "You mean like . . . the *devil?* The bad guy? Am I still drunk, Tony? Or has my hearing suddenly become impaired?"

"Go take a hot shower, David," Tony suggested. "I'll open up a can of soup and be heating it." He looked around and raised his voice so all could hear. "Don't any of you eat or drink anything in this house that's been opened. I think my wife tried to drug or poison me this evening."

Rita looked toward the closed front door. She wondered what was keeping Don?

Now David was totally confused. It showed in his eyes. "I hate to say this, Tony. But I wasn't this confused while I was drunk. Did I just hear you say that Lena tried to poison you?"

187

"Yes. Go on, David. Grab a shower. I'll get you a bathrobe and you . . ."

Gunfire suddenly ripped the night. Rita recognized the booming as that from a .357.

Some hideous, nonhuman screaming cut through the storm. The sound chilled those in the house. Lightning flashed and thunder rumbled. The lights went out.

Those inside could hear Sonny Passon yelling. "Did you get it, Don? Jesus Christ, what was that thing?"

4

As the storm howled and crashed in and around the town of Becancour, Xaviere lay naked on the silk sheets of her bed. She longed for a man, but she knew that could never be until her first mating with Sam Balon. She did not feel it unfair. She knew that as the earth-bound daughter of a Christian warrior and Witch-mother, her duty was to seduce her mortal warrior-father and from that union, bring forth into the world and onto the earth a demon . . . the child of Satan.

"Who's out there?" Romy called from the back porch of the home. He held a pistol in his right hand.

Only the storm replied.

"Dammit, answer me!" Romy called.

Lightning flashed, momentarily illuminating the grounds. Romy could see nothing.

Julie Dorgenois appeared at his side. "What is it, Romy?"

"Jackson, I'm sure. Damn this storm. I've never seen anything like it."

Julie's eyes touched his. "It's time, Romy," she said.

189

"Grandfather Dorgenois is right."

"The old man should have done it years ago. He claims he did not have the strength. But I don't believe that. It goes much deeper, I'm thinking."

"That R.M. is waging a battle within him. And the dark side is winning?" she asked.

Laughter from the darkness of the estate reached their ears.

"Yes," Romy said, his words just audible over the storm.

Across town, in the columned home of R.M. Dorgenois, R.M. sat in the darkened den, listening to the howl of the storm . . . and to the dark howling that silently screamed from within him.

The old man was tired. Very tired. And he knew, now, that he had lost.

His lighter spirit grew weaker as the dark side of his human psyche strengthened and the storm raged outside the home.

"I tried," he murmured. "You know I tried."

The lights flickered on and off.

"But you won't win, Jackson. Romy will put it all together and kill you."

Upstairs, in their bedroom, Colter Dorgenois rose from her chair and locked the bedroom door. She took small box out of a chest of drawers and opened it. She removed a half dozen crosses that had been blessed years back by Father Ramagos. She put the largest of the crosses around her neck. She took several small Bible from the box and placed them around the room, a cross beside each Bible. At the bottom of the box a dagger lay on the silken lining, gleaming up at her. She removed the dagger and placed it on her bed. Once more seated, she pressed the intercom button on the telephone and waited for R.M. to pick up downstairs.

When her husband answered, his voice was thick, slurry.

"Don't come upstairs, R.M.," she warned him. "I would prefer it if you left this house entirely."

"You have to believe me, Colter," the old man said. "I tried. I really tried."

"You lie, R.M. You surrendered."

"I want to *live!*"

"I would rather die secure in the arms of my God than walk the path you have chosen."

"Join me!"

"Never."

"Then you know what I must do."

His wife of sixty years laughed at him. "You are forgetting I am a Laveau. There is nothing you can do to me."

R.M. was silent for a time. But Colter knew he was still on the line; she could hear his heavy breathing.

"*Oui,*" he finally spoke. "*A mon grand regret.*"

"You may regret, R.M. I don't. Our *mariage de convenance* kept your darker side chained for many years, did it not?"

"I despise you!"

But Colter knew that was not R.M. speaking. She knew that was not R.M. sitting down in the den. That was only his shell. R.M. Dorgenois had, for all intents and purposes, died.

"Think of love, R.M."

The thing that sat in the den screamed its outrage at the mere mention of that which it hated.

"Love, R.M.," Colter persisted.

The screaming grew more vile and profane. "*Vous l'avez bien voulu!*"

Colter smiled. "No, R.M. You're wrong. I did not ask for it. My will could control yours, so the Church brought us together—don't you remember?"

She could hear the sounds of objects crashing in the den. "*Il y a longtemps,*" she muttered. "Such a long time ago."

She could hear him return to the chair and sit down. "I don't know what finally broke the soft chains I had around you, R.M. But so be it." Her features hardened; when she spoke, her voice was hard. "Now, leave this house, R.M. Right now!"

That which had been R.M. Dorgenois screamed like the rabid animal it had become.

"I command you in the name of all that is holy to leave this place!"

The screaming abated. Colter could hear something clumping about in the den, moving like a hooved awkward animal.

"*Allez-vous-en!*" She yelled the words.

She heard a door slam. She could sense that the Devil' Own was gone. At least for the moment. She was no afraid. She punched off the intercom and dialed th police department.

"Mrs. R.M. Dorgenois here. Chief Passon, *s'il vou plaît.*"

"*Bon soir*, Mrs. Dorgenois," the dispatcher sai

192

"Chief Passon is not here. He is at Dr. Livaudais's home."

"Thank you." She dialed Tony's home. "Dr. Livaudais? Colter Dorgenois here. You have quite a gathering there, I think, *est-ce que c'est correct?*"

"*Oui, madame.*" Tony switched to Cajun French. "And quite a fright, too, I might add."

"Oh? Are you hurt?"

"No, madame. It's just that . . . some very odd things are taking place about town."

Colter could hear that deputy—what was his name?—Lenoir, that was it, yelling in the background. She smiled at his words.

"Goddamn it!" Don yelled. "I put five rounds into that . . . *thing!* Don't tell me I didn't hit it. I shot 298 out of 300. I hit what I'm shooting at."

"Doctor," Colter spoke. "Tell your deputy to calm himself. He could have hit that 'thing' he spoke of three hundred times and he would not have killed it. If it's what I think it is, and I'm probably correct."

"You . . . know what is going on?"

"Of course I do. Tony," she said, surprising the doctor, for Mrs. Dorgenois was usually very formal, "is that new young man in town with you?"

"Sam Balon. Yes, ma'am." He named the others gathered at his house.

"Come to the mansion, Tony. All of you. Time is short, and we are few."

She hung up.

Sam rode with Tony, Father Javotte in the backseat.

193

"How old is Mrs. Dorgenois, Tony?" Sam asked.

"Mid to late eighties. So is R.M. But you couldn't guess it by looking at them." Tony's eyes widened in shock and he slammed on the brakes, the rear end of his car slewing around on the rain-slick street. "My God! What was that?"

Father Javotte gazed at the man-beast-looking thing caught in the glow of the headlights and crossed himself.

Sam sat and stared at the . . . thing. He'd seen worse-looking creatures up in Canada, when Satan unleashed the creatures from the Pits against him. But this was bad enough for one stormy evening. Even though Sam knew, but did not tell the others, that matters were about to get much worse.

The creature had the head, hands, and feet of an animal; but the rest of him was dressed in a business suit.

"That's R.M. Dorgenois!" Tony said. "He was wearing that suit when I saw him uptown this morning."

The small convoy had stopped behind Tony. The occupants of the cars sat and stared in silent horror at the creature looking back at them.

Don clicked on the outside speaker of his prowl car, the speaker located in the center of the outside bar lights. "That's the same kind of thing I put five rounds into a while ago," he said, his voice splitting the rainy night.

The creature threw back its hairy head and opened its mouth, exposing great fanged jaws. It howled, the howling crawling up and down the spines of the people in the cars.

Rita hugged herself, her palms feeling the chill-bumps that gathered on her bare arms.

Sonny Passon crossed himself and said a small but highly emotional silent prayer.

Andrea Golden closed her eyes and shook her head, hoping it was all a bad dream. But when she opened her eyes, that thing was still there, howling at the dark skies.

Dr. David Whitson, sitting in the car with Sonny, almost lost his just-eaten soup.

R.M. Dorgenois turned and loped away, the darkness taking him into wet arms, melting around him like a shroud.

Tony looked at his hands. They were trembling so badly he wondered if he could drive.

"You want me to drive?" Sam asked.

Tony looked at him. "Jesus, man! How can you sit there and be so calm?"

"I've seen it all before. And I'll see it again—if I live through this fight."

"Well, goddammit! I haven't seen it all before! And I hope I never see anything like that again."

"You will," Sam assured him.

Tony put the car in gear and drove on. A moment later, they pulled into the Dorgenois drive.

Sam closed his eyes and thought of Nydia.

"We're all right, Sam," her voice came into his head. "Little Sam is sleeping soundly and Dog is lying by his bed."

"It's begun," Sam projected.

"I know. Something has been prowling around the house. But it's very afraid and very nervous. It did not stay long. The area is clear."

"You have the car. I may ask you to join us."

"I'll be waiting."

When Sam opened his eyes, Tony was looking at him very strangely. "Don't tell me," the doctor said. "You've been talking to your wife, right?"

"Right."

"Jesus!"

"Yes. I speak often with Him, too."

"Does he ever answer you?"

"In a manner of speaking."

Tony Livaudais could not suppress a shudder.

5

The old woman was busy picking up the broken glass and shattered vases when the small group entered her lovely home.

"Let us help," Sam said.

"I almost have it, young man," Colter said. "But thank you for offering. You're Sam Balon?"

"Yes, ma'am." Sam could feel the strength emanating from the lady. This lady, he thought, is no ordinary person.

"Tony, you and Lena have been here before. You know the way to the kitchen. Perhaps you and the young lady," she looked at Andrea and smiled, "would consent to make us some coffee."

Tony smiled and motioned for Andrea to follow him. In the large and well-equipped kitchen, Andrea looked around.

"I'm hungry," she said.

"Why don't you make up a batch of sandwiches while I fix the coffee?"

The coffee perked and the sandwiches made, the group found seats in the spacious den. The rain still beat at the house, but the lightning and thunder had abated somewhat.

"Mrs. Dorgenois," Sonny said. "We all, uh, saw a . . . well, man, sort of, about a block from here. I . . . uh . . ." He didn't know how to finish it.

Colter did it for him. "What you saw was probably the shell of my husband. What did he look like?"

Tony described the creature.

"Worse than I thought," Colter said, lifting her coffee cup to her lips. She sipped and placed cup back into saucer.

"What do you mean, Colter?" Father Javotte said. He alone would call her by her first name.

She met his dark eyes with eyes just as dark and unreadable. "You alone, Daniel, know more than anyone here. What have you told them?"

"Not much. Most of what I know I can't prove. I know bits and pieces. But I know who you are."

"Do you now?" Her eyes twinkled.

"I know the demon was exorcised from you as a child. I know that you had a vision. I know that shortly afterward, you accepted Christ. I know your maiden name was Laveau."

"Someone in the Church has a big mouth," Colter remarked.

"There aren't that many exorcists, Colter," the priest gently reminded her.

"What do you people do, have conventions?"

"Hardly, Colter. But then, I haven't done anything like that in a long, long time. I'm done with it."

"Bullshit!" the old woman said bluntly.

The profanity shook most of the men in the room. Colter's eyes touched Sam's. The young man was sitting calmly, looking at her. A very strong young man, she thought. And he'd better be.

The old woman looked at the small gathering. "Is this it?"

"Ma'am," David Whitson said. "Is *what* it?"

Sam waved him silent. "No, I don't think so, Mrs. Dorgenois. I believe there are others, including your family."

"Romy will join us later. Probably tomorrow. With his wife. I don't fear for Romy. He pieced together the family puzzle years ago." Her eyes touched Sonny's. "Your department, Sonny?"

"C.D. and Bid are OK, I believe. I don't know about their families."

"Get them. Use that phone." She pointed.

"I have two R.N.'s that . . . I guess are secure. And Dr. Martin."

"When Sonny is finished summoning his people, call yours," Colter said.

"And I shall call Mike Laborne," Javotte said.

"How about the other preachers?" Don asked. "Earl Morris and Cliff Lester?"

The priest shook his head. "I sounded them out repeatedly, over a period of weeks. They do not believe. If it is not too late for them already, they'll come to their senses." The priest folded his arms across his chest and stood his ground.

A strong and stubborn man, Sam thought.

Don snapped his fingers. "Tess Nardana and Matt Comeaux. I'll call them. I saw Matt's car parked over at Tess's house about an hour ago."

"Anyone else that you're sure of?" Colter asked.

"Mrs. Wheeler," Sonny said, off the phone.

Colter smiled. "If anyone attempts to harm that lady, they'll be in for a very rude awakening. Most of you are too young to remember what happened at her place years back."

"Yeah," Sonny said. "I forgot about that incident. Those two escaped cons. They're buried right outside of town, aren't they?"

"Yes," Colter said. "After Mrs. Wheeler shot and killed them both. We'll not be able to convince her to leave her home. All we can do is hope for the best."

The old grandfather clock began chiming in the hallway. The gathering listened. It was midnight.

"That's all we're going to do?" Mary bitched at Jackson Dorgenois. "Just laugh at your brother? What a disappointment."

"We have time," Jackson assured her. "Come on." He took her hand.

"Where are we going?"

"To see an old friend."

They walked through the rainy night. In a few moments they were at the Rogers's house. Jackson scratched on the back screen. Bonnie appeared on the porch. She was still naked.

"I've been waiting for you, Jackson. What took you so long?"

"You're both too impatient," he said. "Bonnie, you remember Mary."

"We've spoken to each other over the years, haven't we, Mary?"

"Yes. At first I thought it was the medicine they were giving me. Then I recognized your voice. That was you who told me how to get out, wasn't it, Bonnie?"

"Yes." She motioned them both in. "Quickly, for the

night is unsafe."

"For us?" Jackson asked, stepping into the house after Mary.

Bonnie closed the door. "For anyone. Strange forces have been unleashed, forces that I cannot identify. And the Christians are gathering at the Dorgenois house."

"We saw old R.M.," Jackson said. He laughed. "Guess who lost the good fight?"

The trio shared an evil bark of laughter. "What forces?" Mary asked.

Bonnie shook her head. Her bare breasts trembled with the movement. "The creatures that have slept for a hundred or more years are awake. And they are very hungry. Both for food and to mate. In their frenzy, they won't recognize us as one with the same Master. Stay inside for the night. They won't move during the day."

"I've seen them in my dreams," Mary said. "Great ugly hairy things."

"Yes. God's rejects. Our Master took them thousands of years ago. As soon as the Master calls for a gathering, we'll meet them and be secure. But for now, they are unpredictable."

Outside, the storm had gathered strength, once more unleashing its fury against the town.

The cats lay silent in their hidden places, waiting out the storm . . . and watching as strange, misshapen creatures rose from out of the ground, coming out of the dark swamps. The Beasts stood in the rain; they were not fearful of this rain, for they knew it had been sent by their Master. They stretched their arms and loosened their muscles. They had been asleep for a long, long time.

And now they were free.

Huge, clawed hands waved through the wet air. Powerful jaws that dripped stinking saliva, snapped at nothing. The fangs of the Beasts were four to five inches long, and yellow. The lightning flashes clearly showed the hideousness of the Beasts. The creatures, well over six feet tall when erect, weighed between two hundred and fifty and three hundred pounds. Their eyes were small and evil, with Hell-sent hate shining blood-red. The Beasts had massive jaws that slowly narrowed almost to a pinhead at the top of the head. Their bodies were covered with thick, coarse hair. The face was evil, part human, part animal.

The cats lay concealed and watched the Beasts as they stretched and growled and snapped and pranced their grotesqueness in a macabre dance. They strutted and leaped in the stormy night.

And the cats did not know what to make of them.

"How small the army," Colter Dorgenois muttered.

"It always is," Sam said, speaking softly. He sat next to the woman.

"You've done this before, Sam?"

"Twice."

"You don't seem afraid."

"Not yet, at least. Only a fool does not know fear when confronting the Dark One."

"You're Catholic?"

"No, ma'am. I don't attend any church on a regular basis."

The look she gave him was a curious one.

"There are other denominations, Mrs. Dorgenois."

"That isn't what I meant by the look, young man. It's very late, and I'm tired." She stood up and rapped sharply on a table with the heavy ring on her right hand.

"People," she said. "I'm only going to say this one time. If there are any nonbelievers among you, I would suggest you make your peace with God right now. For you are in more danger than you have ever faced in your life."

No one moved, no one spoke. The old woman looked at each man and woman. "My maiden name was Laveau. I was born to a witch. I am a witch. I was possessed as a child. I had the potential to do incredible evil as a child, but a very wise and strong priest saw that within me, good was battling evil. It took that man nearly three days to spiritually cut the evil from me. He died within moments after doing it. His name was Ramagos."

She sighed. "My husband, R.M., as is the firstborn male child of each generation, has a birthmark. A birthmark in the shape of a cat. It is a very small marking, but one with powerful meaning. The Dorgenois family moved up here from New Orleans to escape their past and try to rebuild their lives. They have always managed to handle those who were born . . . well, marked by the devil. Usually by pairing the male off with a very strong female, like myself. Jackson Dorgenois was one we could not handle. For those of you who do not know, Jackson killed his parents and then consumed their flesh."

Several of the listeners looked as though they would like to puke.

"R.M. and myself . . . we took Romy to raise as our own. Jackson does not know it, but he will meet his match when he confronts his brother, Romy." The woman began to pace the room as she talked. "Chief Borley and the sheriff agreed to help institutionalize Jackson. Borley and the sheriff died shortly afterward. Who killed them? Satan, probably. Please understand something, people. I wanted, R.M. wanted it also . . . we wanted to come forward with this terrible truth. But who would have believed us, and what would it have accomplished? Nothing. Jackson would have been placed in some state hospital and turned every inmate into Satan's follower. If he had been placed in a prison, that would have been even worse. Where he was, he could be, and was, kept heavily sedated. Someone relaxed just for a second there, and he was gone. It had happened before, so no one became unduly alarmed, since he had never hurt anyone before . . . this time. The reason for that was that he had never been called before . . . called by the Dark One.

"I am an old woman. I am not as strong as I once was. R.M. unwillingly broke free of my control. I could do nothing."

Don Lenoir took his wife's hand into his own and squeezed gently. Frances Lenoir sat in shock, not knowing what to believe.

"Sam Balon told me, just a few moments ago, his thoughts on the situation. I think for the most part, you were correct, Sam." She looked at him. "But something, I don't know what, has speeded up the devil's timetable. If I had to guess, I would guess it was caused by mortals. The mortals in this town, who became impatient. It's happened so many times it must be extremely frustrating for Satan."

Frances Lenoir began crying softly, her face in her hands.

"Father Landry attempted to exorcise Jackson Dorgenois. He failed. It broke his health. He lived for years after that, but that killed him, finally. R.M. has lied to Romy. I overheard him lying to him just the other night and knew that his dark side was overpowering the other side. I called Romy shortly after that and told him the truth. I don't know whether he accepted it all, or not. I can only hope he did."

"The cats, Mrs. Dorgenois?" Tony asked.

"Why they are what they are?" she asked.

Tony nodded his head.

She shrugged. "I don't know. Satan can do anything he wishes with almost any human or animal. Look what he's doing this night with the elements. I don't know."

"Perhaps it's from the Scriptures," Father Javotte spoke. "Revelation. 'And the beast which I saw was like unto a leopard, his mouth as the mouth of a lion.'" It was his turn to shrug his shoulders. "But that would be condemning all cats, and I don't believe that. The Bible speaks disparagingly of other animals as well. I think that the Lord of Flies chose cats in this area because there are so many of them."

"And because of the birthmark," Sam said. "And why did I get the idea, or where did I get it, that the Dorgenoises renounced Satan and accepted God?"

"R.M. planted that in your mind, Sam," Colter told him. "Or Jackson, or the Dark One."

"Yeah," Rita said. "I was there when you said that. Planted it?" She looked at Colter. "Is that possible?"

"Oh, yes, girl," the old woman said, her smile grim. "Believe me, R.M. and I have had some mental battles over the years."

"And the gradual building of horror that I spoke of?" Sam asked.

Colter moved her right hand in that classic French

gesture of *comme ci, comma ça*. "Perhaps that was the Dark One's original intent, Sam."

"So many of my friends . . ." Andrea paused. ". . . Used to be friends have tattoos now. Of a tiny cat." She looked confused. "I've known that all along. Why didn't I say anything about it before now?"

"Perhaps for the same reason I said nothing about the lack of discipline at school," Matt Comeaux said. "I was just discussing this with Tess when you called this evening. I would think about it; then I'd get home, and the thought would be out of my head the instant I walked through the front door. My wife, of course."

"And my parents," Andrea said.

Sam glanced at C.D. His wife sat beside him. "Did you make the stakes, C.D.?"

"Yes, sir."

"Dear God!" Margie said, summing up the feelings of all present. She put her hands to her face and began weeping.

THE FIRST DAY OF THREE

6

The small band of Christians had spent the night at the Dorgenois house. All but Sam. He had borrowed a car from Colter and driven back to the rent house.

Yes, Sam thought, lying in bed beside Nydia. We are a very small band.

There had been no new additions last night. Sam counted them down. Colter, Don and Frances, Sonny Passon, C.D. and Connie, Bid Grenier and his wife, Pat, Susan, Noreen, Margie. David, Tony, and Oscar. Mike Laborne and his wife, Lois. Father Javotte. Andrea. Matt and Tess. Romy and Julie, when and if they joined the group. And the kids. Be thankful, he reminded himself, that there weren't that many kids.

Mrs. Wheeler, he counted one more. Although the old lady had refused to leave her house even after Colter had called her and practically begged her to join them. She would stay in her own home, thank you very much.

Sam quietly got out of bed and looked in on Little Sam. He was sleeping soundly, Dog lying by the side of his bed. Sam glanced at his wristwatch. Eight o'clock. He had not had much sleep, but felt alert and refreshed. He showered and shaved while the coffee was perking, then fixed a cup of coffee and took it outside, to sit on the front porch.

The skies had cleared, the clouds gone, the sun shining. And it was hot and humid, with only a light breeze blowing. The breeze brought with it a very slight odor.

Sam recognized the odor immediately.

The Beasts were up and moving.

Sam sipped his coffee, gathered his thoughts, and tried to ignore the odor that drifted about him.

It was a losing battle. Hopefully, Sam thought, not indicative of the battle facing us all.

Nydia came out onto the porch, a cup of coffee in one hand. She sat down and looked at her husband. "The Beasts are here."

"Yes. I would guess some are very close to this house. Probably over there." He pointed toward the dark swamp.

"I would have sworn we were to have more time, Sam." She sipped her coffee. "I just felt we were to have several months."

"I would have, too. Colter Dorgenois asked me last night if I felt fear. I did not then. Now, I do."

"Yes," Nydia said softly. "Dog was restless last night."

"Are you afraid to stay here, Nydia?"

She smiled as she looked at him. "Husband, I have powers inherited from my mother that you have never seen. I don't think I could use them in any evil manner. But I will use them to protect the good around me. Little Sam's powers, I believe, are awesome. Dog is not of this earth. He never drinks, he never eats. No, I am not afraid."

"You've changed over the past fifteen months, Nydia."

208

"I have discovered a lot of my mother in me. But with the help of God, I have managed to channel that to good use. I remember my mother talking to Falcon while I was held their captive. Before Falcon raped me. One of the few times I ever saw my mother afraid. She could see that I had totally rejected the Dark One. It took me a long time to recall those words of hers, but they finally came to me. She said, 'I do not want to be present when Nydia discovers the powers within her and unleashes them. For it will be awesome.'"

Sam smiled. "I seem to be the low man on the totem pole in this family when it comes to powers."

She leaned over and kissed him. "Little Sam and I must live with a curse, Sam. But you've been blessed. Little Sam and I can fight with powers that came from the Dark One and now have been sworn to God, while you must fight with guile and mortal weapons. The end result will be the same."

"I'll worry about you all," Sam said.

Nydia shook her head. "Don't. There is no need for that. Go and follow the trails that God has marked for you."

Sam went into the house and packed a few things. Then he retrieved his .22 autoloader and tossed several boxes of hundred-pack ammo into the bag. Nydia watched him gather up his few things.

"I'll leave the shotgun for you. And you have your pistol," Sam told her.

"I won't need any of those things," she replied.

"You're certain?"

Her reply was a smile.

She came to him, opened his shirt, and kissed the cross-shaped scar on his chest. Then she raised her head and kissed his mouth. A woman kissing her warrior-man

209

good-bye as he prepared to go into battle.

"Take the shotgun, Sam. You're going to need it."

"All right. I've never seen you so firm in your beliefs, Nydia."

"For the first time, Sam, I know that I am one hundred percent with God."

"And very secure in that belief?"

She smiled. "Oh, my, yes."

Sam opened a hall closet door and took out a leather gun case. He unzipped the case and pulled out a twelve gauge pump shotgun, the barrel cut off to federal standards. He put a half dozen boxes of shells into his bag. He went into Little Sam's bedroom. Dog lifted his head and watched as Sam kissed his sleeping son. Sam petted Dog and left the room. Dog moved closer to the bed and closed his mismatched eyes.

Sam touched Nydia's face. "I may need your help before this is over."

"I'll know, and I'll be there," she said.

Sam walked out the front door and tossed his gear into the back of the car he'd borrowed from Colter. He backed out of the drive, waved to Nydia, and pointed the nose of the car toward town.

Bonnie Rogers, Mary Claverie, and Jackson Dorgenois sat in the den of Bonnie's house. They sat around a freshly drawn chalk circle on the floor.

They waited for a sign.

Lula Magee sat with her back to the wall. The cold tile floor of the lounge should have been cold on her bare

210

buttocks. But it wasn't. There were no human feelings left within Lula. Jules Nahan sat beside her. His dead eyes never blinked, his flesh never twitched as the dozens of cats padded over his naked legs and belly and shoulders. He sat and waited. Walt Davis sat across the barroom, on the floor. With his tongue, he very carefully groomed himself.

Judy Mahon, Don Hemming, and several dozen of their friends slept hard, exhausted from the previous night's festivities and following sexual orgy. It had been a good night for all concerned. Half a hundred new members had been initiated into the coven. It had been good fun for everybody; except that one who had died. Well, that had been his own fault. He shouldn't have begun having second thoughts just at the last moment.

It had been good fun listening to his screaming as the knife cut his flesh. That Jon Le Moyne really knew how to make the pain last and last and last. Then, just as the boy's heart was ready to cease its beating, Jon had cut it out of his chest, still beating. He had passed the heart around and all had gotten a good taste of it. Wasn't bad.

It was even all right when those adults showed up and took their pick of the chicks at the meeting. Turned out the adults were pretty OK people after all.

They didn't have long to wait now. Just over forty-eight hours before the coven would, in a manner of speaking, blow the lid off of Becancour.

Yeah, worshiping the Dark One was a lot more fun than going to Sunday school.

*　　　*　　　*

211

The coven members, those who were active and those who were about to be, although the latter group were not yet aware of it, slept late that morning of the first day of three.

The Beasts lay in hidden places in and around the town. They did not like the sun to touch their hairy bodies, for the sun was sent by God. The darkness belonged to their Master. The Beasts rested for the night.

R.M. Dorgenois lay sleeping in the shed behind a house on the very edge of Becancour. His expensive business suit was muddy and filthy and torn. R.M.'s hands and lips twitched in his evil-tinged sleep, his eyelids fluttered, his entire body trembled in anticipation of the coming night. He licked his lips, his tongue gathering up the last bits of blood that had dried on his lips.

Xaviere Flaubert had not moved from the window in several hours. Her eyes were far-seeing, and she did not like what she was seeing. Did not like it, but knew there was nothing she could do about it. In sixty hours all concerned would know either victory or defeat. She had asked herself the same question a dozen times during the past few hours: Why? Why had the people moved so quickly? Why had they speeded up the timetable that had so carefully been worked out? Victory had been assured them; even with the presence of Sam Balon, victory had been assured. The Master, in his way, had approached all leaders of the Coven, urging them to go slowly.

And for a time, the better part of a year, they had obeyed. And then suddenly, like a wildly careening merry-go-round, events had begun rushing by.

And now it was too late to do anything except stand back and watch it all develop.

Disgusted, she turned away from the tinted window.

Her entourage had stood silently in the huge room, watching her, waiting.

"You're thinking very negative thoughts, Princess," Janet said.

"I do not need *you* to remind *me* of that," she snapped at the young woman.

"Mistress," an older man spoke. "We cannot stop what has begun; but what we can do is join them and attempt to guide the events."

"Go on," Xaviere said.

"Is the Dark One near?"

"Close."

"Then let us summon him."

"Risky."

"But if we wait, and the townspeople grow even more impatient, will it not be too late?"

Xaviere considered that. "Yes," she finally spoke. "We'll need a subject. Have you one in mind?"

"Yes. Things are looking up, I believe. That foolish preacher, Cliff Lester, has begun gathering his flock to the church. He has convinced them that the subtle change in the town is due to the so-called pornographic books and magazines sold in various stores in the area. Lester and his flock are going to have twenty-four hours of singing and praying, with marches in between. They are going to cleanse the town of filth."

"Is that right?" Xaviere said, her lips curving into a smile. "How noble of Mr. Lester and his flock."

"Yes, Mistress," the man said with a laugh.

"God must have loved fools," the Princess of Darkness said. "For He certainly put a large number of them on earth."

"Yes, Mistress. They began gathering at the church at eight this morning. They are going to have something called singin', shoutin', stompin', and eatin' on the grounds."

"What in the hell is that?" Janet asked.

"I have no idea at all," the man said.

Sam began driving the streets of Becancour. The sawed-off shotgun lay fully loaded on the backseat, the .22 caliber autoloader lay on the seat beside him. One thing stuck firmly in his mind: last night, when he left the Dorgenois house, he had driven the same streets, and he had seen no cats. None at all. And he felt it was not due to the weather, for the rain had ceased long before he left.

Now, in the light of day, the cats had once more gathered. They sat silently on the curbs, in the trees, on porches and on roofs, watching him as he drove slowly by.

Why? Sam pondered. Why would they not gather last night as they had done in the previous nights.

Sam did not see one single dog. Not one anywhere. He did not feel the cats had killed the dogs. Instead, he felt the dogs had simply left the town, sensing something they could not cope with. He felt the dogs had moved back into the timber, away from the danger they sensed.

All except Dog. But Sam, like Nydia, felt that Dog was not of this earth.

Even though Sam felt the timetable had, for whatever reason, been moved up, and events rushing toward the inevitable confrontation between Good and Evil, Light and Dark, the town still appeared normal—normal, that is, to anyone not familiar with what was going on.

But Sam could feel the ugly evil surrounding him as he drove the streets. He looked at the people sitting on the porches, looking back at him.

"Gone," Sam muttered. "They're gone. Their souls have turned black."

Then, that little something that had been nagging at him came to the fore.

He stopped the car in the middle of the street.

He could see men and women; he could see lots of teenagers.

But there were no young children.

He drove on, very slowly now, his eyes moving from side to side, studying the people on the porches.

No young kids.

But where had they gone?

Sam had no answer for that, and none came to him.

But he could hope.

He'd mention it to? . . . To whom? The entire group gathered back at the Dorgenois home? No, he didn't think so. He did not know whether he trusted them all. So he would mention it to Father Javotte and perhaps a few others.

He drove the streets, finding conditions much the same wherever he went: people sitting on chairs and in porch swings, staring at him, their faces either sullen or openly hostile.

The sad thing is, Sam thought, many of them have gone over to the Dark Side and didn't know why it happened to them.

Sam recalled something one of his professors had said

215

one time during a small gathering in his home. The man had been a minister for a good many years before leaving the pulpit for a classroom. "It isn't easy being a Christian, Sam. A great many people are kidding themselves, lying to themselves about having accepted Christ. I have had and will continue to have some spirited debates with my good Catholic friends on that very subject." He had glanced around the group, a twinkle in his eyes. "I see several of you who are Catholic. I hope it won't come as a shock to you when I say that I know many, many priests who don't believe that a person can live a lifetime of sin and at the moment of death, be forgiven? Does that shock any of you?"

It had not shocked a single person in the room. It certainly had not shocked Sam, for he had many friends who had either grown up in the Catholic Church or were actively attending it . . . they didn't believe it either.

"Oh, I don't either!" Father Javotte said. "And in that respect, I'm a practicing hypocrite. I personally believe that a person who has been a miserable jerk all his life will die a miserable jerk, no matter what mortal man speaks over them. I certainly am not Jesus Christ, although I know some priests who behave as if they were. But, of course, that is not confined solely to Catholics. You have not had the pleasure of meeting Cliff Lester, have you?"

"No. I haven't. Should I look forward to it?"

"No. That reminds me of something. Oh, yes. Today is the day that Lester and his . . . flock," he spoke the words very dryly, "plan to stage a march through Becancour, protesting the girlie magazines sold in some stores. Little narrow-minded people who are setting

216

themselves up as judges."

"Lest they be judged, Padre?" Sam asked with a smile.

"Yes." Javotte returned the grin. "Feel like going out for a drive, Sam?"

"Why not?" Sam studied the priest. "You seem very calm today, Padre. What do you have up your sleeve?"

"Eh? Oh, nothing, Sam. It's just that I've made my peace with God. I am ready."

"Ready, Padre? I'm . . . not certain I follow you."

Javotte smiled. "I have counted my blessings, and they are many, Sam. I've lived fifty-odd years, and they've been good years. I . . . well, I don't think I'm going to make it through this fight, Sam. I'm ready to go home."

"You can't know that for certain, Padre."

"I was trained as an exorcist, Sam. Believe me, I know."

7

Sonny and Don said they would like to ride into town with Sam and Javotte. During the ride, Sam told them about his sighting no young children during his drive earlier.

"That is odd," the priest said.

They were riding in Don's personal car, radio-equipped.

"You don't think these . . . Satan-worshipers have harmed them, do you?" Sonny asked.

To Sonny and Don and many of the others, including Tony, all this was like a bad dream; a dream conjured up in the mind of a psychotic, surely, but still a bad dream. One that they were hopeful would end very soon.

It would, but for some, not the way they hoped.

"I . . . don't think so," Sam said. "I think they've run off, sensing something. I don't know why I say that. I . . ."

A hard mental thrust visually shook him. Nydia's voice entered his head.

"Sam? I have several hundred children gathered in our front yard."

On my way, Sam thought.

Aloud, he said, "Out to my rent house, Don. Nydia just told me there were several hundred kids gathered out there."

"Guess that explains that," Sonny said. "But why out there?"

Sam thought of Janet's little child, that little girl he'd seen her playing with out in the gazebo. He kept his mouth shut about that. But he was conscious of Father Javotte's eyes on him.

"My God," Don breathed. "Look at the kids."

Nydia met the men, Little Sam by her side, Dog beside Little Sam. Sam looked at the animal. Dog was studying the mass of children, but without particular interest in any one child.

Sam stood with his family while the others questioned the children. Don walked up to Sam, scratching his head.

"It's the damndest thing, Sam. The kids don't know why they came here, or really, remember coming out here. They're just . . . *here*."

"Uh-huh," Sam said. He caught Nydia's glance. She slightly nodded her head.

"One hundred and ninety five kids," Sonny said. "Between the ages of two and ten. Where are the ones under two and over ten?"

"And what are we going to do with them, and where are we going to *put* them?" Don asked.

The cops walked off to speak with the older kids. Sam said, very quietly, "Divide and conquer."

"What do you mean, Sam?" Javotte asked.

"One of those cute little girls is going to be the daughter of Janet Sakall. My daughter." Quickly, briefly, Sam told the priest what happened in New York State almost a year and a half ago.

"Then the child would be one of the very young ones?" the priest asked.

"Not necessarily."

"I don't understand."

"You've seen the beautiful woman at the Dorgenois house, Xaviere?"

"Yes."

"She's about four years old."

"Brothers and sisters," Cliff Lester spoke from the pulpit. "Thank you all for coming." His eyes swept the crowded church. "But where are all the lovely young children?"

"They've all gone, Brother Lester," a woman spoke.

"*Gone?*" Lester thundered. "What do you mean, gone?"

"They all left their homes early this morning. When we tried to stop them, they fought us and ran away."

Brother Lester pounded the pulpit, his face turning beet red. "It's those pornographic-readin' heathens in town! They've seized our children for sex slaves! Why, there is no tellin' what perverted acts have been performed on them by now. It's all them filthy trashy books and magazines that are sold in this community. Lord!" He raised his arms. "Give us a sign!"

Brother Lester about had a coronary when a car backfired out in the street.

Composing himself, he gripped the sides of his pulpit, took a deep breath, and said, "Brothers and sisters, it has come to my attention that there are some in this town who believe that *Satan* . . ." He pounded the pulpit for emphasis. ". . . *Satan* walks among us." He glared at his

220

congregation. He stage-whispered, "Well, I believe it, too."

Collective sigh from the congregation.

"Yes!" he roared. "It's them people who sell and read them filthy books and magazines. They have poisoned their minds and darkened their souls glarin' at them glossies and devourin' them nasty words. And now they've taken our children!" His voice rose to a near hysteria pitch. "Oh, Great God!" he roared. "It is up to us, your mortal servants. to right the wrong, to fight the good fight, to bring truth and light and hope to the members of this community who have strayed so far off the path of righteousness. Today is the day, Lord!" he shouted, pounding the pulpit.

Lester warmed up to the subject. He waved his arms and stamped his feet and got so excited he slipped into the Unknown Tongue.

Some of his flock felt the excitement and rose from their pews, waving their arms and dancing in the aisles and speaking in Tongues. Some of the seated Brothers watched the rolling hips of some of the prancing Sisters. Their thoughts were not exactly pristine.

Cliff Lester really got into the spirit. He jumped from the raised platform, rolled up his sleeves, and joined in the passing parades of Tongue-speakin' Brothers and Sisters.

"I'm calling in some outside help," Don announced. He reached for his mike.

Sam, Father Javotte, and Sonny stood outside Don's car and watched him, saying nothing.

The deputy hesitated. "Well?" he demanded. "Give

221

me some input on this."

"Go ahead," Sam told him. "It should be interesting."

Don lifted the mike to his lips. He cut his eyes, looking at the men outside the car. "I'm going to tell them I've got a bad situation here in Becancour. I'm going to tell them . . ." He replaced the mike on the hook and laid his head on the steering wheel. "I could tell them I've got almost two hundred children who just ran off from home. That's really a felony offense, isn't it? I could tell them that last night there were sex parties all over town, couldn't I? I could tell them that old man R.M. Dorgenois has turned into a . . . werewolf, couldn't I? I could tell them that most people didn't go to work this morning, couldn't I? That the town is full of cats. Somebody worked all this out real good, didn't they?"

"They always do," Sam told him.

"Couldn't we have some deputies and state troopers standing by to move in when the lid finally does pop off?" Don said.

Sonny leaned against the car. "I sure as hell would hate to be the one to talk to the colonel down in Baton Rouge. I'd sure hate to be the one to tell him we need help up here because Satan is in town."

Don closed his eyes and cursed, low and long. "OK, then. Somebody tell me this: why us? I'm not particularly religious. I go to church, but so do, or at least they did, nearly all of those people who have gone over to the . . . other side. And I don't wanna hear Scriptures, Father. You tell me in plain ol' English. Why us?"

A very good question, the priest thought. And one that I have no ready answer for.

He was conscious of Don's eyes on him.

222

"Sam!" Nydia called. "We've got to do something with these children. Many of them are hungry and all of them are frightened."

Sam nodded his head, acknowledging her statement.

Don waited for the priest to reply.

"I don't know, Don," Javotte finally spoke. "I just don't know."

Don wearily nodded his head in understanding. "Well, I don't understand it either, Father. I just hope someone can explain it when this . . . mess is all over."

No one will, Sam thought. Because no one will really understand it. I've been trying to understand this and situations like it for several years. I'm no closer to the truth now than I was then.

Sam looked at the mass of children. There would be no use in trying to ferret out Janet's child. Whatever little friend she had latched onto would be totally within the demon child's power. One child, ten children, all of the children would lie for the little girl . . . not willingly, but because they would have no choice in the matter.

Sam looked at Don, sitting glumly behind the wheel of his car. For a moment, Sam mentally wavered, almost told Don to go on, call in, at least we could get the kids out of here.

But Sam knew that would only delay matters; a day, a week, a month, a year. But this town had been chosen by the Dark One, and sooner or later, Light must combat Dark.

What was it that God's Mercenary had told Little Sam in the boy's dreams? Yeah. Time for Sam to start kicking ass and taking names.

All right. So be it.

223

"Sonny?" Sam called, making up his mind. "How many department stores are open today? Or did you notice?"

"I think every one is open, Sam. There's just no customers."

"There is about to be. You and Don go to the school parking lot and get a couple of buses. Use them to take the kids to the clinic. Any spillover we'll house at the mansion."

"How are we going to get a couple of buses?" Sonny asked.

"Steal them," Father Javotte said.

"Father!" Don protested.

The priest lost his temper. "Dammit, Don! Get it through your head that we're in a war. A war! And we're badly outnumbered. Now move your ass, boy!"

"Yes, sir!" Don said.

The cops noticed the streets were almost completely deserted. It gave them both a very eerie feeling. Sam had asked them to stop by the mansion and get Tony and Mike and go to the department stores, get all the sheets and blankets and pillows they could find.

"You ever steal anything, Sonny?" Don asked the chief.

"Not since I was a kid and we used to swipe hubcaps. That stopped when the cops took me down to the station house and beat the hell out of me. You?"

"I never stole anything," Don said, his voice full of gloom.

"You sound like you're sorry you didn't?"

"No, not really. It's just . . . well, I was so straigh

224

when I was a kid. And it was little bit different than when you were a kid, Sonny. Things were a lot more wide open when I was a kid. But I never did anything wrong. Ol' straight-arrow Lenoir, that's me."

"Is this leading somewhere, Don?"

"I don't know. Maybe. You ever been unfaithful to your wife, Sonny?"

"Only in my mind. Me and Jane been . . . was, that is, married for twenty-two years." He fell silent.

"Did she? . . ."

"Yeah. A couple of times that I know of. I see what you're getting at, but it won't wash, Don. Far as I know, and this bein' a small town, we'd both know, Dr. Whitson's wife didn't run around on him. Frank and Thelma Lovern been like two love birds for as long as I can remember. Same with a lot of people we saw in those pictures."

"Guess that shoots down that theory, doesn't it?"

"Keep trying. Maybe you'll hit on it. God knows . . ." He laughed, somewhat bitterly. ". . . I'd damn sure like to know the why of it all."

"You reckon we ever will?"

"Maybe." He pulled into the bus parking area of the school. "Providing we live through it."

8

For the first time in several days, Xaviere's mood was upbeat. The Princess of Darkness had even attempted several small jabs at humor. Her followers at the old Dorgenois house had laughed loudly and long.

Yes, Xaviere felt good. Those silly, vain Christians had taken in the children—as she had known they would—and Janet's child, Bess, was among them. Bess, with most of the others, were being housed at the clinic. The rest were with that small band of resisters at the newer Dorgenois house, with Colter. Yes, things were definitely looking up.

But she wondered about old R.M. He had been so strong at first; Xaviere had almost given up in her quest to change the old fart into that which she knew he was. Then, suddenly, the old man had shifted.

She shook her head. She didn't understand that part of it. She scratched her head and picked a flea from her scalp, crushing the little insect between two long, sharp fingernails.

The once beautiful home positively reeked of body odors. Cobwebs hung in silver-gray ropes in the corners. And cats were everywhere.

Xaviere was just a bit nervous about the coming night. She knew the Master would be terribly angry if she called him out too soon. And when the Dark One became angry . . . matters could turn very grim—in a hurry.

She lifted her beautiful head and stuck out her chin in a defiant gesture. She had obeyed the Master, following all instructions and procedures to the letter. She did not feel that she, or any of her immediate followers, could have possibly done any better.

But that was not for her to say. She lowered her chin.

Tonight would test that thought of hers.

"You know the kids, Sonny?" Sam asked.

"Most of them. Some of them told me they were here visiting relatives; the ones under school age."

Sam hid a sigh. Neither he nor Nydia had the ability to know for sure which child was the demon-child.

But . . .

. . . there was someone who might.

"He is just a child, Sam," Nydia's thoughts pushed into his brain. "Just a little boy."

"Blessed by God," Sam returned the mental push. "To do God's work."

Nydia was silent.

Sam thought: "Get everything you'll need from the house. Bring my .41 mag and the ammo belt with you. It's time to go to work."

"Dog will never leave Little Sam's side," she reminded her husband.

"I don't plan on him leaving."

At their rent house by the bayou, Nydia began hurriedly packing. She put Sam's big .41 magnum, with a

227

six-inch barrel, into a bag, along with a full ammo belt and half a dozen boxes of ammunition. She finished her packing and looked around the house.

Dog was looking at her.

"Stay with him." She spoke softly.

Dog blinked.

Little Sam walked into the room and looked at his mother. "I'm not afraid, Mother," he said. "I know what I have to do."

"You're very brave."

"No." The little boy shook his head. "I'm just a soldier in a war, that's all."

Nydia took her son's hand and the three of them walked out of the house. Nydia closed and locked the front door.

"I liked it here," Little Sam said.

"So did I, Son."

"Will we ever come back?"

"I don't think so, Sam."

"I don't think we will, either."

Ben Ballatin knew nothing of the troubles in Becancour. Ben Ballatin knew very little of the goings-on in the outside world. He lived deep in the swamps and came to town only when he ran out of essentials: sugar, salt, flour, things of that nature. The swamp was his home, as it had been his father's home and his father before him. Ben did not like the outside world and kept contact with it to a minimum. Only his brother, Maurice, had ever attempted to make his way in that English-speaking world . . . and look what that had gotten him.

Drowned, when he took them northerners out into the

228

bayous to fish. How many years had it been? Ben pondered, drifting along in his pirogue . . . must have been . . . Damn! almost forty years ago. Maurice and their cousin Charles was never seen again no more.

Ben always felt there was something odd about that whole thing. Maurice and Charles knew these bayous like they knew the back of their hands. Ben remembered that day well. There had been no wind, no storms, no bad weather of any type.

Maurice and Charles and them Yankees had just plain ol' vanished. And that didn't make no sense a-tall.

Ben reached for his paddle, then paused as a slight noise reached his ears.

Ben sat very still, for the noise was not something normally heard in the swamps. That was no 'gator or bear; no bird takin' off or divin' for food.

Ben listened. Damn! he thought. That sounds like somebody swimmin'.

But not out here. Not in these waters. Take a damn fool to swim in these dark waters.

But there it was. Sure enough was somebody swimmin'.

Then a low moan came to Ben's ears.

"Qu'est-ce que c'est?" he called.

Ben almost swallowed his dentures when he heard his name spoken, the word floating across the dark waters on the hot, still bayou air.

"'Ay!" Ben called. *"Qui est-ce?"*

His name was once more repeated.

"'Ay, boy! You better talk to me. Damn fool swimmin' out here. You los', boy?"

Then Ben heard splashing coming from the other side of his pirogue. Two people swimmin' out here? he

229

thought. Hell, no! No way. Somebody was playin' tricks on Ben. That somebody pro'bly that damn crazy Billy Carmouche. Fool never did have no sense.

"Billy! Billy Carmouche! You crazy son of a bitch! Git outta them waters 'fore a 'gator done took your leg."

The pirogue rocked side to side. Ben grabbed hold of both sides to maintain balance.

He howled in fright and shock as something wet and slimy and rotten-feeling grabbed his right hand. Ben cut his eyes to see what kind of thing had grabbed him.

He looked into the white, dead eyes of his cousin Charles.

Ben's screaming ripped through the swamp, startling the birds. The birds flapped upward, breaking free of the trees, filled with Spanish moss.

"Git away from me!" Ben screamed. He tried to pull his hand free from the slimy grasp of the thing in the water.

Then the pirogue tilted dangerously toward the other side. Something equally cold and slimy and rotten-feeling grabbed Ben's thigh. Ben's squalling intensified.

"Turn me a-loose!" he screamed.

He dared to look at what had him by the leg. He began shaking as total fear numbed his very being.

It was his brother, Maurice.

Maurice looked at him through dead white eyes. His flesh was fish-belly white and wrinkled. When Maurice opened his mouth, death odors from the rotting cavity surrounded Ben.

A splash came from the front of the pirogue, left and right. Ben lifted his horror-filled eyes. Two kids, a boy and a girl, naked, now clung to either side of the homemade canoe. They motioned for Ben to join them.

A splash right behind him jerked Ben's head around. He was nose to nose, eyeball to eyeball with a naked woman. And he knew who it was, even though he felt what he was seeing was impossible.

It was that Yankee woman who had drowned. And them was her kids hangin' onto the front of the pirogue.

Ben started praying.

The woman threw her arms around his neck and jerked his head back. She kissed him, plunging her slimy tongue deep into his mouth.

Ben's screaming prayers were abruptly silenced by the woman's cold, wet, stinking mouth.

The front of the pirogue dipped and Ben's left leg erupted in a hot spasm of pain. He felt his blood gush from his leg. He managed to look down.

The girl was eating his leg.

Pain ripped through him as the woman began gnawing at his face. His blood gushed and flowed and dripped as swamp-stained teeth ripped and tore his flesh. Ben felt sharp teeth hook onto the flesh just below his eye and the woman's head twist and jerk. The flesh peeled away from his skull as easily as someone peeling an orange.

Ben Ballatin screamed just once more. When his mouth opened and the shrieking rolled over his tongue, the woman's teeth clamped down on his tongue and bit deeply. His mouth filled with hot blood and his head exploded in pain.

Ben flailed his arms and tried to kick out with his pain-filled and gnawed-on legs. The other kid was now in the pirogue, chewing at Ben's legs. Water slopped into the pirogue, mixing with Ben's blood. His brother Maurice reached up with fishy-smelling, ghostly white arms and pulled Ben into the dark waters.

The last thing Ben remembered was his brother tearing at his throat.

"Do they know the entire story?" Romy asked Colter.

"Yes," the old woman replied. "Do *you* now believe?"

Romy nodded his head. Julie stood off to one side, their children close beside her. Her face was white from fear and shock and disbelief.

"It would not be wise for you to return to your home," Colter told the grandson she had helped raise as her own son. "Strength in numbers is not something to be merely spoken of—in our case, it's very true. This bit with the children was a smart move on the part of the other side. They've managed to split our forces and weaken us."

When Romy spoke, there was a bitterness to his tone that cut the old woman. "R.M. could have prevented all this. If he'd just had the courage to come forward and admit what he was born to be."

"Yes," Colter agreed. "But the mortal side of him prevailed."

"How do you mean?"

"He wanted to live, Son. Like everyone else. And, Son, who would have believed him?"

"The Church would have believed him." Romy stood his verbal ground.

"And you believe a priest would have killed him?"

"If the exorcism had failed, yes, I do."

Colter knew there was no point in continuing the discussion. Romy was right, to a degree. But there was still much he did not understand, and probably never would.

She wound it up by saying, "Well, Son, you'll probably have your chance to destroy him, and your brother, too. I only hope you are up to the task when the moment arrives."

"I will be," Romy said, a hard grimness in his voice. He met her eyes. "But I don't have to like what I do."

The old woman inwardly relaxed at that. Now she was ninety-nine percent sure that Romy was free of the curse.

But that one percent would nag at her until it was over.

If they lived through it, that is.

"There ain't no school no more, Brother Lester," one of Cliff's flock breathlessly informed him. "And Sonny Passon and Don Lenoir done stole some of the buses and tooken all the missing kids over to the clinic and to Missus Dorgenois's mansion."

The messenger picked up a piece of fried chicken and gnawed at it.

A guitar's thumping and voices raised in song drifted to the two men.

"'I like the old time preachin', prayin', singin', shoutin','" rose the voices.

"The law is in it with all the rest," Brother Lester said, his mouth full of potato salad. "It figures, though. The law didn't do nothin' when the drinkin' and whorin' and other sinnin' jumped up around here. They probably been doin' sinful things in them cells at the jail. No tellin' what-all's been goin' on over there."

The messenger stopped chewing the chicken leg. He

leaned forward, closer to Brother Lester, his eyes shining. "What do you reckon it was?"

"Haw?"

"What they was doin' over in them cells?"

"Lustful things," Brother Lester said.

"Have mercy!" the messenger said.

"Gimme some more of that chicken over there. Thanks. We got to make plans this afternoon. It's up to us, Elmer. Ain't nobody else gonna do it. We're all alone in this fight."

"We'll stand firm, Brother Lester," he was assured.

"I know you will. Gimme some of that cornbread over yonder. Thanks. We're all alone, Elmer. All alone."

"How about them that's supposed to be gatherin' to fight the devil?"

Brother Lester laughed. "Now, Elmer. You don't *really* believe in werewolves and vampires and all that other nonsense, do you?"

Elmer grinned. "Heck no, Brother Lester. But we're mighty few agin so many in this town. That's all I was sayin'."

"I hate to say this, Elmer, but I think we're gonna have to arm ourselves."

"Hot damn!" Elmer blurted.

Brother Lester gave him a reproachful look.

"Sorry," Elmer muttered. "I got carried away a bit."

"We're all human, Elmer. The Lord forgives you, I'm sure."

"Guns, Brother Lester? But who are we goin' be fightin'?"

"The purveyors of filth, Elmer. Them folks who have failed to heed the Good Book. Them folks who continue to wallow amid the fleshy pleasures of lustful sin."

234

Elmer just *loved* it when Brother Lester got to talkin' like that. Made him feel all gooey inside. "I'm ready, Brother Lester!"

"I know you are, Elmer. But we got to preach and pray and sing and shout and stomp some more. We all got to look for a sign. When it comes, then we'll know it's time to move."

"Amen, Brother Lester!"

9

Delivery trucks from out of the parish made their usual runs into Becancour, servicing all the stores with milk and butter and canned goods and shoes and underwear. Everything appeared normal.

Except . . . the shopkeepers and clerks and so forth seemed, well, odd-acting. They weren't rude or anything like that. They were just, well, sort of distant.

The delivery men and women were, although they didn't know why, relieved when they drove out of Becancour, breathing a sigh of relief when they put the city limits sign behind them.

Then they all, to a person, forgot all about the strange behavior of those they'd met in Becancour. They just completely forgot all about being in Becancour that day.

Sam left Nydia and Little Sam at the clinic. He borrowed a pickup truck from Tony for the duration, leaving Nydia the car and returning the borrowed car to Colter. Sam felt more comfortable in a pickup. He put his sawed-off shotgun in the rear window gun rack, laid his big .41 mag on the seat beside him, and stowed his .22 autoloader in front pocket of the seat covers.

He tossed a dozen sharpened stakes and a heavy mallet onto the floorboards.

"You want to take a ride?" he asked Father Javotte.

The priest eyeballed the stakes and the mallet. "You feel it's time for that?"

"If I know for sure who they are," Sam said, "I'll finish them."

Javotte nodded his head and climbed into the truck.

Sam drove the circle drive and pulled out onto the street, pointing the truck toward Becancour.

"What are your plans, Sam? Today, I mean?"

"Well, Padre," Sam said with a grin. "It's a hot day, and I'd kind of like to have a cool one. How about you?"

The exorcist returned the grin. "I could stand a brew. Drive on."

They drove to Lula's Love-Inn and parked by the side. Sam slipped the light .22 caliber autoloader behind his belt, covering it with his shirt. He slipped a fully loaded spare into his back pocket. "You ready, Padre?"

The priest smiled and reached under his shirt. He produced a short-barreled .38 revolver. "Love will conquer all, Sam. But sometimes it helps to keep an ace in the hole."

The men laughed and got out of the truck, walking to the front door. Sam pushed it open and stepped into the beery, murky barroom, Javotte right behind him. They stood for a moment, giving their eyes time to adjust to the sudden darkness.

Several tables were occupied by smelly men and women; the place reeked of unwashed human flesh. One table was occupied by a group of teenagers. Lula stood behind the bar. Jules Nahan sat on a bar stool. Walt Davis stood at the end of the bar, wearing a T-shirt and faded jeans. His feet were bare. A large cat lay on the bar before him.

Humans and animal stared at Sam and Javotte. Sam closed the door.

Sam and Javotte walked to the bar and took stools close to the front door. Lula walked stiffly toward the men. Sam studied her as she walked. Her eyes were dead, and she shuffled more than walked. And she was filthy, her hair matted. When she opened her mouth to speak, her breath fouled the already stinking air of the barroom.

"What'd you guys want?"

Sam met her gaze and saw a touch of fear in those dead eyes. "Two beers, in cans, unopened."

She nodded her head and flipped open the lid to a cooler. She placed two cans of beer on the bar.

Sam tossed a couple of dollars onto the bar.

Lula pushed the money back to him. "On the house, boys. Drink up and haul your asses outta here. You're not welcome."

"Do we offend you, miss?" Javotte asked gently.

Lula laughed. "That's one way of puttin' it, asshole."

"Bear this in mind, Father," Sam whispered to Javotte. "They accepted the Dark One willingly. They were not forced into anything. Whatever happens to them, they brought it on themselves."

"I have colleagues who would argue that, Sam," the priest returned the whisper.

"They're wrong. I don't have to tell you the devil preys on hypocrites and the morally weak. These people are lost, Padre. Lost forever. You can't—no one can—

238

exorcise an entire town."

"What now, Sam?"

"They want Satan. Let's send a few of them to meet him."

Javotte's eyes flicked around the room. "Two against twenty or so? You like to play dangerously, don't you?"

"Coming to this town was not my choice, Padre. I am what God told me to be."

"And you're not afraid?" Javotte whispered.

"Hell, no."

Javotte chuckled grimly. "Very well. I'm with you."

"Stay loose, Padre." Sam opened his beer and took a pull. He looked around the room. Kick ass and take name-time, he thought.

"Which one of you bastards would like to be the first one to try something?" Sam challenged.

A young man rose from his chair.

"Don Hemming," Javotte whispered. "He's a tough kid, believe me."

"I'm tougher," Sam said.

Javotte smiled and shook his head. He genuinely liked this brash young Sam Balon.

"I'll not only try it," Don said, balling his hands into fists. "But I'll do it."

"Bring your ass over here, hot-shot," Sam said, taking another pull of the cold beer.

Don ran toward the two men, kicking tables and chairs out of the way.

Sam slipped from the bar stool, ducked under the wildly thrown right fist, and slipped under the young man's arm. Sam grabbed Don's belt and tossed him across the barroom floor. Don's butt and back slid across the floor. He came to rest against a wall, by the silent

239

jukebox. Sam reached him before he could gather his senses and get up. His right boot lashed out, catching the punk in the mouth with the toe of leather. Blood spurted and teeth broke off, falling to the floor, glistening wetly as they rolled and clicked.

Don was out of it for a while.

Sam grabbed up a long neck and smashed the half-full beer bottle into the face of the girl who had initiated the confrontation. The girl screamed as the busted glass ripped her flesh. She fell from her chair, both hands to her bloody face. She lay on the dirty floor, sobbing.

The cat on the bar hissed and snarled and sprang at Sam. Javotte's .38 roared in the close air of the barroom. A huge hole appeared in the cat's left side as the hollow-nosed lead exited. The cat was slung to the far side of the room, dead.

The barroom was suddenly very quiet. Those who had chosen the pitted path of the Prince of Darkness sat in shocked silence. Everyone had said this was going to be easy.

Somebody lied.

Don's crying and moaning and the girl's sobbing and blubbering was the only sound.

Sam stood in the center of the room. Javotte noted that the man was not even breathing hard.

"Back out of the door, Padre," Sam told him. "Check the outside before you step out."

Javotte opened the door and glanced out, looking left and right. "It's clear."

"You folks have a real nice day," Sam told the barroom crowd. "Next time is going to be much more interesting, I assure you."

He stepped out into God's sunlight and joined Javotte.

240

The two men walked swiftly to the pickup. Sam cranked up and drove off.

"That was very exhilarating!" Javotte said.

Sam laughed. "And that was good shooting, Padre."

"Thank you. Target shooting is a favorite hobby of mine."

"Could you kill a human being, Padre?"

"We're not facing human beings, Sam. Could I kill an innocent? No. Could I, would I, kill a follower of Satan? Yes."

Sam nodded his head, his eyes and attention on a group of cats padding noiselessly up the sidewalk that ran alongside the street. "They're pacing us," Sam noted. Then he cut his eyes to the other side of the street. He slowed, then stopped the pickup. "No, they're not pacing us. They seem to be going somewhere. Do you get that feeling, Padre?"

The priest watched the parade of cats, lines of them. Hundreds of them had appeared. They were all padding off to the northeast, angling through alleys and side streets.

"Yes. They seem to have a definite destination in mind."

"But where?"

Father Javotte was silent for a moment, his eyes on the cats. "I don't like what I'm thinking, Sam."

"Let me see if I like it or not."

"Let's assume the cats have a destination in mind. It certainly appears that way. Perhaps they are, well, going to a meeting or a gathering of some sort?"

"Go on."

"But animals are not prone to do that sort of thing, right?"

241

"Not to my knowledge. But these cats are under the power of . . ."

Sam let that drift off, the words hanging in the air.

"Precisely," Javotte said.

"He does not make appearances in the daylight, Padre."

"No. I would think not. Perhaps the cats are leaving a bit early, to get a good seat." The priest started laughing, with just a bit of hysteria touching the words.

"Padre?"

Javotte wiped his eyes and sobered. "Forgive me, Sam. The dark humor of what I was saying struck home. I'm sitting here discussing cats going early to a meeting, in order to get a good seat. It would be very easy to lose one's grip on reality in this matter, would it not?"

"Very easy." He put the pickup in gear and moved out. "Let's tag along, Padre. See where they're going."

It was not a long drive. The cats were gathering in a vacant field just a short distance behind the old Dorgenois mansion, just behind Dumaine Street.

"Now we know," Javotte said.

"I've seen this," Sam said, a tenseness in his voice. "They're calling out Satan."

"Tonight."

It was not a question, for the priest could sense the gathering evil.

"Tonight."

242

10

When Sam and Father Javotte drove back to the main
street of town, a Louisiana State Trooper car was parked
by the side of a Mom and Pop convenience store at the
northernmost edge of Main Street. Sam pulled into the
parking area just as a young trooper was walking out of
the store, a soft drink in one hand, a candy bar in the
other.

"You know him?" Sam asked the priest.

"I've seen him in town quite a few times. But no, I
don't know his name."

The trooper, smiling, walked toward the truck. His
name tag read "Norris." Sam and Javotte got out of the
pickup.

"Afternoon, Trooper," Sam said.

"Howdy," Trooper Norris replied. "Ya'll must have
had one whale of a storm around here."

"Yes," Javotte said. "You didn't get any storms in,
ah? . . ."

"Jonesville," the trooper finished it. "No, sir. It's dry
as a bone just a couple miles outside of Becancour.
What's with this town, Father?"

Javotte and Sam exchanged quick glances. "What do

243

you mean?" Javotte asked.

The stocky young trooper took a bite of candy and a swig of soda. "Well, ya'll look clean. But you're the first people I've seen in town that didn't need a bath. Is there some sort of water shortage around here?"

"There's a shortage, all right," Sam said. "But it has nothing to do with water."

"Is that right?" Norris said. "You want to explain that?"

"You wouldn't believe us, Trooper," Javotte said.

"Ya'll got my interest up now. Where was all those cats headin' awhile ago?"

"To get a ringside seat for the big show that's going to take place tonight," Sam said. He could not help but smile at the trooper's expression.

"Say what?"

"You off duty?" Sam asked.

"No. But I will be in four hours. You guys been drinkin'?"

"No," Javotte assured him. "Well, that's not quite true. We each had a short beer about a half hour ago."

"Down at Lula's Love-Inn," Sam said.

Norris eyeballed the priest. Now he was *really* confused. "Father, what were you doin' in Lula's Love-Inn?"

"Confronting a group of devil worshipers."

The trooper leaned forward. "Doin' *what?*"

"The town is possessed," Sam told him.

Norris looked long at Sam. Then he looked at Javotte. "Are you a real priest?"

"For twenty-odd years, Trooper. Are you a religious man, Trooper?"

"I try to go to church a couple of times a month. But

I'm not a fanatic on the subject, no, sir."

"Not one of those who gathered is," Sam mused aloud. "That's interesting."

Trooper Norris devoured the last of his candy bar and took a sip of soda. "Not one of those who gathered . . . *where?*"

"At two places around town," Sam said. "You know Deputy Lenoir and Chief Passon, Trooper?"

"Sure."

"Good, solid, and very dependable men, right, Trooper?"

"All the way."

"Would you believe them if they told you they were convinced that the forces of Satan had taken over this town?"

Trooper Norris backed up a step. He wasn't sure exactly what he was confronting here. For sure, a couple of whackos. But? . . . The doubts lingered in his mind. Something was damn sure wrong with those he'd seen in town—all except these two guys. Sonny Passon was an ex-trooper, highly decorated. If Sonny said something was wrong in town, he'd have to give that some serious thought. Then he'd . . .

. . . do what?

Shit! he didn't know what he'd do.

"The town is possessed?" Norris asked.

"That is correct," Javotte said.

"You got devil worshipers runnin' around?"

"That's right," Sam said.

"I think you're both nuts!"

"You know Dr. Livaudais?" Javotte asked.

"I sure do."

"He's another who is convinced."

245

"Yeah?" Maybe if he could get to his radio, he could call in and have somebody get the hell in here to back him up, 'cause these two Moon Pies might get violent any moment.

The sounds of singing reached Trooper Norris's ears. "What's that?"

"Cliff Lester and his flock. They are preparing to march on Becancour sometime this afternoon."

"For what? Do they think the . . . devil is running around here, too?"

"In a manner of speaking," Javotte told him.

"Where is Don and Sonny?"

"Don is at the clinic. Sonny is at the Dorgenois house."

"Let's go see them."

Sonny talked to the trooper for a moment.

Norris started drumming his boot heels on the floor, his expression a mixture of humor and concern.

Matt Comeaux began speaking.

Norris stopped drumming his heels and sat still.

C.D. picked it up and told what he knew.

Norris started jumping up and down. "Are you *serious?*" he hollered.

"Call Don at the clinic," Sonny suggested.

"I damn sure will!" Trooper James A. Norris stalked to the phone and jerked it up. He paused for a moment. "You're all pulling my leg, right? You been waiting on me to come back in here just so you could pull this on me, right?"

His question was met by a wall of cold silence.

246

He experienced a strange clammy sensation in the small of his back. It started right at the base of his spine and, like a wet snake, began slowly slithering up his backbone.

Norris replaced the receiver in its cradle. His mouth was very dry. He looked up toward the second-floor landing. A couple of dozen kids were standing there, by the railing, looking down at him. Then the awful truth dawned on him. No one was pulling his leg. This wasn't a joke. It was all . . . everything they'd told him . . .

. . . was true.

Trooper First Class Norris cleared his throat and swallowed hard. He thought of a dozen different ideas, rejecting them as fast as they entered his head.

He sat back down in the chair.

"What made you come here?" Sam asked the trooper.

Norris looked at the man. "Why . . . I, ah, don't know. The only time I ever come to Becancour is when there is a wreck involving a fatality. Well, I mean, I patrol the highway occasionally, but usually I leave that up to Don. That's been the deal between the sheriff and my troop commander for as long as I've been a trooper."

"Why?" Sam asked.

Norris thought about that for a moment, then he got the drift of Sam's question. "Oh, there's nothing sinister about it. It's just that Don doesn't have that much to do. *Nothing* ever happens in Becancour."

"James," Sonny said. "You can't remember why you came here?"

"No. I was just . . . driving, then when I looked up, here I was. Am."

"When does your shift end?"

247

"This is my short day. I get off at four o'clock this afternoon and don't go back on until two o'clock Sunday afternoon."

"It will be all over by then," Sam said. "One way or the other."

Norris shuddered and looked at Sam. "Just who in the hell are you, anyway?"

Sam told him. The telling took about five minutes. When he was finished, Trooper J.A. Norris was sweating profusely.

Norris rose from his chair and walked out of the house into the backyard. He just needed to be alone for a time. He sat down in a swing and swung back and forth, slowly. He felt like running off into the woods, waving his arms and shrieking at the top of his lungs.

He began rocking and humming. He stopped his humming when he realized what it was: "Three Blind Mice."

"Who is this highway patrolman?" Xaviere asked Janet.

"Nobody."

"Don't be too sure of that," the Princess gently admonished the young woman. "He didn't just come in here by accident."

"Who here would summon him, and why?"

Xaviere shook her head. "He wasn't summoned. He was sent. He probably doesn't realize he was, but he was sent."

"But why?"

Xaviere shrugged her shoulders. "I am not privy to God's communiqués. Although I doubt it is God interfering."

"The old mercenary?"

"Yes. God turns His back and allows Michael a great deal more license than our Master would ever allow us."

The sky suddenly darkened and lightning licked at the earth, followed by the rumbling of thunder.

Xaviere and Janet both cringed, knowing who had sent the signals—The Dark One.

Winds suddenly entered the aging mansion, whipping the filthy drapes and blowing out the candles in the room, plunging the room into darkness.

The winds whistled and sighed around the ankles of the two young women.

As quickly as the winds came, they went. The candles came back to flame.

Xaviere and Janet both sighed a breath of relief.

TFC James Norris beat it back to the house when the lightning began licking at the earth. Smart-mouthed truck drivers, drunk motorists, and bad wrecks were something he could handle. Wind lightning in the middle of the day was another matter.

The younger kids at the clinic began crying as the brief storm lashed at the outside. With fifteen kids to one adult, those at the clinic had their hands full trying to calm the kids, keep them occupied, fix snacks, and keep the bathroom lines in order. All breathed a bit easier when the skies once more cleared.

"There it is!" Brother Cliff Lester hollered from the

pulpit. "The *sign*, Brothers and Sisters. Gird your loins and prepare to march, carrying the banner of freedom from filth!" The lightning and thunder faded.

Elmer was a little bit confused. He knew how to march, but what was that bit about the loins?

He didn't have much time to think about it, for everybody in the church stood up and began marching and singing . . . the marching in step; the singing in Tongues.

Then Elmer remembered he had forgotten to tell the other men to arm themselves. Oh, well, he mentally shrugged that off as the urge to babble struck him. It wouldn't much matter . . . So he followed out the door.

Brother Lester raced to catch up and move to the front of the line. If they could pull this off, this could be the start of something big in Central Louisiana. TeeVee people might even come in and interview him. Hot damn! he thought.

No one noticed the teenage girl who ran back to the church to use the bathroom. Or the two men who were hiding behind the church . . . waiting.

Twice Trooper Norris had started his car to pull out, just get away from this crazy town. Twice he had shut it down. He looked toward the mansion. That Sam Balon was standing on the wide porch, his arms folded across his chest, looking at him.

With a sigh, Trooper James A. Norris lifted his mike and called into his troop. "Log me 10-7," he said.

"10-4," Dispatch replied. "Have fun, James."

"Yeah," Norris said, with about as much enthusiasm

as someone getting ready for a double root canal. He slowly walked up the sidewalk to face Sam. "Why am I doing this?"

"Somebody far, far away, but yet very close, asked you to do it."

"God?" Norris whispered the word.

"No," Sam said with a smile. "Some call him God's mercenary."

"God has a mercenary?"

"He's a warrior. I've spoken with him several times."

Norris started to sweat again. He reached out his hand and gently touched Sam's arm, as if he expected his hand to go right through; as if Sam might not be of this world.

"I'm human," Sam assured him. "I like a good drink of bourbon, a cold beer, an occasional football game on TV and I really enjoy making love to my wife."

"I'm not married."

"Any special lady in your life?"

"Naw. Nobody ever takes me seriously enough. I been a clown for so long, people never know when to take me seriously."

"Rita thinks you're cute."

"She's *married*."

"She threw her husband out. He's one of those who joined the other side."

That brought it all back into perspective. "Burt s? . . ."

"Yeah."

"Sam? What's the plan?"

"I don't have one. The rules state that I can make no overt hostile move unless first provoked."

Norris stared at him. "The *rules?*"

251

"It's a game, Trooper," Javotte said, walking out onto the porch. "Not one that our God enjoys, but a game nonetheless."

"What are the odds?"

"About a hundred and fifty to one," Sam said. "Against us."

James sat down on the porch. "Why did I have to ask?" he muttered.

11

The line of singing, shouting, arm-waving, and hip-shaking marchers reached a small convenience store located on the northern edge of Becancour's main business drag. The store sold beer and booze and bread and cold cuts and canned goods and gasoline—and girlie magazines. Not the X-rated type of magazines, but those that did "Show it all, man."

Brother Cliff Lester threw open the front door and stepped inside. Taking a deep breath, just knowing this would get him a slot on *Donahue,* he dramatically announced, "We are the Committee for the Removal of All Pornography."

The young man behind the counter, not a part of either side of the invisible struggle going on around him, just knowing that he felt weird, looked up at Brother Cliff Lester. "That spells CRAP, man."

"I beg your pardon!" Lester roared.

"You know, that does spell crap," Elmer said to Sister Sally.

"Hush your mouth, Elmer!" Sister Sally whispered. "We're doin' Lord's work here."

"I don't know," Elmer muttered. "But the fried

chicken was good."

Sister Sally withered Elmer silent with a frosty look.

"Clear that rack of filth!" Lester yelled, pointing to the magazine rack.

"Carry your ass on out of here, you redneck!" the young man told him.

"How dare you speak to me in that manner!" Brother Lester yelled. "Don't you know who I am?"

"I know you're a crazy nut!" the assistant manager said. "Get outta here."

Brother Lester looked heavenward. "Lord, give me patience before I strike this poor heathen hip and thigh."

The young man rose from his stool, walked around the counter, and busted Brother Lester on the snoot with a solid right.

Brother Lester's butt hit the floor as the blood from his bent beak poured. There was a look of astonishment on his face. With both hands to his bleeding nose, he looked around at his flock. "'Eize 'em 'ilthy 'ooks!" he said, pointing to the rack.

Sister Sally, all two hundred and forty pounds of her, bulled her way through the crowd and began snatching up the magazines, ripping them apart. Elmer grabbed one of the glossies.

"Look at them pictures," he breathed.

The young man grabbed up a spray can of Mace from behind the counter and gave Sister Sally a squirt.

Sister Sally hit the floor and went into convulsions.

Only those Brothers and Sisters standing in the door knew what really happened. Those outside saw only that Sister Sally hit the floor and began jerking.

"She's in the spirit!" one yelled.

"And so is Brother Elmer!" another one yelled.

Elmer was on his hands and knees, attempting to gather up as many of the torn pages as possible. He'd never seen anything like this in all his life. He'd never even seen his wife naked. Not that he'd wanted to in the last twenty years.

"'All the 'olice!" Lester said, his voice rising about the hubbub of voices.

"Hey, you silly sanctimonious jerk!" the young man shouted at Lester. "If anybody calls the cops, it'll be *me!* You don't have the right to come in a man's business and start orderin' me around and then wreck the place. Ain't you got no sense at all?"

"Seller of filth!" a man yelled. "Debaser of morals!"

"Get lost and get out!" the young man yelled.

Elmer had crawled behind a soft drink machine and was busy looking. "Ain't that a sight?" he muttered. He turned another torn page and found an article on government. Nobody ever told Elmer these magazines had *words* in them. He began to read. Pretty damned interesting.

"Brother Elmer!" Sister Bertha squalled. "Where are you when we need your strength?"

Elmer scrunched up closer to the machine. If he had any luck at all, they'd forget about him.

The young assistant manager jerked out a pistol. "Ya'll better carry your asses on outta here!" he hollered. "Fore a bust a cap!" He looked down at Sister Sally. And drag that heifer outta here, too."

Brother Lester was on his feet, his shirt front bloody from his busted snoot. "Gather outside, Brothers and Sisters. We'll pray."

The store emptied and the young man began gathering the torn magazines. People like Cliff Lester and those that followed him irritated the shit out of him. Always tryin' to tell somebody else what to do. Worse than the damned government.

He cut his eyes and found Elmer, sitting on the floor, his back to a soft drink machine. "Well, what in the hell are you doing?"

Elmer looked up. "Uh . . . you sell fried chicken?"

The teenage girl did not fully understand what had happened. She had gone back to the church to use the bathroom and something had exploded against the back of her head. She had dropped into unconsciousness. When she had awakened, she was bound, gagged, and blindfolded.

And naked.

Those that had seized her had put their hands all over her body, squeezing and fondling her flesh.

Then she had heard a female voice saying that the girl would do just fine. The Master would be pleased.

Sadie Wesson was scared. She was so scared she couldn't help herself. She wet on herself.

The unseen men around her thought that was very funny.

Colter stilled the ringing of the phone. She tensed as the familiar voice sprang into her ear.

"Hi, Granny!" Jackson said. "My, my, but wasn't grandfather a funny-looking sight last night?"

"Where are you, Jackson?"

"At my darling baby brother's house, Granny dear. Are you ready to die, Granny?"

Colter had motioned for Sam and Father Javotte to pick up the extensions.

"What do you want, Jackson?"

"Why, just some conversation, Granny. Don't you want to talk to your favorite grandson?"

"I would rather see you dead and buried, Jackson."

"Goodness, gracious, Granny!" Jackson laughed. "You have turned into a hard old broad, haven't you?"

She said nothing.

"Some are walking now, Granny," Jackson whispered. "But I think you know that."

"I know, Jackson."

"Why don't you call for outside help, Granny? The more the merrier, as they say."

"You know why we don't, Jackson."

Jackson's laugh was so evil it touched Colter's heart, chilling it. "Oh, I know, Granny. I know. Monday morning, Granny, the pretty little town of Becancour will be back to normal. Everything will be just dandy. Won't it, Granny?"

He's too confident, Sam thought. Much too sure of himself.

Sam caught Javotte's glance. The priest nodded his understanding and agreement.

"I'm going to kill you, Granny," Jackson said. "You . . . are . . . dead!"

He hung up.

"Jackson?" Romy asked.

"Yes."

"Where is he?"

She met the man's eyes. "At your house."

Romy pulled a .38 from his waistband and checked the loads.

257

"You can't kill him with that, Romy," Colter warned him. "Listen to me! You can't kill him with that weapon."

"Listen to her, Son," Father Javotte urged. "Don't be a fool."

"I believe I can," Romy said. Before anyone could stop him, he ran out the front door.

"Romy!" Colter called. But the only reply was the slamming of the door.

All listened as Romy's car cranked into life and roared out of the driveway.

Julie ran toward the front door. Matt Comeaux grabbed her and held her until Colter, Andrea, and Tess could get to the woman and lead her off into a bedroom.

Colter did not tell the woman her feelings: She did not expect to ever see Romy again. At least not alive.

And now she had another worry: Romy and Julie's son, Guy, who was four years old, was marked, and she did not know which side of the line the boy would choose.

She looked around for Guy, but could only spot the oldest child, Cindy. "Where is your brother, Cindy?"

"He's not here, Grandmother," the thirteen-year-old said. "He asked if he could stay over at the clinic. Guy and Little Sam Balon got along real well."

Colter nodded her head and pursed her lips. Guy was marked, but a lot of Dorgenois men were marked; not all turned toward the Dark One.

She felt eyes on her and looked up. Sam Balon was looking at her. He smiled sadly and Colter's heart was suddenly very heavy.

She walked to him. "Must it be children against children, Sam?"

"It's not up to us, Mrs. Dorgenois. We can only figh

258

the evil the best way we know how."

"Romy?"

Sam lifted his heavy shoulders in a shrug. "I don't know. Jackson is very, very confident. That might work against him. I guess there is only one person who really knows what the outcome of all this will be."

Trooper Norris walked up, a sandwich in his hand. "Who's that?"

"God," Sam said.

12

There were strange stirrings in the swamps and bayous that surrounded the town of Becancour. A stillness had fallen over this part of the parish. Not one breath of air was moved by any winds.

The Beasts grew nervous in their hiding places. For they had not been warned of anything like this. Those cats that came under the power of the followers of the Dark One, those that had gathered in great furry masses on the edge of the open field had tensed at some silently received signal. They hissed and spat and arched their backs and yowled and quarreled among themselves. Something was happening and they did not know what it was.

And all around the town of Becancour, a strange phenomena was taking place. In small packs, dogs and cats were gathering. They sat and squatted and lay looking at one another.

For the moment, they had no feelings of animosity between them, only some primitive thought that if they were to survive, they must band together.

The dogs and cats looked at each other and reached silent agreement.

*   *   *

"'O, ou're a 'art of 'his!" Brother Lester said to Tony Livaudais.

"Shut up, you idiot!" Tony told him. "And hold still while I set this busted nose."

"Don't you speak to Brother Lester in that tone of voice!" Sister Alice said.

"The same goes for you, too," Dr. Livaudais informed the woman. He set Lester's nose with one quick motion, and that got Brother Lester's attention faster than a plate full of fried chicken and a bowl of gravy.

"Oowww!" he hollered.

"A little pain is good for the soul, Lester," Tony told him. "It reminds one that we are all mortal beings."

"If I want a sermon I'll tape record myself, Livaudais." Felt good to be able to speak properly. "Before I call the authorities, I demand to know why you have seized all these children."

"I haven't seized anybody, you fool. The children were all gathered out at Frank Lovern's rent house. Almost two hundred of them." Tony explained, briefly.

For the first time, Cliff Lester felt some doubts about his scoffing of Satan being in town. He knew Tony Livaudais was a level-headed and solid-thinking man—even if he was a damned Catholic, and didn't believe in foot-washin', and gettin' in the spirit, and Tongues, and all that good stuff. Anybody that didn't stomp and shout and sing and prance and holler when the Spirit moved you was suspect.

But Brother Lester shook away his doubts and held fast. "That's a bunch of bull, Doctor. What's wrong with this town is all them filthy magazines and books and dirty movies. And we want our children returned, too."

Tony took a deep breath and plunged ahead. "I have

spoken with Sheriff Ganucheau, Lester. I have informed him about these children. I have told him they are frightened and mentally confused. I told him about the strange behavior of many of Becancour's citizens. He instructed me to keep the children here, and the overflow at Mrs. Dorgenois's home. Those are his orders, Lester. And I intend to see they are carried out, to the letter."

Lester thought about that. He didn't want any trouble with the High Sheriff. The High Sheriff didn't like Cliff Lester and Cliff knew it. Sheriff Ganucheau had already warned Cliff, twice, that the next time he heard of Cliff physically interfering with the orderly operation of a legitimate business, he was going to bust Cliff's ass and put him in the pokey.

"OK," Brother Lester said. "Fine. How much do I owe you for fixin' my nose?"

"I'll keep a tally, Lester, 'cause you'll be back here again. I've told you what is taking place in this town, you don't believe it. Fine. You go on sticking your long, semipious nose in other people's business, and the next time you're likely to get it shot off, not just punched. You people, and people like you gripe my ass, Lester. You don't know the meaning of democracy. You want to dictate to everybody else. And to hell with the rights of others. I've said my piece, I've got other things to worry about. Now you all haul your asses out of this clinic."

"You're a heathen!" Sister Alice hissed.

"You're a fool, lady," Tony said. "And I'm sick of looking at your opinionated face. Get out of my clinic."

Romy pulled up into the driveway of his house. No poin

in trying to hide anything; Jackson probably knew he was coming.

Sweat beaded Romy's face as he stepped out of the air-conditioned car and into the fierce heat. He looked toward the house; he could feel the dark evil emanating from the home. He wondered who, besides Jackson, was in there, waiting for him?

Despite the heat, Romy was wearing a sport coat. But this time it wasn't just out of habit. The coat concealed the long-bladed hunting knife in a leather sheath on his belt, carried on his left side.

Laughter reached Romy's ears. Jackson. More laughter reached him; female laughter. Two people in there, at least. No, there was yet another female voice. Three people.

Romy's pistol was in his jacket pocket. He touched the weight of it with his fingertips and began walking up the drive, to the house.

"Come on, baby brother." Jackson's voice reached out and filled Romy's head with the taunting.

Romy stepped up onto the small porch and put his hand on the doorknob. He turned the knob and pushed open the door.

Art Authement sat in his office at the funeral home and wondered where his wife had gone to this time. And he wondered why he was feeling so . . . so *odd*. He thought back to the phone call he'd received from Sonny Passon. Damndest thing, that call. About the devil being in Becancour, and about most of the people being pos-essed. Goddamnedest thing Art had ever heard in all

263

his days.

Art's head came up with a jerk. What the hell was that noise? Sounded like it came from back in the small cooler room; but that was impossible, 'cause Billy Cane was gone on vacation and Art knew there wasn't nobody new in that room, anyways. 'Cept that dead orderly from the hospital. And that brought something else to mind: How come Tony hadn't been over here to do the autopsy? On either man.

It was just damned odd, that's what it was, all right.

And there that noise come again. Sort of thumping noise. Kinda like a drunk person staggering around in a dark room, knocking over things and running into other things.

Or like a person that . . .

. . . didn't have any eyes and . . .

. . . couldn't see.

Like that orderly.

"Shit!" Art said, getting up from his chair. "This business must be gettin' to me. That and all the odd-actin' folks around town."

And, he thought, Sonny's call.

He walked toward the rear of the funeral home. The noise grew louder. Damn sure was something in the cooler room. And making a hell of a fuss, too. Art thought about going back to the front and getting his old .38. But it was probably a big-assed ol' rat was all, and he damn sure didn't want to knock a hole in his cooler.

That brought him up short. Now, he never had been able to figure out why his dad had installed the damn thing. Only funeral home he knew of between Tallula and De Ridder that had a cooler was over to Alex. Having a cooler the size of the one his dad had installed, whe

264

you thought about the size of the town, was unheard of.

The noise had increased. And with it came a grunting kind of sound.

Make Art's flesh seem to crawl; like maggots was workin' live on his skin.

Summoning all his courage, Art threw open the door and clicked on the lights, the switch located on the wall outside the cooler room.

Art Authement started squalling as his unbelieving eyes saw the sightless orderly, his arms stretched out in front of him, come thumping and jerking and staggering toward him.

"*Allez vous-en!*" Art screamed and screamed and screamed.

The orderly, eye sockets empty, lurched toward him.

Art fell down in the hall and the orderly stumbled over him, falling on top of Art, knocking the breath from the man.

Art was now nearly as mindless as the orderly was sightless.

But one was about to change.

Art felt the man's cold hands fumbling around his head, the clammy fingers searching.

Gathering all his strength, Art lunged up from the tile floor, knocking the orderly off him. Art started crawling, trying to get to his feet, but his leather-soled shoes kept slipping on the floor. A cold hand closed around Art's ankle and jerked him back. Art's fingers tried to dig in the tile, trying to get a purchase. No good. Turning, Art lashed out with his free foot, catching the dead man . . . *dead man!* . . . those words rang silently in Art's head. This could not be happening.

But it was.

The orderly fell back as Art's shoe hit him. But the blow didn't seem to bother him at all. He dragged Art to him, his cold fingers digging at Art's face.

Then Art knew what he, it, whatever, was trying to do. Get his eyes!

Art began hitting the orderly with his fists. Nothing seemed to bother the thing. He kicked the thing in the balls. Didn't faze him. Art felt hideous pain as the man's fingers dug under his eyes and popped them out of Art's skull.

The orderly jerked and the optic nerve severed. Holding the precious eyes in one hand, the orderly grabbed Art's head in the other hand and beat his head against the tile floor, until Art was unconscious. The orderly bent his head and opened his mouth, exposing needle-sharp cuspids. He plunged the sharpness into Art's neck and sucked noisily, greedily. When he had consumed his fill, he squatted beside the paleness that was Art Authement and stuck the eyes into his sockets. He got them upside down and right in left and left in right, giving him a rather odd perspective on things, but that was all right, the orderly could see . . . sort of.

He lurched back into the cooler room and pulled out the tray holding what was left of the cat-attacked man found out on the road. He bent down and breathed into the man's mouth.

The man's eyes opened.

Much of the skin on the man's face had been eaten off by the cats; the whiteness of bone glistened dully under the harsh lights.

"Hungry?" the orderly asked.

"Blood," the man croaked.

"Soon. Come on."

With one helping the other, the naked men staggered out of the cooler room and into the hall. The torn man's eyes shone with anticipation at the sight of Art.

"No," the orderly said, some of his words whistling out the hole in his throat. "He is now one of us."

The torn man nodded his head. "Blood," he said.

"Soon. Very soon."

They staggered and lurched and stumbled out of the funeral home.

Art opened his eyelids. Darkness met him. No matter, he thought, sitting up. I know where I am and where I have to go.

It had been so nice of Sonny Passon to call earlier in the day and invite him over to the Dorgenois house. A very lovely invitation.

Art would accept.

Right now.

13

Romy took one step inside and then hurled himself out of the small foyer and deliberately rolled down the two steps into the large hall. His eyes had caught movement to his right as he swung open the door and stepped in.

Jackson Dorgenois with a knife in his hand.

Romy had been only a fair athlete in high school, but he did remember how to roll. He came up facing his brother with the .38 in his right hand. He cocked back the hammer.

Jackson laughed at him.

Romy began pulling the trigger.

Smoking holes began appearing in Jackson's chest as the hollow-nosed slugs impacted with flesh. The booming of the pistol was loud in the home; Romy could see some woman that looked vaguely familiar to him running around with a knife in her hand. Then it came to him who it was: Mary Claverie.

Romy felt sick to his stomach as the blood from his brother's wounds began spurting out of his chest. Jackson staggered backward and fell out of the open front door. He was screaming strangely; not a human sound. But more like a big cat.

Whirling, Romy ducked just as Mary lunged at him with the large knife. He tripped her and she fell heavily, slicing open her arm when she fell on the sharp blade. Her screaming joined Jackson's strange catlike howling.

Jumping to his feet, the empty pistol in his hand, Romy literally ran over Bonnie Rogers, knocking her to the floor. The woman's pale skin, not touched by sunlight in more than two decades, looked sick and evil to Romy. Her eyes were filled with hate and depravity.

She hissed at him, like a cat.

Romy kicked her on the side of the head and ran toward his study. He was conscious of his brother trying to get up off the porch. And even more conscious of the stinking blood that was pouring from Jackson's chest.

Romy jerked over his gun cabinet and pulled out two shotguns, quickly loading one, then the other. He looked up as Jackson appeared in the archway of the study. Jackson was . . . *laughing*.

When he spoke, his voice was very deep and hollow-sounding. "You're a fool, Romy. But then, you always were."

Romy lifted the shotgun, a Browning five shot autoloader and blew his brother clear out of the archway. He dropped the Browning and lifted the Police Ithaca pump, a sawed-off model holding eight shells. He lowered the shotgun as Mary and Bonnie ran to Jackson's side and began dragging him out of the house. As they dragged, they cursed Romy.

Romy knew he should shoot both women, but he could not bring himself to do it. He stood and watched them drag his brother into the car he had noticed parked in the drive, in front of the house. He watched as they drove off, still hurling curses at Romy.

Romy walked back into his study and reloaded his pistol and Browning. He gathered up all his rifles and shotguns and carried them out to his car, putting them in the backseat. That foul-smelling blood from Jackson was very nearly overpowering in its stench. He closed the door to his house and drove back to Colter's house. He could not remember ever being so tired.

"Brother Elmer has betrayed us," Lester told his flock. "He has gone over to the side of filth and sin. But we shall not be deterred from our task. Them dirty books and magazines has got to be dis-troyed. And them that sells them terrible things is just as guilty as them that reads 'em."

"Amen, Brother!" the flock responded.

No one had noticed Sadie was gone.

"We forgot our signs last time out," Brother Lester reminded his flock. "Let's rejoice for a moment and then take to the streets like good soldiers."

Nobody much wanted to shout and prance; everybody was kinda tired and a little dejected. Brother Lester asked Sister Lucille and Sister Edna if they couldn't perhaps whip up some iced tea and look around and see if there wasn't some of them cookies from dinner left over.

"We'll march just at dusk," Lester announced.

As the afternoon slowly waned, a deceptive calmness settled over the town of Becancour. But those who were a part of what was happening, willing and unwilling, on the side of Dark or Light, knew the sudden quiet denoted

270

anything but a calmness.

The cats and dogs worked their way closer to the earth on which they lay. Side by side, the cats and dogs lay touching, each drawing strength and comfort from the other. They waited.

The splashing and sudden eruptions of dead but living flesh from the dark waters of the swamps and bayous had ceased as those fish-belly-white beings had anticipated the call from the minions of the Dark One and surfaced— free from their watery confines at last.

Lula's Love-Inn was filled to capacity and beyond. Wall to wall packed with unwashed human flesh. They sat at tables and at the bar, they lined the walls and leaned against the silent jukebox. Men and women and young people with dead evil eyes and willingly lost souls.

They waited for the call to gather.

At the old Dorgenois home, the Princess and her followers had dressed in their finest. They now waited for darkness to fall, for the night to displace day, for all vestiges of sunlight to be gone, for any trace of God's hand to be shrouded in darkness. Only then could they move.

Dave Porter and Bette and Max Encalarde and Louis Black and Frank and Thelma Lovern and Nate Slater and Carl Nichols and Bob Gannon and Mrs. Carmon and a dozen others with souls as black as midnight had gathered at the motel. They waited, breathing the stinking air polluted by their own bodies.

A hundred or more young people had gathered around the local drive-in where they used to bring their girls and drink Cokes and eat hot dogs and hamburgers and french fries. They sat in their cars and trucks and on their motorcycles and looked at Mr. Janson—the guy who owned the drive-in. He stood inside the little building where all the good stuff was cooked and stared back at the sullen young people. Janson didn't know what in the hell was going on, but these damned kids were making him very uneasy, he knew that for an ironclad fact.

"How we gonna do it?" a teenager asked another.

"Slow," his companion replied. "Pay him back for all them greasy, overpriced burgers."

"How 'bout them kids in there with him?" another asked.

"They had their chance. They turned us down, didn't they?"

"Yeah," a girl spoke from the truck parked next to the car. "Now it's too late."

"When?" the question was tossed out.

"Full dark."

Mrs. Wheeler sat on her front porch and listened to the silence around her. She was old enough to remember when conditions came very close to paralleling what was now taking place in this small, quiet off-the-beaten-path town. She had forgotten all about that. She'd been just a little girl . . . ten years old, maybe. Sixty-five-odd years ago.

She could remember that her parents had been very frightened that day and longer night. But when God's dawn broke free, everybody seemed to settle right down. And it had never happened again.

Until now.

Mrs. Wheeler didn't think the next dawn would im-

272

prove a damn thing.

Not this time.

Mrs. Wheeler sat with a shotgun across her lap. Her eyes moved from left to right. Those young punks were back; they thought they'd been slipping up on her, but she had seen them.

Mrs. Wheeler waited.

Old Man Jobert had been drinking all day. Good homemade wine that he'd made hisself. Jobert lived a few miles out from Becancour, off the road and 'bout a mile inside the deep swamp. Jobert had fought in the big war, back in '44, and then, with a taste for adventure in his mouth, he'd joined up with the French Foreign Legion and got his ass shot in Southeast Asia.

Damn kids comin' back from Vietnam couldn't tell him nothin' about that miserable place. Jobert had been fightin' there when some of them were in diapers.

Jobert took another swig of homemade wine and opened his war trunk, carefully, lovingly, taking out his French Foreign Legion uniform. That he was still able to get into the thing showed what hard work done for a man.

He dressed up and put his kepi on his head. He felt like marchin' and singin' the old songs this night. So, by God, that's what he'd do. Just pole over to the road and march into Becancour; maybe go to Lula's and have a drink or two with the boys.

For some reason he could not fathom, Jobert strapped on a pistol and cartridge case, and picked up his old .30-06, slinging a bandoleer of ammo over his shoulder.

Brother Lester and his flock were just about ready to go. They had their placards and signs and had changed socks and shoes for the big march.

"Brothers and sisters!" Brother Lester shouted. "Let's *march!*"

Backslider Brother Elmer stood on a deserted street corner of Becancour and wondered how come the town was so quiet?

And in the Becancour cemetery, Bob Savoie opened his eyes and began pushing at the lid of his coffin.

SECOND NIGHT OF THREE

"It's so quiet, Sam," Romy said, stepping out of the house to join Sam on the porch.

"Wait a few hours, it won't be then."

"I still can't believe what I saw happen with Jackson. I just can't believe it. It simply is not *possible*."

"Get it through your head that Jackson is not a human being. Colter believes he sold his soul to the devil when he was just a child. I don't know; I can't say."

"Julie says that our son is . . . not of this earth."

"No," Sam said bluntly. "He is not."

"How can you be so sure?"

"Because Nydia told me. Little Sam told her. Dog told Little Sam."

"A *dog* told your son!"

"Yes."

"How?"

"I don't know. I was not there. Both my wife and son have powers that are not of this earth. So, too, does Dog. I rather doubt that Dog opened his mouth and spoke English to my son, but somehow he got the message across."

Sonny Passon, Trooper Norris, and Father Javotte had stepped outside to the porch. They stood quietly, listening.

Both Passon and Norris could not suppress a chilling shudder at the words.

The last rays of sunlight had vanished; deep purple was now mixed and mingled with darkness. And Sam knew that it was no longer God's land. It now belonged to the Dark One.

He said as much, his voice low-pitched.

"How could anyone kill a little child like my Guy?" Romy asked.

"If he can be killed," Sam said, "he will not be a little child. He will be transformed into the demon that he was born to be. And it will not be me who kills him."

"Then . . . who?"

"Little Sam," Sam said softly.

Brother Lester and his placard-carrying flock had marched up to the main street of town. There they stopped and stared in amazement. The street was so empty someone could have fired a cannon down it and not hit a thing but air.

"I knowed we'd picked the wrong time for this here parade," Brother Ira grumbled. "This here street is as empty as Will Jolevare's head."

"Be quiet," Lester said. "I hear singin'. Probably comin' from a jukebox in one of those damnable saloons."

The singing drifted to the Brothers and Sisters of Lester's CRAP.

> *"Sautons ensemble! Sautons ensemble!*
> *Legionnaires, nous ne reviendrons pas.*
> *La bas, les ennemis t'attendent*
> *Sois fier, nous allons au combat."*

"It's that drunken old fool, Jobert!" Lester said. "Come on, soldiers of the Lord. Forward, *march!*"

The line straggled onward, without much enthusiasm, and without a single citizen-soldier in step. Looked like a bunch of duck hunters after a bad hunt.

Aging Legionnaire met the members of CRAP in the center of the street.

"Get out of the street, you old sot!" Lester hollered.

Jobert slipped his rifle off his shoulder and stood his ground. *"Non, bordel de merde!"*

"What'd he call me?" Lester asked.

"He called you a damned shit," Brother Benny informed the lay preacher.

"How dare he?" Sister Bertha squalled. "Get out of the way, you old fool!" she screamed at Jobert.

"You get out of the way, *putain de merde,*" Jobert replied.

"What'd he call me!" Sister Bertha shrieked, her voice very nearly capable of cracking brass.

Brother Benny took a deep breath. "He called you a shitty whore!"

With a war whoop that would have awed Cochise, Sister Bertha put her act in gear and charged, all two hundred odd pounds of CRAP.

Jobert might have been drunk, but he wasn't stupid. Jobert, soaking wet, might have weighed one thirty-five. No way he could halt the charge of this moose coming at

277

him. So he sidestepped and stuck out his boot. Sister Bertha went rolling up the street, making as much racket as an empty fifty-five-gallon drum tossed off a moving truck.

The march was forgotten and placards tossed aside when Brother Lester shouted, "Get that heathen! He's assaulted Sister Bertha."

Jobert slung his rifle and took off running, cutting into a dark alley, very much aware of Brother Lester's footsteps close behind him.

A shadow fell across the open end of the alley. Jobert put on the brakes and stood staring in horror at the thing that loomed up in front of him, blocking the escape route.

Brave Legionnaire he was, but fighting Arabs and Vietnamese was one kind of battle . . . Jobert didn't even know what this thing was!

Squalling, Jobert turned around and literally ran right over Brother Lester, knocking the leader of CRAP sprawling, amid the beer cans and whiskey bottles.

The huge Beast stepped into the alley. He was still fifty feet or so from Lester, who was trying to get up.

Brother Lester lost his religion for a moment. "Goddammit!" he hollered. "Do I have to do everything all by myself?"

The Beast stepped closer. Brother Lester got to his feet and turned around just as Brother Benny and Sister Alma reached him. They saw the Beast at the same time.

"What in the blazes is *that!*" Brother Benny said.

Sister Alma took one look at the Beast and let out a shriek that rattled windows. Before the echo of her squalling had died away, Brother Lester, Brother Benny, and Sister Alma had cleared the alley and were rapidly closing in on Legionnaire Jobert, who, considering his age, was moving quite well.

All four of them ran into Lula's Love-Inn.

The altar was a heavy oak door placed on concrete blocks and covered with black fabric. Torches, which would be lighted later, were placed in a circle around the altar. A few of the faithful had begun to gather. All around the edges of the open field, animal eyes stared unblinking at the scene.

And beyond the cats, on the fringes of the swamp, staying together, many of the Beasts had gathered. They stayed together, not trusting the hundreds of cats that ringed the field, not really understanding why the little furry things were here at all. As a food supply, the cats were quite tasty, but not the favorite food of the Beasts.

When they did eat, the Beasts much preferred human flesh. With a single thought of food, thick ropes of stinking saliva dripped from the massive jaws of the Beasts, the saliva dripping onto the great hairy chests, dribbling through the thick mat of hair.

The Beasts and the cats and the few human servants of the Lord of Flies who had gathered in the field patiently waited. It was nearly time for the Black Mass to begin.

"Oooo!" the boys around Mrs. Wheeler's home called out in the night. This was good fun, they had all agreed. And it would be even more fun when they grabbed the old witch and tortured her to death. "Oooo!" they hooted and called, believing they were frightening the old lady.

Mrs. Wheeler clicked her shotgun off safety and took a firmer grip on the old wood of the stock. If those crap-headed, spoiled, pampered, and good-for-nothing punks out there felt they were scaring her, they had a very large surprise waiting in store for them, she thought.

And those in the houses close to the home of Mrs. Wheeler listened to the sounds of the night. Many of them were still in limbo, mentally and physically undecided as to what path to take: Light, or Dark. All over the small town, those humans who were wavering between worlds were being forced to choose. Only the very strongest would be able to choose the path of truth and light and freedom.

The majority would bend to the will of Satan.

"Die, old woman!" a girl called from the night-shrouded side yard of Mrs. Wheeler's home. "Now you die!"

As she waited, the retired schoolteacher began remembering bits and scraps of conversation she'd heard as a little slip of a girl, sixty-five or so years back. She knew that nearly everything one heard, saw, or read was retained in the brain, but seldom brought forth. So she did not struggle to pull the words from her mind; just let them surface naturally.

". . . them things out in the swamps ain't God's work," she recalled some long-forgotten friend of her parents saying.

"They belong to the devil," her mother had said. "My *grand-mère* said they've been here forever."

"Oooo! Oooo! Oooo!" the young Satan-worshipers in the yard called.

"Hell with you," Mrs. Wheeler muttered, and forced

herself to recall more of the long-forgotten bits of conversation.

". . . priest said Satan is always very near to his place."

". . . notice how funny a lot of cats were actin' the other night? Priest said the poor animals didn't have no choice in the matter. They follow the actions of their owners."

"Why not the dogs?" That had come from Mrs. Wheeler's father.

"Don't know."

Mrs. Wheeler reached down beside her and lifted her old cat to her lap. She looked at the cat looking at her. "Is that the way it is, Hector?" she softly whispered to the cat.

The cat purred and briefly snuggled close to the old woman. Mrs. Wheeler smiled and shooed the cat inside the house. "You stay in there, Hector. Things are about to get tough out here."

She heard the punks coming closer. Too eager, she thought. This will be a piece of cake.

Her heart was beating faster, and she knew her blood pressure was up, but that was normal, she thought, considering the circumstances.

"Die, you old witch!" a young man shouted, jerking open the screen door.

Without rising from her chair, Mrs. Wheeler lifted the shotgun and blew half the punk's head off. The Satan-lover was flung off the steps and to the ground. The old lady shifted the barrel position and pulled the trigger at a flash of movement in her yard. A horrible, choking scream cut the hot air. Footsteps ran in the night and faded from the old lady's ears. A car was cranked up, tires

281

spinning on the concrete.

All was still.

Mrs. Wheeler rose from her chair, replaced the shells in her shotgun, and went into the house for a drink of wine.

"Going to be a long evening," she said to Hector.

"Now!" The call was shouted at the drive-in. "Get them!"

Trixie screamed as several dozen young people rushed the drive-in's kitchen and office. Janson slammed and locked the front door, yelling for the kitchen help to lock the back door.

Laughter greeted his command. Angry, Janson turned around, the screaming of the carhops a raging mass of confusion in his head.

Young George Lemare stood in the kitchen door, a butcher knife in his hand. He was grinning at Janson.

"This is gonna be fun," George said.

Janson picked up a pot of coffee from the burner and tossed the scalding liquid on George.

Add George's horrible screaming to the confusion.

A brick slammed through the glass-enclosed office, shards of cutting light hurled about; Janson felt a trickle of blood from a small cut on his neck.

Janson picked up a broom, broke off the handle, and slammed the wood onto a young man's head. Blood spurted from the cut and the young man dropped to the floor.

The front door was kicked in, the small room filling with the stench of unwashed bodies. Janson could see

282

Trixie. Her uniform was ripped from her and boys were holding the screaming girl's legs apart, while another kid was raping her.

"Run, Sheri!" Janson yelled at another waitress. "Run for help!"

George was on the floor, on his knees, both hands to his scalded face. He was moaning and crying in his searing, horrible pain.

Sheri ran out into the night, stopped, and turned around, deciding she could not leave her friend, Trixie, alone back there. Sheri picked up a two by four from a pile of scrap lumber and ran back into the enclosure, through the open kitchen door. She smashed the two by four onto a boy's head, hearing the skull pop like a small firecracker. She almost puked when she saw the boy's gray-looking brains as he hit the floor.

Swinging the lumber from side to side, Sheri cleared a path through the confusing mass; she smashed heads and shattered arms and hands and faces with the lumber. Mr. Janson was fighting with half a dozen boys near the front door, and doing a pretty good job of it, too. Mr. Janson had told her once that young people often make a very bad mistake with a lot of older people, 'cause, Mr. Janson said, "Us old dudes don't fight fair."

But Sheri could tell he was losing simply because of sheer numbers.

Sheri smashed the two by four onto the back of the boy who was raping Trixie then, following through, she hit one of the boys holding her flush in the face with the lumber. The boy's mouth shattered in a gush of blood, several of his teeth flying out of his mouth.

Sheri grabbed Trixie's hand and jerked her toward the

kitchen just as Mr. Janson went down under a crushing mass of young men.

The girls ran out the back door into the night.

And with a roar of anger and hate and decades of pent-up evil, Bob Savoie pushed the last bit of earth from him and rose from the casket.

14

Elmer had seen the four people running up the street, but he was a long way from them and didn't really understand what was going on. Whatever it was, it sure had caused them all to shove it in overdrive.

But who was them two guys staggering up the street toward him? Elmer peered through the artificially lighted gloom of night. Why . . . goddamn! he thought. That looks like that young fellow works over at Dr. Livaudais's clinic. But what the hell was wrong with him—was he drunk?

The two men lurched closer. Elmer fought to keep the fried chicken he'd had for supper down. That other guy was tore all to hell and gone. Jesus Christ! half his face was missing.

The orderly and the torn man spotted Elmer. They stopped in the street.

Elmer willed his feet to move, please move, but they seemed rooted to the sidewalk. Elmer could see the orderly's face clearly now. Jesus God! what was wrong with the man's eyes?

The torn man opened his mouth, a low growling sound rolling from his throat. He held out his arms to Elmer, waggling his fingers, beckoning Elmer to come to him.

"Out of my way, you!" Elmer found his voice and the ability to move. He took off across the street at a flat lope. He could see the lights of Lula's Love-Inn. He'd never been in a honky-tonk in his life, but by God, he was goin' to one now.

Just as he pushed open the front door, he could hear Sister Alma squalling. Elmer stepped inside the foul-smelling, dimly lit barroom and his eyes widened in shock.

Jobert had his rifle leveled at a crowd of men and women, holding them at bay, cursing in French and English and German. He'd told Elmer once that a lot of German used to be spoken in the Legion.

Sister Alma's clothing was half-ripped from her, her bare breasts exposed.

Brother Benny's mouth was bloody and there was a red mark on his cheek; looked like somebody had popped him pretty good.

For the first time in Elmer's memory, Brother Lester stood speechless, his mouth hanging open.

Elmer looked at the barroom full of men and women. He knew everybody there, grown up with nearly all of them. But there was something . . . different about them, now. They all, to a person, looked . . .

. . . evil.

"Now you're all ours," Elmer heard ol' Rich Manion say.

"That's your ass!" Jobert told him.

Sister Alma let out another shriek as a cat jumped on her, clawing the woman's face and neck. Elmer grabbed the cat and flung it across the room. The animal hit the wall, fell to the floor, and was still.

"What the hell is goin' on in this town?" Elmer yelled.

One local good ol' boy jumped up and reared back to take a swing at Elmer. Jobert butt-stroked the good ol' boy with his rifle, the man dropped to the floor without making a sound.

"Stand real still," Jobert said, his voice calm and free of any traces of slurring. Jobert was stone cold sober. "The next man or woman that moves gets shot."

Brother Lester appeared to be in some sort of shock.

"That dead orderly from the clinic is right outside the door," Elmer said. "Along with some fellow that's tore up too bad to live. They look like zombies."

"That's what they are," Jobert replied, without taking his eyes from the crowd of unwashed. "Guess what my daddy tole me was true. The dead are walking."

"Uh . . . uh . . . uh . . ." Brother Lester said.

"That makes about as much sense as anything you ever said," Jobert told the lay preacher.

Elmer silently agreed with the man.

Brother Benny didn't know what to say, what to do, or what to think.

Sister Alma was crying, making no attempt to cover her bare breasts.

"Cover yourself, woman!" Jobert said. "'Fore someone decides to give you a feel."

Grunting sounds were heard just outside the barroom door.

"We have time to deal with you later," someone in the crowd said. "But not now. We're being called."

And on some silent signal, the barroom emptied, the men and women and teenagers exiting out the back door.

The grunting outside the door faded as lurching footsteps sounded on the sidewalk.

287

"What the hell? . . ." Elmer said, looking around the empty, still foul-smelling barroom.

"Anybody know where the Christians are gathering?" Jobert asked.

"What?" Brother Lester finally found his voice.

"Satan is among us," Jobert said. "The dead are walking. There's gonna be a *noir messe* somewheres close. Bet on it."

"A what?" Lester said.

"Black mass," Brother Benny said.

"Ridiculous!" Brother Lester spat out the word. "The poor wretched souls in this den of evil were just drunk, that's all. As dark as it is in here, they've probably been watching filthy movies. It's proven that those types of things can cause strange behavior."

"Gets a feller excited, that's for sure," Jobert said. "First few times you watch one. After that, it's boring."

"It's sinful!" Brother Lester shouted.

"Lester, I ain't got time to mess with a fool like you," Jobert replied. "I repeat: does anybody know where the Christians are gathering?"

"What do you think *we* are?" Brother Lester shouted. "We're Christians!"

Jobert shook his head. Time was wastin'. "No, Lester, you're not. What you are is a hypocrite. And if I have to explain that to you, well, then you're a bigger fool than I think you are."

"The Dorgenois house," Elmer said, before Brother Lester could get cranked up and start preaching.

"Which one?" Jobert asked.

"Missus Colter's house."

"And the clinic," Brother Benny said.

"Then that's where we'll go," Jobert told them. "Let's do 'er, boys and girls."

"I will not!" Brother Lester said. "I shall return to my own home where my good wife is waiting."

"Uh, Brother Lester," Elmer said.

"What?"

"She ain't gonna be there."

"I beg your pardon!"

"I seen her about half an hour ago. She was with Co Wilson and that Cuvier boy. Her drawers was tied to the ratio antenna. They was headin' thataway." He pointed.

Brother Lester stepped toward Elmer, his hands balled into fists.

"Don't do it, Cliff," Elmer warned, his voice low. "'Cause I'll sure whup your ass if you try it."

Brother Lester backed off. "My Lucille is a good woman, Elmer. Don't bad-mouth her."

"I ain't bad-mouthin' her, Cliff. I'm just tellin' you what I seen. And I did see it. Ugly as your wife is, there ain't no way I could be mistooken."

Jobert laughed. "For a fact, Lucille could hire her face out to frighten little children." He looked at Cliff Lester. "Your other woman, now, Cliff, that's a different story, ain't it?"

Brother Lester's face turned beet red in the darkened barroom. He opened his mouth to speak, then thought better of it.

"Like I said, Cliff . . . you're a hypocrite. I'm headin' for Colter's place. Anybody goin' with me?"

Elmer and Benny stepped forward. Sister Alma looked at Brother Lester with tears in her eyes. "Is it true, Brother Lester? Do you have another woman?"

"The flesh is weak, Sister," Cliff managed to say.

She slapped him.

The celebration of the Black Mass takes many forms, and is used for many things. It may be called to celebrate the absence of Satan; to simply worship the Dark One; to offer up a sacrifice . . . or to call for Satan's appearance.

The Black Mass is, however, a perversion of the Roman Catholic Mass. It starts with the same ceremony as practiced in the Roman Church . . . but is said backward. The officiating priest can be anybody, but often is an unfrocked priest or a person who has rejected the teachings of the Church. The location can be anywhere, but the time is always at night. The altar must be black-draped. Those attending must stand with their backs to the altar and to the inverted cross and to six black candles.

If the devil is asked to appear, in whatever form, and the choice is solely the decision of the Dark One, a sexual offering must be made, and a human being sacrificed; then the blood and semen are mixed in a silver chalice and either sprinkled onto the heads of the followers gathered . . . or drunk by those in attendance.

After the praising of the Dark One, the sign of the cross is made by all, on the ground, with the left foot.

And then Satan will appear.

The field behind the old Dorgenois mansion was now filled with black-clothed believers in the Dark Arts. The young people from the drive-in had dragged the badly beaten and barely conscious Janson out of a pickup truck and dumped him on the ground, in front of the altar. In front of where the naked and spread-eagled Sadie Wesson was tied.

The low, babbling murmur of voices, the yowling of cats, and the growling of Beasts suddenly ceased as a dozen black-robed people appeared at the edge of the field.

Xaviere Flaubert was at the head of the small procession, followed closely by Janet, Jon Le Moyne, and the others of her personal entourage. Jimmy Perkins brought up the rear, shuffling along, his dead eyes shining through the darkness.

Sadie Wesson's fear was so great she was almost mindless as she struggled against the ropes that bound her to the altar. She had screamed so much her voice was nearly gone, her throat raw and painful. But her eyes watched as Jon Le Moyne took his preassigned place at the base of the altar and removed his robe, standing naked in the hot night air.

Janson moaned in his dark pain and tried to crawl toward the altar to help the girl. A teenage girl stepped out of the near darkness with a knife in her hand. Bending down, she sliced the man's ankle tendons and cut through the upper muscles in both his arms, leaving Janson helpless on the ground. He looked up at the girl through pain-filled eyes. He knew her. Had known her all her life.

"Are you a Christian?" the girl asked him.

"Yes," Janson managed to say. "I am, and proud to be one."

The girl turned to the crowd. "What to do with this one?" she shouted.

Xaviere stood apart, letting the girl handle the show in

291

her own way.

"Give him to the cats!" several voices called out from the dark throng.

Janson was dragged to the edge of the clearing and left there. In seconds, his naked body was covered with cats. They tore at his flesh while the crowd enjoyed the man's horrible screaming.

Across the clearing, the Beasts stirred and looked at each other, anger clear in their eyes. The man should have been tossed to them, not the cats.

Hate bubbled from their throats, a low, menacing sound in the night.

And it did not go unnoticed by Xaviere.

But at this stage of affairs, there was nothing she could do except continue. Matters could not be halted now.

"Let it begin!" Xaviere called out.

Jon Le Moyne crawled onto the altar, positioning himself between Sadie's legs. He looked at the Princess.

She nodded her head.

Jon lunged forward, impaling the girl. Her hoarse screaming shattered the night as her virginity was torn from her.

As Jon hunched upon her naked flesh, the girl began praying. The praying amused those watching and listening. They began hooting and calling out profane insults.

Jon's buttocks tightened seconds before ejaculation. He shuddered as his semen flowed from him, mixing with the girl's blood. He carefully withdrew his massive and now softening organ and several followers of the Dark Side rushed forward with dirty silver chalices, to gather up the mixture leaking out of the nearly unconscious girl. That done, they stepped back and waited.

Jon donned his black robe and withdrew into the gloom of sultry night.

Xaviere stepped up to the altar, a dagger in her hand. She began drawing hideous designs in the girl's living flesh. The blood oozed and spurted and poured from the cuts, and was quickly gathered in cups and bowls by the faithful followers who hovered close by.

Mercifully, Sadie dropped into unconsciousness long before the ceremony was concluded.

Sadie's body lay chalk-white in death on the bloody altar.

The semen and the blood was mixed, and all gathered were allowed to sip from the chalices. That done, on silent signal, the throng turned their backs to the altar as a wooden cross was driven into the ground, inverted. The candles were lighted.

Xaviere stepped out of her robe, to stand naked in the candle- and torch-lit night. "Belzebuth," she called into the flickering gloom. "Hear me, Supreme Head of the Infernal Empire, founder of the Order of the Fly."

Dark clouds swept the skies.

"Hear me, Satan, my beloved Prince."

The clouds moved closer to earth, their gray darkness fouling the night with a filthy stench.

"Come to us, Eurynome, you Prince of Death of the Grand Cross of the Order of the Fly."

The black-clothed throng began stamping their feet in rythm.

"Moloch, Prince of Tears. Come!" Xaviere called into the night.

The earth shook with the stamping of feet.

"Pluton, Prince of Fire, Governor General of the Blazing Land. Come!

"Lilith, Prince of the Succubi. Come!"

The cats were sitting in rows, their heads moving in time with the rhythm of the stamping feet.

The Beasts were stamping their hooved feet and swaying back and forth, growling and snapping their jaws.

"Leonard, Grand Master and Knight of the Fly," Xaviere called. "Come!

"Baalberith, Grand Pontiff and Master of Alliances. Come to us with the others. We are calling you.

"Oh, Goddess Proserpine, you beautiful Arch-Demoness and Princess of Mischievous Spirits—come!"

Savage lightning licked the skies, searing the odious clouds. Vague, ill-defined shapes began appearing, seeming to gather shape as the rainless storm intensified.

"Adrameleck of the Order of the Fly, come to earth once more. Astaroth of the monies, come. Nergar of the Secret Police, come with them. Baal of the Armies of Darkness, come. Belphegor to Martinet, come, come to us. From Verdelet to Antechrist . . . come, come, come at my calling."

Xaviere paused for breath, then invoked the call that was the most dangerous of them all.

"I, the Princess of Satan, Daughter of the Prince of Darkness, do conjure thee all named in the name of The Master of Darkness to appear before me. If you fail to do so, Saint Michael the invisible, the Archangel, will cast thee into the deepest of all the pits of Hell. Come thou then, all named, come thou, come and do my will."

Excrement fell from the dark, foul-smelling cloud. Urine fell as rain on the heads of those gathered in the field.

With dripping excrement falling all around her, the

yellow rain soaking her flesh, Xaviere raised her arms high above her head and screamed in victory.

The cats broke their ranks and raced about in frenzied circles of madness, yowling and hissing and spitting.

The Beasts danced and pranced and thumped their great hairy chests. They leaped high into the air, spinning and snarling in happiness.

"Now!" Xaviere screamed. "You are here!"

The face of Satan appeared.

15

Rita began screaming, the frightened sounds coming from the rear of the mansion. Trooper Norris jerked out his .357 and ran through the house, to the source of the squalling.

If he had thought the stinking storm that had appeared out of nowhere and just as quickly vanished was awesome and unthinkable, the thing that stood grinning at him from the backyard was mind-boggling.

"Dear God in Heaven!" James whispered.

"That's Mr. Authement!" Rita practically screamed the words, pointing at the sightless man on the back steps.

Sam and Father Javotte had joined them on the back porch.

Art opened his mouth and hissed at the gathering. A noticed that his tongue was blood-red, almost glowing i the night. And his teeth were pointed, needle-sharp.

He moved toward Rita and the trooper leveled his .35 and began squeezing the trigger, putting all five round into Art's chest.

The owner and director of the funeral home wa knocked back by the slugs, but not down. He shook h head for a moment, and then grinned at the men and women.

J.A. Norris looked at his pistol in total disbelief.

Father Javotte reached into his pocket and removed a small vial of liquid. Muttering a short but very sincere prayer, he shoved his way past the still-astonished trooper and threw the liquid onto the nonhuman creature.

Art screamed and hissed and spat like a big cat in terrible pain. Wherever the liquid had landed, smoking holes appeared in his flesh. Howling in pain, Art ran off into the hot, murky night and disappeared into the timber behind the expensive home.

"I shot that fucker five times with hollow-noses," Norris said. "Five times, all in or around the heart area from a distance of not more than five yards, max. Didn't even knock him down." He looked at Javotte. "And you throw some sort of liquid on him and he acts like it was dynamite. What was that stuff?"

"Holy water," the priest said. "I stopped by the church this afternoon and stocked up, so to speak."

"I hope you filled up a tanker truck with it," the trooper said.

Rita's shaking was visible to them all. Norris stepped close to her and put his arm around the woman. "Hey, Rita. We're gonna make it. Believe it, honey. 'Cause I think you gotta believe it."

He walked with her back into the well-lighted house.

Javotte looked at Sam. "Did you feel it when the Dark One made his appearance, Sam?"

"Yes. And not only Satan, but all his aides and chieftains as well. This is going to be a struggle right up to the last second, Padre."

"I never doubted it. But why do you think so?"

"Because he wants to destroy Nydia, Little Sam, and me."

Jackson Dorgenois lay on the floor. He knew he had come close to final death several times, and that had confused him, for he had been promised eternal life when he gave his soul to the Master of Filth. Then Jackson began to understand the Why of it all.

The Master had not guaranteed him eternal life in any one specific form.

Despite his pain, Jackson had to laugh, his laughter drawing some curious looks from Bonnie. They were alone, Mary having gone to the gathering in the field.

"Something amusing, Jackson?" Bonnie asked.

"I'm goin' to die, Bonnie. At least this form of me is going to die."

"I know. I sensed it. You are to be what you have always wanted to be."

Jackson closed his eyes. "At last," he whispered.

A huge dark shape appeared on the front porch.

Brother Cliff Lester had walked slowly through the darkened streets of Becancour, back to his church. He had been walking when the stinking storm had erupted, showering him with urine and shit.

But as usual, Brother Lester got it all wrong. "It's punishment on the town for toleratin' all them nasty, filthy books and magazines and sex movies," he had muttered. "God has sent the devil into this town. He has

298

allowed Satan to enter as punishment. The town has become a haven for sinners; for them that has sold their souls into darkness."

"Amen, Brother Lester!" The voice had sprung out of the darkness.

It was Sister Edna and Sister Bertha and Brother Ira. They stepped out to meet him.

"'Bout forty of the flock is a-waitin' at the church," Ira said. "The rest has forsaken us, runnin' in fear."

"They are like lambs runnin' toward the wolves," Brother Lester said.

"Amen!" Sister Edna said, and began to get in the spirit right there on the street.

"No time for that now!" Brother Lester calmed her before she got carried away. "We've got to make our plans, Brothers and Sisters."

"You lead and we'll follow!" Sister Bertha said.

That made Brother Lester feel *good!*

"Please help us!" Sheri called toward the back door of the clinic. "For God's sake, please, somebody, anybody!"

Don Lenoir ran outside and peered into the murky gloom of evil night. "Who is it?"

"It's Sheri, Deputy. From Janson's Drive-in. Please help us. Trixie's been raped and they've taken Mr. Janson."

"Might be a trap," Bid Grenier said, stepping out to stand by Don.

"Cover me." Don ran toward the ill-defined shapes huddled close to the street. When he saw Trixie's torn uniform and the blood all over Sheri, he knew the girls were in trouble and it was no trap.

He led them into the clinic and closed and locked the back door.

"'Allo, the house!" Jobert called. "You dere, Madame Dorgenois, *Nous y voici!*"

"Is 'at you, Jobert?" Colter called, cracking the front door just a bit.

"'At's rat. Me and some folks come quick to rat here."

"You best be on the right side, Jobert," Colter told him.

"I sure hope we are, madame. One thing for sure, though, we got shut of 'at fool Cliff Lester. He din believe no devil was in town."

"Anybody smart enough to get rid of that idiot Lester has to have full possession of his faculties," Colter said. "That man is an insult to the ministry."

"I concur," Javotte said.

"Come on in, Jobert!" Colter called. "We're going to need all the help we can get."

Inside the expensively furnished home, the front door closed and locked, Jobert stood with Colter for a moment. "Was 'at what I thought it was fallin' from the sky a while ago?"

"Yes." She smiled and sniffed daintily. "You must have sought shelter, Jobert."

"Did for a fact." He introduced his little group.

"Mr. Jobert," Sam said. "What do you suppose this Lester person will do now?"

"Sam, I reckon only the Lord could answer that. If the Lord even pays any attention to people like Cliff Lester,

300

that is."

Elmer and Alma and Benny shuffled their feet and looked awfully uncomfortable.

"I shouldn't 'ave said that," Jobert apologized.

"It's all right, Jobert," Elmer said. "For right now, I just wish somebody would tell me what in the world is going on."

"Come on into the den, Mr. Elmer," Colter said, waving her hand. "I'll let Sam Balon explain. I'm an old woman, and I'm tired. I'm going to bed."

As the hands of time marched steadily toward the hour of midnight, a quiet calm settled over the town of Becancour. The field where Satan and his aides were summoned lay quiet in the night, all trappings of black magic had been removed. The Beasts had slipped back into the timber and the swamps surrounding the town. The cats had broken up into small groups and scattered about the town. Xaviere and her entourage had returned to the Dorgenois mansion. They were certain now of victory.

A group of Satan's believers had gone to Janson's Drive-in and cleaned up the mess; the drive-in now looked perfectly normal. A closed sign was hung in the door.

The Devil worshipers had broken up their gathering and most had returned to their stinking, filthy homes. The Master had asked that Becancour appear normal to any salespeople or route men who might travel through the next day. The Dark One had promised victory; had told them all that from this moment on, day or night was

301

acceptable for activities toward total victory . . . just be discreet about it. There was no need to rush.

The clouds had swept away, the stinking storm had vanished, and the skies had cleared.

A great black panther now roamed the streets of the small Louisiana town; a huge cat with strangely human eyes. A pale lovely woman walked with the panther, a white hand sometimes on the great cat's neck.

The woman and the panther prowled through the murky darkness.

Lula's Love-Inn was filled with unwashed human flesh. The men and women and boys and girls sprawled on the floor, exhausted after a night of sexual perversion.

The young assistant manager at the convenience store who had popped Brother Lester on the snoot had fought his last battle; what was left of him lay in bloody rags in a ditch not far from his home.

The cats had eaten well that night.

Guards had been posted at Colter's home; the others slept fitfully.

Don and Sonny had moved their radios to the clinic and to Colter's home, to keep some appearance of normalcy in case someone in what they now all called "the outside world" tried to contact them.

Mrs. Wheeler slept very lightly, her shotgun and pistol close by her bed.

Brother Lester and his flock had gone to their homes and found weapons, then returned to the church. Brother Lester had jerked and moaned and spoken in Tongues and had a vision. In his so-called vision, an angel had appeared, giving him instructions. Brother Lester now knew what he and his followers must do.

They must destroy the residents of Becancour, for the

angel had said so. What remained of his flock was the hard-core, the fanatics, the intolerant of anyone not believing as they did, and if Brother Lester said he had a vision . . . Brother Lester had a vision, and that was that.

And at the clinic, a small form was changing shape, while outside, in the hot darkness, the dead were walking.

16

Dog growled low in his throat. Little Sam opened his eyes.

"Not yet," the child whispered to Dog. "But soon. Very soon."

Dog looked at him through his mismatched eyes. Little Sam nodded his head. Dog lay back down on the tile floor of the clinic room and closed his eyes. Child of God and animal of God waited for the Dark One's demon to make its move.

An hour passed, no one noticed the almost invisible mist that crept throughout the clinic, hugging closely to the floor.

No one except Nydia, Little Sam, and Dog.

All the others were deep in sleep, all touched by the mist, deepening their sleep. At the back door of the clinic, Don had slumped to the floor, his chin on his chest, asleep. At the front of the clinic, Dr. Oscar Martin was stretched out on the floor, asleep.

On a couch in the waiting room, Guy Dorgenois sat up as the mist touched his bare feet.

But it was not the Little Guy Dorgenois his mother would have recognized.

The mist had crawled up the child's legs, scaling them, turning the feet into hooved, pointed, and clawed extremities. The mist crept onward, slicking the scales with slime, turning the arms into ropy muscles, covered with coarse thick hair. The neck and head had changed, the neck shortening, the head enlarging. The teeth were thick and misshapen and pointed, the mouth wide, the lips heavy and cruel. The nose had flattened, more like a pig than a human. The eyes were set wide apart and crooked. The ears were large and pointed, the top of the head hairless, covered with scales that oozed slime. The hands were clawed and powerful, with long yellow pointed fingernails.

Guy Dorgenois had become what Satan had decreed he was born to be.

The demon child slipped from the couch and walked toward the front of the clinic, its front-hooved and back-clawed feet clicking on the coolness of the tile floor. The demon squatted over the sleeping Oscar Martin and bent its head, sinking its teeth into the doctor's neck. With a sharp twist, the doctor's throat was ripped open, the hot blood gushing in torrents. That which had once been Guy lapped at the blood, feeling strength enter its squatty, powerful body.

Guy peeled flesh from the doctor, stuffing the bloody strips of meat into its wide toothy mouth, chewing greedily, savoring the hot flesh. It smacked its lips in satisfaction and peeled more meat from the body, eating faster now as more strength filled the demon. Guy broke off the doctor's fingers, one by one, and stuck them into its mouth, shredding the flesh from them, cracking the bones and sucking out the marrow. The demon ripped open Oscar's stomach and began pulling out ropes of intestines, stuffing them into its mouth, smacking as it glutted itself on flesh and blood and organs.

Little Sam and Dog and Nydia lay in the air-conditioned coolness of the clinic and listened to the spawn of Hell stuff its belly.

Nydia knew her powers were, at the least, equal to Little Sam's. But she knew, without knowing precisely how she knew, that this was her son's fight, and his alone.

The sounds of the demon's eating faded. Seconds later, his hooved and clawed feet were heard on the clinic floor. Little Sam looked at Dog looking at him. Little Sam nodded his head. The animal growled low, not liking what he sensed; but he obeyed. He rose and backed away from the open door.

Little Sam swung his feet off the bed and quickly dressed in his little jeans and shoes. Looking once at his mother, the little boy stepped out into the hallway.

There was twenty feet between child of Hell and child of God. Little Sam stood alone, facing the creature in the darkness of the hall. The demon opened his hideous mouth and howled at Sam. Slime dripped off the scales and hair of the creature to fall in stinking puddles on the tile.

The demon's eyes began to shine with a strange and eerie light.

Little Sam's eyes began to shine with a pure white light.

Light of God met the corruptive light of Hell. With eyes locked, the small boy and the demon quickly found that one could not best the other in this manner.

The demon, screaming its hate, charged Little Sam Sam sidestepped and tripped the demon, sending i sprawling and howling and sliding down the hall

306

Creature of Hell leaped to his feet, its clawed hands, the claws needle-sharp, whipping the air as it advanced on Sam. Sam stood his position in the hall. Waiting.

The demon charged, howling and slobbering, the spittle running in foul streams out of its mouth, its hooves and claws scratching and tearing the tile as it came.

Little Sam faked the little demon, stepping as if to once more trip the creature, and just at the last split second, darting back the way he had come. Off balance, the demon stumbled as it tried to recover. It made the mistake of stepping into the room with Dog. With a growl of intense hate, Dog's massive jaws opened and clamped down on the demon's leg. Dog tore off a hunk of scales and hair and meat. The demon screamed in pain.

Dog spat out the mess in disgust.

The demon raised his muscular arms and charged Little Sam. Sam met the charge and kicked out with one shoe, the toe of the shoe catching the creature between its legs, almost lifting it off the tile. Shrieking in pain, with stinking puke rolling out of its mouth, the demon tumbled to the floor, for the moment, helpless.

Little Sam's eyes began glowing with a fierce new intensity, the light white-hot from the powers bestowed upon him from beyond the Heavens. The demon's hair was the first to begin smoldering, then burst into flames.

Satan's own began squalling as the flames moved over his hideous body, finally covering the head. The sounds of his cooking brains bubbled throughout the clinic.

The mist had abated, those asleep coming awake and running to the sounds of battle. They stood and gazed in awe at the little boy with the glowing eyes. Then their eyes shifted to the awfulness on the floor.

Sam turned, the light in his eyes fading. "Guy Dorgenois," he said. Then turned and walked back into his room, to join his mother and Dog.

Little Sam put his arms around his mother's waist and began crying . . .

. . . just like any other normal little boy.

Bonnie and the great panther had paused, briefly, at the home of Mrs. Wheeler, but neither one wanted to tangle with the old woman . . . just yet. The great cat and the woman looked at the sprawled bodies of the young people in the front yard. They moved on, to prowl silently through the hot, still night.

The cats rested throughout the town.

The Beasts prowled the fringes of the town, occasionally finding one or two cats by themselves. The Beasts silently killed them and ate them.

For even among the ranks of the followers of the Dark One, there is jealousy.

And the night grew very hot, and very still. The town of Becancour lay like a ticking time bomb, ready to explode.

THE SECOND DAY OF THREE

"It looks so quiet and so peaceful," Matt Comeaux said, gazing at the just broken dawn of day.

"It won't be for long," Sam said, stepping out onto the porch. He carried a wooden mallet and a half dozen sharpened stakes.

Father Javotte was with him, his arms full of stakes, a mallet in his hand.

With the exception of Tess and Colter, who were with the children in the house, the others gathered on the porch. Their eyes were on the stakes in the hands of the men.

"Might as well get my feet wet," Trooper Norris said. "I got a pretty good idea why you got those stakes, but lemme ask a question."

"Why wait until the day?" Javotte asked.

"Yes, sir."

"Because most likely, unless Satan has changed the rules of the game, those truly possessed will be forced to sleep during the day. We can find them asleep, and kill 'em."

"The rules of the . . . game? Just like maybe one troop plays another in softball? A . . . game?"

"The oldest game in the world's history," Sam said. "God versus Satan."

Norris nodded his head and swallowed hard. "Whenever you guys are ready."

Sam looked at Jobert. "Jobert? I'll ask you to stay here and guard those in the house, with Chief Passon."

"Honored, Sam," the old ex-Legionnaire said. "I did not surrender at Dien Bien Phu, and I shall not surrender here."

"I'll go with you, too," Matt said. "If I might make a suggestion? . . ."

"Sure."

"I'll ride with Father Javotte, you with Trooper Norris. We might be able to . . ." He shook his head and swallowed. ". . . accomplish more by splitting up."

"Good idea," Sam said, handing the Louisiana trooper a half dozen stakes. "You ready?"

"I reckon."

"They are coming, Princess," Janet told Xaviere.

"They are fools!" The Princess of Darkness spat the words. "Overconfident mortals who shall soon be destroyed."

"The Dorgenois demon faced no mortal," the Princess was reminded.

Princess Xaviere's smile was ugly. "But the priest and Sam and the others coming this morning are mortals. The Master promised us victory this time."

"Yes, Princess. But of course. And there is still my daughter, Bess."

"She can destroy the Balon Bastard tonight. Advise

her of that."

"Look for them in sheds and in darkened houses," Sam told the trooper. "Be very careful and don't let one bite you."

"Just like in the movies, I'll become one?"

"Just like in the movies."

"What in the hell is that down there?" Trooper Norris pointed.

Sam squinted his eyes against the bright sunlight. The temperature was already, before seven o'clock, in the nineties.

"I don't know."

"Oh, shit!" the trooper said. "That's Cliff Lester and his bunch."

"They've got enough guns, that's for sure."

Norris let off the brake and moved his patrol car forward, stopped in the middle of the street. He and Sam got out to confront Cliff Lester.

"Get out of our way!" Brother Lester shouted at the men. "Or we'll roll right over you. We are the Army of the Lord."

"I thought that's what we were," James Norris muttered.

"I wish you would all join us," Sam said. "We'd stand better chance of defeating Satan."

But he knew when he said it, his words were falling on deaf ears.

"Satan himself is not here, you fool!" Lester shouted. "Not *personally*. I have been instructed by an angel from the Lord to destroy all the residents of this wicked city.

This city has become a modern-day Sodom and Gomorrah. It is wicked and depraved and sinful. Now stand aside, we are on our way to burn the library."

"The *library?*" James blurted. "What's wrong with the library?"

"Nasty, filthy, wicked, lustful, profane books!" Lester shouted.

"Amen!" came the chorus.

"You ignorant redneck," James said. "Dumb white trash, that's all you are."

"I'll smite you hip and thigh!" Lester shouted, raising a club over his head.

Lester found both eyes suddenly crossing, as they looked down the barrel of Norris's .357. Man could sure get that gun out in a hurry.

"Lower that club, you hillbilly," James told the lay preacher. "Or I'll blow your head off."

"You heathen!" Lester said. But he lowered the club.

"Now you listen to me," Sam told the leader and the followers. "You're not burning *any* buildings. The buildings are not our problem. And be advised of this too: there are lots of people in this town who are not on either side . . ."

"If they are not on the side of decency then they are on the side of filth and perversion!" Sister Bertha howled from the crowd.

"That's right!" Lester stood his ground. "There is no middle road."

James said it first. "They don't understand, Sam. They're all about three bricks shy of a full load."

Lester glared at the trooper. "No," he hissed at James and Sam. "It is you who do not understand. Neither you. Pornography has brought this plague upon us. T filthy words and dirty pictures are to blame. The mark of Cain is on this town, and on its people . . ."

"It's not the mark of Cain, Lester," Sam said. "It's the Mark of the Beast."

"Stand aside!" Those behind the man lifted their shotguns and rifles and pistols.

Sam waved the so-called religious mob to move on past them.

They marched on, singing.

"Now we got that to deal with, too," James remarked.

"Yes," Sam agreed. "They're so opinionated and prejudiced they don't realize they're wrong."

"Yeah. But do you realize who is gonna be caught up in the middle of it?"

"Yes. Us."

17

Matt Comeaux and Father Javotte came face to face with a group of young men and women. Among them, Ted Wilson.

The punk grinned at Matt. "Hello there, Teacher. I hoped it would be me who got to you."

The wild-eyed group of young men and women could not see the pistols stuck in the back pockets of Comeaux and Javotte; most of them were looking at the stakes in the men's hands.

"It isn't too late for any of you," Javotte said. "Let us help you, and you can then help us destroy the evil."

The crowd of young people laughed. Ted said, "Stuff it, Teacher!"

Javotte flushed, reaching the end of his patience.

Ted glared at Matt. "You stayed on my back for years, you bastard. You steady picked on me all the damned time."

"I tried to give you an education, Ted. I tried to make you see there is something beyond high school sports. I guess I failed."

"I guess you're gonna die, Comeaux!"

"We're all going to die, Ted." Matt spoke softly, but

314

his words were hard-edged. He stood with a stake in his right hand, a mallet in his left.

"Oh, my, how profound, Teach." He cut his eyes to Javotte. "You gonna pray for my lost soul, Zorro?"

Javotte shook his head. "No. I think it's far too late for that."

"Man's got some smarts, people," Ted said, jerking his thumb toward Javotte. He looked at Matt. "Got any last words, Teach?"

Matt's smile was rather sad. "You poor young fool."

Ted was genuinely astonished. "*Me!* Man, we're in control of this town, and you feel sorry for me? You really are some kind of nut."

"Just a Christian, Ted," Matt replied.

Ted lunged at the former principal. Matt lifted the stake and held firm, allowing Ted to impale himself on the sharpened stake. The point of the stake took the unwashed, undisciplined follower of Satan in the hollow of his throat, exiting out the back of his neck, slightly to the left.

Ted gurgled and bubbled and staggered backward, his eyes wide with the shock of finally realizing he was not immortal. He was going to die.

Matt pulled a .38 from his back pocket and shot another believer in and practicer of the Dark Arts between the eyes. The range was so close that powder burns were evident around the small hole that leaked blood and fluid. The young man dropped to the ground and kicked and trembled for a moment, then lay still as death took him winging into the foul arms of that which he considered his God.

Javotte brought his hammer down onto the head of a young man, wincing as he heard the skull pop under the steel head. The young man slumped to the ground, in a kneeling position, sort of like he might be praying in death.

Both Matt and Javotte seriously doubted that.

What remained of the gang of thugs and would-be toughs, male and female, split.

A scream ripped through the hot early-morning air. It echoed around the men, confusing them as to direction. Again, the scream clawed the air in almost mindless terror.

Javotte pointed. "Over there!"

Priest and schoolteacher ran toward the shrieking. They ran around the corner of a house just as the screaming ended with a flat bubbling sound.

R.M. Dorgenois knelt on the ground, sucking the blood from a woman he had pinned to the ground with one hairy and clawed hand. He had ripped the woman's dress from her, shredded her panties, and was attempting to mount the woman, his ragged and filthy suit trousers down around his ankles. The woman managed to scream once more while he sucked her blood from the puncture wounds in her neck.

"Too late for her," Javotte noted as the woman physically and mentally succumbed to the powers of that which lay beyond the realm of understanding.

Murmuring a prayer, Matt Comeaux ran up to the old man and lifted a stake high. He brought the stake down hard, driving the point through the man's back.

R.M. lifted his animal-like head and roared and howled as Matt worked the stake back and forth, pushing forward as he worked.

R.M.'s strength was enormous. He rose to his knees and tried to arch his back, anything to relieve the awful pain.

Matt summoned all his strength and pushed the stake further into the man's chest, the point finally reaching the heart.

A yellowish, sickeningly odious liquid gushed from R.M.'s mouth. He howled an animal-like wail as his clawed hand tried to work its way behind his back to grasp the stake.

Matt could hear the sounds of hammering but dared not lift his eyes to seek the source. He felt he knew. He held onto the stake and worked it back and forth, enlarged the gaping wound, pushing the stake deeper and deeper into the heart of the spawn of Hell.

R.M. gave one final shriek of pain and slumped to one side.

Leaving the stake piercing the dark heart, Matt looked toward the priest. Javotte was hammering a stake into the heart of the woman, whose features were already being altered by the forces of Darkness. Hair was rapidly covering the woman's face and arms, her fingers were resembling claws. Her hands were clutching the stake being pounded into her chest. Blood was pouring from her mouth and chest. She hissed and howled and screamed curses upon the priest.

The point of the stake penetrated her heart. The woman jerked on the ground, then lay still, her claws falling away from the stake.

Both Javotte and Matt stood back, sweating and panting, and watched in horror and fascination as the features of R.M. and the woman began to change. In seconds, the man and woman had changed into human form. It was such an unexpected metamorphosis neither man could do anything except stare in shocked silence for a long moment.

Javotte's voice brought the teacher out of his staring.

"Watch out! To your left!"

Matt spun around, reaching for his pistol. Matt paused, again staring in disbelief. He was looking at a huge black panther. No panthers that size in this area for years—more years than Matt had on him.

"Look at his eyes," Javotte whispered.

Matt looked. They were human eyes.

And they were very hypnotic in their unblinking stare. So hypnotic, neither man could see the woman slipping up behind them.

Some primal sensing came to the fore in Matt's head. He turned just as Bonnie Rogers was stepping up behind Father Javotte, a knife in her hand, preparing to plunge the blade deep into the priest's back.

Matt shot the woman three times in the stomach with his .38. The slugs knocked her back and down to one knee. She came up snarling just as the black panther jumped at Javotte.

Javotte held up a cross and stood his ground without flinching.

The sunlight glinted off the gold cross, the reflected light hitting the leaping panther in the face. The panther screamed in rage and fright and disgust at the sight of the gold cross. His front paws clawed at the hot air and the panther twisted to one side to avoid the hated cross. He landed lightly and jumped for the bushes behind the house. Matt fired just as the panther disappeared, but not before the men heard a squall of pain from the great cat.

They turned to look at Bonnie Rogers.

She was gone.

Sam and Trooper Norris were having no luck in seeking

out and destroying the Satan worshipers. They had broken into several houses and half a dozen sheds, all empty, or merely filled with frightened and very confused people.

"Who are they, Sam?" Norris asked, back on the road.

"In limbo. They'll probably try to stay in hiding until this is all over."

"Unless Lester and his kooks find them first," the trooper said.

"Yeah. And speaking of Lester's bunch . . . look over there."

Brother Cliff Lester and some of his flock had broken into a small shop that specialized in used books, hardcover and paperback. They were piling the books onto the street.

"Gonna be a bonfire soon," the trooper remarked. "You want to try to stop it?"

Sam shook his head. "We've got more important things to do than deal with those bigoted fools. The Beasts and the cats and the coven members will deal with them, I should imagine, in time."

James looked at Sam, a strange look in his eyes. "We think we're on the side of God, they think they're on the side of God. It's a weird world, Sam."

Sam smiled. "Stick around, James. It's going to get a lot stranger."

18

Brother Luther reported back to Brother Lester. He told Brother Lester about the upside-down crosses he'd seen around the town. The devil's paraphernalia, and such like that there.

"We've all seen it on the TeeVee," Brother Luther said. "Maybe there is something to what that there Sam Balon's been sayin'."

"What do you mean, Luther?" Lester asked.

"Witches and werewolves and the like. Like that thing you and the others seen last night in the alley."

Brother Lester was interested. Might be something worth listening to here. "Go on."

"Folks is hidin' in their houses, Brother Lester. Shunnin' God's light of day. What does that mean to you?"

Lester put a hand on the man's shoulder. "Brother Luther, you are right. If it was good enough for them folks up in Salem years ago, then it's good enough for us today."

"Uh . . . what folks up where?"

Brother Lester waved that aside. "Gather the Sisters

Brother Luther. Tell them to drop whatever they are doing and return to the church. Get some fresh-washed sheets and begin making robes for us, in various sizes. We must be pure, Brother Luther, both inside and out." He glanced at his watch. Early. "We'll meet at the church at noon. Tell the men to start gathering firewood and pile it down by that field next to the church."

"Yes, sir, Brother Lester. Uh . . . Brother Lester, what are we goin' to do with firewood?"

Brother Lester's smile was that of a zealot, certain of his convictions, sure his feet were planted firmly on the pathway to Heaven.

"How does one destroy a witch or a warlock, Brother Luther?"

Luther thought about that for a moment. He was a good hunter, he was a right good farmer and a fair welder . . . but durned if he knew how to . . .

He grinned, the answer coming to him. He suddenly frowned. "But how do we know we're gettin' the right folks, Brother?"

"Filthy, trashy, nasty books and magazines, Brother Luther. The wearin' of obscene clothin', and the thinkin' of impure thoughts and the actin' out of impure deeds." The others had gathered around their spiritual leader. "Backsliders, Brothers and Sisters, them folks who has ceased the attendin' of church, who allow their children to run wild, who hang out in bars and the like." He slowly turned, eyeballing each Brother and Sister. He winked and smiled at them. "You all know the types."

"Amen!" Sister Bertha shouted, and began to get into the spirit, waving her arms and shouting.

Brother Luther began stamping his feet. "Burn!" he

proclaimed. "Burn, burn, burn!"

The other forty-odd members of Brother Lester's flock began gettin' down, waving their arms and shouting.

"Burn, burn, burn!" they shouted.

And the devil began laughing.

What was left of Dr. Oscar Martin was rubber-bagged and stored. The charred remains of Guy Dorgenois were tossed into the garbage bin outside the clinic. The story of what had happened went through the crowded clinic like wildfire, eventually reaching the children. Only one child had to feign shock at the story; she knew now it was solely up to her. She would destroy Little Sam Balon . . . that night.

Salespeople and route men reached the cutoff road leading to Becancour. Minutes apart, they pulled over and stopped, mulling things over in their mind. It was a long, boring drive to Becancour, and one more day wouldn't make all that much difference. One by one they turned around and traveled on down the main highway. Hell with Becancour.

Everyone that is except the breadman and the milkman. Everyone has to have fresh bread and fresh milk. They thought about skipping Becancour; though hard about it. The bread man even turned around twice in his confusion. Turning around, he missed seeing the mail truck as it barreled on right past the turn-off not even looking at the southbound road to Becancour. But in the end, the breadman and the milkman rolled toward Becancour.

The milkman and his helper had the windows down and the radio on, turned up loud, the rock and roll music blaring. The bread man had a box of X-rated movies in the truck; he'd picked them up from a friend in Ferriday and was going to have some guys over this weekend for a stag party. Drink some beer and watch some skin flicks.

That was the plan, anyway.

The bread and milk rolled on toward Becancour.

Preacher Earl Morris just didn't feel quite right; hadn't felt right since that night he'd come to under the carport wondering how he'd gotten there. And his neck had hurt, too. Two little tiny marks on his neck. And he'd been having some wild, wicked thoughts . . . and he enjoyed those thoughts.

His wife had locked herself in her bedroom . . . Jesus! when had she done that? He couldn't remember. Last night? The day before? He couldn't even remember why she'd done it.

"Hey, Ann!" he hollered. "Get on out here, baby!"

A sobbing sound drifted to him from up the hallway.

"Stupid bitch!" he muttered.

Preacher Earl Morris knew he had a sermon to write for Sunday, but right now he didn't give a damn if he ever again even entered a church. Just the thought of doing so was strangely repugnant to him.

Dark, savage, primitive thoughts roared through the man's head. "Hey!" he shouted. "You gonna come out here and take care of me or not, baby?"

"Get out!" his wife screamed at him. "I don't know you anymore, Earl. Get out and leave me alone."

Rage filled the man. He jumped from the chair where he'd been sitting for? . . . He didn't know how long. Hours, surely. Couple of days, maybe. He walked swiftly up the hall and kicked in the door to his wife's bedroom. He was screaming and cursing and using language he had never before used in his life.

She flew at him, striking him with a hand mirror. He wrested the mirror from her and threw her to the floor. Then he did something he thought he'd always wanted to do. He wasn't real sure he'd always wanted to, but what the hell?

Laughing at her screaming, the man brutally took his wife.

He looked around at a noise behind him. Mayor Will Jolevare and his wife, Betty, were standing in the doorway.

"Wanna swap wimmen?" Will asked, his voice odd sounding to Earl.

"Hell," Earl said. "Why not?"

They were running about two hours late, due to their indecision at the crossroads, but the breadman and the milkman finally pulled into Becancour. The bank time and temperature read 11:00 & 96°. The milk truck radio was blaring rock and roll music as both trucks pulled into the small convenience store where Lester had confronted the assistant manager and Elmer had backslid—so to speak.

But the store was closed.

Milkman looked at breadman. "I didn't think this place ever closed."

"I've never known it to close. Must be an illness in the family, maybe?"

"Yeah."

Then the men were conscious of a mass of whiteness moving around them. It momentarily startled them.

"What the hell! . . ." the milkman's helper said.

"Listen to that music," Sister Sally said. "The devil's music."

"Are you people in a play or something?" the bread man asked Lester.

Lester looked like a small snowstorm in his white robes. "Why are you here?" he demanded of the route men.

"We're here to deliver the Liberty Bell, you patty-cake," the breadman said. "What the hell do you think we're here for?"

"Yeah," the milkman's helper said. "So buzz off, Snow White."

Lester listened to the music coming from the milk truck. He frowned at the lyrics . . . those that he could understand, that is. "Satan's music. Obscene. Destroy the radio," he ordered.

"Now, you wait just a minute!" the man who owned the truck said.

He was too late. The music stopped abruptly under the head of a hammer.

"Hey!" the helper called, running to the cab of the truck. He tried to pull the white-robed flock member from the cab. The man kicked the young helper in the face. Blood popped out of busted lips.

325

Sister Estelle let out a whoop.

"Get out of my truck!" the breadman hollered at her.

"Filth!" Sister Estelle squalled. "Nasty movies in here, Brother Lester!"

Lester walked to the truck and looked at the box of skin flicks. "Purveyor of filth!" he said, looking at the bread man. "That's why you were so concerned about the store being closed, wasn't it?"

"Huh?" the breadman said.

"How many other stores do you service with this fleshy filth?" Brother Luther questioned.

Breadman looked at milkman. "I'm leavin', man. You with me?"

"Let's go."

"Grab them!" Brother Lester yelled. "Take them to the field."

The three men were seized, their hands tied behind their backs.

"Destroy the store," Brother Lester ordered. He remembered Sam's warning. "Not with fire. With axes— and the trucks, too."

While the store and the trucks were being beaten broken, hacked, and axed, the three men were led off.

"I think," the milkman's helper said, "that we are all in deep trouble."

"Shut up!" Sister Helen told him. "We're doin' th Lord's work this day."

"Not no Lord that I ever heard of," the milkman sai accurately.

With the sounds of axes and hammers and tire iror ringing off of metal and wood and shattered glass, th breadman asked, "What are you people going to d

326

with us?"

"You will confess your sins before a court of True Christians," Brother Lester told him. "And then your flesh will sear with the fires you love."

"These people are nuts!" the milkman's helper summed up.

19

The police radios at the mansion and the clinic were filled with chatter, but none of it directed at the cops in Becancour. It was as if they did not exist.

Sonny Passon said as much.

"Maybe we don't no more," Jobert spoke softly.

"What do you mean, Jobert?" Colter asked.

"I don' know, for really, madame. It's jus' a feelin' I got. One that I can't hardly put into words."

"Like we have been forsaken, Jobert?"

"No. Not that. I don' think my God is gonna forsake me. But I kinda believe that He is leavin' the fight—this fight—up to us." He shook his head. "I ain' sayin' this rat."

"You're thinking there will be no outside help; is tha' it, Jobert?"

"Yeah. I don' think none of us could get out if we tried And I don' think nobody else can get in. I din feel thi way a short time ago. But now I do. An' I don know why. jus' do."

C.D. walked to the picture windows of the huge de and looked out. "I just wish they'd make their move. just feel so . . . so *helpless* here. I'm confused, I'm scare

328

and . . . I don't understand it."

Sam and the others returned. Sonny looked at Sam, unspoken questions in his eyes.

"We got a few of them" Sam said. "Too few to suit me."

"Tonight," Javotte said. "Tonight is when we'll face the real Hell."

"I believe that, too," Sam said.

"It's like a pressure cooker out there," Matt said. "Just building and building up steam. Something's got to set it off."

"I think tonight," Jobert said. "I don' know why. But tonight it blows."

Tess Nardana began silently weeping.

Princess Xaviere stood at the window in her room and looked out over the hot, still town. An evil smile caressed her lips. Everything was just perfect. The violence, for the most part, had been kept to a minimum—not like it was back in New York State. And now the so-called Christians were at odds with each other. Not only here, but at nearly all levels of government around the nation. Narrow-minded, hypocritical, and thinly disguised intolerance of all beliefs other than what those in power believed in was coming to the fore.

And that was good. Her Master had told her so. The Dark One had told her he had seen this take place many, many times, all over the world. The Prince of Flies had seen it many times over the centuries. Xaviere knew that whenever one group tries to suppress the rights, beliefs, privileges of another group, that suppression only serves to heighten the desirability of that which the intolerant want to censor.

Morality cannot be legislated, but the new Puritan wave that was stomping around the nation, like that fool Cliff Lester, was too blind and bigoted and ignorant to see that.

Xaviere rubbed her hands in glee and laughed and laughed. The evil laughter floated around the filthy room.

It was just too good to be true.

But it was true.

And she loved it!

"You're all right," Bonnie said, stroking the head of the great black panther. "And so am I. We have both achieved our dreams, Jackson. We are immortal."

The great cat licked Bonnie's hand with its rough tongue and purred.

At Lula's Love-Inn, those who had slept the sleep of the exhausted were awakening. They stretched their arms and loosened sore and tightened muscles. The place reeked with the odor of dozens of unwashed bodies.

"Tonight," Walt Davis heard the silent call from the smoking pits. "Tonight."

"Tonight," the others repeated.

Dave Porter stroked the flesh of the young girls who had serviced him the previous night. One of them responded and shifted positions. Her long unwashed hair fanned Dave's flesh.

"Tonight, baby!" Dave groaned. "Tonight."

"Tonight," Nydia said, looking at Little Sam.
Her son nodded his head.
Dog growled.

A Beast tore a hissing cat apart and stuffed its mouth full. The Beast smacked its lips in satisfaction. It belched a foul odor and devoured the other half of the cat.

The Beast did not know why it hated the little furry creatures . . . but it certainly did, and so did the other Beasts.

Tonight, it managed to think, tonight the cats would be fair game. The Master had not signaled otherwise, and until he did . . . the hunt was on.

Javotte looked at Sam. "Tonight," the priest said.
Sam nodded his head in agreement.

"Confess your sins!" Brother Lester shouted at the three men.

The men had been stripped and tied to poles driven into the ground. Dry wood had been piled around them, knee-high, and then soaked with kerosene.

"You're crazy!" The milkman screamed the words. "What in the hell is the matter with you people?"

"Confess!" Lester hollered, his face sweaty, his eyes shining with the light of a zealot. "Tell us of your sins."

"What happens to us if we do?" the breadman asked.

That confused Brother Lester. He thought for a moment and shook his head. "Confess!"

The milkman sealed the fate of them all. "You goddamned sorry no good motherfuckers!" he yelled at Brother Lester's flock.

"See! See!" Brother Lester shouted. "Listen to the filth rolling from his mouth. Burn, burn, burn!"

Torches were lighted as some of the Brothers and Sisters got in the spirit and began prancing and talking and shouting nonsense.

Brother Lester grabbed a torch from the hands of a man and tossed it into the kerosene-soaked wood piled around the milk man. "Scream your praise to Satan as the fires of the Lord sear your sinful flesh! Burn, burn, burn!"

A few more of the Brothers and Sisters got into the spirit and began dancing around the screaming, burning man.

Anguished screaming filled the heated air as the men's flesh began cooking and bubbling and peeling, exposing the raw meat of their bodies. The men's hair exploded a the flames reached higher. Brains and eyeballs began cooking and melting, the eyeballs running down th men's seared cheeks.

Sister Bertha began tossing the X-rated films into th flames, her shrieks of uncontrolled Phariseeism almos overriding the now-fading screaming of the men bein burned alive.

"Rejoice, Brothers and Sisters!" Lester shouted. "W have begun ridding the world of sinners. Tod Becancour, tomorrow . . . *the world!*" he scream flinging his arms high over his head.

The bonds holding the cooked meat that was on

human parted as the flames reached them. The men toppled forward into the burning wood.

"Burn, you heathens!" Lester shouted. "Burn!"

Mary Claverie had slept, awakened, then slept a bit longer until the noonday heat became too fierce for her.

It was then she remembered one of the reasons she came here.

Her Brothers.

It seemed like to Mary that someone was trying to tell her something in some almost inaudible voice in her head. It seemed to Mary that the voice was telling her to wait, don't go just yet.

But Mary didn't want to wait. She loved the Dark One, loved all that he stood for, but this was important, too. She picked up her pistol and stepped out into the noonday heat. She remembered the way to her old home, and knew that Clarence lived in the old place. Clarence was the oldest, so it was only fitting that he be the first.

No one attempted to stop Mary as she walked the hot streets. She paused once, sure she was hearing some sort of singing floating on the air—singing and screaming. But she mentally brushed that aside. Who would be singing now?

Screaming, yes. Singing, no.

It was not a long walk to Mary's childhood home. The place had not changed that much. Mary stood for a moment outside the home. She could sense the fear emanating from within. She smiled at that. Clarence had been appalled years back—Mary couldn't remember how many years—after her rape, when Mary began renouncing God and praising Satan. Her brother had begun shouting all sorts of religious junk and his minister had spoken from the Bible.

She wondered what had happened to that old poot of a preacher?

Mary walked up the sidewalk, her pistol in her hand.

The fear smell grew stronger. Mary's own stinking body odors paled against the fear odor.

The front door opened and there he stood. Dear Brother Clarence. His eyes widened as he recognized the ragged, wild-eyed woman standing before him.

"I might have known you'd have something to do with . . . whatever is happening to this town," Clarence said.

"Don't you know?" Mary asked, thinking: what a dope.

"No," Clarence said, his voice dull.

"Will and Jack with you?"

That startled the man. "Will and Jack? Mary, they died years ago, within eighteen months of each other."

Mary started laughing. That was even better.

"You find it funny your brothers have died?"

"Hysterical, Brother dear." She put the pistol back into her dirty purse. "Would you like to see ou brothers?"

"*What?*"

"Are you deaf as well as stupid? You heard me Clarence."

"I should call the doctors at the hospital. But . . ." H looked puzzled for a few seconds. "I don't know th number," he said lamely.

"You don't know a lot of things, Clarence. But tonigh for a very short time, I'll see if I can't clear them up f you."

334

Clarence's wife—Mary forgot her name—joined him on the porch. She was as dull-looking as Clarence.

"Where are your kids, Clarence?' Mary asked her brother.

"All grown up, Mary. What's going to happen tonight?"

She waved her hand at him, turned around, and walked away. She ignored his calling for her to turn around, talk to him.

At the corner, she paused, trying to remember which way to the cemetery. It came to her.

She walked to the outskirts of town and entered the cemetery. Chuckling, she located the caretaker's building and broke the lock off the door. She stepped into the building and located a shovel. She was whistling a dirgelike tune as she walked the grounds. She had absolutely no idea where her brothers were buried.

Shovel in hand, Mary prowled the cemetery like a ghoul—ragged and dirty and stinking, her eyes inspecting each headstone for names. She knew a lot of the names, and spit on several of the graves.

Then she found the family plot. She dropped the shovel and clapped her hands in glee. Good ol' Jack and Will. Oh, she thought, what a surprise was waiting for them.

She began digging.

20

The sun beat down on Becancour with a merciless intensity, sending the temperature soaring upward. The heat did nothing to alleviate the sickly-sweet odor of burned flesh that wafted over the town, floating on the almost breezeless air.

The grunting sounds of men and women joined in all varieties of sexual positions mingled with the smell of burned flesh and the odor of many unwashed bodies.

No one walked the streets, no one drove the streets. The clerks in those stores that were open did nothing except sit and stare dully out the windows. There were no customers to buy their wares, no one just browsed through the aisles.

At the clinic and at the Dorgenois house, those gathered tried to rest, to conserve and build strength for the night that would all too soon be upon them. But real rest, for most, was very elusive. For they sensed, felt, *knew,* the night and the following dawn and day would bring horror that none among them had ever before experienced. None, except Sam Balon and Nydia.

And all marveled at how Sam and Nydia and Little Sam and even Dog could sleep so soundly.

Mary Claverie continued her digging. The heat did not bother her at all. On and on through the hot afternoon she dug; first at one grave, then at the other, so she could time the rebirth, and claim two more souls for the Dark One. She sometimes laughed as she worked.

Ex-City Patrolman Louis Black made the mistake of going to the home of Old Mrs. Wheeler. He stood out on the front yard, close to the front porch, and began taunting the old woman. He heaped verbal filth upon her, the profanity rolling from his mouth in stinking waves.

Mrs. Wheeler, with a sigh, rose from her chair and opened the screen door.

She shot him with the shotgun, the buckshot striking him in the legs, knocking him sprawling. Screaming in pain, Louis managed to crawl off, out of range. As he crawled, his blood stained the grass beneath him. He crawled on, until he came to a house he thought was deserted. Slowly, painfully, he pulled himself up onto the porch. He moaned as hands found him and pulled him inside. He looked up into the eyes of Art Authement. Art bent his head and kissed the man, his lips moving over the lips and down to his neck.

And Brother Cliff Lester was having another of his semifamous visions.

"World power," the soothing voice whispered to

Brother Lester. "Fame and riches. Sound good?"

Lester agreed that, yes, it shore did.

"Your own television show, carried coast to coast, border to border."

"Oh, my, yes!" Brother Lester whispered to the voice.

"People flinging themselves at your feet, begging for forgiveness—from *you*. Like that, old friend?"

Shore did, for a fact. Hallelujah.

"What you have done today was good, a start, but only a small start. There are many more in this town who must be punished. Do you agree?"

"Shore do."

"You must do exactly as I say. For I speak only the truth."

"Right, right! Lay it on me." As Brother Lester moaned and jerked and spake in tongues, his flock were working themselves up into a murderous frenzy. Their joyful noisemaking was muted in Lester's feverish brain as the voice spoke.

The voice gave Brother Lester instructions, and Brother Lester loved it.

His moaning and jerking ceased. He opened his eyes and sat up. "Lo," he shouted. "I have spoken with an angel."

Not exactly an angel.

"I know now what we must do!"

His flock waited.

Lester told them.

They gasped.

"What angel told you this?" a daring flock member asked.

"Do you dare question *me!*" Brother Lester shouted

The questioner lowered his head.

"That's better," Lester said. "Cleanse yourselves, mentally and physically. For we must hurry."

And Mary pried open the lid to Will's casket. She grabbed his rotting head and kissed his cold lips.

Will opened his eyes.

"Hi, Brother!" Mary cried. "Welcome back!"

21

Sam visited the clinic and spoke softly with his wife and son, in private.

"You've seen a small taste of Hell, Son," he told Little Sam. "But in a few hours, Satan is going to unleash everything at his power. You've been a brave boy, now I must ask you to be braver."

"I will, Father. I promise."

"You've spotted the devil's child?"

"When she walked in with Guy, Father."

"She won't be as easy as poor little Guy."

"I know. But Dog will help me."

Sam patted the big head of the animal. He lifted hi eyes to Nydia. "You're going to be very busy tonigh love."

"I know."

Sam kissed his son and his wife. He stood up. "I'll se you all tomorrow."

Sam spoke briefly with the remainder of the adults the clinic. "Hang in there," he said.

They all watched the husky young man leave th building. Sam stood outside for a moment, in the almo unbearable heat of mid-afternoon. The odor of evil was almost as intolerable as the intense heat.

He walked to the borrowed pickup truck and got behind the wheel, wincing as his hands touched the hot steering wheel.

With a long expelling of breath, Sam started the pickup and rolled out, heading for the main drag of town. He saw nothing and nobody. He didn't even see a cat.

But he felt the evil all around him, slithering about like some dangerous snake, the forked tongue sliding rapidly in and out past the eternal smile of the serpent.

He drove the main street, stopping at the sight of the nearly destroyed convenience store. Parking, Sam got out and inspected the milk truck and the bread truck. And that odd smell he'd been smelling for several hours was stronger.

He knew what it was.

He drove toward the stronger odor, stopping about a block from Cliff Lester's church on a side street. There, out in the field, he saw the three charred poles.

With a sigh, Sam backed up and turned around. He didn't have to go inspect the poles; he could smell what remained of cooked human flesh.

"The damned fool," Sam muttered. "Why can't people be Christians without being fanatics?"

He wasn't expecting any reply and none came. This was to be his fight; he had sensed that from the outset. But to even the score some, God had lined up some strong and stable people to fight with Sam.

Sam had to smile—what a bunch he had with him. A pretty good cross section of America. Some homemakers, doctors, cops, teachers, businesspeople, a whole gang of kids, some teenagers, a priest and a preacher, one very old lady, and Jobert.

Sam liked the ex-Legionnaire; no back-up in that old boy. None at all.

Sam glanced up at the sky. Couple more hours until dusk. Couple more hours until . . .

. . . He wondered how many of those Christians gathered at the mansion and the clinic would live to see the dawn?

Sam wondered if *he* would live to see the dawn? He quickly put that thought out of his mind.

He once more drove the main street of Becancour, looking for? . . .

. . . He wasn't sure. Something that might give an indication of what might be coming at them when night wrapped its dark arms around the land, and the forces of evil were unleashed, to come screaming and howling at the small army of Christians.

But the silent streets and empty-appearing businesses and homes gave no ready answer to Sam's questions.

Alone, Sam thought. We are visibly alone in this fight.

But not really alone. God is with us, watching, silently giving us strength. And Michael, the Mercenary, is sitting beside Him, furious that He will not allow the archangel to leave Heaven to join in the fight.

With a sharp cracking sound, Sam was jerked from his musings. The side window of the pickup was spider-webbed from a large rock thrown at the truck. Sam braked and pulled over to the curb. He got out, a sawed-off shotgun with extended magazine in his hand. He borrowed the shotgun from Deputy Lenoir. Sam's .44 mag was in leather, belted around his waist. He looked toward the mouth of an alley. A dozen or so people, ranging in age from late teens upward stood there, grinning and hooting and cursing him.

"Get the bastard!" a man shouted. The crowd of unwashed rushed Sam.

Sam leveled the shotgun and began pulling and pumping. The buckshot knocked the charging mob backward and to the hot street. Blood splattered the storefront and the big windows were shattered from the buckshot that did not enter and tear nonhuman flesh. For that is how Sam viewed anyone who practiced devil worship . . . Nonhuman.

One screaming, wild-eyed young man almost reached Sam. The man's hands were reaching for him as Sam lifted the muzzle of the 12 gauge and pulled the trigger. The buckshot struck Satan's dupe in the hollow of his throat, almost completely tearing off the head.

A young woman leaped onto Sam's back. Sam fell back on his hard-earned Ranger training and flipped the woman from him, sending her sailing through the air to crash through a store window, the broken glass ripping her unwashed flesh, staining the show area with crimson.

The shotgun empty, Sam tossed it onto the hood of the pickup and jerked his big .41 from leather. He shot a middle-aged man between the eyes, popping his head back as if struck with a hard-thrown brick.

The crowd vanished as suddenly as it came. The sidewalk and street were filled only with the dead and dying; the moaning of those badly wounded verbally clawed the hot, still air.

Sam quickly reloaded the shotgun and laid it on the pickup's bench seat. He punched out the empty brass in the cylinder of the .41 mag and reloaded, all the while keeping a watch for any more attackers. None came at him.

He did not concern himself with the dead or wounded. He knew the Beasts and cats were close by, watching.

They would eat them.

THE THIRD NIGHT OF THREE

Sam had inspected the mansion at least a dozen times in a three-hour span. He had corrected a half dozen mistakes before he was satisfied the mansion was as secure as it could possibly be.

It also came as no surprise to him that the phones in Becancour still worked. The Prince of Filth was making sure as much remained normal as was inhumanly possible.

Sam called the clinic and spoke with Nydia.

"We're as ready as can be, Sam," she assured him.

"I know the demon child has not yet made any move." was not a question; a statement of fact.

"She's making plans. She is not aware I can read her thoughts."

"She's stronger than Little Sam, you know."

"I know. Dog is with him constantly. It will be all right, Sam."

And with that, Sam knew it would be. He felt that Little Sam would not come out of the battle unhurt, either mentally or physically, but then, no one would.

"I love you, Nydia."

"And I love you, Sam."

They both hung up and turned to face the night.

Brother Lester and his hardcore band of Brothers and Sisters, all resplendent in their freshly washed robes, had finished trashing a local store that sold paperbacks. Nothing had been spared. Since many of them had difficulty reading anything, any cover with anything that could be remotely construed as suggestive was either ripped apart or burned. Any cover that dared show the bare curve of a woman's breast or the skin of a thigh was met with whoops of disgust from the Brothers and Sisters; after all, *they,* and they alone, knew what was best for everyone else.

The Brothers and Sisters moved on, hell-bent on their appointed mission to rid Becancour of anything they considered filthy.

Sister Pauline was a bit tardy in joining the others on their Heaven-sent quest toward Truth, Light, and gross Intolerance. She was totally absorbed in reading what was left of a paperback in a store they had just trashed.

She did not notice the dozens of cats that had crept into the trashed store, all of them moving silently toward the woman.

Suddenly something furry brushed against her ankle.

"Rat!" she hollered. The book went one way and Sister Pauline went the other.

The book survived; Sister Pauline did not.

The cats swarmed Sister Pauline and brought her belly-down on the trashed floor. The cats howled and hissed and spat and clawed. Her snow-white robe was quickly turned red with her blood. The cats clawed at her eyes. Sister Pauline would never again have to worry about reading another offensive word.

While the cats were busy tearing out hunks of Sister Pauline, they did not notice the huge shapes that cast giant shadows enter the rear of the store. The cats gorged themselves, their fur becoming matted and slick with blood.

A low growl stopped the cats from their feasting.

As one, they spun and spat their anger at the Beasts that were lumbering toward them.

Cats met Beasts in the center of the trashed store. But it was no real contest.

The cats could not claw through the thick skin of the Beasts; at best they were able only to inflict very minor wounds on the huge creatures of Hell. The cats were ripped apart and slung about the littered store. Then they were eaten. Only a few escaped the raging jealousy of the Beasts.

The Beasts lumbered toward the torn body of Sister Pauline.

They feasted well that early evening of the last night.

Janet's demon child, Bess, did not wait until the full dead of night to launch her attack on the Blessed child, Sam. While the adults were setting up guards around the clinic, Bess slipped away from the crowded room she occupied with half a dozen other kids and made her way to where she knew Little Sam was waiting, with that strange dog. She also knew that the turncoat witch, Lydia, had left her son alone, with that dog, and had done so deliberately.

Bess, with her young and evil mind, matured by a hundred thousand years of depravity, did not understand that move. But that didn't matter; she knew the task before her, and meant to see it through.

She felt that Guy's changing into his real self had been a mistake. Bess planned to stay a little girl, since her mother had told her that little boys were taught from an early age not to hit little girls. Only at the last moment, when she struck the fatal blow, would she change. And by then, she would be too powerful for any of the others to stop—including Nydia.

Bess didn't know Little Sam as well as she thought she did.

Like his father, but learning it at a much earlier age, Little Sam had been born to combat Evil. Little boys or little girls . . . it made no difference to Little Sam.

Little Sam looked up at the open doorway when Bess stepped into his room. Dog never took his eyes off the girl.

"My fight," Little Sam said.

Dog shook his great head as if to say, "I hear the words but that's about it, little buddy."

The smile that formed on the lips of Bess was Evil at its darkest. Sam slipped off the couch and faced the girl.

"Why don't you yell for your mother to come help you?" Bess asked.

"I don't need her help." The boy returned the whisper.

"You're a foolish little boy," Bess taunted him. She hissed at him like a cat, the expulsion of air fouling the windowless room. Her breath was that of a hundred thousand years of evil, straight from the burning pits of Hell.

Little Sam leaped at the girl and kicked her, knocking her sprawling on the tile. Before she could recover from her shock of having a little boy attack her, Little Sam kicked her again, this time in the stomach.

Bess squalled in rage, her face changing, her anger betraying her plans to contain her inner self. She leaped to her tennis-shoe-clad feet, her face a mask of evil, her eyes burning with hate. She spat at him, the spittle a yellowish stinking glob that clung to the wall like a leech.

Little Sam infuriated the girl when he laughed at her.

She sprang at him. Little Sam sidestepped and Bess crashed into the wall, stunning herself with the impact.

When she picked herself up, Little Sam knew that playtime was all over.

The little girl was no more. In her place stood a haglike creature that only vaguely resembled something human. The cackling laughter that sprang from the mottled mouth was followed by puffs of breath that smelled fresh from a stinking grave. The creature spoke to Little Sam, but the boy could not understand the words. They were from a time and place that had long since died and vanished from history.

Dog ran out of the room and clamped his powerful jaws round one ankle of the creature and twisted and jerked, pilling the Godless creation to the floor. The hag attempted to break free from Dog's powerful jaws. But Dog held fast. The sounds of ancient bones splintering and shattering filled the corridor. The hag shrieked her pain. Dog jerked once more and ankle separated from leg. A thick yellowish fluid leaked onto the floor from the severed ankle. Dog slid backward, his paws trying to gain some hold on the slick tile. He spat out the stinking foot and charged.

More than a hundred pounds of God-sent dog hit the creature as she was attempting to get to her one remaining foot. The force of Dog's charge knocked the creature across the corridor. Little Sam lashed out with one shoe and caught the thing on a kneecap. The kneecap shattered. Little Sam reached down and grabbed a wrist and twisted. The wrist broke free.

Little Sam dropped the wrist to the floor as the creature went scurrying down the hall, trying to reach the exit door.

His nails clicking on the tile, Dog reached the creature before she reached the door. The animal grabbed onto a foot and pulled the hag back. Twisting his head, he broke off the one remaining foot. Frances Lenoir picked that time to step into the hall. The hag sank her yellow teeth into the woman's ankle, biting deeply. Frances screamed in pain as the yellow teeth began working higher and higher up her leg, over the calf, and digging and biting into the softness of inner thigh.

Some adults left their posts until Nydia ordered them back. Only Don Lenoir failed to obey Nydia's orders. The deputy stood in horrified shock and watched as his wife within seconds, was consumed and transformed and altered and finally absorbed by the now bloody creature.

They became as one.

"Frances!" Don screamed in rage. He pulled out his .357 and emptied it into the creature.

The heavy hollow-nosed slugs knocked the hag back the floor, momentarily stunning her.

Little Sam was the first to react. The little boy ran down the hall to the lobby. He jerked a sharpened stake out of a large potted plant and raced back up the hall. He jumped at the creature just as she was sitting up, laughing and howling and spraying the walls with a stinking yellow fluid. The stench was awful.

The point of the stake hit the hag in the center of her

chest and drove deep. She howled and hissed and clutched at the stake with her gnarled hands. Little Sam worked the stake in deeper, sweating from his exertions.

That which had once held the human form of Bess rained Hell's curses down on the little boy's head.

Little Sam spat in the creature's face.

Where the spittle struck, pockets of steam rose from the hag's skin.

The hag's hands left the stake and tried to reach Little Sam. Dog leaped and ripped one arm to the bone, tearing great hunks of flesh from the arm. Dog jumped over the vibrating stake and tore at the other arm, shredding it, rendering both arms useless.

Little Sam worked the stake in deeper, finally piercing the evil demon heart.

The shrieking abruptly ceased; the hag began changing. The creature spun back in time, almost too fast for human eyes to follow, until all that was left was the human form of Frances . . .

. . . with a stake sticking out of her bloody chest.

Don fell to the floor beside his wife and began weeping.

Little Sam walked up the hall, Dog by his side. Little Sam's part was over. He had passed the test. God's little warrior and his animal friend could now rest.

22

"Oh, my God!" Jobert screamed. "'At's Charles an
Maurice Ballatin out dere!"

Sam ran to the second-story window and looked out
Jobert was trembling beside him. "Who?"

"Cousins of Ben Ballatin. Them people drowned year
ago, with them Yankees come down here to fish."

"Padre!" Sam yelled. "The Undead are walking."

"I see them," the priest said, no fear in his voice.

The second-floor porch decking prevented Sam fro
seeing what the priest was doing.

Father Javotte stepped out onto the main porch, a lar
cross in one hand, Holy Water in the other. Javotte lift
the cross.

"Back," he spoke. "Go back to your graves and re
There is time for you yet. God forgives what you are n
responsible for. Go back into the waters."

All the outside lights were on, flooding the groun
with harsh light. The naked, wrinkled, fish-white walki
dead were strangely frozen in the light.

Ben Ballatin stepped into the light, bloody and to

and ripped . . . and dead.

The kids appeared, naked and chalk white and wrinkled.

"All of you," Javotte said, his words gentle but yet firm, "return to your final resting places. Go, while there is still time."

The woman appeared in the light. She walked to her children and stood between them.

"Take your children and go with God. Your sins are forgiven. For you are blameless. Go, go."

The woman took the hand of the girl, then the hand of the boy. They walked out of the harsh light and into the darkness.

Sam and Jobert had joined Father Javotte on the porch. Sam held stakes; Jobert had fixed a bayonet onto his rifle, the long needle pointed FFL bayonet of years past.

The walking dead screamed, the foulness of the bayou bottom momentarily engulfing those on the porch.

Naked and screaming, the men charged the porch.

Father Javotte tossed Holy Water on one man. The man was suddenly pockmarked and smoking where the water touched his fishy skin. The undead exploded on the front yard, rotting organs and ropy intestines flung about.

Jobert impaled Ben Ballatin on his bayonet, the needle point sinking deep, piercing the heart. With Ben's hands ripping the rifle barrel, Jobert drove the bayonet in to the hilt. Ben died on his naked feet.

Sam plunged the stake into the chest of the third man. The point hit a bone and was deflected off, the point exiting out the man's upper back. The Undead jerked free and ran howling off into the night.

"Two outta t'ree ain't bad," Jobert said.

Brother Malcolm stepped out of the line of singing and prancing and dancing so-called social reformers. He walked into an alley to relieve himself.

Brother Malcolm almost fainted when a great black panther appeared a few feet from him. The panther snarled, exposing long fangs that glistened in the darkness of the alley. And if that wasn't enough, a stark naked, ghostly white woman appeared beside the panther. She crooked a finger at Brother Malcolm.

"Come," she said, her voice low and seductive.

"Not on your life, lady!" Brother Malcolm said, then split as fast as lightning into the mouth of the alley.

Brother Malcolm had been quicker even than the panther, getting the jump on the big cat as he hauled his tail out of there. With his robes held high, his red, skinny knees flashing in the streetlights' glow, Brother Malcolm passed the entire line of white-clad Brothers and Sisters. He raced past Brother Lester.

"Come back here!" Lester shouted. Lester knew nothing about the naked woman and the great black cat.

"Screw you!" Brother Malcolm yelled, fleeing for his life.

"Heathen!" Lester shouted. "Backslider! Coward!"

But Brother Malcolm was gone into the night, heading for the clinic. Brother Malcolm had had quite enough of Brother Lester and his nutty ideas. He had taken no part in the burning of those men; indeed, had known nothing of it until it was all over. It had been Brother Malcolm who had vocally questioned Lester's so-called conversation with an angel.

Hell with the whole bunch of them.

Brother Thad turned around to see what in the world might have caused Brother Malcolm to behave so strangely.

It was to be Brother Thad's last look at anything.

Snarling, the panther leaped at Thad. One clawed paw ripped Thad's face, shredding the flesh and tearing out one eye. Thad did not have the time to even scream his pain and terror before the panther tore out his throat and lapped at the sudden gush of hot blood.

Bonnie grabbed Sister Ilene and flung her to the hot concrete of the street. Falling on top of the woman, Bonnie's teeth flashed in the night and sank into the woman's throat. Bonnie sucked greedily as the woman's legs kicked and jerked and trembled.

And she became one of Them.

Brother Lester whooped his fright and took off running, holding his robes up high. That angel hadn't said a damned thing about this.

Brother Johnny ran into an alley and straight into a pack of cats. The cats rode him down, scratching and clawing and biting. Brother Johnny howled his death cry.

The line of social reformers broke into a mass of panic and confusion. White-robed men and woman ran in all directions.

Sister Millie ran into an open doorway. Too late, she realized she had stepped into a honky-tonk. Rough hands grabbed her, stripped the robe from her. The nightmare was just beginning.

Sister Bertha was holding her own. After whacking

355

several smelly men over the head with a stick of wood found in the gutter, the large lady was wisely left alone by those that prowled the darkness. Sister Bertha went off in search of Brother Lester.

Brothers Luther, Ira, and Eb, and Sisters Estelle, Helen, and Rose had taken refuge in the office of a service station, after Brother Eb, very unChristianlike, broke the lock on the front door and illegally entered.

The six of them huddled together on the floor, behind a desk and a cigarette machine they had pulled together. They were confused and very frightened. And closer to death than they realized.

Xaviere was in a blue rage, storming around her quarters, throwing vases and cups and anything else she could get her dirty hands on.

Guy had failed, Bess had failed, those called from the dark waters of the bayous had failed. The Beasts and the cats were at war with each other; Jackson and Bonnie had gone off on their own—as had Mary—and so far, at least that damned old woman and her shotgun had managed to remain alive and openly taunting the Master's followers.

Goddammit!

If she failed here, in this hick town in the backwater of Louisiana . . .

. . . Xaviere did not like to think about that.

But why did she think of it? Failure had not entered her mind before now.

Her hands, clawlike in her rage, gripped the sides of table. She concentrated, her mind sending out message to the Beasts to attack the strongholds of the little ban of Christians. But the Beasts ignored her calling. The jealousy of the Beasts had overwhelmed all else in the tiny brains of the creatures. Theirs was one single thought: Kill the cats.

And that they were doing, killing and feasting and enjoying every second of it.

The Princess of Darkness picked up a brush and hurled it through a window.

Leave! The voice entered her head. Get out!

Xaviere spun around, her face mirroring her rage. "No!" she screamed. "No. There is still this night before us."

No good! the heavy voice told her. Another time, another place. For us, it is over here.

Xaviere held her head high. "I am staying here, Master."

There was a long pause. Then the voice once more entered the brain of the Princess. You are that certain, daughter?

"Yes."

I will give you a few more hours. But you must leave before daylight. Is that understood?

"Yes, Father."

She felt the Dark One's presence leave. And Xaviere knew that unless the force of Darkness held the victory their unwashed hands, the Master would not return. She drew a cloak around her bare shoulders. "Janet!" she called.

"Yes, Princess," the girl said, stepping into the darkened room.

"I shall lead. Inform the others."

The young woman hesitated. Her child had been killed

357

that night, and she was experiencing something totally new: sorrow. She wanted to tell the Princess that while she did not feel Sam Balon to be unbeatable . . . they had lost this fight.

But Janet had been born to serve the Princess.

"Yes, Princess. Right away."

Javotte's head jerked up, his eyes holding a strange light "What did I just experience . . . just a few moment: ago?"

Sam stood in the center of the study at the Dorgenoi mansion; he was listening to his wife's voice. The projection ended.

"The Dark One is gone," Sam said. "But his minion remain. The fight is not over."

"But the odds have swung in our favor," Colter sai

Sam thought of the many still lurking out in the darkness. He thought of the Beasts and the cats. He thought of the walking dead. The total Godless that lay i wait for any sign of carelessness.

"Yes," Sam said. "I believe the odds have swung our favor. But don't get careless. It's far from over.'

A wild shrieking ripped the outside darkness. woman's insane laughter followed. Colter walked to window and looked out. It was to be her last gazing at th world. A huge black shape crashed through the windo showering the old woman with deadly shards of gla Dripping fangs and flashing claws ripped the old woma drenching the floor with her blood. The panther tore her throat and leaped for Romy just as Trooper Nor lifted his shotgun and began pulling and pumping.

358

The buckshot tore into the black panther, the force of the buckshot knocking it off its leaping path and flinging it to one side.

A naked woman, pale and dark haired and evil-eyed grabbed Rita Dantin from behind. The patrolwoman reacted as taught. She flipped Bonnie over her shoulder, sending the naked woman sprawling and squalling to the floor. Remembering what Sam and Father Javotte had told her, she turned and grabbed an umbrella out of its stand. Before Bonnie could recover, Rita drove the point of the umbrella into the woman's chest.

The small round rib shield stopped the point just before entering Bonnie's heart. The naked woman kicked out with her bare feet, bruising Rita's legs. Sonny Passon ran up and emptied his .357 into Bonnie's head. The Ruger Security-Six cracked in one long roll of thunder. Bonnie's head was shattered, bone and bits of brain bouncing on the floor.

The head was ruined.

The heart beat on.

The great black panther rose from the floor, the hide and hair dripping blood. It shook its head and leaped back out the window, disappearing into the night.

Sam and Javotte rushed into the wide hallway just as Bonnie was getting to her feet. Bent over, trying to gain balance, Bonnie lifted her head and hissed at the small band. She spat at them, snarling like a human cat.

Sam drove a stake through her back. Using all his massive strength, Sam drove the stake clear through the woman, the point rupturing the heart and exiting out between the woman's breasts.

Bonnie Rogers, a victim without initially being a

359

villainess, died on the floor of the lovely home.

"Drag her body outside and dump it," Sam said.

Julie Dorgenois, her face pale but her hands holding a shotgun, said, "I've heard of Bonnie Rogers all my life. But this is the first time I have ever laid eyes on her."

"Let's hope it will be the last time," Sam said.

23

Those at the clinic had answered the frantic calling and pounding at the emergency door entrance. Brother Malcolm leaped inside and slammed and locked the door behind him.

Despite the terror and awfulness and hideousness that the night held tightly around those besieged and barricaded Christians, Tony had to smile at the man's attire.

"Love your outfit," the doctor said.

Brother Malcolm muttered something that did not contain a single word that could be found in the Bible.

Mary Claverie led her staggering, stumbling and lurching brothers toward town. She was having a high ol' time that evening. Most fun she'd had since she was a little girl and held that boy's head under the water down at the swimming hole. Drowned him deader than Hell. Said it was an accident and everybody believed her.

Voices had told her to do that, too. Mary had always

obeyed the voices. But the voices had changed during and after her time in the old Dorgenois home. And Mary had changed, too.

"Hey, Brothers!" Mary shouted. "Isn't this fun?"

"I've been a fool," Lester said.

"Now, now, Brother Lester," Sister Bertha soothed him.

"No, let me finish. I have been a fool. For God's sake, Bertha! Do you realize we actually burned three human beings to death!"

"They were wicked, evil men, Brother Lester," Sister Bertha held on.

"That's not for us to decide, Bertha. Neither of us are judges of men. That was no angel who spoke to me. That was *Satan!*"

Sister Bertha paled. "But those men were sellers and readers of filth!"

Lester was silent for a time. Silent for so long that Sister Bertha shook his shoulder to see if he was still conscious.

"Yes, yes, Bertha. I'm here. Bertha, if we get out of this alive, I have a suggestion."

"Yes, Brother Lester?"

"If we make it out of this, let's worship the Lord, sing our praises to Him, have socials and eat lots of good food and . . ."

Sister Bertha waited breathlessly for a revelation from her pastor. "Yes, Brother Lester!" she blurted.

". . . And do our best to mind our own damn business!"

Sister Bertha fainted.

"A woman coming up the walk, Sam!" Matt called from upstairs.

"I've been expecting her," Sam called. "Is she alone?"

"Yes. Who is she?"

"The daughter of Satan."

Sam walked to the front door and opened it. Xaviere stepped inside.

"Don't you ever take a bath?" Sam asked.

"Terribly sorry if I offend you, Daddy dear. But I have business to discuss with you."

Sam smiled. "Yeah. I just bet you do." He turned to the crowd gathered on both sides of the hallway. "May I present Xaviere Flaubert, Grand Princess of Filth, Daughter of Satan, Princess of the Smoking Pits . . ." He looked at Xaviere. "Have I left anything out?"

"Your sarcasm is not amusing," Xaviere said shortly.

Trooper Norris held a sharpened stake in his hand. He locked eyes with the daughter of Satan. She smiled at him. "Don't be a fool, whoever you are. Only two Beings can destroy me. Satan, and . . . that other thing."

"God," Sam finished it.

Xaviere spat on the floor at the mention of His name. She glanced into the study, seeing Colter's dead body. She smiled with satisfaction and again looked at Sam. "Deal, Sam?"

"No deals, Xaviere. Just like upstate New York. I don't deal."

"I had to ask. You know as well as I it's all part of the game."

"I know. Satan gave you a few more hours, right?"

The dark-haired, black-robed young woman shrugged her shoulders. Her body odor was nearly overwhelming. "Put that hidden thought out of your mind, Sam. You can't kill me."

"I know. Finally. I know."

He also knew Nydia was listening.

"You're a confusing man, Sam," Xaviere said. "And I don't understand you. Your God is not promising you anything except a place in . . ." She lifted her eyes upward. ". . . up there. My Master would give you eternal life here on earth. Riches, women, fame, whatever you wanted. Slaves to do your every bidding. Yet you refuse it. I'll make a bet with you, Sam. I'll bet you I can tempt at least one man and one woman here to join me. Wager?"

"What are we wagering, Xaviere?"

"You know," she said coyly.

Sam shook his head. "The answer remains the same as always, no."

Her eyes narrowed and her cheeks flushed with anger, but that was her only sign of her hatred for Sam Balon. She glanced at Trooper Norris. "Join me. Name your pleasures. I guarantee them for all time."

"Naw, lady," James said. "I'll take my chances come Judgment Day. Thanks just the same."

The stake in his hand exploded in flames. James dropped the burning stake and stomped it out with his boots.

"Guess she can't take a joke," James muttered.

Xaviere polled the men and women. She had no takers.

Xaviere's shoulders slumped. She shook her head; her

matted and filthy hair hardly bounced with the movement. "The night is not over, Sam," she said, glaring at him. "Nor," she smiled, "that part of the day that belongs to my Master. I shall not say good-bye, Earth-Father, for we shall meet again. Another time, another town. And . . . I think you know that eventually I'll kill you. Yet you keep on. Why, Sam, why?"

"Because my God tells me to do so, Xaviere."

"And I do because my Master tells me to do so, Sam."

"And therein lies the difference, Xaviere. My God is not my Master. He is my Maker, but not my Master."

Xaviere waved her hand. She vanished.

Only her odor remained.

From somewhere, Xaviere laughed. "Tricked you again, Sam."

The house filled with cats.

Clarence Claverie and his wife sat on the couch in their living room. They were both too frightened to utter a sound.

Will and Jack stood over them, the rotting grave scent of them filled the room.

"Uh . . . uh . . . uh!" Clarence finally managed to gasp.

Mary laughed and clapped her hands. "Give your brother and his wife a great big kiss, boys!"

The walking dead leaned forward.

Preacher Earl Morris and Mayor Will Jolevare and Funeral Director Art Authement and Ex-patrolman

Louis Black and a few others lurched and staggered toward the clinic. They surrounded the building and began beating at the windows with sticks and clubs, shattering the glass. Those inside jabbed at them with stakes and sharpened broom handles.

"Die, die, die!" the Undead called, their voices as dead as their souls.

Those inside responded with gunfire. The slugs and buckshot ripped the dead flesh and knocked them spinning . . .

. . . only to rise and charge again and again.

The side door of the clinic shattered. A Beast filled the doorway with his obscene bulk. It roared and screamed its hatred and lumbered up the hallway.

But Sam had told those few allies that the Beasts were not immortal and Don Lenoir and Bid Grenier and Mike Laborne and Brother Malcolm met them with gunfire. Soon the stinking bodies of the Beasts had piled up, blocking the shattered entrance.

At the old Dorgenois house, Xaviere was near exhaustion, standing trembling in her quarters, in her mind, seeing and hearing all. It had taken nearly all her powers to force the Beasts and the cats to cease their personal war and do her bidding.

But even after all that, the little bands of Christians were holding their own. More than that . . . they were winning!

"Walk!" she silently screamed, projecting the order through the darkness of night. "Walk and attack. Kill them all!" She vocally screamed the last. Exhausted, she collapsed on the floor.

Janet ran to her side, knelt, and took the youn

woman's hand. She called for Jimmy and for Jon Le Moyne.

"We're leaving," Janet told them. "Make ready. We must be out of this area by first light. We don't have much time. Move very fast."

"Close the study doors!" Sam yelled. "Trap the cats in there."

The heavy oak doors were closed and locked. Anything that could be piled against the doors to secure them was dragged out of the hall and foyer and stacked against the doors.

The cats almost completely covered the mansion. Those inside could hear their hissing and snarling and spitting on the walls and roof. They could hear their claws digging and scratching, seeking entrance. The mansion seemed to breathe with the cats.

Sam had prepared as wisely as he could, with what materials he had on hand. He had tried to cover every window that could not be guarded, nailing boards and anything else that could be found over the windows.

For the moment, everything seemed to be holding. But he knew it was only a matter of time before the sheer numbers of cats overwhelmed them all.

A cat managed to work its way through two hastily nailed boards. The head, then the clawed paws. It snarled and spat and ripped the air with claws. Several hundred more were pressing close behind it.

James Norris stuck his shotgun into the cat-filled cavity and pulled the trigger, for the moment clearing that hole of cats.

"Water!" Tess panted the words. "Hot water—boiling water."

Several rushed to the kitchen and began boiling water on the stove. Hot water taps were turned on full blast and containers filled and handed out. The scalding water was tossed onto the cats. They howled and ran, some blindly, into the heated night.

A new sound was heard coming out of the hot night. The sounds of barking and hissing.

Those in the house stopped their frantic work to stare through the cracks in the windows. They stared in wonder and shock and disbelief.

Dogs and cats had appeared behind the attacking cats; the newly arrived dogs and cats seemed to be cooperating with each other in their assault on the devil's cats. It was a dog and cat fight to end them all . . . literally.

The snarling and barking and hissing and yowling filled the night around the mansion. The blood odor grew thick.

It was impossible for those in the house to determine what side any cat was on—they all looked alike. But one thing was certain, the cats that attacked the mansion seemed to be losing . . . and pulling away from the house and grounds.

A crashing sound came from the back of the house. Sonny Passon whirled around, his face paling at the sight before him.

"That's Bob Savoie!" he whispered, his words barely audible above the yowling and barking and hissing and screeching outside the mansion.

His clothing hanging in stinking rags from him, his white, seemingly sightless eyes staring, the soles of hi shoes flopping, Bob Savoie lurched and staggered toward Sonny. Matt Comeaux darted past the chief, a stake in his hand. The schoolteacher drove the sharpened stake deep into the chest of the walking dead, the point penetrating the darkly beating heart. Bob's cold hands closed around the neck of Matt Comeaux and clamped down in a death grip.

Sonny and C.D. and Tess beat at Bob's arms, attempting to break the hold. They could not. James Norris ran out of the kitchen, a heavy butcher knife in his hand. "Get out of the way!" he shouted.

Raising the knife above his head, the trooper brought the heavy blade down, completely severing one arm, slicing just above the elbow. Still the dead fingers held fast.

James sliced off the other arm and Bob Savoie fell back, finally dead.

The others ripped loose the fingers, breaking them off and dropping them one by one to the floor. The fingers crawled around like large white worms. One tried to crawl up Tess's leg and she screamed and kicked it away.

"Burn them!" Sam yelled. "Burn them!"

Matt was helped to a chair, the marks on his neck raw and red and turning blue. He struggled for life-giving breath.

Then those in the house felt it.

The silence around them.

They walked to the windows and looked out into the lighted night. The grounds were littered with the bodies of hundreds of cats and dogs. Nearer the house, a line of dogs and cats stood, facing the bloody battleground, guarding those in the house.

"Call the clinic," Romy said. "See about them."

"They need help," Sam said, hearing Nydia's voice in his head. "It's far from being over." He grabbed up an armload of stakes. "Holy Water, Padre?" he asked the priest.

Javotte nodded.

Sam said, "James, Padre, Romy, Tess . . . let's go."

24

Gangs of wild-eyed men and women and teenagers, some armed with clubs of all kinds, beat at the cars and pickup as the small band fought their way through the night, shattering windshields and side windows as the small team drove past them. Gunfire from the vehicles slashed at the night, rolling thunder boomed from the muzzles of pistols and shotguns.

"It's insanity!" Romy yelled.

"Hang on!" Sam told him. "The worst is yet before us."

Romy crossed himself and in the next instant shot a man between the eyes.

A teenage girl leaped onto the hood of the pickup truck. Her eyes were savage and filth rolled in profane waves from her mouth. She beat at the windshield with a claw-hammer.

Sam slammed on the brakes, sending the girl sliding off the hood. He swerved around her. The car behind him ran over her, crushing her beneath the tires.

"Connie," Sam heard Romy whisper. "I was her softball coach two years ago."

"She just struck out," Sam said shortly.

"I can't take any more of this!" Romy screamed.

Sam's right hand left the steering wheel and struck the man on the mouth, backhanding his head back, bloodying his lips.

"You'll take it or you'll die!" Sam said. "Think about that."

Romy began praying.

The small convoy reached the clinic. The men jumped out, weapons of the Lord in their hands.

The men and women attacking the clinic turned to meet them.

Those inside the clinic rushed out, boxing in the attackers.

It was a quick, bloody, and savage few moments. The night grew eerily silent. Someone vomited on the ground. Others were weeping; some gasped for breath in the ho night. Others were trembling uncontrollably.

Father Javotte, his clothing splattered with bloo walked among the carnage. "The Claverie brothers," h said, his voice carrying through the night. "All three c them."

"This is Mr. Authement," Romy said.

"Earl Morris and his wife," Mike Laborn said.

"Cliff Lester's wife here," another called. "Lucille

"Mayor Jolevare and Betty here."

Other names were called out. But a lot were missin And Sam knew they would have to be dealt with at fi light. He looked up as Nydia joined his side. He glanced Father Javotte. "Take care of Little Sam for us, Pad We have things to do while it's still night."

"All right," the priest said.

Sam glanced at his watch. Just about an hour u

dawn. "I think we're going to be too late."

Sam and Nydia drove to the old Dorgenois home, parking in the drive. The gates had been opened, slung back hastily. Weaponless, husband and wife walked through the large old home. The inner foulness was hideously offensive to both of them. They prowled every room, opened every door, looked in every closet, under every stinking bed and pile of filthy clothing. Nothing. The home was deserted.

On the ground floor, Sam found a box of matches and set the drapes blazing. As he did so, a hot, stinking wind picked up outside.

Sam lost his temper. "Do *something!*" he shouted. "We're only human. We're mortals. *Help us!*"

The sounds of a hard slap was heard, the sound of it thundering across the skies. The stinking wind ceased. The night was dead calm.

Nydia looked at Sam. "I don't believe I would have had the courage to speak to Him in that tone of voice."

Sam allowed himself a very small and tight smile. "It worked, didn't it?"

Hand in hand, the couple left the burning house and walked out into the now-flame-lit night.

THE LAST DAY

At dawn, the men and women and few teenagers who ha
been barricaded at the clinic and in the Dorgeno
mansion split up into teams. They all carried stakes. The
started at the south end of town and worked north, goir
from house to house, store to store, building to buildin

It seemed the awful screaming and the seeming
endless hammering would never end.

But it did, finally. And finally, the population
Becancour changed.

For the better, most thought.

But the searchers, bloody and weary, never found
great black panther. And they never found M:
Claverie.

And Dave Porter had vanished.

They found the orderly from the clinic and retur
him to the grave, with a little bit of extra wood in
casket.

But they never found the torn man.

Carl Nichols was in the principal's office at the
school, snarling and spitting and hissing like a cat.

Matt Comeaux ended Carl's life.

Sister Ilene was found by Cliff Lester and F:

Javotte. Javotte handed the man a stake.

Half a dozen times the searchers felt eyes on them, silently watching. Sam told them they were probably feeling the dead orderly's eyes.

And probably always would.

It was high noon and very hot when all felt they had found all they were going to find.

Mrs. Wheeler joined them, a shotgun still in her hands. The old woman looked at the blood-splattered men and women.

"Now comes the interesting part," the old woman said.

"What do you mean?" Don Lenoir asked.

"Explaining why we did it."

25

Romy Dorgenois didn't mess around. He went straight to the top.

"Are you serious?" the governor asked.

"Yes, sir," Romy spoke into the phone. "And I woul[d] suggest you do something very quickly, for the bodie[s] are going to be presenting quite a health hazard befor[e] very long."

"I'll be there just as fast as I can," the govern[or] promised.

Attorney General Millet and Governor Andrews a[nd] Colonel Piper of the Louisiana State Police made a fly[over] of the town before landing at the small airstrip. Colo[nel] Piper had ordered the troop commander of that area [to] meet him . . . and bring every goddamned trooper [he] could find.

"Look at the bodies down there!" Attorney Gene[ral] Millet breathed, gazing down from five hundred fee[t at] the town of Becancour.

"Please God," Governor Andrews muttered. "[No] press on this. Please?"

On the ground, Colonel Piper met the troop commander. "You say you had a man in here while all this was going on?"

"Yes, sir. Trooper James A. Norris."

"Get him!"

After listening to James for ten seconds, Colonel Piper took off his hat. Twenty seconds later he threw the hat on the ground. A minute later he was jumping up and down on it.

"Goddammit, Norris, you are a Louisiana State Trooper. You do not go around hammering stakes into peoples' hearts." The colonel paused. "Did you read them their rights?" The colonel frowned. "What am I saying!"

"Are you ill, sir?" Norris asked.

"Am *I* ill? You've been seeing hobgobblins and vampires and zombies and werewolves and, and, God only knows what else, and *you're* asking *me* who is ill?"

"Perhaps you'd like to sit down in the shade, sir?" Norris suggested.

Colonel Piper went wandering off, muttering to himself. He was very, very glad he was retiring that year. Most happy.

Louisiana State Health officer, who asked to remain anonymous, offered to make a suggestion.

"I wish somebody would," Governor Andrews said.

"A water-borne bacteria, sir. Somebody poisoned the water supply. I would suggest we get the bodies buried as quickly as possible and then seal off the town."

Governor Andrews looked at Father Javotte. "You don't like that idea, Father?"

"Burn them," the priest said.

"Father Javotte!" Governor Andrew said. "This is not the dark ages. I can't give any orders to burn human bodies."

"You'll live to regret it," the priest warned.

The tone of the priest's voice caused the governor to shudder.

Thousands of pictures were taken, of the dead humans, the cats, the Beasts, the bloody stakes, the torn bodies. Senior State Troopers from all over the state were called in to body-bag the dead.

The press was squalling to be allowed in.

They were kept out while helicopters hovered above the town to prevent light aircraft from doing any flybys

Those residents of Becancour who had been caught in limbo were interviewed. They could remember nothing They didn't even know what day it was. They wer confused and disoriented.

The President of the United States called the governo of Louisiana.

"What's going on down there?" the President aske

"Voodoo, black magic, devil worship, zombies, wer wolves," the governor replied.

There was a long pause from Washington, D.C. Th the President laughed. "Well, that's what you get wh you have such a large percentage of registered Dem crats."

The governor, a Democrat, said, "I suppose that is good an explanation as any, Mister President."

26

"Where will you go and what will you do?" Father Javotte asked Sam and Nydia.

Little Sam and Dog were in the car, waiting.

"We will go wherever there is a need for our services," Nydia said. "We will do what has to be done."

"I don't have to tell either of you that it isn't over here."

"It will never be over here, Padre," Sam said. "We didn't get them all. But you will. You and Tony and Sonny and Don and the others. You've got a fight ahead of you."

Javotte nodded his head. "I wish you all would stay. We could use your help."

"You don't need us," Nydia told him. "You all know who they are. They'll surface again."

They were all conscious of Lula and Jules leaning against a building, watching them.

A teenage girl walked over to Lula, holding something

379

in her hand. She spoke to Lula and the three of them laughed. The girl stepped away and held up a can of spray paint. On the bare wall of the building, she spray-painted the outline of a large cat.

And somewhere back in the dark bayous . . .

. . . a big panther screamed.

SPINE TINGLING HORROR
from Zebra Books

CHILD'S PLAY (1719, $3.50)
by Andrew Neiderman

From the day the foster children arrived, they looked up to Alex. But soon they began to act like him—right down to the icy sarcasm, terrifying smiles and evil gleams in their eyes. Oh yes, they'd do anything to please Alex.

THE DOLL (1788, $3.50)
by Josh Webster

When Gretchen cradled the doll in her arms, it told her things—secret, evil things that her sister Mary could never know about. For it hated Mary just as she did. And it knew how to get back at Mary . . . forever.

DEW CLAWS (1808, $3.50)
by Stephen Gresham

The memories Jonathan had of his Uncle and three brothers being sucked into the fetid mud of the Night Horse Swamp were starting to fade . . . only to return again. I had taken everything he loved. And now it had come back—for him.

SIGHT UNSEEN (2038, $3.9)
by Andrew Neiderman

David was a smart one; he had a gift. The power to read people's minds. To see the future. To know terrifying things. Like who would live. And who would die . . .

THE ALCHEMIST (1865, $3.9)
by Les Whitten

Of course, it was only a hobby. No harm in that. The small alchemical furnace in the basement could hardly invite suspicion. After all, Martin was a quiet, government worker with a dead-end desk job. . . . Or was he?

Available wherever paperbacks are sold, or order direct from Publisher. Send cover price plus 50¢ per copy for mailing handling to Zebra Books, Dept. 2091, 475 Park Avenue South, New York, N.Y. 10016. Residents of New York, New Jersey Pennsylvania must include sales tax. DO NOT SEND CASH.

ASHES
by William W. Johnstone

OUT OF THE ASHES (1137, $3.50)

Ben Raines hadn't looked forward to the War, but he knew it was coming. After the balloons went up, Ben was one of the survivors, fighting his way across the country, searching for his family, and leading a band of new pioneers attempting to bring American OUT OF THE ASHES.

FIRE IN THE ASHES (1310, $3.50)

It's 1999 and the world as we know it no longer exists. Ben Raines, leader of the Resistance, must regroup his rebels and prep them for bloody guerrilla war. But are they ready to face an even fiercer foe—the human mutants threatening to overpower the world!

ANARCHY IN THE ASHES (1387, $3.50)

Out of the smoldering nuclear wreckage of World War III, Ben Raines has emerged as the strong leader the Resistance need. When Sam Hartline, the mercenary, joins forces with an invading army of Russians, Ben and his people raise a bloody banner defiance to defend earth's last bastion of freedom.

BLOOD IN THE ASHES (1537, $3.5)

As Raines and his rugged band of followers search for land that has escaped radiation, the insidious group known as The Ninth Order rises up to destroy them. In a savage battle to the death is the fate of America itself that hangs in the balance!

ALONE IN THE ASHES (1721, $3.)

In this hellish new world there are human animals and Ben Raines—famed soldier and survival expert—soon becomes the hunted prey. He desperately tries to stay one step ahead of death but no one can survive ALONE IN THE ASHES.

Available wherever paperbacks are sold, or order direct from Publisher. Send cover price plus 50¢ per copy for mailing handling to Zebra Books, Dept. 2091, 475 Park Avenue So New York, N.Y. 10016. Residents of New York, New Jersey Pennsylvania must include sales tax. DO NOT SEND CASH.